*Transnationalism &
Genre Hybridity*
IN NEW BRITISH
HORROR CINEMA

HORROR STUDIES

Series Editor
Xavier Aldana Reyes, Manchester Metropolitan University

Editorial Board
Stacey Abbott, Roehampton University
Linnie Blake, Manchester Metropolitan University
Harry M. Benshoff, University of North Texas
Fred Botting, Kingston University
Steven Bruhm, Western University
Steffen Hantke, Sogang University
Joan Hawkins, Indiana University
Agnieszka Soltysik Monnet, University of Lausanne
Bernice M. Murphy, Trinity College Dublin
Johnny Walker, Northumbria University

Preface
Horror Studies is the first book series exclusively dedicated to the study of the genre in its various manifestations – from fiction to cinema and television, magazines to comics, and extending to other forms of narrative texts such as video games and music. Horror Studies aims to raise the profile of Horror and to further its academic institutionalisation by providing a publishing home for cutting-edge research. As an exciting new venture within the established Cultural Studies and Literary Criticism programme, Horror Studies will expand the field in innovative and student-friendly ways.

Transnationalism & Genre Hybridity
IN NEW BRITISH HORROR CINEMA

LINDSEY DECKER

UNIVERSITY OF WALES PRESS
2021

© Lindsey Decker, 2021

All rights reserved. No part of this book may be reproduced in any material form (including photocopying or storing it in any medium by electronic means and whether or not transiently or incidentally to some other use of this publication) without the written permission of the copyright owner except in accordance with the provisions of the Copyright, Designs and Patents Act. Applications for the copyright owner's written permission to reproduce any part of this publication should be addressed to the University of Wales Press, University Registry, King Edward VII Avenue, Cardiff, CF10 3NS.

www.uwp.co.uk

British Library Cataloguing-in-Publication Data

A catalogue record for this book is available from the British Library.

ISBN 978-1-78683-698-4
eISBN 978-1-78683-699-1

The rights of Lindsey Decker to be identified as author of this work have been asserted in accordance with sections 77 and 79 of the Copyright, Designs and Patents Act 1988.

Typeset by Chris Bell, cbdesign

Printed by CPI Antony Rowe, Melksham

Contents

Acknowledgements   vii

List of Illustrations   ix

Introduction: Frights, Film Culture and Genre Hybrids
Examining Transnational Genre Hybridity in
New British Horror Cinema   1

1. **The 'Bastard Child of Mainstream Cinema'**
   Middlebrow British Film Culture, Transnationalism
   and Horror   25

2. **The Golden Age of British Cinema is Undead**
   British Zombies and the Social Realist Impulse   63

3. **Hybrid Hoodie Horrors**
   Genre Localisation and Britain's Moral Panic   101

4. **'A Famous Corpse'**
   Resurrecting Hammer's Transnational Appeal   141

Conclusion: British Horror's Perpetually 'Dying Light'   177

Notes   189

References   219

Filmography   239

Index   249

Acknowledgements

This book is the culmination of a series of unlikely events, and I'm grateful to everyone who has supported me along the way. In particular, thank you to Roger Hallas for working with me to transform the seed of an idea about genre hybridity in British horror films into the full-length study from which this book stems. Truly, I could not have asked for a better mentor. I would like to thank Steven Cohan and Kendall Phillips for their expertise, feedback and support, as well as Linnie Blake and Chris Hanson for their valuable comments on the project in its earlier stages.

Thank you to Sarah Lewis, the head of commissioning at the University of Wales Press, for her interest in my project and for helping to shepherd the project through the publication process. Thank you to the reviewers for their time and feedback.

I would like to thank my colleagues at Boston University's Department of Film & Television for their interest in and support for this book.

Thanks to all of the various folks who have given me feedback on various pieces of this project at conferences, particularly Johnny Walker, Ann Davies, Rachel Fabian, Justin Smith, Dana Och and Geneveive Newman.

I would be remiss if I did not thank Dustin Potter, Staci Stutsman, Melissa Welshans, Peter Katz and Sarah Barkin for listening to me as I worked through ideas at various stages in this project.

And finally, thank you to my students – I try to touch on the concept of transnational genre hybridity in nearly every course I teach, and I have really enjoyed our conversations about it across the years.

List of Illustrations

Figure 1. The cover of the October 2002 issue of *Sight & Sound*. 58

Figure 2. Shots from *Pure Rage* (top to bottom: talking-head interview, lap dissolve, shot from *28 Days Later*). 71

Figure 3. Top, *Attack the Block*, Moses, played by John Boyega, being pursued by the flattened, undifferentiated mob of aliens. Bottom, *Assault on Precinct 13*, the gang members emerge from the shadows in the mid-ground in the police station parking lot. 130

Figure 4. Top, Jennet's smoky black ghost hand on Kipps's left shoulder. Bottom, the smoke-like ghost of Kayako hovering over Sachie. 161

Figure 5. Top, Nathaniel in *The Woman in Black*. Bottom, Toshio in *Ju-on: The Grudge*. 163

Figure 6. The cover of the November 2012 issue of *Sight & Sound*. 178

Figure 7. Whitehead's body is turned into itself. 181

Figure 8. From left to right, top to bottom, making an eye in *Under the Skin*. 183

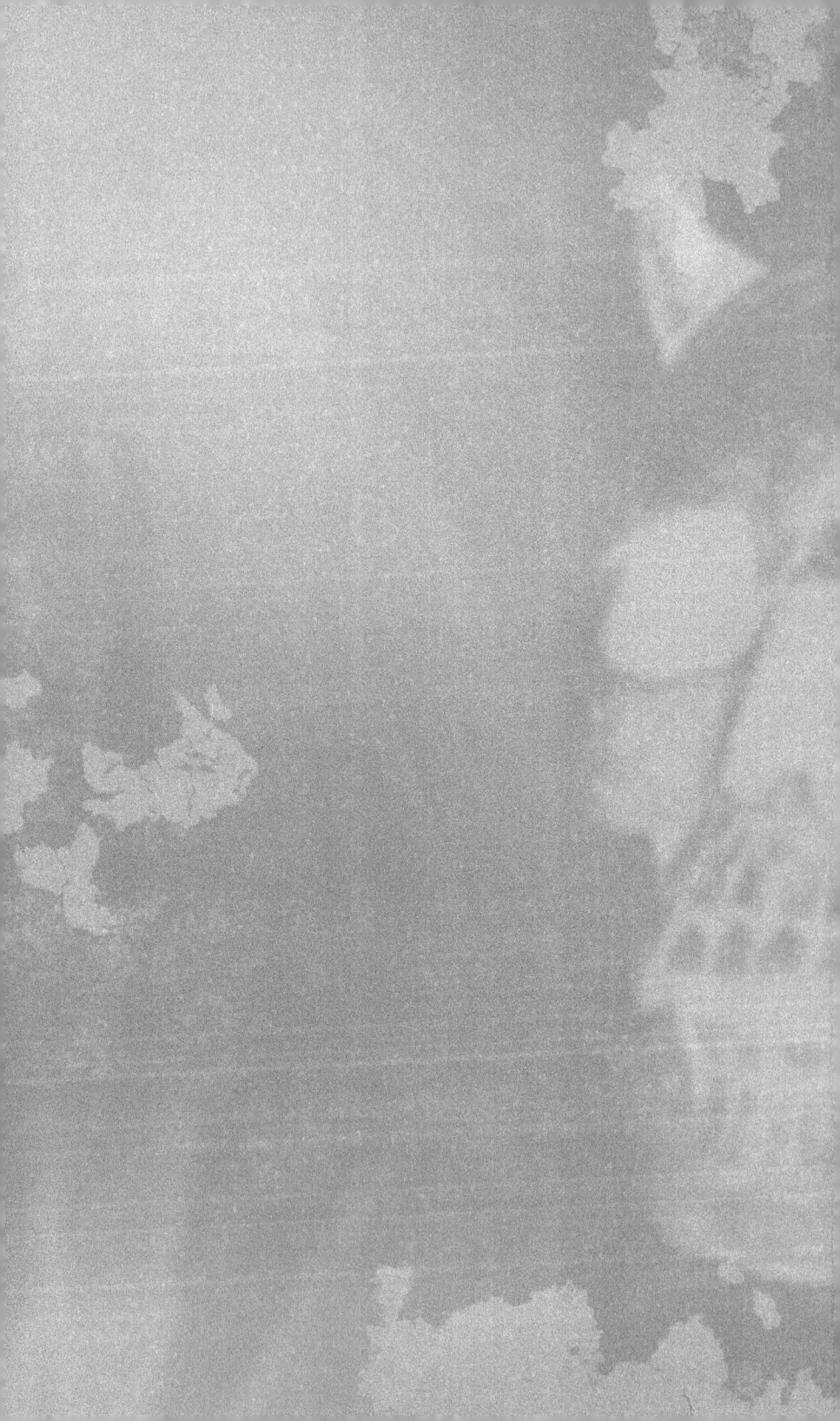

Introduction: Frights, Film Culture and Genre Hybrids
Examining Transnational Genre Hybridity in New British Horror Cinema

> Although the increased visibility of British horror cinema in the new millennium has made it difficult to ignore, it is significant that the films with the greatest critical and cultural impact have been those with the highest levels of generic impurity. Whilst the similarly Romero-influenced *Shaun of the Dead* and *28 Days Later* benefited from their borrowings from other genres – respectively, comedy and post-apocalyptic science fiction – the British horror film still lacks critical respectability. A slightly different fate has befallen films that can be more closely identified with the science fiction genre. Although fewer in number, these have enjoyed greater prestige. (James Leggott, from his *Contemporary British Cinema: From Heritage to Horror*[1])

THE ABOVE QUOTATION from British cinema scholar James Leggott's excellent *Contemporary British Cinema* primer, published in 2008, crystallises the key concerns of this project by bringing together new British horror cinema of the 2000s, genre hybridity, transnationality and middlebrow British film culture. Leggott cites the fact that the most critically significant British horror films of the first decade of the 2000s were genre hybrids – characterised by, as he puts it, 'generic impurity'. He casts this hybridity, or 'impurity', as negative. It likely helped Edgar Wright's *Shaun of the Dead* (2004) and Danny Boyle's *28 Days Later* (2002) but not enough to make them as prestigious as more straightforward genre films that fit more solidly within a single genre like science fiction. More importantly, this excerpt positions *Shaun* and *28 Days Later* as transnational hybrids, primarily influenced by American director George Romero's zombie films but made better by their fusion with genres Leggott has earlier framed as explicitly British. However, this recourse to home-grown genres could not save these Americanised British horror films – indeed, the transnationality of the genre hybridity seems to be part of what keeps the films from critical respectability, in opposition to films seen as more uncomplicatedly British. But this respectability is being adjudicated and found wanting within the context of a particular strand of British film culture, one which dominates many discussions of British film, academic and otherwise, and has influenced Leggott's writing here: middlebrow British film culture.

In this book, I theorise the ways that transnational genre hybridity can function in a film through formal elements and genre tropes. I use the 2000s British horror resurgence as a vital case study through which to investigate this phenomenon. The term 'resurgence' has been used fairly widely in popular and academic publications to discuss the British horror boom of the 2000s. While Geoffrey Macnab may have been the first to mention the 'UK horror picture' and its 'remarkable resurgence', it appears that Anne Billson's review of David Pirie's *A New Heritage of Horror* was the first instance of the full phrase 'British horror resurgence'.[2] In part, this period of British horror cinema presents such a compelling site because of middlebrow British film culture and its relationship with both the horror genre and the British film industry. The British film-makers whose work I examine in this book used transnational genre hybridity in several key ways within a set of prestigious and successful new British horror films. This allowed these film-makers a means to respond to discourses circulating about the industry and genre within middlebrow British film culture. In doing so, transnational genre hybridity became a tool for cultural engagement as well as cultural legitimation. Film-makers could respond to a key strand of film culture that was discussing and shaping their work, which further allowed them to influence several of the discourses about British horror circulating within that film culture.

Films that engage in transnational genre hybridity draw on formal and narrative tropes from specific genres associated with foreign national cinemas and combine them with tropes from long-standing and emergent genres from their own national cinema. This transnational genre hybridity is not simply postmodern intertextuality but a deliberate strategy through which to engage with the film's own national cinema and film culture, as well as discourses circulating about both the national and transnational within that industry and culture. This combination creates genre hybridity that also marks out that film as firmly transnational. Consequently, a study of transnational genre hybridity cannot only be a textual study of formal and narrative generic elements within a film or set of films – it cannot only be an elaboration of a film's intertextuality. It must also be a study of the film's paratexts, including promotional and supplemental materials like trailers, posters, behind-the-scenes DVD featurettes and press interviews from directors, the cast and crew members. Because transnational genre hybridity engages with discourses circulating within associated national film cultures, a study of the phenomenon must also be a study of film culture and the relevant discourses within that culture. This hybrid methodology, combining more traditional textual analysis of films with the study of paratexts and film cultures, allows for more nuanced readings of films as texts and illuminates how these uses of transnational genre hybridity allow films to engage with specific film cultures and to what ends.

'Transnational' has come to mean many things, but I use it here descriptively to refer to how a film's genre hybridity positions it with regard to nation. In the twenty or so years since it emerged, transnational cinema studies has provided a much needed corrective to what Andrew Higson dubbed 'the limiting imagination of national cinema'.[3] Much film studies scholarship in this area has productively focused on the transnationalism of remakes, co-production, distribution, exhibition, reception and stardom; brought attention to postcolonial, diasporic and non-Western cinemas; and examined films that narrativise cultural and geographical border crossings.[4] At the same time, while an entire journal is dedicated to transnational media, *Transnational Screens* (published by Routledge, 2010–present), academics are still debating the meaning and utility of the term. This is most notable in the work of scholars like Deborah Shaw, Will Higbee, Song Hwee Lim, Mette Hjort, and Iain Robert Smith and Austin Fisher.[5] However, despite the field having blossomed and expanded to cover an impressive number of cinemas and methodologies, the relationship between transnationalism and genre has gone relatively unexamined.

Shaw comes closest to my concerns when discussing 'transnational modes of narration' in terms of films following certain film language conventions, like those of art cinema, and 'transnational critical approaches and transnational influences', including the intertextuality made possible in a global film industry.[6] With the term transnational genre hybridity, I bring together these ideas in a new way to think through the ways that strategically using transnational intertextuality and shared film language conventions associated with different cinemas allow film-makers to comment upon the relationship between their national industry and other national or regional cinemas, or even global cinema.

Breaking the word transnational into its component parts, *trans-* and national, allows some further specificity here. 'Transnational', as a polysemic term, has numerous potential meanings, in part because of the different ways that the prefix *trans-* can signify: through or *situated across*, so as to thoroughly change or transfer and on the other side of or beyond. Focusing on the different meanings of this prefix, then, 'transnational' can be used to describe a film, or set of films, situated across national cinemas. These films can draw on the tropes, genres or national concerns of multiple national cinemas; they may address the relationship between particular national cinemas, whether to emphasise differences or break down borders. 'Transnational' can also designate a film that *thoroughly changes* some aspect of nationality. For example, a film may engage in localisation by taking a stylistic device or genre associated with a foreign national cinema and changing it to better fit pre-existing national film traditions or with contemporary cultural concerns. A film could also take up and change a pre-existing national genre, or style, to make the film itself more exportable, or more in line with the style or concerns of a particular foreign cinema or audience. 'Transnational' can also be used to describe a film that moves *beyond* the national to address the regional or global. This could mean positioning the film as part of a regional tradition or hailing a global audience familiar with a multiplicity of national cinemas and global genre trends.

In using the term transnational, I am also concerned with how we can push against, as Mette Hjort puts it, '"transnational" as a largely self-evident qualifier'.[7] I mean this in the sense that 'transnational' is sometimes used to imply a shared definition that is subsequently not provided; this vague usage can lead to imprecision, as well as implying that 'transnational' denotes one specific situation. So, while I examine select genre hybrids of the British horror film resurgence in this project, the specific ways that these films signify as transnational has implications for how transnationalism can operate in film more broadly and how we can study and use the term itself. Indeed, I have used it to discuss Iranian-American director Ana Lily Amirpour's *A Girl Walks Home Alone at Night* (2014) and its hybridisation of 1950s Hollywood teen films, Italian spaghetti Westerns and Iranian New Wave aesthetics.[8]

British horror cinema of the 2000s represents a particularly fruitful site for examination for a number of reasons. The horror genre seems particularly suited to the strategies of transnational genre hybridity. Horror is concerned with hybridity, focusing on liminality and the uncanny. Also, the late 1990s ushered in an international boom in horror, with the rise of Asian horror and a renewal of interest in and access to European horror. This flourishing of international horror led to industrial and national cross-pollination (for example, the spate of American remakes of J-horror films) that helped to position the horror genre as a key site of transnational exchange. And horror has a celebrated history of genre impurity; many of the most well-regarded horror films, from *The Thing* (John Carpenter, 1982) to *Let the Right One In* (*Låt den rätte komma in*, Tomas Alfredson, 2008), are genre hybrids. In terms of other British genres, non-horror films of this time period have not, for the most part, been notable for their genre hybridity. Transnational concerns have often been explored via the experiences of immigrant and postcolonial populations – as with Stephen Frears's *Dirty Pretty Things* (2002), Saul Dibb's *Bullet Boy* (2004) and, more light-heartedly, the films of Gurinder Chadha – or treated in a superficial and commercialised way, as with films like *Slumdog Millionaire* (Danny Boyle and Loveleen Tandan, 2008) or *The Best Exotic Marigold Hotel* (John Madden, 2011).

This period of British horror cinema also provides a useful lens through which to examine transnational genre hybridity because the idea of 'British cinema' is so vexed in the first place and Britain's film culture and industry are not completely separate entities. Several academic projects have set out to define British cinema. In his 1995 book *Waving the Flag*, Andrew Higson suggests that analysis of British cinema ought to take into account the films that are watched in Britain, including those produced and made outside the UK.[9] From a different angle, in 2007 the UK film industry established a 'cultural test' to assess whether a film is British enough to receive funding from the UK government based on: content (setting, characters, subject matter); its representation of the diversity of Britain's culture, heritage and creativity; its use of British studios and shooting locations; and its involvement with British creative talent for production and post-production.[10] The discursive construction of British cinema has been integral to UK film policies and defining British cinema since it was enacted.

Sarah Street, drawing on Benedict Anderson's idea of the nation as an 'imagined community', discusses British cinema in terms of how it, and other 'cultural referents', construct a 'dominant conception of what it is to be British, a collective consciousness about nationhood', though her work focuses on films defined as British through their UK government registration.[11] John Hill talks about British cinema as linked to 'nationalism and myths of national unity' but argues it can increasingly 're-imagine the nation, or rather nations within Britain, and also to address the specificities of a national culture in a way which does not presume a homogeneous or "pure" national identity'.[12] These critics focus on British cinema's ability to draw from and constitute national identity and dominant cultural constructions of the nation. And while Street focuses on films produced in Britain, Hill discusses three potential foci of examination: production, audience or the representation of nation.

As Susan Hayward notes, 'there are no easy definitions' for what constitutes a national cinema.[13] All of these definitions work alongside others to constitute multiple and shifting discursive constructions of British cinema, defined not only by the films that compose it and the people who make those films but by industry figures, the government legislating around the industry and the critics and academics that discuss the industry and its films. While Street, Hill and Higson's definitions work for their studies, this book is not focused on defining British cinema or what it ought to be. I am not British; I live and work in the US, so the stakes of my definition are necessarily less personal and political than that of Street, Hill and Higson. While British cinema could be defined as the products of the British film industry, transnational film production has made such easy definitions untenable. If a British director makes a film financed primarily by a Hollywood studio, with editing done in Britain and effects done by a company run out of Spain, is the film British?

For the purposes of this book, I want to consider how a film's intertextuality positions it as part of a national cinema, as well as how a film addresses issues prevalent in its contemporary national cultural discourse (that is, how it reflects local concerns). British cinema, then, is constituted by the films produced by the British film industry that are in some way legible, to a person with a reasonable level of knowledge about the industry and history of British cinema, as having come from that industry or British culture more broadly. Britishness is then also partly determined by British film culture. Legibility is often achieved primarily through British direction or production, but it can also be achieved in part through some combination of industrial factors and setting (the UK), topic (e.g. British politics), characters (e.g. British hoodies), theme (e.g. laddish masculinity or postcolonial race relations), genre (e.g. the heritage costume drama, the social realist drama) and marketing campaigns (trailers and posters that explicitly or implicitly reference the 'Britishness' of the film).

While work on British cinema has, at least partly, shifted from national cinema studies to address the transnational, recent scholarship on British horror has remained invested in the national, likely because the Britishness of British cinema has so long been a focus of British cinema studies. Asserting the Britishness of British horror allows scholars to claim both academic and cultural legitimacy for horror and its study. Thus, Ian Conrich praises 2000s British horror for its use of British locations; John Fitzgerald notes specific films' connections to British culture, while Steven Gerrard makes similar connections to subgenres; David Pirie takes heart that 'the great English horror myths are still here'; and James Leggott sees horror as redeemable for its 'naturalistic edge' (i.e. link to the tradition of British social realist film-making) and national socio-political commentary.[14] While I am also clearly invested in the Britishness of 2000s British horror, my focus is on how genre hybridity works to actively position these films as British for specific ends. Here, Britishness as a quality is not a prescriptive label applied to denote general approval. Instead, transnational genre hybridity can operate as both a cultural and an industrial strategy through which film-makers can encourage audiences to view a film as asserting its Britishness through the use of formal and narrative conventions from specific British films and genres. Within the context of British film culture, this assertion of Britishness affirms the film's cultural relevance (and thus critical and cultural worth) within and to that culture.

In terms of the overlap between industry and culture in the UK, most basically, there are voices within British film culture who are also part of the film industry. In addition, the industry has historically relied significantly on governmental funding and oversight, and certain segments of British film culture have actively worked to sustain the industry by shaping the governmental and cultural conversations about it. This is particularly true of middlebrow British film culture. Lucy Mazdon has discussed the British middlebrow as 'fluid' and historically contingent, but also 'a means of negotiating pleasure and improvement' related to 'cultural advancement'.[15] Mazdon looks to the BFI and BBC as examples of the middlebrow, casting *Sight & Sound* as more concerned with arthouse cinema than 'mainstream middlebrow commercial cinema'.[16]

However, I posit a slightly different framing, drawing on Janet Harbord's work in *Film Cultures*.[17] Harbord looks at the site of the film festival as an institutional site of taste-making – a particular strand of film culture – to show how film cultures produce cultural discourses that film-makers can engage with through their work. Putting Mazdon and Harbord in conversation, I examine British middlebrow film culture as a key context that provides an additional set of meanings that are key to understanding how transnational genre hybridity is operating in 2000s British horror cinema. For my purposes, British middlebrow film culture includes sources that place more emphasis on improvement and cultural advancement and in doing so elevate 'artsy' commercial cinema alongside art cinema, like *Sight & Sound*. This definition includes publications like *Sight & Sound*, newspapers like *The Guardian* and *The Independent*, industry publications like *Screen International* and a variety of writers working within film journalism and even academic film studies. This strand of film culture is positioned as professional and aimed at the cineliterate.[18] Traditionally, middlebrow British film culture has emphasised the cultural importance of taste, aesthetics and auteurism, as well as espousing a general suspicion about the potential value of genre cinema. The players in middlebrow British film culture have a vested interest in British cinema, whether that means trying to define British cinema, critiquing government regulation (or lack thereof) or debating the best way forward for British film-makers, the industry or film policy.

Of course, there is not a single, monolithic British film culture; the strand I examine is one of several. There are horror fan communities in the UK that organise, or organised, around magazines like *Shivers* (published 1992–8 and featuring writer Kim Newman), *Dark Side* (published 1990–2009, 2011–present) and the US magazine *Fangoria* (1979–present). Mainstream commercial film culture within Britain is more genre-friendly and can tend to be focused on box office totals and stars – this strand would be represented by magazines like *Empire* and *Total Film* (for the most part), radio programmes like BBC Radio 5 Live's *Kermode and Mayo's Film Review* and television shows like the BBC's *Talking Movies* and BBC Two's *The Culture Show* (again, to some extent). By defining middlebrow British film culture as the segment of film culture in the UK that concerns itself with British cinema, I am necessarily constructing a particular frame around the applicable contributing texts and leaving other texts aside that are no less worthy of study but are not directly relevant for my purposes. There is clearly room for additional reception studies work in the area of British film cultures.

Transnational genre hybridity in 2000s British horror cinema is a reaction to several discourses circulating in middlebrow British film culture at the time. By drawing intertextually on a variety of British film traditions, some more and some less exportable – from the Second World War's Ealing comedy cycle to the BBC's *A Ghost Story for Christmas* series – the films I examine position themselves in a lineage that confers both prestige and cultural capital. Using recognisably British film genres to reframe foreign horror subgenres allows these films to respond to discourses about horror and anxiety over the 'Britishness' of British cinema that circulated in British film culture at the time, attempting to legitimise the horror genre through association.

While the British industry and film culture did not use the term transnational genre hybridity, they did demonstrate a clear awareness of the phenomenon as it manifested in many of the most critically, and often financially, successful British horror films of the time. As James Leggott's quotation above shows, early films like *28 Days Later* and *Shaun of the Dead* were marked out as genre hybrids. *The Independent*'s Ryan Gilbey called *28 Days Later* 'a zombie movie, but not your common-or-garden-kind' à la George Romero – one incorporating Britain's 'tradition of desolate, appalled surrealism' as seen in films like Patrick Keiller's difficult to classify *London* (1994) or Lindsay Anderson's *O Lucky Man!* (1973).[19] *Shaun of the Dead* was marketed and largely received as the first 'zom-rom-com', combining Romerian zombies with the British romantic comedy tradition, then most recently manifested in Richard Curtis's spate of 1990s and early 2000s rom-coms like *Notting Hill* (1999). James Watkins's hoodie horror *Eden Lake* (2008) was dubbed '*Deliverance* meets *Lord of the Flies*', a 'very English *Apocalypse Now*' with 'hints of Peckinpah's *Straw Dogs* and perhaps even Dennis Potter's *Blue Remembered Hills*'.[20]

The 'genre-bending rocket of a film' *Attack the Block* (Joe Cornish, 2011) was compared to *Independence Day* (Roland Emmerich, 1996), *Assault on Precinct 13* (John Carpenter, 1976) and even *E.T.* (Steven Spielberg, 1982), but also Ealing's *Hue and Cry* (Charles Crichton, 1947).[21] The paratexts around James Watkins's later collaboration with the revived Hammer Studios, *The Woman in Black* (2012), placed simultaneous emphasis on the film as a new take on British author Susan Hill's classic Gothic novel and the influence of the visuals and atmosphere of Japanese horror films of the 1990s and 2000s (J-horror).[22] Finally, there are *A Field in England* (Ben Wheatley, 2013) and *Under the Skin* (Jonathan Glazer, 2013), critical darlings despite their meagre financial returns, framed through their art-cinema/horror hybridity, as well as their geographical and temporal settings, as both British and European. This scope, starting with *28 Days Later* and ending with this pair of arthouse horror films, allows me to map the way these films respond to and shape the discourses around horror until a point where the genre achieved a modicum of cultural legitimation within middlebrow British film culture, by 2013.

Of course, not all films of the British horror resurgence of the 2000s engage in transnational genre hybridity; not all are genre hybrids, and not all that are genre hybrids combine foreign and British genres. The resurgence produced hundreds of films – over 1,000 features between 2000 and 2019 based on Internet Movie Database (IMDB) data – most of which were released straight-to-DVD or VOD. Others followed a predictable pattern of limited success on VOD or straight-to-DVD release within the US, which led to a limited theatrical release in the UK or Europe. The ease of entry allowed by the proliferation of relatively inexpensive digital film-making equipment allowed for the boom in production, while streaming services like Netflix, Amazon, Hulu and Shudder created new pathways to distribution, as well as helping international fans coalesce around instantly-accessible, low-budget horror.[23] Most of these films circulated primarily within informal fan film cultures and were disregarded by both mainstream commercial and middlebrow British film cultures.

I have chosen films that best illustrate different uses of transnational genre hybridity and thus have had to exclude some important films, notably including Neil Marshall's *Dog Soldiers* (2002) and *The Descent* (2005), Gareth Edwards's *Monsters* (2010), Ben Wheatley's *Kill List* (2011) and *Sightseers* (2012). A British focus also precludes Irish and Irish-set Ireland/UK co-productions like *Grabbers* (Jon Wright) and *Citadel* (Ciarán Foy, 2012). Ending around 2013 also means missing out on women-directed British horror like Alice Lowe's *Prevenge* (2016), Kate Shenton's *Egomaniac* (2016) and Aislinn Clarke's Ireland/UK co-production *The Devil's Doorway* (2018). I am fully cognisant of the fact that all of the films I'm examining here were directed by English men born between 1956 and 1974, who are presumably also cis-gender and straight, or at the very least are not out as belonging to the LGBTQIA+ community. The whiteness, maleness and Englishness of this set of film-makers reflects not only the dominant composition of British cinema directors, but also British horror, as well as the preferences of middlebrow British film culture during the 2000s (though hopefully that is changing, as more women directors, directors of colour and directors from Scotland, Wales and Northern Ireland are funded and recognised for their good work).

It is not my aim here to provide a representative sampling or survey of the output of 2000s British horror. M. J. Simpson's *Urban Terrors* provides a thorough survey of the films coming at the very start of the resurgence.[24] John Fitzgerald, James Rose, Ian Cooper, James Leggott and Barry Forshaw each devote a chapter, or a significant part of one, to 2000s British horror in their books on British cinema or British horror, covering the main trends and numerous films.[25] Steven Gerrard dives into several of the key subgenres of new British horror, showing how each ties to contemporary British cultural fears.[26] Instead, the films that I have chosen for this study (1) demonstrate transnational genre hybridity, and (2) were widely discussed within, and important to, middlebrow British film culture during this time period. Of course, it is no surprise that these films would have especially interested this segment of the national film culture, as the transnational genre hybridity displayed by each film works to engage with the conversations and debates taking place within that film culture at that time.

British horror films have been a controversial topic in middlebrow British film culture, and often mainstream British culture, since at least the 1950s, when British horror as-such came into its own with films like Hammer Studios's *The Quatermass Xperiment* (Val Guest, 1955). The relative dearth of horror films in previous decades can be attributed in part to the harsh censorship faced by British film-makers, who had to submit scripts to the censors in pre-production. As Peter Hutchings has noted, films that the censors perceived to contain 'the potential to disturb social, political or moral order did not reach the screen'.[27] This climate persisted until after the Second World War, when censors no longer felt such a strong moral imperative to prop up national morale, and the competition posed by television caused a shift in cinema audience demographics away from families. The film industry responded by producing more explicit films, and the censors responded by creating the X certificate in the early 1950s to acknowledge the changes occurring in the film industry and in cinema-going practices.[28] After Hammer's success in the late 1950s, other studios and film-makers began producing horror films as well, including

Amicus Productions's anthology horror films and Tigon British Film Productions's exploitation horror.

I would be remiss if I did not mention Alison Peirse's excellent work tracing a counter-history to the traditional British horror history, which is dominated by Hammer. Peirse's research has revealed a cycle of British horror films in the 1960s that provided women audiences with particular pleasures related to expressing negative emotions and watching women behave badly. These films have often been deemed psychological thrillers, a term often used to culturally elevate horror films by distancing them from that label. These films, like *The Innocents* (Jack Clayton, 1961), *The Haunting* (Robert Wise, 1963) and *Séance on a Wet Afternoon* (Bryan Forbes, 1964), drew on 'nervy black and white European horrors' like *Les Diaboliques* (Henri-Georges Clouzot, 1955) and *Eyes Without a Face* (*Les yeux sans visage*, Georges Franju, 1960).[29] Peirse offers a powerful critique of the horror histories written by men, and largely including films made by and targeted at men.

Horror became 'one of the most commercially successful areas of British cinema' from the 1950s to the 1970s, when a financial crisis hit the film industry and studios like Hammer fell into insolvency.[30] However, despite modest financial success, horror remained largely critically disreputable – as I. Q. Hunter has noted, even now-classic British horror films like Michael Powell's *Peeping Tom* (1960) were regarded as 'beyond trash', as 'abject and excremental'.[31] British horror film-making withered away in the decades of the 1980s and 1990s. This marked decline reflects the general disastrous dwindling of British film production and domestic exhibition in the 1970s. As David Pirie notes, at least 138 British feature films came out in 1957, the year Hammer released *Curse of Frankenstein*, while twenty-four films were released in 1981.[32] Surveying this 'wasteland', as Pirie terms it, it is unsurprising that criticism of British horror at the millennium was rather despairing.[33] Steve Chibnall and Julian Petley's 2002 edited collection, *British Horror Cinema*, begins and ends with essays that reflect on what they saw as the bleak future of the genre. Petley and Chibnall's introductory chapter argues that though 'genre films can be a very effective means of exploring difficult and disturbing subjects', that is not true of 'the horror genre in Britain today'.[34] In the final essay of the collection, Richard Stanley goes so far as to write an obituary for British horror, arguing it is no longer British 'in any significant way'.[35]

More recent work, though, has called these despairing conclusions into question. James Rose's *Beyond Hammer* defends a string of

British horror films since the fall of Hammer, arguing that the films have maintained three key elements of Hammer's films: monsters that are 'perversions of rational humanity' rather than supernatural beings; engagement with the realist mode to situate horror in real public and private British spaces and places; and engagement with the historically relevant cultural fears.[36] However, Rose's study follows the tradition of British horror scholarship's persistent elevation of Hammer by using the studio's films to legitimise new horror. Linnie Blake also devotes a chapter of her larger project *The Wounds of Nations* to 2000s British horror. The project focuses on how national traumas manifest in horror films and how those horror films help audiences work through those traumas. New British horror, Blake argues, works through 'the trauma wrought to long-established modes of masculine selfhood by the socio-economic and cultural', as well as imperial, changes that have occurred in Britain since the 1970s. These self-reflexive films, like *Deathwatch* (Michael J. Bassett, 2002), *Dog Soldiers* (Neil Marshall, 2002) and *Shaun of the Dead*, present 'fusion monsters' that must be defeated by new 'fusion heroes' who actively hybridise older models of masculinity with newer modes to both 'conquer the monster and become a man'.[37] Using trauma studies methodologies allows Blake to produce a nuanced understanding of how 2000s-era British horror responds to changing conceptions of masculinity. My work builds on the threads of her work that examine hybridity in the British horror film and draw out allegorical resonances between generic hybridity and hybrid cultural identities.

Johnny Walker's excellent, in-depth study, *Contemporary British Horror Cinema*, represents one of the most sustained, wide-ranging looks at the full complement of British horror, from straight-to-DVD and streaming/VOD options to theatrically exhibited, more mainstream, productions.[38] It takes up a New Film History methodology and focuses heavily on empirical research into industry history, bringing in cultural history along the way. Drawing on primary research into the funding structures that helped to enable horror's return, as well as primary interviews with industry personnel, the book paints a picture of an industry wherein horror had become associated primarily with home video and online streaming and thus also associated with the video nasties controversy of the 1980s. This served to further deride horror as a genre for, and capable of creating, sadists and deviants. Fan film-makers' nostalgia for these nasties, Walker argues, manifests in the resurgence, particularly in the depiction of masculinity, cult film fandom, teens and the working class. Walker also examines and argues for the relative irrelevance of Hammer Studios's brand name in the modern marketplace – another reflection of the influence of nostalgia for the nasties, considering that by the 1980s, Hammer's originally classic films had lost much of their capacity to scare, or were dismissed as camp fare. While both of our books touch on similar key topics in British cinema during the time period, like laddish masculinity, the moral panic over hoodies and Hammer's return, it would be difficult to write a book about the period and genre that does not address those topics. Walker's industry analysis helps inform my discussions of the British film industry in this book, but my approach is more transnational and theoretical in focus and my focus on film cultures more explicit.

This is in part because British horror has long been discursively constructed within middlebrow British film culture as a genre that exists primarily to titillate sadists and social deviants – unable to explore issues of cultural import like more socially purposive and prestigious films have done.[39] In the early 2000s, new British horror was largely cast as hypothetically useful only (if at all) as a way for up-and-coming, potentially auteur, directors like Jonathan Glazer and Lynne Ramsay to produce 'large-scale films with international appeal' that could 'break away from the UK's glut of low-budget comedies and gangster flicks' – but only when those future auteurs could produce individualistic films rather than the 'more generic end of the spectrum'.[40] Early praise for the horror resurgence was tainted by an anti-horror discourse that positioned 'more generic' films as necessarily lesser than and in opposition to work from directors of burgeoning cultural and/or artistic worth. However, the discourse around new horror films was beginning to change. The relaxation of horror film censorship by the British Board of Film Classification (BBFC) beginning in 1999 and the establishment of events like Film4's FrightFest Film Festival in 2000 indicate that the anti-horror discourse was fading at the turn of the century. This shift is embodied by a number of the films of the resurgence, which deploy horror conventions as a means of exploring broader cultural issues in explicit projects of meaning-making. Three of the earliest films of the resurgence, *28 Days Later*, *Dog Soldiers* and the lesser-known *Deathwatch*, for example, all critique the efficacy and humanity of institutional military power, likely in relation to the UK's military involvement in conflicts in places like Kosovo, Bosnia and Sierra Leone.

There are three specific discourses circulating in middlebrow British film culture that are relevant to this project: the anti-horror discourse, discussed above; the saved/doomed discourse, a binary discourse that positions

British cinema as either saved or doomed; and a related anti-Americanisation discourse. While the saved/doomed discourse has not been written about in a sustained scholarly way, James Russell alludes to the discourse in a weary way in his chapter in *The Routledge Companion to British Cinema History* (2017), saying that in his discussion of Hollywood Blockbusters shot in the UK, he will not be 'rehearsing concerns about the threat of "Americanization"'.[41] Also, Mark Kermode has a chapter in *The Good, The Bad and The Multiplex* on the tendency of British critics to simultaneous predict the imminent death and potential rebirth of the film industry.[42] Especially irksome to Kermode is the tendency for a film's American success to spur calls of 'The British are coming!'[43] This equation is particularly problematic for Kermode because he sees US acclaim mainly for films that sell images of British royalty or heritage, and he does not see US acclaim as having tangible benefits for other types of British film which may be more relevant to the average British viewer, and better. Kermode concludes that he would like to see a return to a thriving exploitation market in the UK, which would be better suited to the UK industry's constant financial woes.[44] I would argue, though, that by 2011, the UK had already seen this resurgence of exploitation in many of its straight-to-DVD and VOD horror films; Kermode's lack of recognition of this fact actually places his chapter on the doomed side of the saved/doomed discourse he critiques.

Similarly, a general attitude of defeatism regarding the contemporary British film industry and displeasure regarding perceived or potential Americanisation pervaded middlebrow British film culture in the 1990s and 2000s, and this is part of what makes the anti-Americanisation discourse so important to the strategic transnational genre hybridity used in new British horror of the 2000s. This discourse both manifested and shaped anxieties about the future of British cinema in a global marketplace that was largely seen as dominated by Hollywood films, which took home the majority of profits at the British box office, and multinational corporate control over exhibition and distribution. As Mark Glancy notes, critics began to discuss the 'fad' of American films' popularity as early as 1910, and within the UK political sphere, Americanisation had been discussed in foreboding tones since the mid-1800s.[45] The term Americanisation, from its birth as a neologism, has been essentially negative. As Genevieve Abravanel shows in her study of the discourse of Americanisation in Britain, it has been used to mean 'the rise and spread of American-style capitalism and the mass entertainment that often followed in its wake' and as a 'rough synonym for standardization or what F.R. Leavis' would later call '"levelling down"'.⁴⁶ Between the world wars, critics began to express concern that the US was 'colonizing Britain and the world through its mass media', with one *World Film News* critic lamenting what was seen as the success of the 'American drive to obliterate every vestige of a native British film industry'.⁴⁷

It seems clear that the increasing visibility and vitriol of the discourse around Americanisation between the wars related to shifting attitudes toward Britain and British film itself. According to Tom Ryall, since the mid-1920s production crisis, British films had often been 'dismissed in vituperative terms' within British film culture, while the critical and financial success of Second World War-era British films brought with it a concern for 'the promotion of an indigenous cinema' that 'neither retreated into a narrow parochialism nor attempted to copy the Hollywood film'.⁴⁸ The success of the industry was seen as something to be nurtured and protected, and this situation, coupled with the Second World War-era ascendancy of American (and diminishment of British) world power, would have made it easier to cast American cinema as a negative colonising force. By the 1950s, Abravanel argues, Britain had shifted from a discourse that highlighted 'Britain's worldly predominance to its minor role in a global American Age'.⁴⁹ This discursive shift in power reflected the sense of defeat felt in the UK as the empire slowly dissolved.

And, after the prominent Second World War-era myth of class levelling in Britain was no longer necessary or expedient, fears about Americanisation expanded to encompass class fears: the mass media of the supposedly classless United States would 'flatten social difference' in the UK and threaten the cultural and economic power of British elites.⁵⁰ The discourse of Americanisation was, almost from the start, a discourse of anti-Americanisation, flexible and capacious enough to encompass fears of reverse colonisation, anxieties about Britain's waning global power and the persistent idea that the working classes needed to be kept in their place, for their own good and to enable elite dominance. Within British film culture, Americanisation has been blamed (alongside the government, film industry and directors themselves) for 'holding back the development of both the indigenous film industry and an authentic film culture'.⁵¹ This anti-Americanisation sentiment persists within middlebrow British film culture, as well as occasionally popping up in mainstream culture and even academia.

The fact that 2000s British horror cinema provided a vital space for film-makers to engage with these discourses helped to contribute to the destabilisation of the persistent anti-horror discourse. The transnational genre hybridity of these films shows that British film can draw on foreign, and even American, genres and film traditions without losing the ability to assert a substantive connection to their nation of origin, whether in terms of film history, film culture or contemporary socio-political concerns. All of this makes this set of films a key case study through which the methodologies of genre studies and film culture studies can extend previous work done on the transnational, as well as British horror. With this book, I aim to make interventions in several film studies subfields, primarily transnational cinema studies and British cinema studies. I also seek to contribute to horror studies. Several important works have looked at the industrial context for horror – such as Richard Nowell's edited collection *Merchants of Menace* – or taken a transnational approach to horror – as with Dana Och and Kirsten Strayer's excellent edited collection, *Transnational Horror Across Visual Media*, and Sophia Siddique and Raphael Raphael's collection focused on the grotesque body, *Transnational Horror Cinema*.[52] By examining the relationship between films and their film cultures through a transnational lens, I show that hybrid films call for hybrid methodologies, and this is of particular import in horror studies, as few genres are so prone to and interested in hybridity.

A final note on audience: because this book is not simply intended for British cinema scholars, or indeed British academics, I have included more information on the culture, history and industry than would be traditionally seen in a book dealing with British cinema. I have done this in order to make the book more accessible to readers from transnational cinema studies and horror studies, as well as readers from outside the UK.

Chapter Breakdown

This project is divided into five chapters. Chapter 1, 'The "Bastard Child of Mainstream Cinema": Middlebrow British Film Culture, Transnationalism and Horror', provides key context for the film culture discourses around transnationalism and horror – the discourses that new British horror directors and studios would counter using transnational genre hybridity. I map how the anti-horror, saved/doomed binary and anti-Americanisation discourses manifested during major British film industry events of the 1990s and 2000s, establishing the import and history of these discourses that the films I examine in later chapters engage with. I do this primarily by analysing publications important to middlebrow British film culture, such as *Sight & Sound*, *Screen International* and *The Guardian*. Analysing how publications, as well as individual film critics and scholars, responded to these events and tracing the three key discourses, I demonstrate how they helped to create an environment wherein horror cinema could be revived and flourish.

Throughout the 1990s, the anti-horror discourse in British film culture softened. In the early 1990s, horror most often conjured images of impressionable children and working-class youth inspired to commit acts of violence after seeing them on screen. However, after much resistance within British film culture to these simplified claims about media and violence, the BBFC relaxed their censorship of horror films (in part signalled by their release of *The Exorcist* (William Friedkin, 1973) for in-home viewing in 1998, ten years after it had been removed from store shelves and banned). The establishment of FrightFest, and its growing recognition within both British film culture and the film industry, further demonstrates and contributed to the decline of the anti-horror discourse. On the other hand, anti-Americanisation remained strong throughout both decades, as did the saved/doomed binary. Just as Nick James argued that British cinema had, by 2001, surrendered to complete Hollywood domination, Ryan Gilbey could write in 2010 that while *28 Days Later* kickstarted a 'new wave' of British horror that continued unabated, those films could not 'compete with the good-looking US model populated by, well, good-looking US models'.[53] While horror films only briefly figured in to the saved/doomed discourse with early entries *28 Days Later* and *Shaun of the Dead*, their general exclusion allowed them room for the sort of experimentation that manifested in their transnational genre hybridity. All of these changes enabled the British horror film to become the most prominent genre of the decade, increasingly positioned as an integral part of British cinema's past, present and future – a genre no longer for sadists only.

The book's four other chapters argue how and to what ends key films of the resurgence employ transnational genre hybridity to negotiate their relationship to these discourses and work to culturally legitimate the genre within British national cinema. Each chapter focuses on a specific manifestation of transnational genre hybridity as exemplified by particular films: 'transnational' as *between*, as *changing thoroughly* or as *beyond*. In each chapter, for each film, I examine how and to what ends these films hybridise the narrative and formal tropes of foreign genres with those of traditional or emergent British genres. While these strategies position each film differently in terms of the national and the transnational, they all enable the films to be positioned as part of British cinema while also commenting upon the film industry that produced them.

Chapter 2, 'The Golden Age of British Cinema is Undead: British Zombies and the Social Realist Impulse', focuses on how, through the use of transnational genre hybridity, a film can be positioned as situated *across* nations, which allows the film to act as a commentary on the relationship between those two film industries. Focusing on the zombie films *28 Days Later* and *Shaun of the Dead*, I map how both films visually and narratively cite scenes from American director George Romero's original *Dead* trilogy (1968, 1978, 1985) while also signalling their engagement with British cinema by drawing on British genres and a more general impulse within British cinema toward topical social realism. *28 Days Later* reframes Romero's zombies by drawing on the cinematographic and visual tropes of heritage cinema, as well as Second World War melodramas. In addition, it participates in contemporary debates around media effects, surveillance culture and animal activism in the UK – particularly through the film's revision of the zombie. *Shaun of the Dead* draws on a range of British comedy styles, including the gentle, but sometimes dark, humour of post-Second World War Ealing comedies, the satire of Monty Python and the men-centred humour of two-man comedy teams like Morecambe and Wise. The film also contributes to discussions around Britain's then-new service economy and associated shifting conceptions of masculinity.

In reframing Romero through British traditions, both films engage with the discourses I examine in my first chapter. *28 Days Later* participates in the anti-Americanisation discourse by delivering a subtle critique of the potential negative influence of Americanisation on the film industry and British audiences via its revision of the zombie, changing Romero's slow-walking intestine-chewers into sprinting, blood-spewing infected that allegorically resonate with the malleable, violent youth and working classes envisioned in the kind of anti-horror media effects discourse that spurred the 1980s video nasty panic and the Bulger murder panic of the 1990s. *Shaun* addresses the same discourses but delivers a different critique. By paying homage to Romero without becoming Americanised, and while remaining within British comedy traditions, *Shaun of the Dead* critiques the anti-Americanisation discourse that positions British film as something tainted by Americanisation, as an industry where Americanisation is inevitable and disastrous.

In Chapter 3, 'Hybrid Hoodie Horrors: Genre Localisation and Britain's Moral Panic', I contend that as the resurgence progressed and the hoodie horror cycle emerged, directors used transnational genre hybridity to take foreign genres and *change them thoroughly* to fit into an emergent domestic film cycle, as well as better addressing domestic cultural concerns – in particular, the moral panic around racialised, working-class teens (commonly referred to as hoodies). Specifically, I look at *Eden Lake* and *Attack the Block*, exploring how these films rework the narrative and visual tropes of 1970s American backwoods horror and cult action films to fit into the British hoodie film cycle. Doing so allows the films to participate in, and potentially critique, the then-ongoing moral panic over hoodies that was simultaneously represented and perpetuated by the hoodie cycle, which depicted the lives and crimes of that population.

Eden Lake combines the concerns of the British hoodie cycle with the tropes of American backwoods horror films like *Texas Chainsaw Massacre* (Tobe Hooper, 1974) and *The Hills Have Eyes* (Wes Craven, 1977), following a young couple on a journey into the British countryside, where they are terrorised by the local hoodie gang. *Eden Lake* taps into the discourses of middle-class anxiety about the working class in backwoods horror but shifts from a very American-coded politics of eugenics to a more localised politics of place – monstrosity becomes an infectious part of working-class spaces. Backwoods horror films depict the conflict between a privileged middle class who invades (and uses for leisure) the home spaces of a population that has little hope of economic mobility; these working-class Others are depicted as innately monstrous, and this monstrosity is used as cause for and symptom of their exclusion from the national economy. *Eden Lake*, on the other hand, shifts the politics of its class conflict to better fit the hoodie panic – monstrosity, rather than being innate, is positioned as an integral and infectious part of spaces that have been culturally coded as working class. The solution to the 'hoodie problem' then becomes one of fencing off land to preserve safe, elite spaces that are free from the aggressive contamination of the working classes (a truly repellent message that is in line with much of the rhetoric around hoodies in British culture at the time).

On the other hand, *Attack the Block* draws on 1970s cult action films like *The Warriors* (Walter Hill, 1979) and *Assault on Precinct 13*, from the name of the gang leader, Hi-Hatz (Jumayn Hunter), to the film's climax, when the heroes and main criminal come together to risk their lives creating an explosion to defeat a larger threat to the broader community.

While the politics of cult action films tend to be ambiguous at best – for example, in *Assault on Precinct 13*, Wilson may help save the precinct, but he is still an admitted killer who has no backstory to ameliorate his crimes – *Attack the Block* works to humanise its hoodie protagonists, who see the error of their ways. The film does not condemn the hoodies or their community but the anonymising living spaces (tower blocks) that keep them from seeing themselves as part of their local, regional and national community. While *Eden Lake* perpetuates the hoodie panic by endorsing protective ghettoisation and condemning working-class spaces as dangerously infectious, *Attack the Block* critiques the panic itself and works against this reading of space by encouraging youths, and viewers, to fight against anonymity and for community.

In Chapter 4, '"A Famous Corpse": Resurrecting Hammer's Transnational Appeal', I argue that, once the resurgence was well underway and established, film-makers used transnational genre hybridity to highlight the global appeal of their films by positioning them as *beyond* the national and hailing a transnational audience. Specifically, I examine how Hammer Studios, whose celebrated horror films of the 1950s and 60s are often thought of as synonymous with British horror, attempted to reclaim its cultural clout domestically and abroad with *The Woman in Black*. Aesthetically, the film draws upon not only the internationally prestigious British heritage film but also a multiplicity of Gothics: Britain's historical Gothic, Hammer's Gothic, the global Gothic of millennial Japanese horror films and the safe Gothic appeal clinging to Daniel Radcliffe's star image after he played the boy who lived in the *Harry Potter* franchise. At the same time, discourses around the film efface its connection to less exportable domestic Gothic media, like the BBC's *A Ghost Story for Christmas*, and the film draws on historical Gothics in a largely superficial way where they are evacuated of their original meanings. *The Woman in Black* has, for example, little in common with the heaving bosoms and virile masculinity of Hammer classics like *Horror of Dracula*. Instead, these Gothics are drawn upon to position the film as appealing to an explicitly transnational audience. The use of J-horror tropes set up the film as beyond the familiar British Gothic for British audiences, just as the links to classic Hammer, however superficial, position the film as similarly exportable. The international popularity of J-horror, combined with Daniel Radcliffe's star text, helps frame the film as appealing for foreign audiences. Transnational genre hybridity allows the film to draw upon the cultural capital of Hammer's former glory while also casting off the weight of those associations and appearing as a new, culturally legitimate face of Hammer and British horror more broadly.

I conclude the book with a final reflection, 'British Horror's Perpetually "Dying Light"'. Film-makers' strategic use of transnational genre hybridity had an immensely positive impact on British horror, and British horror remained strong before the COVID-19 pandemic (ongoing as of this writing), both in terms of output and critical success – a hard shift away from theatrical exhibition and toward streaming platforms has changed the financial landscape and to some extent obscured the genre's profitability behind streaming service's claims of proprietary data, so financial success is trickier to substantiate but seems likely, since quite a few film-makers have been able to put out several films in the last decade. Indeed, 2013 was seemingly a horror jubilee: FrightFest had a banner year of films, the BFI hosted a Gothic cinema season and critically acclaimed films continued to roll onto screens (cinema and computer). However, while transnational genre hybridity had helped bring horror back from the dead, middlebrow British film culture's celebration of the genre would be short-lived. In 2014, middlebrow critics would become distracted by 'elevated horror', which, ironically, is a cycle largely associated with American films, such as David Robert Mitchell's *It Follows* (2014) and Robert Eggers's *The Witch* (2015).

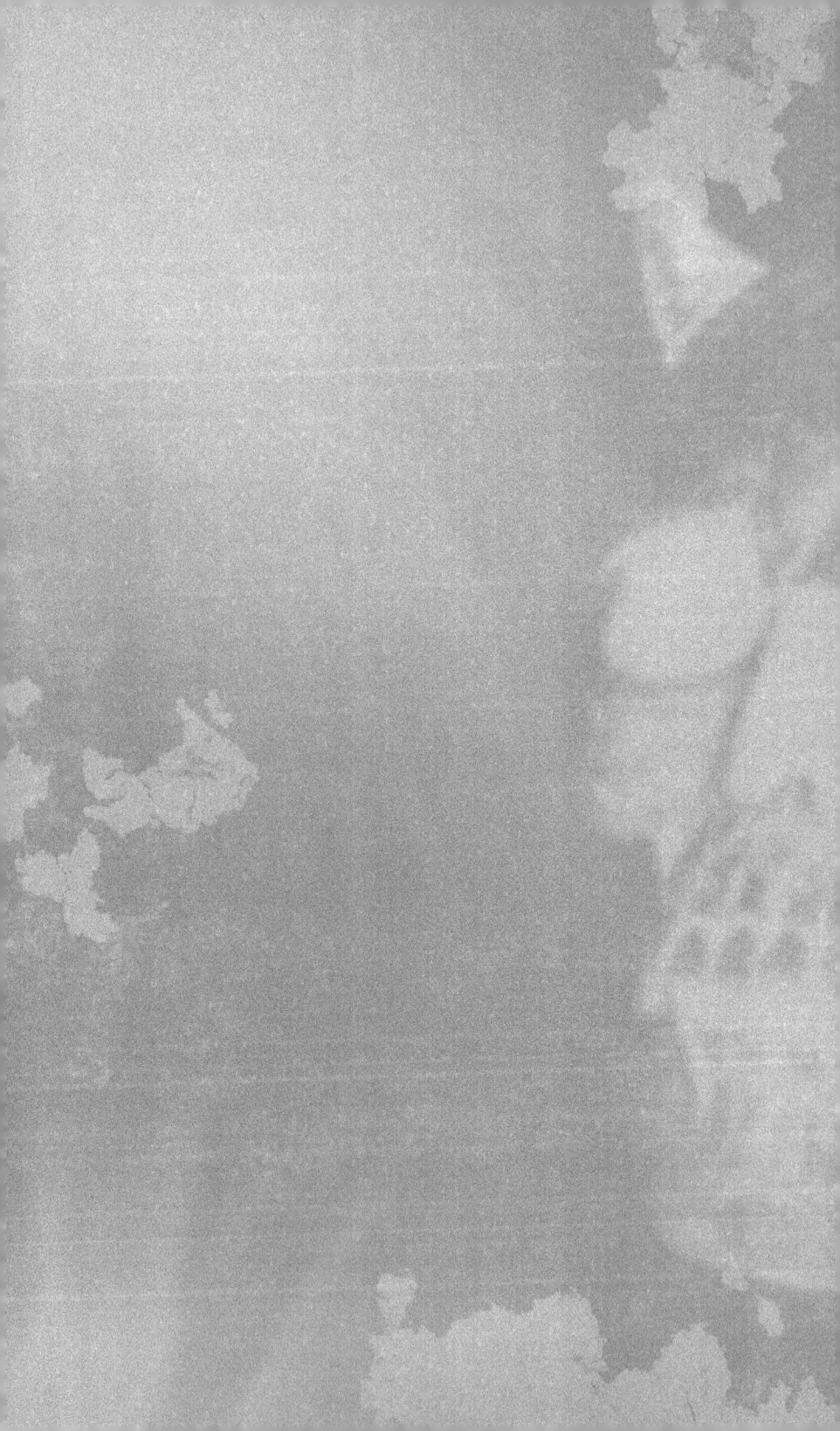

1

The 'Bastard Child of Mainstream Cinema'

Middlebrow British Film Culture, Transnationalism and Horror

THE HORROR GENRE has historically been treated in the UK's highly censorious media culture as a 'bastard child of mainstream cinema'.[1] As a result of this inferior status, British horror films have generally been less subject to the pressures of the saved/doomed binary discourse circulating in middlebrow British film culture. This discourse frames individual films and small cycles of films as having the power to save or doom the film industry. Because they were not subject to these pressures, British horror films have had more latitude to take creative risks (restricted, of course, by the lower budgets typical of the genre), but they have also been subject to an anti-horror discourse that has circulated within this strand of film culture, as well as in the mainstream press. I argue that these discourses produced in British horror film-makers a desire to create horror films that were more than just gore-fests to be cut by the British Board of Film Classification (BBFC) and that engaged with social issues relevant to British audiences in the 2000s. By drawing on foreign and British genres, these films position themselves as specifically British products with a place in British national cinema, asserting the resilience and vibrancy of British cinema and the British film industry in opposition to the critics who predicted its imminent death and irrelevance. The films also counter discourses that position horror as a genre bereft of cultural capital or relevance.

To establish the import of these discourses and their impact on the post-2000s horror resurgence, I map how these discourses operate in middlebrow British film culture of the 1990s. I focus on important moments in this film culture – and the history of horror in the UK. These moments include the meeting on film at Downing Street in June of 1990; the establishment of the Department for National Heritage (DNH) in 1992; the James Bulger case, subsequent media fallout and renewal of the video nasty-era debates on film censorship from 1993 to 1994; the General Agreement on Tariffs and Trade (GATT) talks in 1993; the change of the DNH to the Department for Culture, Media and Sport (DCMS) and initiation of the National Lottery Film Franchises in 1997; and the further relaxation of censorship after James Ferman's retirement from the BBFC in 1999. All of these events stirred up discussion within middlebrow British film culture and helped to shape the three key discourses.

Sight & Sound magazine, published by the British Film Institute (BFI) since 1932, is critically important here, as it is read by and directed to a British and international audience of cine-literate people with an active interest in the film industry. As Christophe Dupin and Geoffrey Nowell-Smith note in their examination of the BFI, 'anybody in Britain whose interest in the cinema extends beyond what's on at the local multiplex will at some point in their lives have taken advantage of some service or activity performed or supported by the BFI'.[2] The remit for the BFI through most of the 1990s was to help Britons become cine-literate, and, as the BFI's flagship magazine, *Sight & Sound* became a sort of governmentally sanctioned shaper of culture. So, it only makes sense to examine it at length as a major source of and influence over middlebrow British film culture.

Sight & Sound has also been a key popular publication for nationally and internationally acclaimed critics and academics, from Mark Kermode and Nick Roddick to bell hooks and Linda Williams. Writers for *Sight & Sound* are often BFI employees who had previously worked in other areas of the organisation, British and American film scholars, or journalists. Several writers, like Kermode, have experience working in the British film industry itself, usually in production. **Sight & Sound** also hosted key debates that shaped film studies within the UK in the late 1970s. The magazine underwent major changes during the 1990s to increase flagging subscriptions and counter a sense that their focus on arthouse cinema was no longer cutting edge.³ These changes included: replacing long-time editor Penelope Houston, whose leadership had (unfairly) fallen into disregard, with Philip Dodd; switching to a more journalistic monthly publication schedule, replacing the more academic quarterly schedule; and integrating the *Monthly Film Bulletin* (MFB) into the magazine, combining the magazine's traditional feature stories and arthouse leanings with the MFB's wide-ranging film reviews and commitment to popular cinema. These changes, as well as the content of the magazine itself, reflected and contributed to changing discourses circulating in middlebrow British film culture in the 1990s.

I also consider film-related articles in the London newspaper *The Guardian*; this newspaper shared writers with *Sight & Sound* in the 1990s and was a key source of film news, particularly in terms of government policy changes affecting film. Their Letters to the Editor section hosted key debates about the revival of the video nasty panic in the early 1990s. However, I am not solely concentrating on officially sanctioned cultural and journalistic sources. I also examine *Screen International*, the UK's leading trade publication, which publishes on the global film industry on a weekly basis and features 'insider' information from people working in the film industry. It is not uncommon to see letters or columns written by important members of the British film industry, including producers and directors managing various UK studios.

Finally, I also consider academic sources, such as *Screen*, a highly regarded UK journal that focuses on film and television. *Screen*, like *Sight & Sound*, started the 1990s by announcing its intent to change itself to better fit contemporary needs. The journal has had a long and storied history, including as the forum for significant debates that advanced and shaped film studies in the 1970s, not unlike *Sight & Sound*. I examine various edited collections and single-author publications that were key to ongoing and emerging discussions about British cinema in the 1990s, several of which were published by the BFI. While the scope of my study does not go back far enough to accommodate significant inclusion of foundational texts of British cinema studies, like Raymond Durgnat's *A Mirror for England* (1971/2011) or Charles Barr's *All Our Yesterdays* (1986/2008), I examine American academic Lester Friedman's edited collection with British, British expatriate and American contributors, *Fires Were Started* (1993/2006), one of the more important collections on British cinema published in the 1990s. The collection came under fire for the national make-up of its contributors, a fact that figures into my analysis.

The publications I examine skew mostly toward the middle class in terms of their audiences and writers. Based on readership data for 1990 and 1999, readers of *The Guardian* in the 1990s were primarily men, ABC1, thirty-five and older; readership shifted in the decade to skew even more toward the ABC1 and over thirty-five, but in terms of gender, men's readership went down slightly while women's readership rose slightly.[4] Based on 2012 data surveying their print and online readership, the readers of *The Guardian* are considered to 'have a passion for arts and culture' and be particularly loyal to *The Guardian* as their newspaper of choice.[5] Readership data for the 1990s is not available for *Sight & Sound*; however, based on the fact that it has not radically changed its format since its reboot in the early 1990s, it is fair to extrapolate the magazine's readership statistics based on available data. According to data from the early 2010s, *Sight & Sound*'s readership is principally comprised of college-educated ABC1 men of age thirty-five and older; as *Sight & Sound* puts it, 'film industry insiders, students, academics and serious film fans'.[6] *Screen International* is a global film industry trade publication, 'the voice for the industry outside Hollywood', aimed at industry insiders and other interested parties, including academics. Their readership, based on available data from 2011, skews toward European CEOs, producers and distributors, though certainly academics doing industry studies would be another audience.[7] In terms of *Screen* and the books I examine, both the specialised topic and level of film studies jargon deployed in the texts implies a primarily academic audience.

It is of note that the horror genre is somewhat seldom mentioned in British film culture, and because of this, the absence as well as presence of discourse features in this chapter. I do not substantively discuss of horror until the section on the James Bulger case, the cultural moment that brought the spectre of the 1980s video nasty crisis and horror cinema back into the discourse after a period of relative silence. Taking *Sight & Sound* as a case study is particularly instructive here. From its first revamped issue in May 1991 to December of 1999, the magazine published eighty-five issues. In total, there were 663 feature stories – of these, only around 4 per cent, a mere twenty-eight feature stories, focused primarily on a horror film, a director of horror films or the horror genre itself. Horror films fared slightly better in terms of the magazine's cover; nine cover images, a little under 11 per cent of all covers for the period, showed a still from a horror film or a photograph of a director and an accompanying headline linking the director to a horror film or the genre more broadly.

This relative silence on horror was also true of academic work. David Pirie's *Heritage of Horror*, published in 1973, was one of the first books to focus a critical, analytical lens on British horror films.[8] Charles Barr wrote a substantial part of one chapter on horror in his foundational study *All Our Yesterdays*, but there would be no full-length study of British horror until Peter Hutchings's *Hammer and Beyond* in 1993.[9] It was not until the 2000s that a substantial number of scholarly books were published on British horror, such as Jonathan Rigby's *English Gothic: A Century of Horror Cinema* (2000), Steve Chibnall and Julian Petley's *British Horror Cinema* (2002) and *A New Heritage of Horror*, Pirie's 2007 update of *Heritage of Horror*.[10]

Downing Street and the Establishment of the Department for National Heritage (DNH)

As has been widely noted by scholars and critics writing about the British film industry, the Thatcher years were a strange and somewhat hostile time for British cinema. American funding had largely disappeared in the UK, as major US studios invested in the re-emerging studio system forming as multinational corporations consolidated their power in Hollywood. The main cash infusion from the US to the UK film industry came from the US films that were shot and had post-production done in the UK, at famous UK studios like Pinewood and Thorn-EMI Elstree.[11] For funding, UK film-makers turned to one of their biggest sources of competition in the previous decade – television. Channel 4, in particular, helped to fund numerous films, a number of which were successful at the box office (for example, Merchant/Ivory's *A Room with A View* (James Ivory, 1985), which secured 10 per cent of its budget from Channel 4) and many of which were implicitly critical of Thatcher's neoliberal economic policies and anti-communitarian beliefs (for example, Peter Greenaway's *The Draughtsman's Contract* (1982), which received 50 per cent of its funding from Channel 4, and *My Beautiful Laundrette* (Stephen Frears, 1985), funded entirely by Channel 4).[12]

In office from 1979 to 1992, Margaret Thatcher and her government enacted a variety of policies to reduce public subsidy of the film industry, and the industry itself went through a volatile period of successes and failures. The early 1980s saw a rise in the international visibility of British cinema, with critical successes such as *Chariots of Fire* (Hugh

Hudson, 1981), winner of multiple awards from Cannes, the Academy Awards and the British Academy of Film and Television Arts (BAFTA), and Richard Attenborough's *Gandhi* (1982), which also won multiple Academy Awards and BAFTAs. The second rise of the costume drama had started in the previous decade but found its greatest success in the heritage films of the 1980s, with films like *A Room with a View* winning at the Academy Awards and the BAFTAs and making over $23 million at the US and UK box offices.[13]

But these successes occurred despite the UK government's actions. The Thatcher government's first action regarding the film industry did not occur until almost the end of its first term in office, when in January 1983 the government suspended the quota that had been in place, in various forms, since 1927, meaning that cinemas were no longer required to apportion a certain percentage of screens for British films.[14] It was not until its second term that the government released its long-awaited White Paper on film policy on 19 July 1984.[15] When the White Paper was introduced into the House of Commons that day by the Minister of State for Industry and Information Technology (it was, for some unknown reason, not available to all members of the House of Lords, though the Minister's statement from the HC was read into the record of the HL), speakers argued that British cinema's 'renaissance' could only be supported by fully eliminating the screen quota; ending the heavy tax burden the Eady Levy placed on cinema owners, which had been used to fund British film production; privatising or abolishing several groups tasked with the oversight of the film industry, including the National Film Finance Corporation (NFFC), the British Film Fund Agency (BFFA) and the Cinematograph Films Council (CFC); and 'free[ing] the film industry from Government intervention and from an intrusive regulatory regime dating from the days of the silent films'.[16]

Only with these changes could the British film industry, it was argued, properly take advantage of pieces of the recently passed Finance Bill, such as the business expansion scheme and an option to delay tax payment on profits until after a film's expenses had been paid.[17] The elimination of these supports represented an attack on what had, since 1950, been 'the major components of state policy' on film.[18] While the Eady Levy and quotas had become ineffective, with the Levy rewarding high-grossing films rather than films that needed the funding and the quota system failing to stimulate British film production as intended, the government wanted the film industry to be subject to the free market and so did not set up newer, better alternatives to the Levy and quota that would have brought them in line with the practices of the modern film industry (for example, updating the Eady Levy to include not just cinema receipts but profits from television and video).[19] Of course, this was part of Thatcherite economics and one of its key contradictions, in that institutions that were not succeeding in the free market with minimal governmental support were thought able to succeed only once that little support was fully withdrawn.

Despite negative reaction on the part of MPs from both houses – HC MP Mr Bryan Gould of Dagenham asserted that the policy would 'inevitably bring much closer commercial and cultural surrender to the Americans' – the White Paper's suggestions became law in the 1985 Film Act.[20] The Act created the British Screen Finance Consortium (BSFC), later shortened to British Screen, a privatised group the Thatcher government helped to form to take over the functions of the NFFC. This new business would receive a minimal yearly government grant for five years, at which time it was expected to have established itself as self-sustaining. Rank, EMI (soon to be bought by Cannon) and Channel 4, all key players in the UK film industry, signed on to contribute financing for a set period: three years for Rank and EMI and five for Channel 4. While it did not become self-sustaining in the 1980s, British Screen did play a more intensive role in the British film industry than anticipated; while the Thatcher government had expected British Screen would play a 'modest' role, instead it became a key player in British film finance. In 1988 alone, British Screen contributed funding to 25 per cent of films that began production that year.[21] Also in 1985, exhibitors and distributors in the UK launched the British Film Year in a bid to increase cinema admissions, which had reached their nadir at 54 million the year before. Cinema attendance did begin to increase in 1985 and would continue to rise until the early 2000s.[22] However, rather than increasing because of the British Film Year campaign, it is perhaps more likely that, as Phil Hoad argues, the arrival and proliferation of the US-style multiplex was key to this rise in cinema attendance.[23]

While cinema-owners were reaping increased profits from both the rise in attendance and the elimination of the Eady Levy, funding for British film production fell after 1985, as the Thatcher government continued to phase out government supports. A particular blow was the gradual elimination by 1986 of the tax shelters that had operated as one of the more important motivators for film producers in the UK since 1979. This tax shelter had made it so that the first-year profits of a film would not be taxed if the production company spent a matching sum on other pictures that year.[24] A number of British production companies, including Goldcrest, Virgin, Palace and Thorn-EMI, drastically scaled back, went bankrupt or stopped work in production altogether. This lack of domestic funding contributed to the decision by British Screen to take on the management and distribution of monies from the European Co-Production Fund in 1991. This additional funding led to more co-productions between UK and European producers, often resulting in Europuddings (unoriginal, mediocre films produced through European co-production). However, it also made British Screen an even more important source of financing for the British film industry.

In June of 1990, the Thatcher government arranged a seminar on the film industry at Downing Street; the seminar was likely convened because of the confluence of the steep decline in British film production – fewer than thirty films had been produced in 1989 – and a growing demand for cinema in the European market. At the meeting, British producers put forward their case for the cultural relevance and economic potential of British cinema, if only it had adequate government supports. While the government did not go so far as admitting the toll their aggressive free market policies and elimination of tax reliefs had taken on the industry, they did promise to form working groups to study and recommend changes to funding and the tax code, including potentially directing funding from television and video to film production and making it easier and faster for producers to write off production costs. The government also established the British Film Commission (BFC) as a consequence of the seminar, whose remit was to encourage inward investment by framing the UK as a centre for international production, encouraging foreign producers to use the UK's filming locations, physical studio spaces, pre- and post-production services and crews. The meeting was seen as a clear indication that film was back on the UK political agenda, and it was even suggested that the industry could become 'the Hollywood of Europe'.[25]

The discourses surrounding the Downing Street seminar were permeated and surrounded by an anti-Americanisation sentiment, as well as the fatalism of the saved/doomed binary. Writing before the seminar, *The Guardian*'s Derek Malcolm asserted that the seminar would take place in large part because Thatcher was afraid of 'the Americans . . . invading Europe as never before'; about the film industry, he says 'We can never be Hollywood, England, and being Channel 4, England is not the answer'.[26] Malcolm positions Hollywood as an almost colonial power here, tapping into resentments around the post-Second World

War rise of US cultural imperialism and the UK's simultaneous imperial decline. At the same time, Hollywood's comparative economic freedom and ability to produce films aimed at a wide international audience were a sought-after goal that Malcolm painted as the ideal, but unachievable, scenario. Rather than celebrating what well-regarded films funded by Channel 4 had achieved at home and abroad, on cinema and television screens, the modern UK industry was denigrated as unable to appeal and ultimately unsuitable.

Screen International's announcement of the seminar, titled 'UK Film Back on Political Agenda', ran on the front page, but just above a longer story that takes up the centre of the page, 'US Product Gains Ground in European Territories'.[27] While the UK story is attributed to staff reporters, the article on US product gets a proper byline by Ralf Ludemann; all of the stories on the front page except the UK story have a byline that attributes a specific writer. While this may have just been coincidence, the result is to make the UK story appear less important. In the top article, Thatcher looks for 'ways of saving the industry' (though not through 'additional state funding for film production'), while, in the lower article, Hollywood's dominance of European screens is illustrated by the fact that in the UK in 1990, only five UK films made the box-office top ten in European cities, while forty-four US titles made it.

As if to further illustrate the disparity between the industries, the London Top 10 appears to the left, featuring six US films (one, *Pretty Woman* (Garry Marshall, 1990); two, *Harlem Nights* (Eddie Murphy, 1989); four, *Internal Affairs* (Mike Figgis, 1990); five, *The Hunt for Red October* (John McTiernan, 1990); eight, *Look Who's Talking* (Amy Heckerling, 1990); and nine, *She-Devil* (Susan Seidelman, 1990)), one Japan/US co-production (ten, Akira Kurosawa's *Dreams* (1990)), one US/UK co-production (six, *The Witches* (Nicolas Roeg, 1990)) and two UK productions (two, *Nuns on the Run* (Jonathan Lynn, 1990) and seven, *The Krays* (Peter Medak, 1990)). That three of the non-UK films were directed by British directors would likely have been an additional source of frustration given long-standing worries around British directors being seduced to the Hollywood 'dark side'. The top left article spot is taken by a story predicting that a particularly high box office over Memorial Day weekend presaged a most profitable summer at the US box office. Both via its layout and through the unspoken link between the stories, this magazine page positions US box-office domination as, if not to blame for UK decline, then at least intricately entangled in the problems of the UK film industry. The visual rhetoric of the page seems to say that UK films cannot take centre stage, centre page or a central place in the UK box office (let alone any other box office) when US films are allowed to continue to dominate.

This discourse remained strong, as evidenced by the February 1992 editorial in *Sight & Sound*, where, on the eve of the election, editorial staff bemoaned the dangers of *Pax Americana* and the 'US stranglehold over distribution, production and exhibition'.[28] As noted by Nowell-Smith in his examination of the BFI, anti-Hollywood rhetoric had once been common in *Sight & Sound*, which had historically been criticised by the BFI for writing disparagingly about popular Hollywood films.[29] The magazine's shift in 1991 to a monthly format and incorporation of the more populist MFB, as well as new editor Philip Dodd and a more trans-Atlantic cast of writers (for example, B. Ruby Rich, John Powers and Peter Biskind), was seen as ameliorating this anti-Hollywood discourse, but the discourse persisted nonetheless.[30]

For a variety of reasons, mostly owing to a passing of responsibility from minister to minster (twelve in total), the working group on funding formed by the Downing Street seminar had not yet produced results when John Major's new Conservative government, fresh from a surprising general election victory, established the Department for National Heritage (DNH) to oversee the government's interaction with the British film industry in April of 1992.[31] The department was run, at least for the first five months, by controversial politician David Mellor, who colloquially christened his role, Secretary of State for National Heritage, as 'Minister of Fun'. Moving film industry oversight from the Department of Trade and Industry (DTI) to a Department for National Heritage has clear implications about the shifting view of the film industry in the government – Major's government saw film not just as another commercial sector of UK industry that needed to sink or swim based on its free market viability but also a key contributor to culture, a repository and recorder of the nation's heritage. This shift in attitude also meant a shift of focus from privileging distribution and exhibition to placing more value on production. The DTI had been focused on profit, perhaps understandably given their mandate as a department meant to foster trade and industry, and been less sympathetic to producers' arguments about the cultural value of film.

Response to the creation of the DNH, like the Downing Street seminar, was permeated by the anti-Americanisation discourse, though, unlike with the seminar, the saved/doomed binary was present in both its hopeful and sceptical forms. In a feature on the Conservative election victory and plans for the DNH, *Screen International* noted 'reason for optimism in the British film industry' and quoted BFI director Wilf Stevenson, who saw the election as 'a great opportunity to look again at the way film is positioned in Britain'.[32] Even if the DNH did nothing for the industry, there was hope that the stability provided by a majority government would stabilise the economy and instil confidence in London financiers and investors, including those in the television industry, who would then, *Screen International* dared to hope, invest in production, exhibition and distribution of UK films. Michael Relph, then-head of Primrose Hill Studios, responded to the feature in the Letters section with even more positive feelings on the Conservative election and plans for the DNH. To Relph, the feature story did 'not sufficiently emphasise the significance' of the shift of film industry oversight from the DTI to the DNH, which he saw as, 'at last, . . . a vital change'.[33] The feature's reserved optimism is clearly not enough for Relph, who sees the DNH as a long-awaited saviour of British film production.

Relph's distrust of the DTI is palpable, and this distrust stems from their profit motive and what he sees as their willingness to capitulate to American cultural and economic imperialism. He writes, 'distribution and exhibition have always been susceptible to purely commercial criteria and if it has been more profitable for them to deal mainly in American product then they could be assured of DTI approval – just as it has approved the takeover of Rover by Ford'. Here, the dominance of Hollywood films on British screens and in British VCRs becomes analogous to the American buyout of a culturally iconic vehicle company. The clear implication is that American films shown on UK screens were usurping the rightful place of domestic product. British films were positioned as analogous to the Rover: iconic, more rough-and-ready than American products (a Rover is more capable of handling most situations thrown at it than a glossy, showy Mustang, for example) and expressing the British 'national attitude to life'. Relph saw the creation of the DNH as heralding an era where 'the cultural importance of maintaining a healthy production industry in Britain will take precedence and the way in which distributors and exhibitors contribute to this will be as important as their commercial well-being'. Relph felt the DNH could save the British film industry, creating a balance between economic imperatives and the nationalistic cultural imperative to privilege British over American products.

Sight & Sound's editorial staff had a less approving view of the formation of the DNH, stating in the June 1992 editorial on the collapse of Palace Pictures, which had been the UK's largest independent producer and distributor of films, that 'the title of the department, we ought to be frank, is not encouraging and it is easy to imagine some of the unfortunate ways it might develop', one of which being 'that the arts could be packaged as a heritage attraction, with anything that can't easily be seen in these terms discarded'.[34] For them, the DNH's David Mellor's immediate task was to ensure that the 'crisis at Palace doesn't also signal the last rites for film made in Britain'. Their concern here falls into the doomed side of the saved/doomed binary. Considering that Palace, though they had a solid video distribution arm, had started struggling almost as soon as they had moved into production in 1983, particularly with the musical *Absolute Beginners* (Julien Temple, 1985), considered 'one of the more notorious failures in British film history', the equation of Palace's success with British cinema's very existence is hyperbolic.[35] In addition, while they did distribute films from British directors like Mike Leigh and Peter Greenaway, much of Palace's profits came from the distribution of American independent films from John Cassavetes, the Coen brothers and John Waters and international arthouse films from directors like Rainer Werner Fassbinder, Nagisa Oshima and Bernardo Bertolucci.[36] In June of 1992, the unexpected and intense success of Neil Jordan's *The Crying Game*, which Palace had a hand in producing, was still months away. Yet, the editorial staff's reaction is a commonplace response within British film culture to any perceived loss or failure in the British film industry or of British cinema – apocalypticism.

The James Bulger Case and Another Moral Panic

In February of 1993, the brutalised body of a two-year old boy was found on the railway several miles from the shopping centre where he had disappeared two days beforehand. Public and journalistic outrage quickly escalated when the suspects in the boy's killing were found: two ten-year-old boys, later identified after their trial as Robert Thompson and Jon Venables. The two boys were charged on 20 February 1993; their trial, which started on 1 November 1993, lasted just twenty-four days. Upon their conviction, the judge addressed the courtroom: 'It is not for me to pass judgment on their upbringing, but I suspect exposure to violent video films may in part be an explanation'.[37] With these words, Justice Morland reignited the decade-old video nasties panic, leading to a firestorm in the popular press, debate and new legislation concerning increased film and video censorship from Parliament and the BBFC being given increased powers of censorship. In citing the viewing of violent films as a cause for real-life violence, Morland also tapped into one manifestation of the long-running anti-horror film discourse in British culture.

The original video nasties panic that the Bulger murder revived had its origin in the 1980s but was part of a rising tide that had been building since the 1970s against the filmic depiction of violence, sex and sexualised violence, particularly the violence rather typical in horror films. The BBFC has, since its establishment in 1912, had the role of classifying films to designate an appropriate audience, cutting films to achieve a certain rating (either desired by the Board or by the film's producer or distributor) or banning films outright that are considered unfit for public consumption. In the 1970s, facing pressure over the depiction of the 'permissive' culture coming out of the social movements of the 1960s, the BBFC overtly (and unashamedly) adopted the practice of allowing the perceived 'artistic quality' of a film to determine whether it would be banned, cut or rated and passed as-is, meaning that artistic films were more often allowed to cross a number of 'unwritten but . . . well-understood boundaries of taste' regarding sexuality and physical and sexual violence.[38] While some horror films like *Straw Dogs* (Sam Peckinpah, 1971) were seen as '"very serious films with something to say about the problems of violence in modern society, and employing violence to make their point"', an increasing majority of horror films of the period, like *Last House on the Left* (Wes Craven, 1972), were seen as catering to and exploiting the low taste of the masses without any 'greater merit'.[39] The Board's singling out of horror films as low culture was hardly new, as the Hammer films of the 1950s and 1960s had met a similar response from a number of critics. Rather, their linkage of horror and irredeemable violence shows the sustained negative view of what had become typical horror tropes, an attitude that would carry into the 1980s and 1990s and shape both the video nasty panic and the post-Bulger panic.

The 1970s also saw other developments that would shape the 1980s video nasty policies, namely the appointment of James Ferman as BBFC Director in 1975. Ferman further cemented the previously unwritten morality policies of the BBFC by working with the government to bring films under the purview of the Obscene Publications Act (OPA) in 1977, a move which effectively allowed the BBFC to police films on the basis of their potential to corrupt the morals of or produce depravity in viewers.[40] In the early 1980s, the BBFC began to give a 'greater degree of consideration' to the questions of '*when* and *if* children should be exposed to certain material'. They were responding to the same conservative discourses of simultaneous distrust and protectionism towards children and the working classes, bolstered by the Thatcher government's election, that would lead to the banning and confiscation of 'video nasties'.

The video nasty controversy was influenced by the BBFC's growing conservatism and the increased conservatism under Thatcher, but it was also shaped by technology and industry. By the end of 1979, there were 250,000 VCRs in use in the UK, and 80 per cent of videos watched were rented. Because 'major distributors [were] worried about both video piracy and denting their theatrical audiences', video distribution was dominated by independent distributors and the rental shelves were stocked with exploitation films, including cheap horror and pornography.[41] As Mark Kermode notes, distributors saw a 'potentially lucrative business opportunity' in the unregulated video market and seized the chance to 'release on video movies which the BBFC would certainly not pass for theatrical distribution', including films like *The Driller Killer* (Abel Ferrara, 1979) and *I Spit on Your Grave* (Meir Zarchi, 1979).[42] This situation meant that content that had long been censored, and essentially kept out of Britain by the BBFC and the OPA, was easily accessible and accessible in the home, where it could be viewed by anyone, potentially including children, teens and the working classes.

The press campaign against the video nasty started in earnest in May 1982. There had been earlier articles about the 'supposed threat to children posed by their easy access to video cassettes of all kinds', but it was not until May of 1982 that the discourse solidified and *The Sunday Times* introduced the term 'video nasty' in an article that cautioned readers about 'How High Street Horror Is Invading the Home'.[43] A month later, *The Daily Mail* would start a campaign for the censorship of these 'video nasties', as well as the destruction of video cassettes currently in circulation, whether privately owned or on store or video rental shop shelves. The video nasty panic built on the fears generated by the threat to government censorship. So, while the press is often blamed for generating the moral panic, in truth, as Julian Petley notes, it was a confluence of circumstances and discourses that led to the media panic, the Director of Public Prosecutions issuing a list of films he felt were in breach of the OPA (films which were subsequently banned and stripped from the shelves of video stores) and the resulting Video Recordings Act (VRA) of 1984.[44] The VRA granted even more censorship power to the BBFC by requiring all videos to be submitted to the BBFC for approval and rating before distribution could occur in the UK, making them the 'official state video classifier'.[45]

The video nasty panic and its resulting legislation was also heavily shaped by anti-horror discourse in British culture. As Julian Petley notes, from the start of the press campaign, 'video nasty' was synonymous with 'horror', despite the fact that the films singled out by the Director of Public Prosecutions on his list of videos in breach of the OPA were not solely (though they were mostly) from the horror genre.[46] Petley would know, as he was one of the only British film scholars of the time who took up the task of critiquing the video nasty panic for its decidedly backward and classist notions about the working classes, publishing in *Screen* (he was also on the editorial board at the time), *MFB* and *The Listener* (a BBC magazine known until the late 1980s for its intellectual and artistic leanings). In his article for the *MFB*, published not long after the VRA was passed, Petley points out that 'horror film has always had precious few friends among the British critical fraternity, and so the unwillingness of most critics even to look at (let alone defend) so-called "video nasties" [was] hardly surprising'.[47] Indeed, Petley's three pieces are virtually the only critical analytical writing published on the topic at the time by British scholars, and his efforts to publish further on the topic were both discouraged and rejected by key publications in British film culture like *Screen*.[48]

Given the links between the 1980s video nasty panic and horror, it seems unsurprising that Justice Morland's remarks about violent videos and the Bulger case in 1993 restarted the video nasty panic and brought the associated strains of anti-horror discourse to the fore. Across the country, the British press 'consistently demonized horror videos' from the end of the trial through the passing of legislation in April 1994 that gave the BBFC the power to rate films differently for cinema exhibition and video distribution.[49] This demonisation even applied to high-profile, award-winning horror films generally thought to be more artistic or culturally worthy, like *The Silence of the Lambs* (Jonathan Demme, 1992).[50] The day after the verdict, writers at *The Guardian* were already presenting one of the convicted boy's fathers as 'a film buff with a penchant for horror' who 'regularly hired videos for the night'.[51] They also pointed out that during the course of their investigation, the police looked into the father's rental history and found 'several horror films', including *Child's Play 3* (Jack Bender, 1991); the writers further speculated, incorrectly, that 'one could draw some parallels between the film's plot and James Bulger's death', as the film has a scene set near 'the tracks of a fun-fair ghost train where' the villainous doll, Chucky, is killed. The article's linkage of the working-class community where the boys grew up with horror (at the video shop, a 'focal point of the local community', 'kids would browse through the horror stacks, discussing their favourites knowledgably') draws on and perpetuates the suspicions more explicitly voiced in the 1970s and 80s: that horror films cannot be viewed by the uneducated masses, children and the working classes, without leading them to mindlessly repeating the violence they see therein.

Horror films, as in the 1980s panic, were singled out. Just pages later, *The Guardian* reported that MPs had demanded governmental action 'over horror videos in the light of the part they may have played in the James Bulger murder'.[52] It is of note that the article also says that the father of one of the boys 'claimed his son watched only cartoons'. The use of 'claimed' works to undermine and throw suspicion on the father's words, and this suspicious and dismissive attitude is rooted in the writer's anti-horror bias. After all, cartoons have long contained levels of violence that would be openly condemned if they were at all taken seriously, as horror films are, and research has shown that if they were 'treated as more than a joke, then cartoons [would] number amongst the most violent programmes on television'.[53] Horror films are often only marginally more realistic than cartoons; aside from being live-action, horror films and cartoons share key unrealistic features, such as the ability for characters to survive what would usually kill someone (whether it is Jason or Freddy coming back to life or Wile E. Coyote surviving long falls from cliffs), as well as a penchant for depicting characters without moral compunction (again, whether it is Wile E. Coyote's repeated attempts to kill The Road Runner or Hannibal Lecter stealing Chilton's pen so he can kill his guards and escape). *The Guardian*'s review of *Child's Play 3* on 26 November, which mentions the Bulger case, ends with a line that resonates all too well with depictions of violence in cartoons: 'The film shows blood, but little pain'.[54] At least horror films show the blood – cartoon violence rarely results in anything so close to a consequence.

While there was hardly an equal debate between the swelling ranks of conservative groups and MPs who shouted for legislation banning the video release of any film rated 18 or higher and those who opposed such measures, there were at least more writers opposing radical censorship in the 1990s than in the 1980s. Julian Petley again rose to defend horror films from the video nasty label, writing in *The Guardian* as well as organising a conference on media effects, though that was not reported on in *Screen* until the following summer due to publishing schedules.[55] But Petley was not a lone voice this time. David Elstein, the director of programming at British Sky Broadcasting (BSkyB), which coincidentally aired *Child's Play 3* twice around the end of the Bulger trial, noted that 'anyone looking at the film dispassionately cannot fail to notice that nothing that happened to James Bulger is depicted in any way'.[56] He goes on to say that clearly few reporters 'actually watched the film, and those who did wilfully misrepresent[ed]' what is a 'fairly routine horror film'. Petley wrote in soon after, answering Elstein's rhetorical question about why the judge and media felt they could blame horror videos: the reason the judge in the Bulger trial felt able to blame violent videos was that 'ever since the "video nasty" panic of the early eighties, horror videos have presented an easy target for those seeking facile explanation of and solutions to the allegedly rising tide of violence' in British society.[57]

Other publications ran stories critical of the panic as well. The writers of two *Screen International* opinion columns stood firmly on the side of film, if not explicitly the side of horror. One column chastises British society for shirking its 'responsibility to its artists not to let them become governed by the political issues of the day', and the other criticises the UK for coming 'so close to such shameful censorship' (meaning the banning of videos rated 18 or higher) as a 'blatant sop to public opinion still seething at the murder' of James Bulger.[58] In both columns, the *Screen International* writers refuse to give credence to the anti-horror discourse, instead historicising this second video nasty panic and explicitly calling attention to the way that film acts as an easy scapegoat for politicians who would rather not do the hard work of reducing violence. While neither column explicitly mentions horror films, the fact that they do not clearly differentiate horror from the rest of film can be seen as implicitly supporting horror as simply another film genre that is equally culturally worthy of freedom from censorship and scapegoating. *Sight & Sound* also ran an editorial that lamented that the UK was 'back in that barren territory in which violent films – and more particularly videos – are routinely assigned the blame for criminality', while distancing itself somewhat from the horror genre by calling *Child's Play 3* 'a second-rate horror movie' (or perhaps just honestly evaluating what was a rather run-of-the-mill film).[59] Here, the editorial staff, like the writers for *Screen International*, implicate British politicians in the perpetuation of criminality and violence that comes about when they blame a false source. These publications represent a real change from the 1980s, when editors shied away from publishing anything critical of the video nasty panic.

Perhaps in part because of the raised voices in key publications in middlebrow British film culture, the media furore and conservative campaign to have all films rated 18 and over banned from video distribution did not win legislatively when Parliament decided the issue in the spring of 1994. The plan would have had dire consequences for the horror genre in the UK, as access to horror would have had to go almost completely underground. The plan would also have had a tremendously negative impact on the burgeoning video industry, and this potential loss of economic opportunity played a key part in the defeat of the types of amendments and laws proposed by *The Daily Mail* and like-minded parliamentarians. Rather, the government legislated and made statutory an already-common practice at the BBFC: the Video Recordings Act was amended to require the BBFC to classify videos with 'special regard' to whether the depiction of 'criminal behaviour', 'illegal drugs', 'violent behaviour or incidents', 'horrified behaviour or incidents' or 'human sexual activity' could stimulate or encourage said behaviours in 'potential viewers'.[60]

So, while the BBFC was technically given increased powers of censorship, the consequences of the law were less radical than conservative campaigners had hoped for, as the BBFC had gained the power to do something they claim they had already been doing.[61] While the BBFC continued to be more conservative in their ratings for video distribution than for cinema exhibition, the renewed focus on the BBFC in the press would lead, in the coming years, to increased scrutiny of what were perceived as inconsistencies and a general liberalisation of BBFC policies under James Ferman. The mainstream and middlebrow British film culture publications concerning the murder of James Bulger and subsequent renewed video nasty panic reflect both the persistence of the anti-horror discourse and the changing, and shrinking, of the spreadability and credibility of that discourse. Horror may still have been a reviled, bastard genre in comparison to mainstream genres, but it was less so than a decade earlier.

The General Agreement on Tariffs and Trade (GATT) Talks

In November of 1992, it was confirmed that the UK would join Eurimages, a body that operated as the Council of Europe's financial support fund for European co-productions. David Mellor's personal and financial scandals had led to his removal from his place at the DNH, and his replacement, Peter Brooke, along with starting the procedures to join Eurimages, froze film funding at its then-current levels. He also vowed to continue the government's support of British Screen, though without increasing their rather low amount (£2 million). Given this continued lack of real national financial support, middlebrow British film culture seemed abuzz with scepticism as the long-dragged-out Uruguay Round of the General Agreement on Tariffs and Trade talks, which started in 1986 with the aim of settling fair trade agreements between the member countries on a vast number of goods and materials, approached yet another final deadline in December of 1993.

Part of the reason the talks had dragged out so long, and one of the last issues to be resolved, was the issue of audio-visual industries. The American negotiators were displeased with and unwilling to let stand the government subsidies and quota schemes commonly used by European governments to support their national film and television industries. The subsidies and quotas were seen by the Americans as needlessly and inhospitably punishing the American film industry. What the US government wanted was a policy wherein the US would open its film and television market to other countries only if those countries allowed the US similarly open access to their film and television markets, not restricted by quota or unbalanced by government subsidy. However, on the European and British side of the question, the Americans were seen as wanting unfettered access to European and UK television and cinemas, which was seen as a move that would inevitably quash existing industry in those regions (particularly since US films already took in a disproportionately large share of the yearly UK and European box office). It was also felt that previous GATT talks had allowed American products to penetrate too deeply into the British market.[62] America's demands on this front were largely seen as going against a fundamental GATT principle that had existed since their original inception in 1947: the promotion of fair, not necessarily free, trade and competition.

There was a stalemate on the issue up until nearly the end of the talks, and rather than craft a mutually agreeable solution, the GATT talks ended with the television and film industries left out of the agreement entirely, which meant that individual countries and the various cooperating organisations of nations in Europe could continue their current subsidies and quotas, and even expand and enlarge those practices. The decision to leave out the film and television sectors also meant a concession that these industries were more than just trade but also possessed cultural components that required at least some economic protectionism in the face of the better-capitalised and more stoutly structured Hollywood. While some sectors of middlebrow British film culture remained civil about the GATT talks, others turned to bombastic, anti-Americanisation rhetoric. *Sight & Sound*'s editorial on the talks falls into the former category, acknowledging the claims of both sides and ultimately concluding that the world of film is one of 'dizzying complexity' where 'responsibilities do not stop at protecting [one's] own hide' and 'we are all likely to swim or sink together', mirroring the magazine's focus on the global film industry.[63] On the other hand, *Guardian* staff writers wanted to see the GATT talks end in an agreement that would allow countries to 'build up industries reflecting their own potential expertise' and warned that if the talks did not result in an agreement, the US would 'bludgeon . . . individual countries into bilateral agreements'.[64] *Screen International* quoted esteemed French actor and director Claude Berri (of *Jean de Florette* (1986) and *Manon des Sources* (1986) fame) as saying 'We shouldn't allow them to deal with us the way they dealt with the Redskins'.[65] While the use of this slur is beyond offensive, it works to frame the US as an invading colonial force that will take over European and British screens before killing off much of the local industry and isolating what remains. This type of hyperbolic rhetoric escalated until the GATT talks were discussed in terms reminiscent of messaging around the Second World War as a fight to stop future generations of children from speaking German; Michael Billington, in a *Guardian* feature, called the talks 'an historic last chance to prevent future European generations from being turned into little more than surrogate Americans'.[66]

Anti-Hollywood, and anti-Americanisation, sentiment ran high in middlebrow British film culture during the GATT talks. The prevalence of this discourse is also highly ironic, though. As Michael Relph of Primrose Hill Studios noted in his opinion piece for *Screen International*, it made little sense for the British film industry to pressure the government to 'attempt to barricade [their] cultural independence at GATT and then leave it in the hands of US charity at home'.[67] By 'charity at home', Relph was referring to the fact that the investment in exhibition that led to rising admissions in the 1990s was initiated by a partnership with US exhibitor AMC, so that even if the UK won a victory at GATT, they would still rely on partnerships with US companies for exhibition. As Relph's subheadline asserts, 'criticizing the US cannot hide the UK's grass-roots problems', including a lack of investment in new film talent and production. Within the discourse around GATT, as Janet Harbord notes in her book *Film Cultures*, America was not figured as a nation of individuals, or a collective culture, in the way that the other nations involved saw themselves. Rather, America is seen as a 'representation of multinationally based corporate empires', wherein 'the multinational company pursues interests external to particular national affiliations' while 'its corporate ownership resides largely within the domain of the USA', so that Europe and the UK's 'resistance to the liberalization of trade is a resistance to multinational corporate power'.[68] What seems at first glance like a cultural argument, then, against worldwide US cultural hegemony, can also be seen as a veiled economic argument, wherein the real threat was an economic hegemony of the multinational corporation and the ways those corporations changed the flows of capital to siphon away national powers of economic self-determination.

Despite the relative success of the talks, where the 'American cultural invasion' was at least prevented from becoming more pronounced, early the next year there were sensationalised headlines in *The Guardian* wondering provocatively, and apocalyptically, 'if the cameras must stop rolling across the Continent' as 'America's cultural invaders snatch the big box office'.[69] *Sight & Sound* implicitly questioned the cultural imperialism of American films in UK cinemas when they asked whether British cinema 'made for the multiplex' like American cinema was 'a matter for celebration'.[70] However, others, such as prominent producer David Puttnam (*Chariots of Fire*), saw the GATT talks as a reminder that the UK and European film industries had some culpability for American dominance at the box office. He asserts that 'If our European industry made more films [audiences] wanted to see, they'd be encouraged to pay and see them'.[71] While this equation is rather facile, given the realities of UK funding structures, Puttnam's desire for UK film-makers to take advantage of new technologies and opportunities to make a film industry of the future rather than one rooted in tradition and nostalgia represents a key iteration of the saved side of the saved/doomed discourse: the industry can be its own saviour, if only it can take a 'courageous leap of confidence. If [the industry] can't deal with the future by coming in through the door, then for God's sake let's try crashing in through the window'. The fact that *The Guardian* can proclaim doom while Puttnam heralds a new future shows that the saved/doomed binary discourse pervaded middlebrow British film culture, and, moreover, that both sides of the binary were applied to the same events, so that the industry was constantly discursively positioned in a dialectical state where it was simultaneously both saved and doomed.

It is within this context that Lester Friedman's collection *Fires Were Started: British Cinema and Thatcherism* was published in 1993 (by University of Minnesota Press in the US, University College London Press in the UK). It started some fires of its own within middlebrow British film culture. British academic and cultural critic Andy Medhurst, writing for *Sight & Sound*, delivered one of the earliest reviews of the book; he starts the review with a rather extended metaphor that snipes at Friedman and his co-authors:

> Sometimes one is so caught up in one's own social or cultural circumstances that it becomes impossible to adopt a perspective. At such moments, it can be helpful to ask: how would this look to a visitor from outer space? For students of British cinema, that question is no longer purely rhetorical. The publication of this book demonstrates that the Martians have finally landed. Unfortunately, the little green men and women forgot to pack any decent maps or phrasebooks when they blasted off for Planet Thatcher, with the result that, for the most part, their versions of events will be unrecognizable to its inhabitants.[72]

Medhurst frames the academics writing the book as alien invaders who have either little or incorrect knowledge of the industry but who feel entitled to make claims anyway. However, a little under half of the contributors, seven of the seventeen, grew up in the UK and/or went to university there. Based on their faculty profiles at their various institutions, US contributors were Lester Friedman, Leonard Quart, Mary Desjardins, Barry Keith Grant, Susan Torrey Barber, Tony Williams, Chris Lippard and Guy Johnson (while I could find no existing faculty record, Johnson was pursuing his PhD from the University of Southern California when he contributed to the collection). Contributors who grew up in and/or went to university in the UK were Peter Wollen, Thomas Elsaesser (who got his PhD from Sussex), Paul Giles, Andrew Higson, Antonia Lant, Jim Leach and Michael Walsh. Other contributors include Brian McIlroy (Canadian) and Manthia Diawara (born in Mali, he did his early schooling in France and earned his PhD in the US, where he now teaches).[73] If anything, this delegation would be only half 'alien'.

Medhurst's contrary tone continues throughout the review, as he posits a number of counter-assertions meant to show the shoddy academic work done in the book but which mostly show the influence of the anti-Americanisation rhetoric swirling in the discourses of middlebrow British film culture in summer 1993. Some of his call-outs are correct (or at least probable), if quibbling – is *Wish You Were Here* (David Leland, 1987) set in East Anglia or West Sussex? When the article is about temporality, not geography or place, this seems a somewhat petty point to press.[74] He disputes Mary Desjardins's claim that the Kray brothers remain 'working-class heroes', but the Kray brothers' status as working-class heroes seems more than probable.[75] When Ron Kray died in 1995, the BBC obituary noted that the 'Krays have reached iconic status, revered by some and scorned by others', and a post-arrest 'industry has grown around them with books, T-shirts, television specials and a film starring pop star twins'.[76] *The Independent*'s obituary notes that the Krays were 'idolized by many as icons of safer, predictable days' and had friends and fans who mounted 'frequent campaigns to get [both brothers] released'.[77] Oddly, considering his criticism, Desjardins's essay is the only one he praises that was not written by an already-famous academic or well-known UK scholar of British cinema (the others he praises being Peter Wollen, Thomas Elsaesser and Andrew Higson). But Medhurst makes solid points about the collection's neglect of Mike Leigh and existing British cinema scholarship from British scholars.

However, Medhurst's other complaints are often uncharitable readings, in particularly his issues with Susan Torrey Barber and Manthia Diawara's chapters. Barber writes that the Thatcher administration 'instituted Clause 28 banning homosexual depiction in the arts'.[78] Medhurst interprets this phrasing as Barber saying Clause 28's 'primary intention' was to ban homosexual depiction in the arts. While Medhurst is correct that this was not the primary intent of Clause 28, that was not Barber's assertion, and it is true that Clause 28's text prohibits the local governments of England, Wales, Scotland and Northern Ireland from 'publish[ing] material with the intention of promoting homosexuality'.[79] Given the government's subsidising of the film industry, however small in the early 1990s, it does not seem improbable that Clause 28 could have been used as a justification to prohibit the depiction of homosexuality on film, as the clause bans the use of government money for positive depictions of homosexuality. Medhurst chastises Diawara for claiming '*Love Thy Neighbour* and *Mind Your Language* were BBC sitcoms', but Diawara calls on those two shows as examples of shows that use 'racist stereotypes of blacks in Britain' – he only mentions sitcoms in afterward, when discussing Channel 4's nonracist sitcoms as challenging damaging depictions of Black people.[80]

Medhurst ends his essay claiming that 'this collection is more interesting as a demonstration of American academic imperialism than a contribution to the study of British cinema'.[81] However, considering that, as previously mentioned, seven of the seventeen contributors grew up in the UK and/or went to university there, and two others were from Canada and Mali, respectively, Medhurst's assertion that the collection demonstrates American academic imperialism is suspect. However, what is most significant is that he has construed this collection as American, as alien, as Other. The anti-Americanisation discourse in middlebrow British film culture leading up to the GATT deadline that December was of such force and saturation that even Medhurst, a usually accurate and judicious scholar, produced rhetoric inflamed by that sentiment.

Indeed, the attacks on Friedman's collection continued from other writers within middlebrow British film culture. *Times Literary Supplement* writer Christopher Bray attacked the book for not being concerned enough with aesthetic evaluation, even as he noted that this is rather typical of academic books engaged in cultural critique.[82] Bray concluded that though British cinema was then and always had been 'in a miserable state', at least *Fires Were Started* 'takes British cinema seriously', 'despite its simplistic politics and aesthetics'. While this review is less negative than Medhurst's, it still delegitimises the main political and scholarly aims of the book by asserting that the best approach to British cinema is an aesthetic one. In her review in *Screen*, Jane Sillars identifies *Fires Were Started* as American repeatedly – the book is 'an American collection containing an uneven mixture' of overviews and single-director studies, 'a US collection addressing British film' wherein 'it is too easy to pick out simple errors'.[83] In a deeply ironic move, after implying that Malian-born critic Manthia Diawara is uncomplicatedly American, Sillars notes that the collection was best when 'the differences between cultures [were] acknowledged rather than when writers simply [tried] to translate or transcend this difference'.[84] (Of course, I cannot and am not trying to make claims about Diawara's personal conception of his national identity in the early 1990s, or imply that immigrants are not American; I'm simply acknowledging that nationality is more complicated than where one currently resides.) Like Medhurst, Sillars praises one woman scholar, Antonia Lant, and heavy-hitters Wollen and Elsaesser. And like Medhurst, Sillars brings up several valid critiques of the collection, particularly its examination of a mostly English cinema that is then made to stand in for British cinema as a whole without an examination of the fractured and fractious nature of what constitutes

'Britishness'.⁸⁵ While some of her criticisms are valid, Sillars tends to collapse all of the writers under the heading 'American' and to collapse the scholarship done in the collection under the category 'American'.

The collection has become an important touchstone in British cinema studies, despite the occasional errors made (and mostly corrected for the second edition, published in 2006) by its contributors. At this date of writing, Google Scholar shows 375 citations alone for Andrew Higson's article in the 1993 edition.⁸⁶ While these British reviews present valid critiques of the collection, they are also permeated by the anti-Americanisation discourse then circulating in middlebrow British film culture during the lead-up to the GATT talks.

The Department for Culture, Media and Sport and the National Lottery Film Franchises

In 1993, the new National Lottery created another potential funding source for the British film industry, with funding to be distributed by the Regional Arts Councils (RACs). However, as Maggie Magor and Philip Schlesinger note in their critical review of UK film policy's relation to taxation, this money tended to go to capital projects far more often than film projects.⁸⁷ After several studies by governmental advisory committees, the Arts Council of England (ACE) commissioned their own study into whether the Lottery could be used to help sustain vertically integrated companies within the UK that could produce enough product and profit to encourage private investment.⁸⁸ The report produced positive results, and ACE set about putting their plans into action. Thus, in 1997 the National Lottery Film Franchises were born, with The Film Consortium, Pathé Pictures and DNA Films receiving sustained cash infusions from the Lottery totalling over £92 million over the course of six years. Films made outside these franchises remained eligible for funding on an individual basis. At nearly the same time, the UK elected Tony Blair's 'third-way' New Labour government in a landslide victory, ending the long era of Conservative Party rule by Thatcher and Major.

There was, throughout middlebrow British film culture, a mix of hope and doubt, summed up well by one *Guardian* headline: 'Boom or Bust Time for British Movie Makers'.⁸⁹ While this line implies both hope (boom) and doubt (bust), it also implies an urgency, the common feeling in middlebrow British film culture that the industry would either be irrevocably saved or doomed in the coming months rather than continuing to exist in its current state. Louise Tutt, writing in a page one article for *Screen International*, quoted Simon Perry, then CEO of British Screen, as saying people there were 'overjoyed', not because they thought their budget would increase but because they 'expect[ed] the dialogue to be better' with New Labour than the Conservatives.[90] In August of 1997, *Sight & Sound*'s editorial staff wrote that 'never in 18 years of Tory rule – and barely within living memory – [had] British film-makers found themselves with so much to do, so little to complain about'.[91]

However, these ebullient expressions of the saved side of the saved/doomed binary were accompanied by their constant companion, complaint and calls of doom. The *Sight & Sound* editorial writers, perhaps despite themselves, find things to protest in the same editorial, including the experimental nature of a new tax write-off for film. They also fret over the ability of UK films to succeed in the domestic market, despite their clear success abroad, particularly given the difficulties of finding distribution when a film's television rights have been pre-sold to acquire production funding. Writing for *Screen International* in the same month, Stuart Kemp worries that 'while UK films have an increasingly high profile at festivals, do they really have a market abroad?'[92] It is hardly surprising, given the pervasive nature of the saved/doomed discourse in middlebrow British film culture, that two articles published in the same month could simultaneously declare the British cinema's success with international audiences and wonder if UK films could please those same audiences.

When the Blair government renamed the Department of National Heritage, christening it the Department for Culture, Media and Sport, there was little analysis, at least compared to the Major government's change to the DNH. This lack of response may have been because, unlike the Major government's name change and shifting of responsibility for the industry from the Department of Trade and Industry, changing the DNH to the DCMS did not involve substantively changing film industry oversight. It did, however, reflect changing attitudes toward film between the Major government and Blair government, as well as revealing a shift in the industry itself. Coming out of the 1980s, the heritage costume drama had been the most prominently internationally successful genre of the decade. Even non-costume films like *Chariots of Fire* tapped into a nostalgia for Britain's past. It is little surprise, then, that for the Major government, British cinema was concerned with national heritage; in this context, the Department for National Heritage possessing responsibility for the industry makes a great deal of sense. However, while heritage costume dramas continued to be successful in the 1990s, from Merchant/Ivory's *Howards End* (James Ivory, 1992) to *Mrs Brown* (John Madden, 1997), the runaway international success of the decade lay with romantic comedies like Working Title's *Four Weddings and a Funeral* (Mike Newell, 1994) and *Notting Hill* (Roger Michell, 1999). Both were films that depicted (a sanitised, whitened) modern British culture, and this emphasis on Britishness was underscored by how the films' leading ladies, both Americans, interacted with and viewed the culture they found themselves in. The shift from Heritage to Culture, then, can be seen not only as a consequence of a tradition-minded Conservative government versus a forward-looking New Labour, but also as representing the shift in the international image of British cinema, which was no longer dominated by heritage concerns.

There were several events that were genuine cause for concern, however. The closure in September of Rank Films' distribution and production arms was a significant blow to the industry, not just because it represented the expiration of a once-key British player in the industry but because Rank had been considered one of the potential distributors to take on Film Franchise products. By October 1998, writers at *Sight & Sound* were wondering in the table of contents if 'the British confidence bubble burst before the mini-studios [were] even up and running'.[93]

There was also an ongoing meltdown at the BFI in 1998. As Nowell-Smith notes, deputy director John Woodward, in response to the DCMS Film Policy Review, which advised the BFI to concentrate more on education and access to films, had attempted to retrench the BFI's activities and in doing so had reorganised the departments.[94] This reorganisation did little to stabilise the BFI's finances but did further delineate between production, exhibition, education, and the archiving and collecting of materials. Near the end of the year, the BFI was 'not only financially insecure and organizationally in chaos, it was also intellectually debilitated', as throughout the 1990s the organisation had been unable to stop a 'steady haemorrhage of qualified staff' and 'intellectual capital'.[95] This was partly self-inflicted, though, as the BFI fired Colin MacCabe, who had most recently worked as Head of Research and Education, without notice. The BFI's rebranded mission was inching it closer to being primarily an educational body and further away from substantive contribution to British film policy, even through culturally applied pressure.

The Relaxation of BBFC Censorship and the Departure of James Ferman

In 1998, the BBFC, and James Ferman in particular, was under attack from the conservative press. In late 1997, Ferman had liberalised the type of pornography that could be licensed under an R18 rating, in an attempt to curb black market pornography. However, Ferman had not consulted the Home Office, and Home Secretary Jack Straw publicly criticised the BBFC for allowing in videos 'which would otherwise have been prevented from entering the country under obscenity laws'.[96] The *Daily Mail* was waging a series of morality campaigns that led Ferman to claim his successor would need 'a flak jacket'.[97] As Mark Kermode and Julian Petley noted in their article on the BBFC at the end of the century, 'the beleaguered BBFC [found] itself attacked from both sides: by libertarians who argue[d] that the private ownership of videos should be their own affair, and by tabloid newspapers who [sought] to attract a censorious readership with moral campaigns such as those mounted against *Crash* and [then] *Lolita*'.[98] By March of 1998, the R18 guidelines had been returned to their previous, more censorious state, and the police had been emboldened to conduct a raid on the home of David Flint, a historian of pornography.[99] Also, Ferman had announced his intent to quit the BBFC by the end of the year. He had survived two video nasty panics with a clean reputation as a strict censor, but his tenure would not survive what seemed to be a third moral panic in the making.

In part, this brewing panic was signalled by a Home Office study released in early 1998 that again drew a link between film violence and violent behaviour in children and teens. However, while most newspaper headlines were quick to read the report selectively, the report itself only found a potential link between 'vulnerable' youths and screen violence. *The Guardian* was quick to jump on the media effects bandwagon. Kamal Ahmed, in his provocatively titled article 'Film Violence Link to Teenage Crime', writes: 'Although admitting that most teenagers were unlikely to be affected by violent films, the authors of the Home Office study said that for those in a "vulnerable" situation, films that glamorised killing could encourage them to commit more crimes'.[100] Despite the fact that the study found that nine out of ten young people were not negatively affected by screen violence or prone to imitate it, Ahmed (and a number of colleagues) chose to twist the results of the study until they fit into old cultural scripts from the video nasty panics of the 1980s and

90s. The article's near-hysteria is poignant when contrasted with *Screen International*'s take on the study, which, to them, showed 'no causal link between violent videos and violent behaviour'.[101] Thus, it is unsurprising that Ahmed's article also participates in the anti-horror discourse; it starts with a summary of the *Child's Play 3* controversy and its supposed link to the murder of James Bulger, including Justice Morland's famous quotation. With the controversy between the BBFC and Home Office over censorship, and this study, the country seemed poised to repeat history.

And yet, it did not. Though Ahmed's article claims that the study 'reignites the debate on film violence and teenagers', little substantive action was taken, and the panic fizzled before it caught flame. Unlike in the 1980s and early 1990s, the outcry was 'largely confined to the pages of the *Daily Mail*, who were busy attacking Adrian Lyne's *Lolita* (1997), shifting their concern with children from violence to sexuality and sexualisation.[102] Home Secretary Jack Straw appointed Robin Duval to take over from Ferman, then largely turned away from the BBFC to deal with more pressing concerns.[103] In early 1999, Andreas Whittam Smith had taken over as president of the BBFC, with Robin Duval replacing Ferman, and as *The Guardian* notes, 'Everything was in place for a dramatic clampdown on sex and violence', but the clampdown never materialised.[104] Instead, the Smith/Duval BBFC certified for release long-withheld horror titles like *The Driller Killer* (Abel Ferrara, 1979; cleared for video release after distributor-initiated cuts), *The Texas Chainsaw Massacre* (Tobe Hooper, 1974; cleared for uncut cinema exhibition) and *Straw Dogs* (cleared for video release). The duo even released *The Exorcist* (William Friedkin, 1973; cleared for video release), a move surprising and noteworthy enough that *Sight & Sound* devoted an entire cover to the fact. Atop the iconic still of Father Merrin (Max von Sydow) standing beside a lamppost, picked out against the dark by a beam of light, the magazine ran a single, simple headline: 'The Exorcist returns'.[105]

The relaxation of censorship for these horror films provoked 'no public or media outcry whatsoever'.[106] The anti-horror discourse prevalent toward the start of the decade had quieted (though not disappeared). Robin Duval, in an interview with Julian Petley for *Sight & Sound*, confirmed the new BBFC attitude toward horror, saying that since his and Whittam's tenure commenced, 'the Board has actually taken a fairly relaxed view on horror films', so much so that he 'struggle[ed] to think of a single mainstream horror film that [they had] interfered with'.[107] Of course, this is not to say that the BBFC had ceased to censor horror films, or that horror films had lost their ability to shock or outrage. In 2002, Duval and the BBFC agreed to finally, after thirty years of censorship, pass Wes Craven's canonical, influential and highly disturbing horror film *Last House on the Left* (1972) for video release, with cuts. However, the distributor held out for an 'intact release', and despite Mark Kermode's 'expert evidence' on the cultural and historical value of the film, the Video Appeals Committee overseeing the appeal 'actually concluded that more cuts were needed' than those the BBFC had asked for.[108] However, the BBFC did experience a significant change of opinion on horror, and this change serves as a good indicator of the continued diminishment of the anti-horror discourse in British film culture, which by the end of the 1990s was even less pronounced than in the early 1990s, around the Bulger case, and far less prominent than with the video nasty panic of the 1980s.

This shift was indicative of a larger shift within British film culture; the establishment of Film4's FrightFest Film Festival in London in 2000 is perhaps the most visible, public confirmation of this larger attitudinal shift. The festival's first year line-up emphasised global horror, including American films (*Pitch Black* (David Twohy, 2000)), Japanese films (*Ringu 2* (Hideo Nakata, 1999) and *Audition* (Takashi Miike, 1999)), works by Italian *giallo* masters Mario Bava and Dario Argento and, most importantly for this study, *The Lighthouse* (1999), Simon Hunter's British horror film. *The Lighthouse*, also known as *Dead of Night*, was a low-budget slasher, but it also, as its titles indicate, was self-reflexive about its place in British cinema history (*Dead of Night* also being the title of a celebrated British anthology horror film from 1945, directed by Alberto Cavalanti, Charles Crichton, Basil Dearden and Robert Hamer and produced by Ealing Studios). While *Sight & Sound*'s review of *The Lighthouse* accused it of being 'nakedly derivative' of *Alien³* and DePalma's *Dressed to Kill*, it also begrudgingly admitting that 'commercially-minded directors like Hunter had a place' in the industry.[109]

Part of the reason for this relaxation on the part of the BBFC, aside from Straw's shift in attention and the softening of the anti-horror discourse in Britain, may be New Labour's plan for the film industry, which revealed itself gradually from 1998 to 2000. The reorganisation of the BFI, firing of Colin MacCabe and rebranding of the BFI's mission in 1998 put the organisation on a path toward increased focus on educational outcomes. As Nowell-Smith notes, by April of 2000 it was clear that the DCMS had removed the BFI's remit over British film culture, and a once key player was 'turned into little more than a delivery mechanism for a strategy' that was 'part of New Labour's plans for the "creative industries"'.[110] Thus, the rebranding of the BFI's mission placed it in a hierarchy that favoured developing 'a sustainable domestic film industry', with 'film culture firmly in second place'.[111] And yet, this shift of focus placed more power in the hands of a body that would have considerable influence and effect on the British horror resurgence, along with British film more broadly, in the first decade of the 2000s: the UK Film Council.

The 2000s Horror Resurgence

Financial changes throughout the coming decade, as well as the continued softening of the anti-horror discourse, played a key role in enabling the 2000s horror resurgence. In 1999, Polygram Filmed Entertainment and its subsidiary Working Title, the studio that produced *Four Weddings and a Funeral* and *Notting Hill*, were sold to Universal in a move that, to many, dashed the hopes for a British producer and distributor that could compete with Hollywood in the UK market. In 2000, British government-supported funding for the film industry was consolidated, bringing together British Screen, the National Lottery and BFI Production under the auspices of the newly established UK Film Council (UKFC). The UKFC would thus take responsibility for the lottery funds used to support the film industry, amounting to some £145 million in 2000. This consolidation left some members of middlebrow British film culture nervous that a single funding source would be 'more vulnerable to powerful lobbying and "safety first" measures' that could quash the risk-taking they saw as necessary to a dynamic industry.[112]

Some of this negativity was likely also due to the fact Alan Parker, a so-called 'Hollywood director' and fervent advocate for commercially viable cinema, was chosen as the first chair for the organisation.[113] Parker is somewhat infamous for supposedly declaring, in the 1980s, that he would leave the country if Peter Greenaway was allowed to make another film, but, once taking over at the UKFC, he 'admitted that the Film Council would indeed be looking for the new Greenaways'.[114] The UKFC's merits and demerits would continue to be debated throughout the first decade of the 2000s.[115] However, by the time that the UKFC suddenly closed in 2011, with the BFI absorbing most of the organisation's duties, opinion had largely turned in favour of the UKFC and British cinema. *The Telegraph* published a public letter from fifty-three actors who worked within the British film industry, many of whom were well-known or up-and-coming, condemning the closure and giving the UKFC credit for 'any success we have had in our acting careers'.[116] Signatories included Bill Nighy, Sir Ian Holm, Thomas Turgoose, Saoirse Ronan, Emily Blunt and Kelly Reilly. The council's chair, producer Tim Bevan, went so far as to say that British film had become 'one of the UK's more successful growth industries' under guidance of the UKFC.[117]

During its tenure, the UKFC helped fund the production of hundreds of British films. While IMDB data is incomplete here, it lists the UKFC as a producer or miscellaneous funding source for over 200 British features released between 2000 and 2016. Indeed, the formation of the UKFC allowed director Danny Boyle to secure additional funds for *28 Days Later* (2002), which I discuss at length in the following chapter. The UKFC also provided the newly rebooted Hammer Studios, which was bought out and put back into production in 2007, with funding for their first critically and financially successful film of the twenty-first century, *The Woman in Black* (James Watkins, 2012). As Johnny Walker notes, 'the UKFC continued to show faith in the commercial prospects of the horror film', funding a diverse range of British horror films through its New Cinema Fund (for 'innovative, lower-budget films'), Premiere Fund (for bigger releases) and Distribution and Exhibition Fund (which helped fund distribution of UK and foreign films within the UK).[118]

Adding to this new focus on horror in the 2000s, London's Fright-Fest sprang onto the scene in 2000. This event was organised by people working within the British film industry: Paul McEvoy (film producer), Ian Rattray (film distributor) and Alan Jones (film journalist). The festival's burgeoning audience over the decade necessitated two changes of venue, moving from Prince Charles Cinema to the Odeon West End in 2005 and from the Odeon to the Empire Cinema in 2009. Channel 4's Film4 signed on as a headlining sponsor for the festival in 2007, praising FrightFest as 'this country's most well loved and respected premiere event for horror film fans' and beginning to schedule complementary programming on Channel 4 during the festival.[119] FrightFest was an important platform for British horror across the decade, both in terms of showing films and hosting events that allowed directors and actors to interact with fans. In 2002, Danny Boyle brought the first reel of *28 Days Later* to FrightFest; 2008, 2009 and 2010 represented banner years for British horror at the festival, with the screenings of *Eden Lake* (James Watkins, 2008), *The Broken* (Sean Ellis, 2008), *The Disappeared* (Johnny Kevorkian, 2008), *The Dead Outside* (Kerry Anne Mullaney, 2008), the BAFTA-nominated television program *Dead Set* (EP Charlie Brooker, 2008), *Colin* (Marc Price, 2008), *Dead Cert* (Steven Lawson, 2010), *Cherry Tree Lane* (Paul Andrew Williams, 2010) and *Monsters* (Gareth Edwards, 2010). As the festival grew in prestige, it gained yearly coverage from *The Guardian* and *The Independent* in 2004.

The softening of the anti-horror discourse in middlebrow British film culture is also reflected in *Sight & Sound*. In October of 2002, *Sight & Sound* ran an issue containing a four-feature article British Cinema Special (see Figure 1). This issue was significant because, throughout the 1990s, even issues featuring headlines and covers that implied the issue was especially about British cinema did not usually contain more than one or two feature stories on British cinema. The June 1991 issue proclaims the 'Twilight of the English' atop a still of Helena Bonham Carter in *Where Angels Fear to Tread* (Charles Sturridge, 1991) but only had one feature (of six total) on British film. This trend persists in the November 1993 issue, with a cover image of Mike Leigh, the headline 'Mike Leigh "Naked"' and a total of two (of seven) features on British film, and the October 1996 issue, with a cover image of Christopher Eccleston, the headline 'Britgrit' and one feature (of six total) on British film. The best ratio is achieved in the September 1998 issue, which has a cover image of Jonathan Rhys Meyers from *Velvet Goldmine* (Todd Haynes, 1998), the headline 'Wham Bam Thank You Glam: "Velvet Goldmine"' and two features (of five total) on British film.

Thus, it becomes clear why a four-feature issue on British cinema was significant when it finally came out in 2002, and the issue's cover presents an interesting object of study. It features two critically acclaimed British directors, Mike Leigh and Lynne Ramsay, as well as former television-drama turned feature film director Marc Evans, whose *My Little Eye* is cited by the cover as '2002's scariest movie'. The magazine's headline reads: 'The confident new face of British cinema'. While 'new' in the headline may refer to a new confidence in British cinema, Mike Leigh's established reputation serves to emphasise the 'newness' of Ramsay and Evans. Ramsay had made her feature film debut in 1999 with the critically acclaimed *Ratcatcher*, while Evans had critical success with his drama *House of America* (1997) before *My Little Eye*. However, Mike Leigh was, is and has been for some time, an acclaimed director. In the

Figure 1. The cover of the October 2002 issue of *Sight & Sound*.

1970s, he directed several television plays for the BBC, including *Nuts in May* (1976), a well-regarded comedy, and by 1993 he had won the Best Director award at Cannes for his film *Naked*. The cover acknowledges Leigh's status as proven veteran with his caption: '*All or Nothing*: his best yet'. Perhaps that is why Leigh's visage is to the left, followed by Evans in the centre and Ramsay to the right – the image positions the directors from most to least established. Evans's inclusion is of note, considering the previously cited dearth of articles (not to mention covers) on the horror genre in *Sight & Sound* in the 1990s. This inclusion is both prescient (given the rise of horror in the coming years) and reflective of the softening of the anti-horror discourse.

Inside the issue, there are feature articles on new films by Ken Loach, Mike Leigh and others, an assessment of the recently shut-down Film4 production outfit, a look at Ramsay's latest film *Morvern Callar* and an article about how *My Little Eye* plays with notions of violence and voyeurism in the internet age. What is most striking about these features is their participation in the 'saved' side of the saved/doomed binary – a positive tone pervades. The introduction to the special issue perhaps best shows this:

> With the winding down of FilmFour still fresh in the memory, it might seem an odd moment to devote an issue of *S&S* to celebrating current British cinema . . . [The demise of FilmFour has] occasioned familiar complaints about the British film industry's inexhaustible capacity to self-destruct. But there's another story to British cinema right now. Forget, for a moment, the gloomy outlook of the trade papers, and consider the evidence on screen . . . Here you'll find British directors on exhilarating, ambitious form . . . But in wider terms it's perhaps not too fanciful to suggest they signal a new direction for British cinema. For what unites these films – a risk-taking rigour and willingness to provoke and make demands on audiences – are precisely the qualities that have recently been in short supply.[120]

Against the 'familiar complaints' about the doomed nature of British cinema and the film industry, this special issue asserted that British cinema and the industry were headed in a new and exciting direction, not because of gains in British production or distribution but because of the content of the films making it to screens.

Sight & Sound identifies these new films as taking risks, as asking audiences to think rather than consume. Though the implication that films previously made little to no demands on audiences is more hyperbole than fact, the issue's focus on social realist and arthouse types like Leigh and Ramsay alongside horror like *My Little Eye* shows the diminishment of the anti-horror discourse. The genre hybridity of *My Little Eye*, with its mix of horror tropes and documentary style, albeit heavily mediated through the lens of reality television, was a risk, even after the success of the American found-footage horror film *The Blair Witch Project* in 1999 and the fact that similar ideas had already been circulating in the straight-to-video market. It is hard not to see *My Little Eye* as a cultural critique not wholly unlike those delivered by lauded figures like Loach and Leigh, considering the film is about voyeurism and violence and was made in a culture with a long-standing obsession with the censorship of film violence, particularly in horror. Placing Evans alongside film-makers like Leigh and Ramsay shows how shifting conceptions of what British cinema could be, as well as the decrease in anti-horror rhetoric, had changed enough to allow new horror to be framed as part of a culturally engaged British cinema that might save the industry.

Even the rhetoric around video nasties had quieted to such an extent that *The Evil Dead* (Sam Raimi, 1981) was allowed national exhibition in 2002. Johnny Walker identifies the screening of *The Evil Dead*, shown on a double-bill in British cinemas with *The Lighthouse*, as a key moment in the softening of negative attitudes toward horror.[121] This was a national, eight-week release on twenty screens; before 2002, video nasties had only secured successful runs in arthouse cinemas and at film festivals.[122]

The three main discourses examined here played a vital role in setting a cultural climate that could allow for the British horror resurgence of the 2000s. The changing cultural attitudes toward horror films, and the softening of the anti-horror discourse in British film culture, mainstream and middlebrow, had a hand in enabling creatives within the British film industry to frame their horror films as more than horrific violence for degenerate audiences. The gradual shift in discourse meant that horror films were increasingly seen, like other film genres, as potentially culturally worthy and able to be culturally and socially relevant (to more than youth violence statistics). However, horror films were still subject to biases and censorship and were not yet widely included in the saved/doomed discourse that pervaded discussion of British films from other genres. This comparative lack of pressure allowed for the sort of experimentation that would produce *28 Days Later*, a genre hybrid that took advantage of new digital video technology to produce a film whose cinematography evoked the gritty, bleak look of social realist dramas. These films were produced from and received into a film culture that, in 2000, was asking itself whether Britain still had a 'film culture' and answering 'if we do, it is already American'.[123]

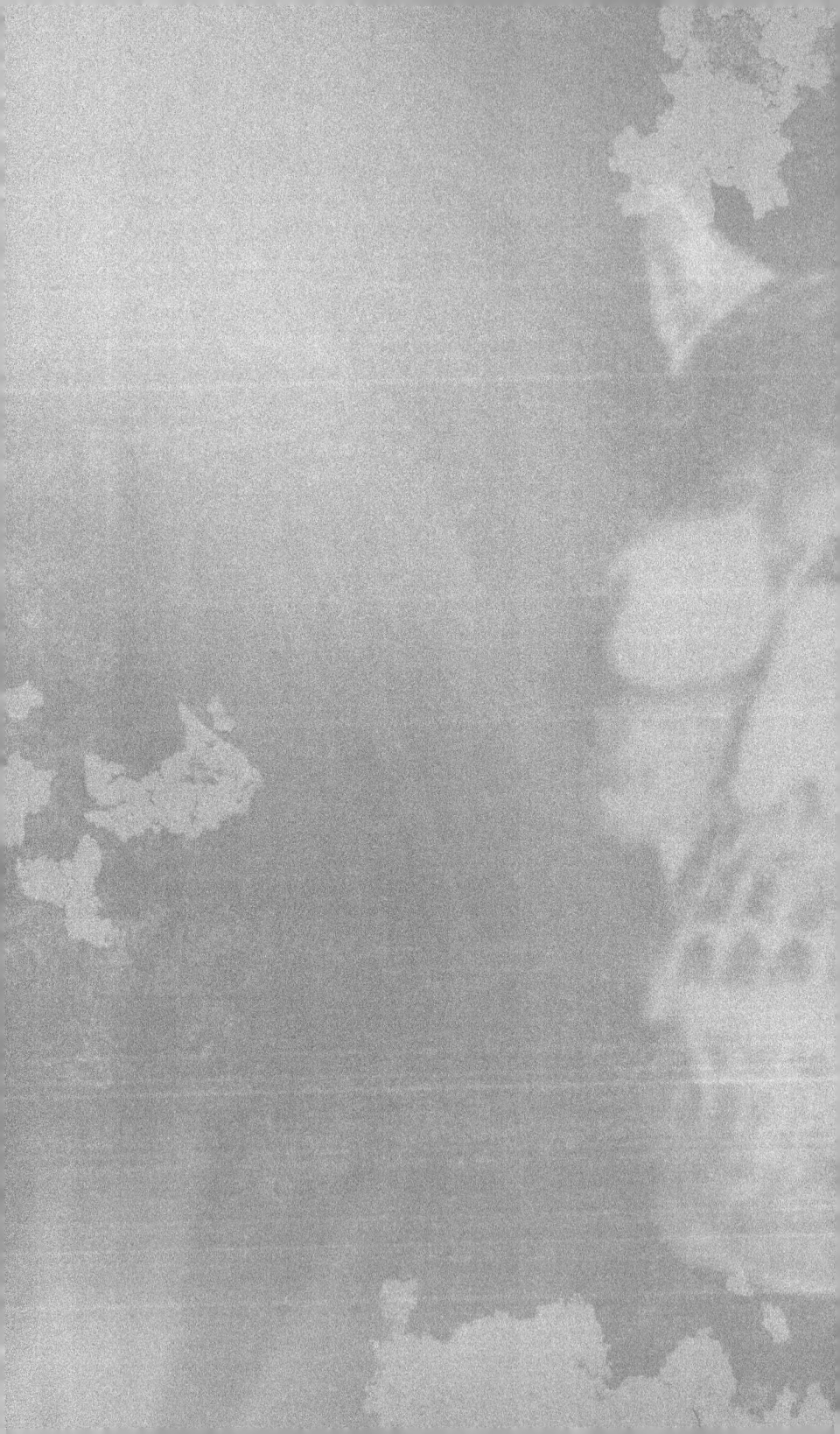

2

The Golden Age of British Cinema is Undead

British Zombies and the Social Realist Impulse

The belief that generic forms can be intentionally used as a vehicle for serious concerns has been the downfall of many a director (think Coppola's *Dracula* and *Frankenstein*) . . . By all means let's project our own private fears onto the public canvas of horror movies. But let's not try and fit cultural ambitions into the readymade mould of genre cinema, like the toy inside a Kinder Surprise. (Nick Roddick, British film critic[1])

I like to play around with genre, though . . . The genre hooks are MacGuffins that give us a route into exploring ideas. (Danny Boyle, British film-maker and director of *28 Days Later*[2])

THE TWO QUOTATIONS above embody a contradiction at the heart of 2000s British horror: though British horror had long been discursively constructed within middlebrow British film culture as a genre unable to successfully explore issues of contemporary national cultural import, a number of British horror films of the period do exactly that while also receiving substantial box office revenue and/or critical acclaim at home and abroad. Although Boyle was not directly responding to Roddick, we can read these quotations as representative of the dialogue between middlebrow British film culture and British horror film-makers in the 2000s. Middlebrow British film culture continued to cast British horror as culturally marginal and mere entertainment, useful only (if at all) as a 'public canvas' upon which individual viewers could project their fears. In this metaphor, the viewer is the artist, the true author of meaning, projecting his or her fears onto the waiting (and wanting) medium. The horror film, then, is cast as an incomplete text; like the screen upon which films are projected, horror is framed as a non-space waiting to be endowed with meaning. In direct opposition to this attitude, British horror films were engaged in explicit projects of meaning-making, playfully deploying the conventions of the genre as a means of 'exploring ideas'.

This chapter examines how two early films of the British horror resurgence, specifically *28 Days Later* (Danny Boyle, 2002) and *Shaun of the Dead* (Edgar Wright, 2004), engage in transnational genre hybridity as a means of initiating and participating in the dialogue just described. Both films' generic hybridity positions them as *situated across* the two nations, tapping into a meaning of *trans-* that allows the films to comment on both nations' film industries and the relationship between them. Both films draw on the tropes of British genres, including comedies and what Andrew Higson calls 'melodramas of everyday life' that flourished during and after the Second World War, to reframe the US zombie horror subgenre.[3] Specifically, the films reframe the then-prevailing zombie paradigm embodied by George Romero's original *Dead* trilogy (1968's *Night of the Living Dead*, 1978's *Dawn of the Dead* and 1985's *Day of the Dead*). While both films draw on a variety of genres, by hearkening back to the Second World War, both films position themselves in relation to what is commonly referred to as the Golden Age of British film-making, a move that associates the films with prestige and cultural capital. By reframing the Romerian zombie paradigm and aligning themselves with a celebrated national cinematic heritage, they respond to the anti-horror and anti-Americanisation discourses circulating in middlebrow British film culture at the time by attempting to legitimise the horror genre by association. That the horror genre provides a vital space in which to undertake in this work significantly troubles the anti-horror discourse. In addition, the films' transnational genre hybridity shows that British films can draw on American genres and film traditions without losing the ability to assert a substantive connection to their nation of origin, whether in terms of film history and film culture or contemporary socio-political concerns.

The relationship between the British and American film industries, and these films' engagement with that transnational relationship, is a key context in which the films of the British horror resurgence are imbricated but which remains largely unacknowledged within critical and academic work on the films. Scholars writing on *28 Days Later* have tended to either examine the film's specifically British cultural elements or gloss over those elements in favour of finding universal messages. Critics focusing on specifically British meanings have focused mostly on cultural anxieties regarding gender, race, class and adulthood. Linnie Blake argues that Jim (Cillian Murphy) from *28 Days Later* represents a 'third way' for masculinity, neither oppressed nor oppressive, rejecting militarism and machismo in favour of 'social cooperation and personal self-sacrifice'.[4] Nicole LaRose contends that the film presents a critique of the Anglican Church and British military, while Barbara Korte argues that the film taps into Blair-era political discourse in Britain that posits 'the multi-ethnic society as a vision for the future'.[5] Writing on *Shaun of the Dead*, Blake argues that the film explores 'how late-capitalist society infantalises its males, bombarding them with mass cultural simulacra of their own desires' to keep them isolated and powerless.[6] Kim Edwards sees *Shaun* as an indictment of London's 'slothful . . . and dissolute society'.[7] These critics read the films productively within both a historical and national context, while Johnny Walker notes, from an industry angle, how both films tried through their marketing and content to attract a horror audience with intertextuality and a broader audience that included women, who were not traditionally seen as horror fans by studios or promoters.[8]

However, other critics tend to put aside the films' national context in favour of a universalised message about culture, which can flatten out historical and cultural specificity. Peter Dendle places *28 Days Later* in a larger argument about the arc of American zombie films, arguing the film represents cultural anxiety over 'an over-leisurely society' driven by 'unchecked power and its desires for consumption'.[9] Gretchen Bakke explicitly groups *Days* with 'US Action Cinema'.[10] Nick Muntean and Matthew Payne read the zombies of *28 Days Later* as representing post-9/11 anxieties over terrorism.[11] However, terrorism was a concern in Britain long before 11 September 2001. From the long history of conflict between the UK government and the Irish Republican Army (IRA), to an international tragedy like the 1988 Lockerbie bombing, to the 1999 nail bombing in Soho, the UK has its own historically (and culturally) contingent relationship with terrorism. Even Michael Newbury's excellent argument about how twenty-first century zombie films like *Shaun* and *Days* resonate with cultural anxieties about industrial food systems, disease and junk food concentrates on an American context, leaving out British cultural factors such as the rise of animal rights activism in the late 1990s and the bovine spongiform encephalopathy (BSE; colloquially known as mad cow disease) outbreaks common after the mid-1980s.[12] While there can be merit to approaches using broad Anglo-American or Western cultural schema, these approaches can gloss over cultural and historical specificity for the sake of generalisation. There is a sense that by participating in the zombie genre, *Days* and *Shaun* are more readily and acceptably placed under American or broader cultural rubrics.

I argue that rather than taking an approach that reads the films in either an exclusive British context or a more generalised (or American) context, the films must be taken explicitly as transnational. As Paul McDonald has argued, 'the presence of Hollywood entertainment [in the UK] is just one example of how the popular imagination of UK residents is continually formed through transnational flows of symbolic goods', so that 'Hollywood film is today as much a part of British culture as fish and chips or warm beer', just as Hollywood is 'part of the very substance of the [British] film industry'.[13] In addition, the films themselves, via their transnational genre hybridity, point toward this approach, so that the films are considered not just in terms of their relation to the American zombie subgenre but also in terms of their national and cinematic contexts as British films. Moreover, because of how the industries are imbricated, and the lively discourses around this imbrication in middlebrow British film culture, the additional consideration of how the films respond and fit into British film culture is also an important layer of meaning.

This chapter delineates how each film attempts to claim filmic and cultural legitimacy by reframing the Romerian zombie films through specific British genres, in addition to participating in British film's social realist impulse by explicitly addressing contemporary British social issues. In using the phrase 'social realist impulse', I am not trying to claim either film as realistic or to designate either as a social realist drama of the New Wave, Ken Loach or Mike Leigh varieties. Rather, I reference the long-standing discourse within British film culture that elevates films that are deemed realistic, either in terms of form (location shooting, a detached and observational camera, the use of Northern accents, etc.) or attention to social problems (often the lived realities of working-class people). *28 Days Later* belies this engagement through its resonance with late-1990s and early-2000s British discourses about media effects, surveillance culture and animal activism. The film's links to British film traditions are further cemented by the way the film draws on Second World War melodramas of everyday life and the heritage film. *Shaun of the Dead*, on the other hand, engages with debates around Britain's new service economy and shifting conceptions of masculinity, as well as drawing on a range of British comedy styles, including Ealing comedies of the 1940s and 50s; Monty Python and their absurdist satirising of institutional authority and norms; and television two-man comedy teams like the Likely Lads or Morecambe and Wise. The boundaries between film and television are more permeable in the UK, so that it is not uncommon for actors, directors, screenwriters and other talent to work in both film and television, just as it is common for television programmes to spawn films, as with both Monty Python and the Likely Lads. Thus, *Shaun of the Dead* reshapes the boundaries of British 'film' tradition to include media more broadly. By combining British comedy styles with tropes of the American zombie film, *Shaun* pays homage to Romerian zombies without becoming Americanised and so critiques discourses bemoaning the inevitability of Americanisation in British film culture. *28 Days Later* responds to the same discourses by adopting British traditions to revise the figure of the zombie itself to deliver a subtle critique of Americanisation.

28 Days Later and Conceiving of a World beyond Britain

Before discussing how *28 Days Later* ultimately critiques Americanisation through its deployment of British film traditions and contemporary cultural concerns, I delineate how the film participates in the discourses of Americanisation present at that time in British film culture, as well as reframing Romero's zombies. Early British reviews and fan responses to *28 Days Later* displayed both a defence of the film's perceived Britishness and a distaste for Americanisation. The film relays the story of Jim (Cillian Murphy), a former bicycle courier and his companions Selena (Naomie Harris), Frank (beloved character actor Brendan Gleeson) and Frank's daughter Hannah (Megan Burns), a ragtag group who leave zombie-infested London to seek safety with soldiers outside Manchester. Writing just before the film's debut in the United Kingdom, Stephen Applebaum of *The Scotsman* linked *28 Days Later* specifically to anti-Hollywood sentiment, positing that Boyle's expensive Hollywood flop *The Beach* likely led him toward 'star-shy casting, comparatively small budget, British setting and raw digital cinematography'.[14] Applebaum further speculated – incorrectly – that the film was unlikely to do well in the United States because, unlike Hollywood films, the violence is not sexualised or seductive but 'shocking and repulsive'. *Time Out*'s Tom Charity had similar doubts about the film's ability to succeed abroad, calling the film insular and saying it 'barely conceives of a world (or indeed a market) beyond Britain', though for Charity, as for Applebaum, this is one of the film's strengths.[15] *Mail on Sunday* writer Jo Wiltshire takes a similar stance, arguing that though the ending's 'glimmer of hope' could read as pandering to 'Hollywood sensibilities', it is instead an attempt to answer the film's own questions ('are we a greater danger to ourselves than any outside enemy; is "rage" the modern plague?'), which ultimately helps the film avoid 'mindless violence' and 'titillating terror'.[16] In her study of fan response to *28 Days Later*, Brigid Cherry notes that fans privilege the Britishness of the film, particularly the 'aesthetic and narrative breaks with the dominant forms of Hollywood genre', and their descriptions of why they enjoyed the film articulate a resistance to 'Hollywood culture'.[17] For these critics and fans, the film's Britishness is defined through its use of an anti-Hollywood attitude and aesthetic. These responses hearken back to long-standing identification of certain British films, especially those that deploy a realist aesthetic, with a discourse of quality.[18] By extension, this positivity toward what is perceived as an anti-Hollywood approach taps into the anti-Americanisation discourse in middlebrow British film culture.

Of course, not everyone looked favourably on what were seen as the film's anti-Hollywood elements: the use of digital video, avoidance of A-list stars in favour of relative unknowns for the leads and giving smaller roles to familiar character actor Brendan Gleeson and Christopher Eccleston (the head military adversary in the film), a household name in the UK for his television roles. *Screen International*'s Allen Hunter panned the film for just those reasons, concluding that it was unlikely to do well either in Britain or internationally.[19]

However, the film did do well both in the UK and abroad. Like so many films in this transnational era, it depended on Hollywood studio distribution (via 20th Century Fox) and an international audience for economic viability, but it does not simply replicate Hollywood genres. But screenwriter Andrew Macdonald set out to write a new type of zombie film that broke from the established paradigm.[20] The direct intertextual links between *28 Days Later* and each of the three films in Romero's *Dead* trilogy help indicate the film's concern with US cinema. The famous, gleeful raid on the Budgens grocery store in *28 Days Later* directly cites the shopping sprees in Romero's *Dawn of the Dead*, where the protagonists take over a shopping mall. Jim's trip into the abandoned restaurant when Frank and Hannah refuel their car, and the child who subsequently springs upon him, mirrors the helicopter fuel stop in *Dawn* where Peter wanders into an abandoned airport chart house and is attacked by two children. The vicious soldiers and the chained zombie, Private Mailer, cite the similarly callous soldiers and chained zombie, Bub, in Romero's *Day of the Dead*. The soldiers in both films share a deplorably enthusiastic attitude toward sexual violence. Additionally, both Bub and Private Mailer are chained by the neck and allowed vengeance against an unstable and ethically compromised military leader.

The links between Romero's *Night of the Living Dead* (1968) and *28 Days Later* are accomplished not through direct visual or narrative citation, as with *Dawn* and *Day*. Instead, they become clear when looking at how each film consciously shifts away from the then-dominant zombie paradigm – and in the case of *28 Days Later*, the main paradigm was Romero's. While there were zombie films before *Night*, Romero is widely credited with reinventing the film zombie, changing it from the traditional Haitian-inspired voodoo zombie, usually created and controlled by a nefarious character, to the shuffling, flesh-craving modern zombie, who travels in packs to hunt the living.[21] Other types of zombies came into existence on film between *Night* and *28 Days Later*, perhaps most notably in Italian cinema, with purposely reanimated undead in *Zombi 3* (Lucio Fulci, 1988); super-strong ghouls capable of a decent jog in *Nightmare City* (Umberto Lenzi, 1980). There are also the gooey, campy, advanced-decomposition zombies of *Return of the Living Dead* (Dan O'Bannon, 1985). The zombies in *28 Days Later* do not die and come back to shuffle around, moaning and seeking out flesh (like Romero's zombies) but rather remain alive and sprinting (with athletes cast to play the zombies), given purpose by an infectious 'rage' created by scientists whose experiments include exposing chimps to violent media images for extended periods.[22]

While the zombies of *28 Days Later* are not individually created by exposure to media violence, the fact that the experiments that create the 'rage' virus are clearly linked to the viewing of violent images ties the zombies to Britain's media effects discourse – the discourse that implicates violent media in the real-life violation of hegemonic middle-class cultural norms of social behaviour. This discourse is part of middlebrow British film culture's anti-horror discourse, a key motivator in the push for film censorship and part of the cultural logic underlying the video nasties panics of the 1980s and 90s. The zombies of *28 Days Later* represent a new level of zombie violence when compared with their Romerian predecessors. Travelling alone or in packs, Boyle's zombies bite and vomit blood with the goal of infection rather than biting to feed on human flesh. While the eating of human flesh can be seen as a product of desire, in many zombie narratives (and Romero's trilogy), the infected must eat the flesh (or brains) of the living to maintain their undead state. However, in *28 Days Later*, the emphasis is not on sustenance but virus-like transmission. This shift in motivation renders the zombies less human, and less potentially tragic or sympathetic, because their violence is impersonal. It does not benefit them, only making more zombies who will also compete to infect others.

The film's linkage of zombies, violence and infection extends to its paratextual materials, including its making-of documentary *Pure Rage: The Making of '28 Days Later'* (Toby James, 2002), which was shown on Channel 4 on 5 November 2002, the Friday of the film's first opening weekend.[23] It is also included on the film's DVD release, both the UK and US editions. While operating primarily as a promotional paratext, the documentary also argues that 'the greatest danger to humanity is currently from viruses and pandemic infection'. The first twelve minutes of the documentary, fully half of its runtime, discuss pandemics in the early twenty-first century, while the latter half of the documentary focuses on the film itself, showing behind-the-scenes footage and revealing details about the film-making process. Throughout the documentary, there is a slippage between the real-world dangers of infection and the dangers of the film's zombie infection. In addition, there is a visual slippage between real-world news footage and footage from the film itself, both of which are presented as somewhat grainy and desaturated. These slippages position the film, and its concern with infection, as both timely and significant, which in turn works to sell the film and bolster its relation to British film's long-standing concern with documentary and social realism.[24]

The slippage between real-world and diegetic dangers is particularly visible in the lap dissolves from real-world talking head experts to scenes from the film itself. After the first commercial break, the documentary presents a brief talking-head interview with Andy Coghlan, from *New Scientist Magazine* (a popular, general audience UK science publication), who states that 'the threat to us at the moment from infectious diseases is probably as big as it has ever been, and getting worse'. While he speaks, the film lap dissolves from a close-up shot of his face to a shot from *28 Days*

Figure 2. Shots from *Pure Rage* (top to bottom: talking-head interview, lap dissolve, shot from *28 Days Later*).

Later in which Jim enters the church where he first encounters zombies (see Figure 2). A few seconds later, the documentary uses a lap dissolve again to fade from the shot of Jim to an extreme close-up on Coghlan's eyes as he continues to talk.

This same technique is used throughout the documentary, moving fluidly between shots of the real-life experts who provide the documentary with its argumentative evidence about disease and pandemic, including Professor Brian Duerden, microbiologist and then-Director of the Public Health Laboratory Service in England and Wales, and footage from *28 Days Later* that seemingly gives visual evidence to support the real-world claims. The cuts and lap dissolves between interview footage and film footage blend the diegetic world of the film with the real world as posited by the documentary. The talking-head experts bolster the relevance of *28 Days Later* to the real world, but the use of film footage also lends an eerie air of reality to the expert's seemingly unreal and apocalyptic discussions of pandemics.

The visual slippage between news footage and film footage also works to confuse the line between diegesis and reality to endow *28 Days Later* with at least some of the authority vested in documentary's assumed indexical bond. The fact that the film was shot on digital video, so shots have a grainy, documentary feel, is part of what allows the documentary to appropriate them as visual evidence. The documentary spends several minutes discussing the UK's 2001 foot-and-mouth disease crisis. Foot-and-mouth disease is a highly-contagious and variable virus that affects cloven-hoofed livestock. Because the virus spreads so quickly, once a herd is infected, the entire population is usually killed. While the narrator describes the 2001 epidemic, footage is shown from BBC news reports, providing visual evidence of, as the narrator states, 'the slaughter of over 5 million animals', 'more than the entire human population of Liverpool'. When the narrator says that the strain 'eventually resulted in the military being drafted in', the footage cuts smoothly from BBC news footage to shots of barbed wire, fences and guards around the stately pile that the military men take over in *Days*. The film also takes over for the documentary's narrator, as Major West (Christopher Eccleston), the leader of the soldiers, apologises to Jim for having such a small detachment of soldiers and not having helicopters, a field hospital or the easy answer to infection that Jim seeks (that is, a cure or some governmental, authoritative method for survival).

The documentary then transitions directly to footage of Prime Minister Tony Blair as the narrator takes over again, discussing the extreme cost of the infection for the UK's government (over £4.2 billion). The filmic footage here functions as a representation of the failure of Blair's real-world government to deal quickly and effectively with the foot-and-mouth infection; by using the filmic footage rather than news footage, and the film's dialogue rather than scripted narration, the documentary further enacts a slippage between the diegetic reality of *28 Days Later* and the real world. In *Pure Rage*, the promotional address sells the film as relevant to real-world concerns of modern society, as depicting a potential future. At the same time, the documentary's visual rhetoric troubles the boundary between reality and diegesis and in turn further supports the resonance between *28 Days Later* and both the long-standing documentary tradition in British cinema and that cinema's related social realist impulse.

The documentary's invocation of foot-and-mouth disease, widely referred to as 'mad cow' disease, is more than simply fortuitous in connection to the 'rage virus' of *28 Days Later*. Images of cows recur throughout the segment discussing foot-and-mouth, visually evoking the spectre of 'mad cow'. Expert Andy Coghlan brings up variant CJD, specifically defining it as 'the human form of mad cow disease', during a discussion of the easy transmissibility of viruses between humans and other animals. Throughout the 2001 foot-and-mouth epidemic, the spectre of variant CJD was consistently invoked by UK media. As the documentary notes, variant CJD's primary symptoms are 'prominent psychiatric/behavioural symptoms', 'changes in gait', 'hallucinations', 'muscle stiffness' and 'muscles twitching'. Viewers of *Pure Rage*, as well as audience members present during the initial exhibition period for *28 Days Later* in 2002, may well have recalled the more prominent symptoms of variant CJD and connected them to the 'rage virus' of *28 Days Later*. The clips from *28 Days Later* shown in the documentary, in particular that of the zombie priest, show the film's zombies exhibiting similar symptoms, especially their jerky movements. While not outright positing that the zombies of *28 Days Later* have variant CJD, the documentary links the two infections through the resonant discursive link between a 'rage' virus and 'mad' disease. This link further stresses the slippage between the real world and film's diegesis, ignoring the more supernatural elements of the film's plot to make an argument about its timeliness and relevance to its nation of origin and historical moment. Taken together, the film's revisions to the zombie, supported by the film itself and paratexts such as its making-of documentary, represent a critical paradigm shift away from the Romerian zombie and reflect the film's concern with violence's infectious nature, a move which also works to connect the film to UK media effects discourse.

Engaging Contemporary Cultural Concerns on a 'Diseased Little Island'

Violent American films have often been categorically singled-out for blame for real-life British violence, as when Quentin Tarantino's *Reservoir Dogs* (1992) and Jack Bender's *Child's Play 3* (1991) were blamed in the Bulger case for influencing the boys to commit murder.[25] In 1998, Roy Penrose, a senior British police officer and director-general of the National Crime Squad (NCS), claimed that 'gun-toting characters' from 'Hollywood films . . . have encouraged criminals and society in general to become blasé about killing'.[26] This idea pervaded not only the British press in the mid- and late 1990s, but also the British film censors. A few years earlier, James Ferman, the director of the British Board of Film Classification (BBFC), laid the blame for both real-world and filmic British violence on Hollywood, saying that 'the real solution is for Hollywood to wake up with a conscience'.[27] Two years later, Andreas Whittam Smith, then the president of the BBFC, expressed similar concerns over Hollywood violence and its effects on British society, writing that 'to believe that nothing flows from this [violence] is surely implausible'.[28] Much of the writing inspired by the media effects discourse in Britain places the blame for real-life violence not on the perpetrators but on-screen violence, especially violent American films. Rather than addressing sociological factors that often foment violence, such as poverty and oppression, much of the discourse seeks to end real-world violence by restricting or completely withholding access to violent films.

The media effects debate takes on special resonance in the context of the horror genre. As Mark Kermode notes, censorship of horror films in Britain, due to the influence of the media effects discourse, has made it so that historically fans have not been able to see the films as they were intended to be seen, instead only having access to 'BBFC-approved bastardised versions', which have been hacked to pieces by the 'clumsy bludgeoning of genre-illiterate censors'.[29] Regardless of British censors and pundits who think seeing-equals-doing (but only for children and the working class), the fact remains that the American film industry continues to pump out violent films, arguably with increasing violence, and increasingly sexualised violence, with each passing year. Media effects discourse remained a key discourse in British film culture during the pre-production and production of *28 Days Later*, influencing not only what versions of films were exhibited but also British film financing. While the BBFC relaxed their censorship of horror after Ferman's retirement, censorship and media effects remained a BBFC concern, as well as a concern of middlebrow British film culture more broadly.[30]

The opening sequences of *28 Days Later* immediately establish the film's concern with this discourse, as well as surveillance culture. The film opens on an extreme close-up of a television screen. The images on the screen capture frenetic movement and flip from clip to clip so quickly that the viewer is left only with a series of impressions: eye-level shots of mobs; the sound of gunfire; a close-up of a distraught woman and a wailing infant next to an injured or dead man; a high-angle shot of police on horseback, surrounded by an ominous red cloud of smoke; police marching forward in riot gear; people beating a dead body. All of the images appear to have been taken by handheld cameras or cameras positioned above the scene, as from CCTV cameras or helicopter news crews. The constant switching from image to image recalls the frenetic pace of the twenty-four-hour news cycle, originating with CNN, which repeats stories of violence from across the world on a loop. The footage also resonates with images of and from surveillance culture. Framing viewers' gaze via the camera's gaze, these violent images immediately place us in the midst of and implicates us in the discourse of media effects – by showing this violence, the film confronts viewers with the recursive tension implicit in media effects discourse: does media reflect or create violence? When the camera finally pulls back from the screen and slowly reframes downward to reveal other screens and the chimpanzee forced to view these images, the tightly-framed three-quarter shot feels claustrophobic, evoking the affective state of the chimp and soliciting viewer sympathy.

In the next shot, the camera cuts to a high-angle long shot of the chimp, which is strapped to a table, wires snaking away from its head, forced to look at the violent images on the screens. The image evokes American director Stanley Kubrick's *A Clockwork Orange* (1971), adapted from British writer Anthony Burgess's 1962 book. In *A Clockwork Orange*, young criminal Alex is strapped to a chair, with wires snaking away from his head, and made to watch violent images on a screen after being drugged. The drug makes him feel wretchedly ill, which conditions Alex to associate physical illness with the violent images, ultimately making it so he cannot enact or watch physical violence without becoming ill, thus 'curing' him of his violent criminal behaviour. The visual rhyming between the two films implies that the chimp in *28 Days Later* is forced to watch what appear to be real-life images of violence for the same reason that Alex is: to cure it of its violence. However, this chimp is the only one in the laboratory that is acting calmly; all of the other chimps in the lab are only shown screaming and pounding on the sides of their enclosures. Because of its behaviour, there is the possibility that the violent images are not curing the chimp but infecting it with a perpetual rage it had not yet possessed. This interpretation is possible because the film does not clearly reveal the origin of the rage virus, the zombie infection. The only real information viewers receive, from the mouth of the lab tech, is that the chimps have been given 'an inhibitor', are infected with highly contagious rage carried by both blood and saliva and the lab carries out these experiments because 'in order to cure, you must first understand'. It remains unclear whether this inhibitor is the source of the infection or the reason for its transmissibility, which allows the zombie infection, and thus the film, to resist a straightforward allegorical reading, keeping both open to multiple interpretations.

This ambiguity, both in terms of how the intertext of *A Clockwork Orange* functions and in terms of the source of infection, also creates a richer and more complex discursive resonance between the film and media effects discourse. From this opening scene, it is clear that the scientists in this Cambridge lab are studying media effects, the link between viewing and violence. The experiment resonates with the British discourse of media effects in part because the chimp is exposed to media violence in order to understand real-life violence, whether the exposure creates the initial infection or is a potential source for the cure. Further, the intertext with *A Clockwork Orange* not only connects the film to a longer history of British concern about violence but also to the scandal surrounding Kubrick's film. In 1972, when *A Clockwork Orange* was released in the UK, it was immediately implicated in media effects discourse; as Petley notes, the *Evening News* predicted that the film's 'release [would] lead to a clockwork cult which [would] magnify teenage violence' and 'destroy' the 'weak, the impressionable and the immature'.[31] The film was attacked for its ambiguous message – Alex's 'cure' must be reversed for him to live in British society, leaving the film's ultimate message unclear.[32] For the press, this was yet another instance of violent Americanised media corrupting British youth. Because of the complex national status of *A Clockwork Orange*, a British production adapting a British novel and helmed by a famous American director who had recently expatriated himself to settle in Britain, the linkage of the two films also signals the film's related interest in discourses around Americanisation and the influence of the American film industry on British film.

The most individuated zombie attack that occurs in the film also works to strengthen this tie to media effects, particularly in terms of its connection to children. As David Buckingham argues, 'the figure of the child is at the heart of the majority of debates about media effects'; obsessive anxiety about children's exposure to media violence remains because it is seen 'not only to encourage children to commit acts of violence, but as itself a form of violence *against* children, committed by adults whose only motivation is that of financial greed'.[33] In a film so resonant with media effects discourse, it seems fitting that when Jim goes alone to investigate a roadside hamburger joint, he encounters a child zombie. Jim and the boy struggle until Jim throws him to the ground, placing his boot on the boy's chest to keep him still. The camera frames the boy in a close-up, dried blood streaked on his chest and shoulders, fresh blood visible on his face. Here, the sound design exceeds the diegesis, and the child zombie's rage, visually apparent in his thrashing form, becomes verbalised as a high-pitched hiss of 'I hate you'. However, the child does not move his lips, and the voice is not Jim's. The zombie rage of the violent child exceeds the bounds of diegetic sound, much as the resonance of the violent child zombie exceeds the diegesis to intertextually connect to the British discourse surrounding violent children and media effects. The film aligns violent zombies with violent youths, and thus post-Bulger media effects discourse, in the body of this child zombie, in the film's most individuated attack scene.

And yet, it is significant that this child zombie, and the film's zombies more generally, do not lend themselves to a straightforward allegorical reading as media consumers infected with rage after watching too many American or Americanised scenes of media violence. The fact that *28 Days Later* is not open to a simple allegorical reading, that it requires a more careful analysis of its engagement with contemporary issues in British society and film culture, is itself part of the film's modification of the zombie film paradigm, which skew heavily toward allegory. Kyle Bishop notes that more critically acclaimed films of the genre, such as Romero's *Night of the Living Dead*, ascend to 'the heights of sophisticated allegory'.[34] This tendency to produce allegorical zombie films continues. For example, take the Cuban zombie film *Juan of the Dead* (Alejandro Brugués, 2011). Victoria Burnett, writing for *The New York Times*, discusses how the film presents a world wherein '52 years of socialist rule have turned Cuba into a zombie state', literally and metaphorically.[35] The allegorical content is clear. *28 Days Later*, though, does not present a clear allegory. While it may be tempting to read the zombies as an allegory of a commodity- and consumption-obsessed urban bourgeois population, the return of postcolonial repressed, post-11 September domestic terrorists, or the violent product and confirmation of media effects discourse, Boyle's zombies resist such readings by engaging more subtly with contemporary Britain and middlebrow British film culture.[36] Instead, the film asserts its concern with its own status as a British cultural product awash in a sea of violent and sexualised American and Americanised product. The film's concern with media effects also positions it in the long tradition of British films concerned with addressing contemporary social problems.

To show how *28 Days Later* positions itself in relation to the social realist impulse within British cinema, it is essential to examine how the film engages with the hot-button issue of animal activism in the UK. In 1999, several animal activist groups began a campaign against Huntingdon Life Sciences (HLS), a Cambridge-based animal testing facility much like the Cambridge-based lab depicted in *28 Days Later*. What first started as simple picket-style protesting turned violent quickly, with a 'campaign of hate mail and telephone threats' against Royal Bank of Scotland for financially backing HLS (the bank soon withdrew its support), nail bombs sent through the post, physical altercations with HLS employees and protestors setting fire to HLS employees' cars.[37] In the latter part of the opening sequence of *28 Days Later*, rogue animal activists cause the near-apocalyptic infection because of their unwillingness to listen to the lab tech. This scene indicates not only the film's concern with timely British issues but also begins to indicate where the film ultimately comes down in the media effects debate. The real-life activists and the diegetic activists engage in acts of violence, though they only rough up the lab tech in the film, and these well-intentioned but misguided characters nearly bring about the demise of the entire British population. While the zombies are not an allegory of the mindless, violent consumers posited by media effects discourse, the film does not approve of thoughtless or unnecessary violence, violence that, like the activists, will not listen to reason. In its address of not only media effects discourse but also animal activism, the film firmly cements its concern with contemporary social issues and participation in the social realist impulse.

'You'll Never See a Film That Hasn't Already Been Shot': *28 Days Later* and British Film Traditions

The cinematography in *28 Days Later* draws on the aesthetics of British social realism to capture parts of London that are internationally recognisable, even touristy, yet render those spaces uncanny in their desolation. The iconic scene showing Jim's exit from the hospital and subsequent wandering through the deserted and desolate London in the grey light of early morning uses digital video cameras in combination with frequent high-angle long and extreme long shots to provide gritty images reminiscent of those taken by CCTV cameras, evoking both British surveillance culture and the observational documentary camera. The use of natural, early-morning light and location shooting helps establish a grimy tone that is often associated with British social realism.[38] The empty streets in these shots also provide a visual link to photographs of London taken during and after the Blitz. While this era's most frequent filmic representation of London was of the city in flames, as in some of Humphrey Jennings's more surreal films and the newsreels, photographic London was often sparsely populated, the streets strewn with tipped-over buses and rubble from the bombings.[39] A medium shot of Jim's legs as he wanders across Westminster Bridge captures a bevy of cheap London souvenirs strewn about on the road: miniatures of Big Ben, London's famous black taxi cab, the red Routemaster double-decker bus and the national flag. Charlotte Brunsdon notes that these miniatures of Big Ben work as 'little models of national identity, just like the Eiffel Towers in Ealing's *The Lavender Hill Mob* (1951)'.[40] Here, not only is the film drawing on a recognisable metonym for Britishness, but it also evokes another famous British film to position itself within a history of British national cinema.

The camera then cuts to an extreme long shot, wherein Jim is only barely distinguishable, the camera placed to one side of the bridge, taking in the Houses of Parliament and Big Ben. As Brunsdon notes, part of the reason these shots seem uncanny is that they 'reveal the ways in which the city is and isn't made of buildings', so that the city is 'strangely familiar'.[41] The key landmarks that structure our spatial understanding of London remain the same: it is the total lack of bustling crowds that makes the familiar unfamiliar. London is not London, and Britain is not Britain, without its citizens and visitors. A few shots later, the camera captures Jim in a high-angle extreme long shot as he walks past an overturned iconic Routemaster red double-decker bus, another image usually associated with tourism. However, like previous shots, this shot frames the bus to emphasise desolation and destruction. The tipped over bus acts as a visual metaphor for the authority and power of the governmental institutions, like public transport, that have been overthrown; it is a reminder of a time now passed that Jim has been plucked out of. Throughout, the camera placement is framed as detached and observational, further linking the cinematography to the aesthetics of British social realism.

These are hardly the universal settings that critics like Nick James so feared would leach from Hollywood films into their American-funded British brethren.[42] Rendered in such desolation, devoid of humans save for the spectral figure of Jim, these familiar landmarks and sights serve not as iconic eye candy to entice tourist traffic but as a thought-provoking reminder of the consequences of the apocalypse: the collapse of government and traditional institutions of power. In this sequence, the combination of observational camera techniques and traditional images of London serves not as a filmic call to the tourist gaze but to affectively shock the viewer with the uncanniness of the desolation and destruction surrounding these icons.

These 'fly-on-the-wall' (or 'on-the-ledge-of-a-skyscraper') images engage in what Andrew Higson has termed the 'public gaze' common in popular British Second World War-era melodramas of everyday life. Higson uses this term to discuss war-era melodramas that draw on a documentary aesthetic and function like propaganda. The public gaze was used to interpellate viewers into the national community, as it represented a 'sphere of national interest immediately and widely recognizable as over and above antagonistic sectional interests' to promote national unity during the Second World War.[43] The public gaze is juxtaposed with the 'private gaze', a gaze that 'accommodate[d] the private and the domestic, and the emotional capacity of the individual', giving the individual an 'allotted . . . place within the public common, national experience'.[44] The juxtaposition between the public outdoor scenes and private and emotionally laden indoor scenes, between an objective and subjective camera, creates an 'uneasy tension' in Second World War melodramas. Higson finds these modes of gazing employed by films like *Millions Like Us* (Sidney Gilliat and Frank Launder, 1943) and *This Happy Breed* (David Lean, 1944), which represent the nation 'metaphorically as a small, self-contained, tight-knit community, a unity-in-diversity, but one which is structured like a family'.

The private gaze was used to interpellate individuals into the ideology of victory-in-unity represented by the public gaze. As Higson notes, these films were critical to 'securing this consent of private citizens to the national cause' and making sure that social responsibility to one's community was seen as more important than individual desire. As in *Millions Like Us*, the private gaze is used to convey individual emotions that hook the viewer through their melodrama, such as Celia's emotional fantasy scenes where, in close-up, she plays out her desired romance with her new wartime soldier beau Fred. The public gaze, then, is used to reincorporate Celia into the community, to de-individuate her, as in the final scene of the film, where, after Fred's death, a bereaved Celia is surrounded by and integrated via long shot into the community of women at the factory where she works.[45] The tension between the public and private gaze in the Second World War films Higson discusses works to hook audiences with individual characters' emotions to further imbricate the viewer into the films' overriding communitarian ideology.

The public gaze shots in *28 Days Later* have been stripped of the community essential to the creation of a public; any 'public' seen in these shots is as likely to be a dangerous zombie as it is one of the film's protagonists, shattering idealistic conceptions of national unity in the face of crisis. The shots give viewers a supposedly objective view of the deserted city, which is in stark contrast to the point-of-view shots, close-ups and extreme close-ups used in the shot/reverse shot conversations in the intimate, emotional interior scenes that form the 'private gaze'. After Jim stumbles upon several zombies in a church, they chase him and he luckily stumbles across Selena and Mark, who have more experience at killing zombies. They bring him to an abandoned convenience store in a Tube station, where they are momentarily safe. One of the first shots of this scene is from Jim's point of view as his gaze tilts wildly down, then up, to frame Mark's gas-masked face in close-up as Mark tells a terrible joke about a giraffe, ostensibly to lighten the mood. In a modified shot/reverse shot, establishing emotional immediacy by breaking the fourth wall, the camera cuts back and forth between Mark's point of view, with Jim staring, wide-eyed, directly into the camera, and Jim's point of view as Mark takes off his gas mask, pronouncing Jim 'totally humourless' for not laughing at the joke. The lack of connection between the characters, as well as the close-up shots of their faces, emphasises their emotions (Jim's shell-shock and Mark's disappointment).

Capturing the actor's direct gaze into the camera adds further impact to their emotions. A few moments later, the camera switches focus to the conversation between Selena and Jim. Selena gazes directly into the camera in a shot that captures the hardness of her face, especially in the set of her jaw and the flinty spark in her eye. However, the frustration with which Naomie Harris infects Selena's words to Jim betrays another emotion: compassion. In this scene, as in other physically enclosed scenes in the film, close-up shots are used to convey and emphasise the survivors' emotional turmoil.

The public and private gazes deployed in *28 Days Later* result in a productive tension, much like the productive tension they produce in Second World War-era British melodramas of everyday life. The use of the private gaze enables an individualised exploration of the depth of the emotional resonance that the public gaze evokes through its depiction of the desolate London streets, devoid of anything approaching community. The public and private gaze work together to hook the audience through individuated emotion, as conveyed through close-ups of and point-of-view shots from the protagonists. Here, the public gaze does not interpellate viewers into a specifically nationalistic communitarian ethos via shots of British communities, like the Second World War films Higson discusses. Rather, the film uses the juxtaposition between a harshly non-communitarian, evacuated public space and individuated emotional private close-ups to emphasise an ideology of chosen, self-selected community. Much like the Second World War melodramas explore how people deal with national crisis, *28 Days Later* reconfigures the public and private gazes to underscore the different national project it undertakes in its exploration of how Britons deal with a national crisis of apocalyptic proportions.

These films use the public and private gazes differently because of their dissimilar ideological projects and sociohistorical contexts. While the Second World War melodramas of everyday life attempted to communicate a victory-through-unity ideology to bind the nation together, sublimating individual desire to community needs, *28 Days Later* exists in a post-war, post-empire, post-Thatcher climate. Aidan Power's reading of the film is particularly relevant here: Selena, as a Black British woman, and Jim, as an Irishman, 'present a colonized counterpoint to the colonizers [the military]' and 'their ultimate survival signifies further the collapse of Empire' visually represented by 'shots of [the] unattended London war memorial' and 'crumbling edifice of a country manor'.[46] The public gaze – the shots Power associates with old British power and Empire – is undermined by the private gaze, which both looks at and is possessed by postcolonial figures. National unity of the sort embodied by the public gaze in Second World War melodramas is reconfigured as community-less, dangerous. Community must then be self-selected, chosen by and shared among the people who are emotionally individuated by the private gaze. In this way, the use of the public and private gaze in *28 Days Later* works to critique the holdover Second World War ideology of victory-in-unity that Higson identifies, reflecting the sociohistorical context of the film's production. And yet, the use of these public and private gazes connects *28 Days Later* to this history of British cinema.

The film's positioning of itself as part of the tradition of British cinema is furthered by the film's relation to British Romantic-era discourses of the rural and the country house that re-emerged in British heritage cinema. Specifically, *28 Days Later* draws on the Romantic-era notion of the flight to the rural from the city present in heritage cinema. Fred Botting argues that *28 Days Later* presents a Romantic trajectory of escape from the urban metropole (London) to an 'imaginary family and idyllic rural retreat' and as such remains 'within a persistently Romantic cultural fantasy' where an escape to the rural means survival, while the modern metropole means death.[47] When Jim, Selena, Frank and Hannah stop to eat a meal between London and Manchester, they picnic at the ruins of Waverley Abbey, visually evoking tropes of Gothic Romanticism with the ruins and also British heritage film with the pastoral landscape shots of fields of brightly coloured flowers and lush green pastures that evoke a mythic golden age of Britain where everything was green and innocent. Here, the film's deployment of Gothic and Romantic tropes in the idealised rural space operates in a mostly straightforward way. Within this scene, the rural operates as a place of survival, not only literal bodily survival, as the Waverley Abbey ruins are one of the few places where no zombie attacks occur, but also the survival of a more abstract notion of humanity: the affective connections between survivors.

However, the use of the country house, a staple of British heritage cinema, is more self-reflexive. Heritage film traditionally uses a lush *mise-en-scène* and lingering camerawork that explores, and sometimes fetishises, the English country house while the films themselves investigate questions of national identity.[48] Rather than sweeping pans through the house and long-duration long shots of the house and surrounding grounds, the film only has one brief establishing extreme long shot of the house, after which the camera focuses on revealing the nefarious intent of the soldiers rather than fetishising the house they colonised. These sadistic British soldiers put out a radio signal broadcasting a message of safety but try to kill Jim so that they can rape Selena and Hannah. Their attitudes typify the portraits of sexualised violence and overdone machismo critics so object to in British media effects discourse. The soldiers are as or more dangerous than the zombies; they are the film's final barrier between Jim, Selena and Hannah and safety. Their takeover of the English country house, and the extreme threat they pose to the protagonists, ties together British media effects discourse and Americanisation. Here, the film's relation to media effects discourse resurfaces, and its stance on the issue becomes clear: while violence is sometimes necessary, as Jim must adopt a zombie-like rage to save himself and the women, sexualised violence and grandiose machismo inspired by violent media (which is often framed in British film culture as American or Americanised) is not acceptable and must be eliminated, not allowed to take over British film as the soldiers did the country house.

28 Days Later draws on specific contemporary British social concerns and filmic traditions to reframe Romero's zombies, using transnational genre hybridity to generically situate the film across British and American film cultures. This strategy puts the film in a position where it can assert its place in British national cinema in part by asserting its non-Americanised status. The few American critics who panned *28 Days Later* generally compared it to Romero's zombie films and found it lacking because of its genre hybridity: according to them, it is not a good horror film because it is not frightening enough. Owen Gleiberman, writing for *Entertainment Weekly*, does not completely pan *28 Days Later* but does criticise it for failing to acknowledge that it is really just 'a good old zombie freakfest' rather than the artsy, 'extremely topical nightmare' it tries to be.[49] However, Gleiberman is entirely wrong: *28 Days Later* is not just a good old zombie freakfest because it is an extremely topical nightmare. The film deploys conventions of British film traditions and connects to timely British cultural issues to situate itself as participating in multiple discourses of middlebrow British film culture. In doing so, the film acts as a subtle critique of the potential negative influence of Americanisation on not only the British film industry but also the British viewing audience who consume those films at the cinema.

A few months before the November 2002 UK release of *28 Days Later*, Film4, Britain's only mini-studio, described by Geoffrey Macnab as 'a One-stop shop' capable of production, sales and distribution, and with a lab to nurture new talent and 'experimental, low-budget movie-making', went under.[50] According to Macnab, Film4 had not been able to achieve the hopes of one of its vital supporters and founders, Channel 4 chief executive Michael Jackson, who wanted the studio to 'go up against the big guys', 'beat Hollywood' and 'be in the mainstream'. It was in this environment – one neither culturally nor economically sympathetic to its own films and film-making, particularly horror films – that Danny Boyle and his crew made and exhibited *28 Days Later*. The film succeeded critically and financially in the UK and abroad, partly for the same reason *Four Weddings and a Funeral* and *Shallow Grave* (Danny Boyle, 1994) did, 'by drawing on [its] environment [and] the attributes of British culture'.[51] *28 Days Later* also showed that 'a low-budget British film with Film Council support and a good distribution deal could do respectable business at the US box office', opening up the way for films like *Shaun of the Dead*, as well as the films I discuss in later chapters.[52] However, with Hollywood blockbusters bombarding the British box office, few British films could squeeze into the cineplexes, and these exhibition difficulties contributed to the demise of Film4, as well as making it difficult for the films to obtain the type of distribution arrangements that helped *28 Days Later* succeed financially.

'The Zed-Word. Don't Say It!': *Shaun of the Dead*'s Romerian Citations

The Guardian's Andrew Pulver declared in early 2004 that the British film industry '[could] fearlessly assert that it is fully back on its feet', partly because of the success of *28 Days Later*.[53] However, the film's success did little to change the persistent saved/doomed discourse within middlebrow British film culture. *The Sunday Times* writer Stephen Armstrong wrote months later of his hopes that Edgar Wright's zombie comedy *Shaun of the Dead* (2004) might reanimate the 'rotting corpse' of the British film industry.[54] Often labelled the first 'zom-rom-com' (that is, zombie horror/romantic comedy), *Shaun of the Dead* was one of the projects being produced by Film4 when it was reabsorbed into Channel 4's drama department. WT2, the low-budget arm of the studio Working Title, took over primary production of the film. At the time of the film's production and exhibition, WT2 was seen as 'one of the leaders in developing a distinctive UK film voice', a critically necessary project to balance 'the global domination of American cinema'.[55] The film follows the story of Shaun (Simon Pegg), a numbed retail worker who must try to reunite with his disgruntled girlfriend Liz (Kate Ashfield) while also saving himself, his mum (Penelope Wilton) and his best friend (Nick Frost) from the zombie apocalypse in London. The film reunites nearly the entire cast of Pegg, Wright and Frost's television comedy *Spaced* (airing on Channel 4 from

1999–2001), as well as bringing in British television comedians such as Lucy Davis and Martin Freeman (*The Office*, 2001–3), Dylan Moran and Tamsin Greig (*Black Books*, 2000–4), Matt Lucas (*Little Britain*, 2003–6) and Reece Shearsmith (*The League of Gentlemen*, 1999–2002).

Shaun has been compared with *28 Days Later* because both films were early entries in the zombie revival in the early 2000s, and the films also mix tropes of the Romerian American zombie film with British filmic traditions. Tapping into the broader social realist impulse in British film, *Shaun* concerns itself with the rise of the service industry and associated class anxieties, as well as the related shifting gender dynamics that resulted in new laddism. The film draws on various comedy styles to reframe Romero, from the gentler Ealing comedies to the absurdly satirical Monty Python and two-man comedy teams like the Likely Lads and Morecambe and Wise. By paying homage to the American zombie via British comedic traditions from television and film and addressing contemporary social issues, *Shaun* uses transnational genre hybridity to assert its own cultural legitimacy. By situating itself generically *across* both countries without becoming Americanised, the film shows that British films can pay homage to American traditions without becoming Americanised, thus subtly critiquing the discourse in British film culture that treats Americanisation as an unavoidable catastrophe.

Released in 2004, the film was met with robust critical and popular acclaim, much of which centred on its perceived Britishness. This classification remained important in 2004; a few months before *Shaun* was released for UK exhibition, *Guardian* writer Andrew Pulver was bemoaning the death of the British film industry, which he claimed had been suffocated by American film's economic dominance.[56] *Shaun* was one of the first films of the British horror resurgence that critics aligned with the saved side of the saved/doomed binary, and, as such, the discourse around *Shaun* functions as an indicator of the continuing softening of the anti-horror discourse in middlebrow British film culture. David Pirie has argued that historically, 'even at its most successful, the British horror film never was marketed as being British', and the critics and audiences who eagerly crowded into cinemas to see British horror films 'were entirely uninterested in the fact that they [the films] were British'.[57] Thus, it is significant that critics focused heavily on *Shaun*'s Britishness and mostly treated that Britishness as a major attraction rather than a liability.

Paul English, writing for the *Daily Record*, focuses on the film's casting of prominent British television comedy stars for nearly all the lead roles (leaving the secondary roles for major British talent like Penelope Wilton and Bill Nighy) and labels the film a 'very British take on the established zombie genre'.[58] *Mail on Sunday*'s Bonnie Greer gushes that the film is 'refreshing because it is so quintessentially British' – Shaun is 'Basil Fawlty's son, minus the bitterness and aggression' – and it sends up 'the conventions of big budget Hollywood films perfectly', managing to court a British audience while still giving 'a nod to the rest of the world'.[59] In *Screen International*, Wendy Ide laments the 'critical debacle' of the previous month's unsuccessful exhibition of the (notoriously bad) British comedy *Sex Lives of the Potato Men* (Andy Humphries, 2004). She then positions *Shaun* as having 'every chance of breakout success' because of its casting of British television comedians, slacker humour and 'convincing emotional depth', thus proving 'that the move from small to big screen comedy does not always end in artistic failure'.[60] Of course, not everyone enjoyed the film; *Sight & Sound*'s Kim Newman compares the film to Romero's *Dead* trilogy and finds it 'ramshackle in tone and effect, with running jokes that run into the ground, scenes that don't quite know how to end and characters who keep harping on their one-note traits'.[61] Rather than evaluating the film on its own merits (and demerits), comparing it with Romero's entire *Dead* trilogy seems to foreclose on the film as automatically lessthan; Newman appears to have been one of the 'horror purists' whom Ide thought might be displeased with the film's 'predominantly comic tone'.

The film did well at the box office, though, $30,039,392 worldwide. When considering return on investment, *Shaun*'s takings are impressive, with a budget to box office gross ratio of 7.51.[62] Later in the year, the BBC's *Film 2004 with Jonathan Ross*'s audience would vote *Shaun of the Dead* the sixth best film of the year.[63] The film's success would even lead George Romero himself to give Frost and Pegg 'undead cameos' in his next *Dead* film *Land of the Dead* (2005).[64]

Shaun pays homage to Romero's *Dead* trilogy in a multiplicity of ways. Like in Romero's films, *Shaun*'s zombies are slow, travel in packs and want to consume human flesh. Shaun works at Foree Electronics – named after the actor Ken Foree, who plays Peter, one of the two protagonists who escapes at the end of *Dawn of the Dead*. Like Romero's films, *Shaun* does not offer a clear cause for the zombie outbreak but rather a multitude of potential causes. Early in the film, newspapers mention a super-flu, mystery virus and mystery bug, blaming genetically modified (GM) crops. In the television montage near the end of the film, as Liz clicks from channel to channel, the film teases a cause but does not provide it, as Liz flips to the next channel before the speaker can finish their sentence ('as we now know, the phenomenon resulted from the use of highly da-'). *Shaun* also borrows an iconic line from *Night of the Living Dead*; when Shaun is speaking to Barbara on the phone, Ed shouts, 'We're coming to get you, Barbara', which is the line Barbara's brother uses to taunt her at the start of *Night*. Also, *Shaun*'s ending mirrors the endings of the *Dead* films: all four films feature endings where the protagonists flee a confined space, moving upward to escape from zombies who have invaded their supposedly safe space indoors. Like Ben in *Night*, the protagonists flee a basement. And as in *Dawn*, the protagonists contemplate suicide before realising it is not necessary and escape is possible.

Most obviously, though, the film's title, *Shaun of the Dead*, acts as a citation of and homage to Romero's *Dawn of the Dead*. The title functions not only as citation but as shorthand for the film's social critique. Each of the films in Romero's *Dead* trilogy participate in social critique. *Night of the Living Dead* critiques 1960s American race relations and the dehumanisation of Black people by white civilians and the police, as well as critiquing the zombie-like complacency of some Americans in the face of international political turmoil and military incursions. *Dawn of the Dead*, on the other hand, is more interested in critiquing consumerism, both through the protagonists' hoarding and greed and the zombies' attraction to the shopping centre where the film is set and their mindless desire to consume human flesh. *Day of the Dead* presents a (slightly less coherent) critique of US militarisation, as well as unethical medical experimentation.

Shaun of the Dead presents a clear critique of multiple facets of life for the modern twenty-something in the early 2000s London service economy. While critics have interpreted this zombification as indicative of 'the mundane, highly routine nature of modern British life', I argue that the film specifically critiques the debasement inherent in a service economy, the dominant economic system that emerged after the Thatcher government's privatisation of industry had led the country away from an industry-based economy.[65] As Linda McDowell notes, toward the turn of the century, 'the nature of work ha[d] changed – the majority of workers in Britain no longer earn[ed] their living in the manufacturing sector but in service occupations'.[66] In 1998, the Labour government instituted the New Deal, a programme intended to bring unemployment under control by providing the unemployed with job training and employment opportunities through subsidies and the creation of volunteer programmes. Most of these jobs were in the service sector.[67] While unemployment decreased from 6.4 per cent in January of 1998 to 4.8 per cent in January of 2004, most of the jobs taken by those who moved from unemployment to employment were in the service industry.[68] As McDowell notes, increased employment opportunities were superficially a boon, but 'many of these jobs [were] poorly paid and offered on a discontinuous basis', so that for many workers in service jobs and middle management, especially men, 'work [had] become a less certain affair'.[69] With the rise of 'flexible' jobs associated with variable-schedule service work and freelance contract work, work and take-home pay had become less stable, while the shift to service work meant an increasing number of jobs required repetitive, less-skilled tasks.

Shaun is 'of the Dead' – he is marked out as one of the zombies though he is never bitten, aligning his boring, dead-end job and life with zombification and mindlessness. Shaun's pre- and post-zombie apocalypse morning walks to the local shop emphasise this point, as he is so unaware of his surroundings that he does not notice the disaster that has befallen the city. Liz's friend Di gives him the most praise for his ability to imitate the zombies, further supporting the idea that he is metaphorically already zombified. The opening title sequence reinforces the link between zombification and service work, as does the mirroring of the title sequence in the final news montage. The title sequence shows a variety of people performing tasks in a mindless way, staring off into space with a dead-eyed zombie look: an older man pushes shopping trolleys; Mary, the girl who later turns zombie and attacks Shaun and Ed in their garden, scans items at a cash register in a supermarket, with a line of equally numbed-looking women cashiers scanning behind her; a gaggle of men waiting at a bus stop check their phones in unison; finally, club kids stagger home, bobbing their heads in rhythm.

The film's final television montage mirrors these opening titles and reinforce the film's critique of the zombified nature of work in Britain's service economy. The montage shows zombies taking on the drudgery of service work after the infection is brought under control. A politically correct reporter does a human-interest piece on how the 'mobile deceased retained their primal instincts', which makes them 'ideal recruitment for the service industry'. Her voiceover runs over images of one of Shaun's former co-workers pushing shopping trolleys for the same store as the older man in the opening titles. The television montage cuts from this story to a comedy game show where zombies demean themselves by trying to struggle across an inflatable walkway to obtain a piece of flesh;

here, game shows requiring the physical debasement and humiliation of people are positioned as another service that zombies can provide. The montage cuts next to trash talk show *Tricia*, wherein a woman proclaims her love for her husband despite the fact that he is now a zombie – Tricia asks, incredulously, 'you go to bed with it?' Aligning service work with exploitative television entertainment programmes helps deliver a stronger critique here. Not only do many of the money-making opportunities, whether through traditional service jobs or through fringe participation in the entertainment industry, require physical or psychological humiliation, but their mindless nature is antithetical to a robust inner life of the mind. The people in service work before the zombie outbreak were just as zombified as their later infected counterparts, just with considerably higher living expenses. While *Dawn of the Dead* is often read as satirising consumerism and the insatiable desire for things instilled by late capitalism, *Shaun of the Dead* can be read as a critique of the service economy and its tendency to suppress, and sometimes actively disavow, the human dignity and minds of its workers.

'You've Got Red on You': Comedy Traditions and Masculinity in *Shaun of the Dead*

More than simply drawing on Romero's zombie horror tradition, *Shaun of the Dead* reframes that tradition. While the *Dead* trilogy has humorous moments sprinkled throughout the films (mainly in *Dawn*), all of the films are horror, not horror-comedy. *Shaun of the Dead*, on the other hand, strikes an equal balance of horror and comedy, combining the zombie horror film with British comedy traditions. To do this, *Shaun* draws on Second World War-era Ealing comedies, the Monty Python troupe's absurdist satirising of institutional authority and television two-man comedy teams.

The film's reliance on and debt to Ealing is clearest in its plot structure. Ealing Studios produced numerous iconic British films of various genres before, during and after the Second World War (including *Dead of Night* and *Went the Day Well?*), but they came to prominence and are remembered for their cycle of comedies from the mid-1940s to the mid-1950s. In the post-war period, Ealing became a mascot for British cinema.[70] The core comedies consist of eight films: *Hue and Cry* (Charles Crichton, 1947), *Passport to Pimlico* (Henry Cornelius, 1949), *Whisky Galore* (Alexander Mackendrick, 1949), *Kind Hearts and*

Coronets (Robert Hamer, 1949), *The Lavender Hill Mob* (Charles Crichton, 1951), *The Man in the White Suit* (Alexander Mackendrick, 1951), *The Titfield Thunderbolt* (Charles Crichton, 1953) and *The Ladykillers* (Alexander Mackendrick,1955).[71]

As Kenneth Tynan notes, these films generally dealt with the theme of 'the extraordinary and resilient British, coping with a series of perfectly alarming situations'.[72] For example, *Passport to Pimlico* tells the story of the Pimlico district in London; after the Second World War, evidence comes to light that the district is actually part of Burgundy (the French region) – thus, the alarming situation is no longer being a British subject. The district's inhabitants throw off the lingering wartime strictures on trade, despite the fact that the British government continues to try to reign in Pimlico, eventually erecting barriers and controlling travel into and out of the district. Throughout it all, the residents of Pimlico display resourcefulness and stoicism toward obstacles and setbacks like losing power and running out of water. Ultimately, social pressure from London's other inhabitants causes the British government to negotiate to bring Pimlico back into Britain, though the negotiations favour the ordinary Pimlico residents, not the bumbling British diplomats. *Passport to Pimlico* is about 'comic disruption and disorder which [is] resolved by the seemingly inevitable restoration of established conformity and order', delivering a 'moral "what if"' that uses 'realistic settings and configure[s] recognizable characters leading mundane and humdrum lives'.[73]

Shaun of the Dead also plays on this theme of resourceful Brits, who start and end the film with humdrum lives but spend the middle of the film coping with an alarming situation. While it might seem like the zombie apocalypse would be the most alarming situation with which Shaun must cope, it is at least as, if not more, disturbing to Shaun when his girlfriend Liz breaks up with him toward the start of the film, before Shaun is even aware of the zombies. Liz's break-up with Shaun leads to a night of excessive drinking, as well as Shaun's resolution to get his life 'sorted'. The zombie apocalypse is (almost) a convenient coincidence that gives Shaun an excuse to win her back. The narrative of the film supports this interpretation; the film begins and ends with a scene between Shaun and Liz. Twenty-five of the film's ninety-nine minutes go by before Shaun's Crouch End neighbourhood is overtaken by zombies, and it is a full thirty minutes before Shaun realises anything is amiss (that is, when there's a girl in the garden and she gets back up after Shaun accidentally pushes her onto a pole that impales her).

Shaun's life at the end of the film is like his life at the start of the film. He starts in a relationship with Liz, living with his old college friends. He ends the film in a relationship with Liz, and, though they now live together, his best friend (and now zombie) Ed still lives on the property, confined to the shed in the back garden. Shaun's Sunday routine with Liz differs little from his routine at the start of the film, which revolves around acquiring and consuming tea, picking up a newspaper, heading to the pub and then watching television at home. The main change is that if he wants to play video games with Ed, he has to do it in the shed rather than the living room. Yes, his mother, stepfather and former room-mate Peter are all dead, but they did not seem to play a large role in his daily life, and their deaths (though sad) do not figure into his routine. If anything, Shaun's life is more humdrum, as he is more firmly ensconced in a heteronormative relationship. *Shaun* also draws more broadly on 'emblematic signifiers of communal life in many Ealing comedies', such as 'scenes in pubs' and 'offers and acceptance of tea'.[74]

More interestingly, though, *Shaun of the Dead* can be linked to *Whisky Galore*, *Kind Hearts and Coronets* and *The Ladykillers*. As Charles Barr notes, these Ealing comedies 'impose a fatalistic or moralistic ending without thereby renouncing the gratifications that it ostensibly shuts off'.[75] In these films, he argues, 'moral resolutions are imposed in a tongue-in-cheek way, right at the end, without challenging our commitment to their central characters' single-minded projects or even our belief that they really got away with it successfully'. Throughout the film, Shaun struggles with his inability to leave behind his immature friend Ed, commit fully to his girlfriend Liz and thereby conform to societal norms of being 'grown up'. By the end of the film, Shaun seemingly renounces Ed, leaving his zombie-bitten friend to die in the basement of the pub to leave with Liz and keep her safe. The final scene showcases Shaun and Liz, relaxing on the couch in the flat they now live in together. Here, the moralistic ending appears to tell audiences that young men had best grow up and conform to heteronormative societal expectations regarding commitment and the pursuit of leisure activities with one's significant other rather than same-sex friends. A number of critics have fruitfully taken up this thread, exploring how, as Linnie Blake puts it, the film possesses an 'insistently heterosexist logic' that requires Shaun to 'repress . . . his adolescent yearning for homosocial camaraderie and redirect . . . his desire towards heterosexual romance, domesticity and putative paternity' to 'come fully to life and face his destiny and his responsibilities as a heterosexual and a man'.[76]

And yet, the film ends with Shaun popping out to the garden to play video games with Zombie Ed – in other words, Shaun did not abandon his homosocial bond with Ed. Instead, the bond transcended death and zombification. His bond with Liz, on the other hand, was seriously endangered when he failed to remember to book a table at a restaurant. The alarming situation, whether it is the zombie apocalypse or Liz breaking up with him, appears to set Shaun's priorities straight and give viewers a moralistic ending, but in fact his connection with Ed has merely been dampened, shifted out back to the garden shed, where Liz need not feel threatened by Shaun's relationship with Ed, which appears to have changed little. While focusing on the domesticity of the ending and Shaun's firm embrace of heteronormative bliss with Liz via their cohabitation can result in productive analysis, acknowledging the continuation of Shaun and Ed's relationship reveals not only the more broadly heterosexist (or patriarchal) overtones identified by critics but also the perpetuation of the more historically specific heterosexist discourse of new laddism.

As Sean Nixon defines the term in his study of the changes to British masculinity from the 1980s to the late 1990s, new laddism is a heterosexual masculinity that conforms to new social expectations about civility and sensitivity around women but is unambiguously heterosexual and concerned with asserting that unambiguousness through raucous, raunchy and hedonistic behaviour while also valorising 'underachievement, juvenility' and an 'anti-aspirational' attitude.[77] While Nixon interprets the rise of new laddism largely as a response to more fluid sexual scripts associated with the 'new man' of the late 1980s, new laddism can also be seen as a reactionary response to the 1990s Blair-associated crisis in British masculinity. As Linda McDowell notes, 'the growing feminization of the labour market', when so-called masculine industrial jobs were lost and replaced by so-called feminised service industry jobs, 'has led to an interesting debate about the growing "redundancy" of boys and men'.[78] Studies showed that increasingly men either felt 'powerless and redundant in the face of contemporary economic and social changes . . . or responded by constructing an exaggerated version of irresponsible masculine behaviour', new laddism.

Ed's typical behaviour, which consists of living rent-free in Shaun's apartment and playing video games all day while neglecting to perform any domestic labour, from doing the dishes to taking down phone messages, is firmly rooted in new laddism, as is Shaun's behaviour around Ed. As Blake puts it, Ed's life and Shaun's life with Ed is defined by 'a mode of masculinity endlessly trapped in its own fast-receding adolescence', avoiding normative adulthood to live a life of 'computer games and corner-shop lager, fart gags, dead-end jobs and small-scale dope deals'.[79] The final scene's split locations, the flat's living room and the garden shed, spatially map Shaun's divided masculinity. Inside with Liz, he is a new man, adventurously taking two sugars in his tea and planning out a lazy Sunday with his heterosexual domestic partner, while, outside in the garden shed, Shaun can reunite with Ed and their PlayStation, to live anti-aspirationally. However, Shaun is hardly an aspirational go-getter with Liz; if anything, he has sucked her into his apathetic mindset. While Liz broke up with Shaun because she wanted to live a little and try new things, their Sunday plans are strictly mundane. Rather than ending on a note that clearly ideologically sanctions prevailing patriarchal notions of responsible, adult masculinity, the film also privileges Shaun's anti-aspirational mindset and shows go-getter Liz changing to adopt that mentality. Like in Ealing films like *Kind Hearts and Coronets*, the film imposes a moral ending, in that Shaun appears to have changed his ways, but simultaneously undermines that moral ending by allowing Shaun's new laddism to influence Liz and for Shaun and Ed's relationship to continue.

It is tempting to read zombification in *Shaun* as an analogue for the new lad mindset, particularly because Ed, who best embodies new laddism, enacts the same behaviours before and after zombification: playing video games, breaking wind and serving as Shaun's excuse to put off growing up. Video games themselves, as well, seem an apt device through which to imbue zombification; Ed's responses to the game and manipulation of the controller are too quickly done to show thought and instead show reflexes instilled into Ed by the game. However, despite these temptations toward reading allegorically, the film cannot be read as a straightforward critique of either new laddism or the potential mind-numbing effects of video games. Rather, Ed and Shaun's time playing video games is framed as directly beneficial to Shaun and Liz's survival. During the siege at the pub, it is Ed who most successfully directs Shaun's rather haphazard marksmanship as he shoots the zombies attempting to enter the pub. As Ed shouts 'upper left', 'reload' and 'good shot', he repeats Shaun's dialogue from an earlier scene, wherein Shaun gave Ed support as he played a first-person shooter video game. The trappings of new laddism serve the happy couple well, both during the zombie apocalypse and after, as it is Liz's adoption of a relaxed attitude, a lowering of expectations, that assures the couple's continued happiness.

The relationship between Shaun and Ed is connected to the new laddism, but it is also connected to the tradition of the two-man team from television comedies. I draw here in part on Andy Medhurst's discussion of two-man comedy teams in his excellent book *A National Joke*.[80] From Eric Morecambe and Ernie Wise (the benchmark double act in English popular comedy, whose peak years as a comedy act, 1968–83, saw them starring in *The Morecambe and Wise Show*, their own BBC series complete with Christmas special) to more recent acts like Ant and Dec, two-man comedy teams have flourished on British television. Like the Ealing comedies, Morecambe and Wise are national institutions in Britain; it is often cited that in 1977, more than half of the UK's population watched *The Morecambe and Wise Show*'s special on Christmas Day.[81] Often, the comedy between the two men at least partly focuses on 'the ambiguities of their personal closeness' – the 'meanings of masculinity within intensely close yet non-sexual male bonds'.[82] For example, in Morecambe and Wise's comedy, they often shared a bed, and in one memorable sketch, where they discuss their favoured childhood toys, Wise says, 'I had a little Dinky' (a small, die-cast vehicle), to which Morecambe re-joins, 'You still have'.

While the relationship between comics Morecambe and Wise seemed to exist outside the heterosexual agenda, in that neither engaged in a romantic relationship on the show (which was closer to a sketch show than a traditional sitcom), Terry Collier (James Bolam) and Bob Ferris (Rodney Bewes) of *The Likely Lads* (original series 1964–6; *What Ever Happened to the Likely Lads*, 1973–4) explored definitions of masculinity and homosocial behaviour similarly to *Shaun of the Dead*: two men, 'one feckless and unreconstructed, the other seeking conventional respectability and domestic happiness with "the one"'.[83] The comedy comes into play in the tension between Bob's desire to ascend from the working class to the middle class and to settle down with a woman and Terry's salt-of-the-earth disdain for both of those activities.

Like these two-man comedy teams, much of *Shaun*'s humour and appeal derives from the dynamic and patter between Simon Pegg and Nick Frost, and in particular the ambiguity of their close bond. Pegg and Frost developed this dynamic while working with Edgar Wright on *Spaced*, which followed the adventures of flatmates Daisy (Jessica Stevenson) and Tim (Pegg), with Frost playing a supporting role. In *Shaun*, it is the leading woman, Liz, who takes the supporting role, allowing more focus on Shaun and Ed's relationship. Because of their intimacy and its ambiguity, the men's relationship becomes the punchline of several jokes throughout the film. It is Shaun and Ed who spend several minutes working together to figure out how to kill the zombies, first throwing random objects, then sorting through and throwing Shaun's less-valued records before finally breaking into the garden shed and then beating the zombies to death in tandem. Shaun and Ed decide together that the Winchester pub is the safest place to be in a zombie attack. And, as noted earlier, during the siege at the pub, Ed draws on previous their shared gaming experiences to direct Shaun's shooting. Though Shaun and Liz's relationship, and its restoration, is the sought-after ending, Shaun and Ed's relationship sustains and drives the plot forward. At one point, a supporting character, David, accuses Shaun of having a 'tiff with [his] boyfriend', to which Shaun replies disgustedly, 'he's not my boyfriend'. Just after this, Ed sets down a beer he retrieved for Shaun, saying 'Might be a bit warm – the cooler's off'. As Ed and Shaun share a caring look and smile, Shaun replies, 'Thanks, babe'. The comedic focus on Shaun and Ed's 'bromance' is typical of the British two-man comedy team.

However, much of the film's comedy is also absurdist, full of non-sequiturs, reminiscent of Monty Python's comedy. Indeed, the film cites several Python sketches directly, as well as parts of their films. Shaun's walk to his corner shop, in both of its iterations, and his bus ride to work are extraordinarily similar to 'The Dull Life of a City Stockbroker' sketch from *Monty Python's Flying Circus* (1969–74). In both, a man walks from his suburban home to a corner shop and goes to work without noticing the strange things happening around him. Just as the stockbroker does not notice the nude cashier at the shop, the soldiers and grenade on his bus or the couple kissing animatedly on his desk at work, so Shaun misses the zombies he passes on his walk and the carnage in the corner shop, including the blood smeared all over the cooler's glass door. The comedy here is the same – the scenes provoke humour by subverting expectations through their protagonists' obliviousness. This same type of comedy is in play when Shaun and Ed mistakenly think the girl in the garden, Mary, is drunk rather than a zombie, and when, after seeing they will have to cross a street full of zombies, Dianne decides to give the group acting lessons so they can disguise themselves as zombies – they must endeavour to look, as she says 'vacant, with a hint of sadness, like a drunk who's lost a bet'.

Shaun cites Monty Python again when Shaun rescues his mother and stepfather from their home. Shaun goes into the home expecting Philip to be dead. He is not – just bitten. Philip protests against coming with Shaun, saying he is not sick (he ran the zombie bite 'under a cold tap'), and Shaun tries to get his mother to leave Philip behind to die. This scene faintly echoes one of Monty Python's most famous sketches, the 'Bring Out Your Dead' scene in *Monty Python and the Holy Grail* (Terry Gilliam and Terry Jones, 1975), wherein a man tries to pass off a dying old man, who continually protests that he is fine ('I feel fine! I think I'll go for a walk'), as dead. *Shaun*'s use of excessive blood spurting during zombie kills is also visually suggestive of the very red spurting blood used for comedic effect in *Grail*'s infamous Black Knight scene.

Drawing on Monty Python helps *Shaun of the Dead* to not only enact transnational genre hybridity but also marks the film out as interested in transnationality and the medium of film itself. When *Monty Python's Flying Circus* was brought over to the United States in 1974, it garnered 'a fanatically devoted audience'.[84] As Jeffrey S. Miller argues, *Monty Python*'s comedy could 'speak to an American audience first through revealing and criticizing the social and cultural processes in which [it was] created, distributed and appreciated' – that is, the medium of television. The show was successful in sending up other television genres, like game shows and talk shows, because its audiences were televisually literate. Audiences' positive reactions to much of the comedy was shaped by their 'expectations and knowledge of the way television is "naturally" supposed to be and work'.[85] Similarly, *Shaun of the Dead*'s homage to Romero's zombie films, debt to *Monty Python* and references to popular culture hail a cineliterate audience, one who will recognise and laugh at its citations. Whether it is the scene where Shaun and Ed decide the *Batman* soundtrack provides more value as weapon against zombies than as a record but preserve Prince's *Purple Rain*, Ed saying 'We're coming to get you Barbara!', or the final television montage where Coldplay plays Zomb-Aid, *Shaun of the Dead* sets up its audiences to laugh at the uncanny results of the collision between the zombie apocalypse and popular culture.

By reframing an American genre, via Romero's modern zombie films, and using distinctly British comedy traditions to do so, via Ealing, Monty Python and the television two-man comedy team, *Shaun of the Dead* participates in a transnational form of genre hybridity, positioning itself *across* both national cinemas. *Shaun* is an homage to Romero's zombie films without being Americanised. Indeed, it is the film's comedy, drawn from British traditions, that fully allows its commentaries on the service industry and new laddism to manifest, so that the comedy performs a vital role in allowing the film to achieve social relevance and the cultural legitimacy associated with the social realist impulse in British film culture.

Shaun asserts, via its transnational genre hybridity, that British cinema has not become completely Americanised, that it has not only traditions but a present and future and that horror can participate meaningfully in the cultural work of British cinema. In this way, the film also works to critique the anti-horror and anti-Americanisation discourses present in middlebrow British film culture.

Conclusions

While Robert Murphy quipped in 2000 that the British film industry was caught in 'the Hollywood stranglehold', by 2009 he changed his tune, writing that though he could not say that 'all is well with the British film industry', he had to recognise and support 'the emergence of a refreshingly cine-literate generation of actors, directors, writers, cinematographers, with a genuine interest in the cinema and a determination to make individual and distinctive films'.[86] *28 Days Later* was one of the first individual, distinctive films coming out of the British horror resurgence, reworking Romero's American zombie films by drawing on more respected genres, including genres from the Golden Age of British cinema, to assert its relevance to British cinema and British culture more broadly. Furthermore, Boyle's film is not the only British film involved in this sort of engagement with anti-Americanisation discourses within middlebrow British film culture. While *28 Days Later* uses its genre hybridity to critique Americanisation, Edgar Wright's *Shaun of the Dead* (2004) uses transnational genre hybridity to mix tropes of the Romerian American zombie film with British comedic traditions, to different ends. Rather than critique Americanisation, *Shaun of the Dead* pays homage to Romero without becoming Americanised, which serves to critique the anti-Americanisation discourse in which *28 Days Later* participates. *Shaun* shows that engagement with American genres does not have to be negative; there can be a middle ground, or perhaps even a third way, between Americanisation and a nationalistic, supposedly pure British cinema. Both films use transnational genre hybridity in a way that generically positions the films as *situated across* both national cinemas, which allows the films to comment on the relationship between those cinemas and industries. That these films communicate different critiques shows that transnational genre hybridity can function flexibly and does not necessarily signal a single ideological perspective.

Both films went on to inspire a plethora of other zombie films, both in the UK and internationally. The influence of *28 Days Later* can be seen clearly in the way that films like *The Zombie Diaries* (UK, Michael Bartlett and Kevin Gates, 2006) and *Colin* (UK, Marc Price, 2008) use digital video to attempt a gritty aesthetic, as well as using a documentary style of handheld camerawork. Of course, the film also inspired a sequel, *28 Weeks Later* (UK, Juan Carlos Fresnadillo, 2007), though this film borrows only from the general plot and setting of its predecessor, opting for a slicker Hollywood look, using quality film stock and a conspicuously attractive cast, perhaps a consequence of its heavily international co-production. *Shaun of the Dead* also paved the way for a new hybrid genre, the zom-rom-com. Subsequent films have explored the comic potential of attempting romance during the zombie apocalypse, including *Zombieland* (US, Ruben Fleischer, 2009). Other films, like *Boy Eats Girl* (UK, Stephen Bradley, 2005) and *Warm Bodies* (US, Jonathan Levine, 2013), have opted to investigate the potential for zombie-human romance.

Both *28 Days Later* and *Shaun of the Dead* were critical in jump-starting the British horror resurgence of the 2000s. Both films used transnational genre hybridity to respond to the key discourses circulating in middlebrow British film culture. By reframing a largely American-identified genre, the Romerian zombie genre, by drawing from long-standing British visual media traditions, both filmic and televisual, both films comment on the discourse of Americanisation, as well as positioning the horror film as a vital site for cultural work addressing middlebrow British film culture and contemporary social issues. And yet, zombies are not the only monsters used by British horror film-makers to counter assertions that the 'new wave' of British horror films 'simply can't compete with the good-looking US models populated by, well, good-looking US models'.[87] In my next chapter, I address the hoodie horror cycle and how these films used transnational genre hybridity differently from *28 Days Later* and *Shaun of the Dead* to address issues of class and race that began to bubble up in the early 2000s, boiling over in the 2011 riots.

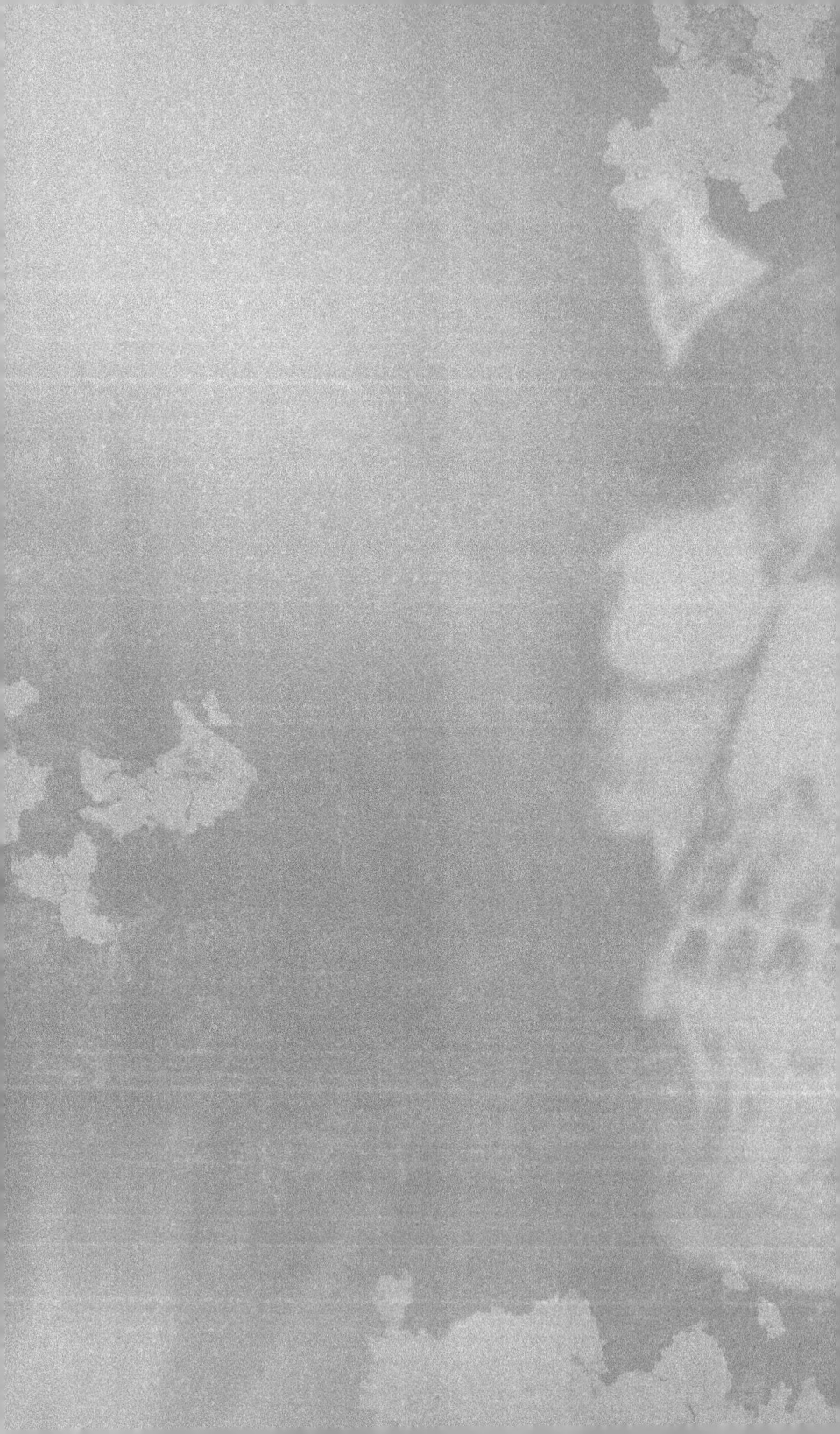

3

Hybrid Hoodie Horrors

Genre Localisation and Britain's Moral Panic

These days, the scariest Britflick villain isn't a flesh-eating zombie, or an East End Mr. Big with a sawn-off shooter and a tattooed sidekick. It is a teenage boy with a penchant for flammable casualwear. (Jane Graham, writing for *The Guardian* in 2009[1])

THIS CHAPTER EXAMINES a second manifestation of transnational genre hybridity in films of the British horror resurgence. Films like *28 Days Later* and *Shaun of the Dead* use both American and British genres to position themselves as *situated across* the two countries to comment on the relationship between the film industries. However, for other films – like *Eden Lake* (James Watkins, 2008) and *Attack the Block* (Joe Cornish, 2011) – the trans- of transnational genre hybridity allows the films to draw on a foreign genre and *change it thoroughly* to address an issue of domestic import. This meaning of *trans-* is linked to change or transfer, as with *transliterate, transmute* or *translate*.

In this way, we could say that the transnational genre hybridity of these films culturally *translates* a subgenre, taking it from its original context and changing it to be better understood within and better serve another culture and its specific national audiences. *Eden Lake* reframes 1970s American backwoods horror, like *Texas Chainsaw Massacre* (Tobe Hooper, 1974) and *The Hills Have Eyes* (Wes Craven, 1977). *Attack the Block*, on the other hand, reframes 1970s cult American gang films, including *Assault on Precinct 13* (John Carpenter, 1976) and *The Warriors* (Walter Hill, 1979). By cult American gang films, I mean the particular subset of action thrillers in the 1970s and 1980s that focused on gangs and came to achieve cult status by the early 2000s. The films of Walter Hill and John Carpenter work well as representative examples here, as, in addition to *Assault on Precinct 13* and *The Warriors*, their films *Escape from New York* (Carpenter, 1981) and *Streets of Fire* (Hill, 1984) also help constitute this group of films. Both *Eden Lake* and *Attack the Block* draw on the narrative tropes or aesthetics of these American films but reshape the films' racial and class politics to address contemporary British concerns by fitting in to the hoodie cycle, a domestic British film cycle concerned with delinquent youths that started during the mid-2000s and encompassed a variety of genres, from horror to teen pics to family melodrama.

Films of the American backwoods horror cycle of the 1970s are invested in showing their antagonists as mentally, physically and/or sexually deviant from middle-class norms to justify their economic, geographic and social marginalisation, using American notions of meritocracy to soothe middle-class fears during the rough economic times of the 1970s. In *Eden Lake*, however, the antagonists' status as working class makes them monstrous, in part because working-class status codes them as less white. As studies on whiteness and class in the UK have shown, drawing here on the work of scholars like Imogen Tyler, Keith Hayward and Majid Yar, working-class status associates white people with people of colour, who are stereotyped as both unduly influenced by American culture and violent media, as well as aspiring to possess the material trappings of the white middle class without a desire to conform to associated cultural norms.[2] The hero of *Eden Lake* is not one of the protagonists, who are themselves presented as pretentious and grasping, but a corporation building a gated community that will re-capture and re-code the working-class space as elite and offer a space of safety by putting up a fence to keep working-class, and many middle-class, people out. On the other hand, the heroes in 1970s American cult gang films often share similar attitudes, characteristics and actions with the villains – for example, both the hero Warriors and their rival gangs rape and murder in *The Warriors* – the result being an ambiguity that troubles the notion of clear delineations between good and evil, particularly based on race or class. However, *Attack the Block* presents a clear political message by showing its hoodie protagonist accept and learn from the consequences of his violence, using the alien antagonists to critique racist stereotypes that are applied to hoodie teens and showing how the solution to the 'hoodie problem' is the acceptance of hoodies into, and hoodies' acceptance of a place within, the broader community.

The problem of space in both of these films is less one of urban versus rural and more of working class (represented by small towns, estate housing and urban tower blocks) versus middle and upper class (primarily rural gated communities and posh urban neighbourhoods). *Eden Lake* and *Attack the Block* both engage with the moral panic around hoodies, and while their responses to the panic are almost diametrically opposed, with one film working to solidify the boundaries of working-class spaces while the other seeks to break down those boundaries, both films create room for potential critical engagement. They can do this by shifting the political perspective of the American genres they draw upon in a way that has eluded other hoodie horror films.

While, for example, the hoodie horror film *Demons Never Die* (Arjun Rose, 2011) borrows from the teen slasher genre made popular by John Carpenter's *Halloween* (1978) and deconstructed by Wes Craven's *Scream* (1996), it does not change the essential politics of the slasher with regard to hoodie teens: teens are delinquent and rebellious, and those who are sexually active or using drugs will pay with their lives for their dissolute behaviour. Similarly, while *Cherry Tree Lane* (Paul Andrew Williams, 2010) takes inspiration from home invasion thrillers like *Last House on the Left* (Wes Craven, 1972) and *Straw Dogs* (Sam Peckinpah, 1971), it does not deviate from the political message associated with that subgenre, wherein a middle-class family is pushed to their limit and wreak horrific vengeance on their attackers that shows the family members capable of the same, if not worse, brutality. These films take their chosen American subgenre and paste it on top of the domestic hoodie context; they operate as statements on the hoodie and merely perpetuate the moral panic around that population, rather than allowing a more nuanced engagement with both the subgenre they draw from and the discourses around the panic itself.

During their initial exhibition periods, reviewers recognised and noted the way *Eden Lake* and *Attack the Block* engaged with both American subgenres and the hoodie panic. Peter Bradshaw, writing for *The Guardian*, commented that *Attack the Block* draws on 'the siege drama – Carpenter's

Assault on Precinct 13' in particular, while addressing 'aggressive youths . . . with a light touch and a cheerful, unfashionabl[e] optimis[m]'.³ *Empire* also picked up on the Carpenter connection, calling *Attack the Block* 'really the best movie John Carpenter never made', 'combining the siege movie mindset of *Assault on Precinct 13* with the grimy sci-fi edge of, say, *Escape from New York*' and setting 'such decidedly American tropes to a landscape that could only be British'.⁴ Similarly, Bradshaw writes that *Eden Lake* juxtaposes Britain's 'perceived social wounds: knife-crime, gangs and the fear of a broken society' with 'inevitable folk memories of *Deliverance*' and 'hints of Peckinpah's *Straw Dogs*', both backwoods horror films.⁵ Even the directors acknowledged these influences. In an interview with the online magazine *Den of Geek*, James Watkins said that he wanted to combine backwoods horror with 'contemporary fears of youth'.⁶ Joe Cornish discusses the influence of *Assault on Precinct 13*, *The Warriors* and similar films extensively during two of the film's three DVD commentaries: the 'Senior Commentary' with Cornish and actors Jodie Whittaker, Luke Treadaway and Nick Frost, as well the 'Executive Producer Commentary' with Cornish and Edgar Wright.

Critics and scholars writing on *Eden Lake* and *Attack the Block*, and hoodie horror more broadly, have often focused primarily on the ways in which these films can be seen as playing into, proving or critiquing the negative rhetoric and moral panic around hoodie youths. John Fitzgerald argues that *Eden Lake* is 'an unsubtle but incredibly effective approach regarding the perceived threat felt by the middle classes from young working-class youth in modern-day Britain'.⁷ For Fitzgerald, the fear inspired by the film corresponds to justified real-life fears, and the 'malevolent, amoral world' of the hoodie is recognisable as an exaggerated reflection of reality. Sherryl Vint focuses on how *Attack the Block* asks viewers to question their 'image of hoodie-wearing, generally non-white, teenagers' and their frequently stereotypical media representation.⁸

On the other hand, Linn Lönroth concludes that hoodie horror films all communicate a conservative and reactionary ideology.⁹ For Lönroth, the films' class ideologies serve the ends of neo-liberal capitalism by demonising the working classes to shift attention away from their exploitation by the economic elites and the way that exploitation produces the inequalities that lead to the very criminal behaviour for which the working classes are demonised. Mark Featherstone expresses a similar sentiment in his study of *Eden Lake*, *F* (Johannes Roberts, 2010) and *Cherry Tree Lane*, seeing hoodie horror as 'a projection of the evil socio-economic system that scapegoats others to hide its own monstrosity'.[10] Featherstone positions the hoodie horror cycle, then, as a means of perpetuating the fear of 'irrational feral youth' as individuals rather than the groups of economic elite or politicians who perpetuate the economic system he sees as responsible for both the discourse of feral youth and the conditions that lead to actual working-class crime.

While these critics have connected the films to the hoodie cycle, they have not attended to the films' genre hybridity, nor the way that hybridity adds to the films' politics, which in turn helps to position the films as culturally relevant to middlebrow British film culture. Johnny Walker, in his article on 2000s British horror, mainly focuses on *Eden Lake* to argue that hoodie horrors are self-aware, as their stereotypical depictions of hoodies make class divisions more apparent and call into question the way hoodies are depicted prejudicially in the news.[11] He also discusses how this self-awareness is achieved through genre hybridity – however, he sees this genre hybridity as the enmeshment of the tradition of British social realism (and its political purpose) and 'genre films designed for pleasure and entertainment'.[12] My argument acknowledges and extends Walker's; I also recognise the call to awareness and action in these films (and traditionally associated with social realism), but I argue that the potential for this awareness and action comes not from hybridity between British social realism and the genre film more broadly but between the tropes of the British hoodie cycle itself and the American subgenres the films also draw from. Further, a focus on these two films provides insight into how hoodie horror changed as it evolved within the broader hoodie cycle: acknowledged as a hoodie horror when it came out, *Eden Lake* premiered when the broader hoodie cycle was still becoming established as a cycle, while *Attack the Block* came out toward the end of the cycle.

'Anonymous, Nonchalant, Menacing': Moral Panic and the British Hoodie Cycle[13]

The hoodie cycle of films, which started with Menhaj Huda's 2006 urban teen drama *Kidulthood*, includes films that take working-class teens of varying levels of delinquency – 'hoodies' – as either their protagonists (as in *Kidulthood* or *Attack the Block*) or antagonists (as with *Eden Lake* and *Harry Brown* (Daniel Barber, 2009)). Hoodies are primarily defined by their class and race; they can be working-class teens of colour, but they can also be white teens whose working-class status makes them discursively racially othered. These racially othered white, working-class people are often referred to colloquially in Britain as 'chavs', a racial slur whose use has risen precipitously since the early 2000s. As Imogen Tyler has noted, like the American white trash figure, the 'chav' figure represents a visible, 'dirty whiteness' that has been 'contaminated with poverty' and associated with working-class, non-white (often Americanised) culture through 'clothing, music and forms of speech', as well as 'geographical, familial and sexual intimacy with working class blacks and Asians'.[14] Tyler argues that this racialisation of the white working class 'is an attempt to differentiate between respectable and non-respectable forms of whiteness' and exclude 'the white poor from spheres of white privilege'. The discourses around 'chavs' and hoodies mark out those in the white middle class as respectable and having risen above the behaviour of the working classes. As Owen Jones and others have argued, since the Thatcher era, UK politicians and the press have framed much of the white working class as a feral underclass – degenerate, unintelligent and uneducated, violent, unhygienic and tasteless.[15]

These representations have also been largely borne out in the representation of working-class people on film. The representation of working-class people as criminals has a long history in British cinema via the crime genre, which has mainly dealt in negative depictions of petty criminals, gangsters, drug dealers and thugs, from Hitchcock's *Blackmail* (1929) to Paul Andrew Williams's *London to Brighton* (2006). Other British films have sought to humanise and complexify the representation of working-class people, including Griersonian documentaries like *Housing Problems* (1935), New Wave films of the 1950s and 60s and Mike Leigh and Ken Loach's social realist films in the 1980s and 90s. And yet, as Stephen Shafer argues, during and after the Thatcher era, working-class people were increasingly portrayed as 'isolated and left outside society' economically, socially and in terms of family.[16] More and more, films both recognised and depicted the real-life marginalisation of working-class people, including their feelings of hopelessness in the face of adversarial government policies. However, while film-makers like Mike Leigh and Ken Loach (and newer voices like Andrea Arnold and Shane Meadows) continued to aim at inspiring class consciousness through their films about working-class people and their problems, that aim was not shared universally, particularly not by films like the politically vacuous *Lock, Stock and Two Smoking Barrels* (Guy Ritchie, 1998) and the saccharine *Little Voice* (Mark Herman, 1998) and *Billy Elliot* (Stephen Daldry, 2000). The hoodie film represents one of the newer incarnations of this longer history of working-class representation on film, and the depiction of teens rather than adults plays into what critic Máire Messenger Davies sees as the post-Bulger murder demonisation of British youths in the media and by the UK government, for example via the introduction of measures, like Anti-Social Behaviour Orders (ASBOs), that disproportionately affect teens and children.[17]

The figure of the hoodie and the rhetoric around it developed quickly. In 2003, when inducted into the *Longman Dictionary of Contemporary English*, 'hoodie' still simply meant a hooded sweatshirt or jacket, 'commonly worn by rappers'.[18] By 2005, due to media coverage of a number of violent incidents involving teens wearing hooded sweatshirts, the term 'hoodie' had become so associated with this population that popular news outlets were using the term metonymically in 'the great "hoodie" debate', despite the fact that the hooded sweatshirt continued to be a popular item of clothing across a number of populations, including adults.[19] The debate over whether hoodies, and teens in hoodies more broadly, were degenerate criminals or misunderstood teens came to the fore in mainstream discourse in 2005 when the Bluewater Shopping Centre in Kent instituted a controversial ban on 'wearing clothing which deliberately obscures the face such as hooded tops and baseball caps', in a move to cut down on violent incidents perpetrated by teens at the centre, as well as to make the environment more 'family-friendly'.[20] Much of the press reaction to the ban demonised the hoodie-wearing youth as criminals attempting to hide their identities from CCTV and intimidate adults.

The criminal activity most associated with the hoodie in the mid-2000s was happy-slapping (inflicting unmotivated violence on a randomly chosen person, usually an adult stranger, and recording it with phones to share with friends and the internet). While incidents began in late 2004 and were originally teen-on-teen or child-on-child violence that cropped up on London playgrounds, the fad soon spread across the country, and happy-slappers set their sights more often on adults. As the fad grew, happy-slappers began to seek out adult victims in parks and other public areas less likely to be observed by the watchful eye of police and CCTV.[21] By 2006, the fad was so pervasive in public discourse, and violence so associated with teens, that in one episode, The Doctor of *Doctor Who* (the David Tennant version) arrives at a UK school expecting 'happy-slapping hoodies with ASBOs'.[22]

Inserting itself into this discourse around hoodies and contributing a variety of perspectives, the hoodie cycle produced films in a number of disparate genres, including teen films, social realist dramas, comedies, crime films and horror films. There are many films in this cycle, but a few examples include: the teen films *4.3.2.1* (Noel Clarke and Mark Davis, 2010) and *Shank* (Mo Ali, 2010); the social realist dramas *Better Things* (Duane Hopkins, 2008) and *Fish Tank* (Andrea Arnold, 2009); comedies like *Anuvahood* (Adam Deacon and Daniel Toland, 2011); and crime films like *Harry Brown* and *Ill Manors* (Ben Drew, 2012). Even hoodie horror itself is not confined to a single subgenre. There are home invasion films like *Cherry Tree Lane* (Paul Andrew Williams, 2010); slashers like *F*, *Demons Never Die* and *Comedown* (Menhaj Huda, 2012); backwoods horror films like *Summer Scars* (Julian Richards, 2007), *The Reeds* (Nick Cohen, 2010) and *Eden Lake*; gothic films like *The Disappeared* (Johnny Kevorkian, 2008) and *Heartless* (Philip Ridley, 2009); and sci-fi/horror hybrids like *Attack the Block*. There are also films that resist easy classification, like *Tower Block* (James Nunn and Ronnie Thompson, 2012) or the truly execrable *Community* (Jason Ford, 2012).

I use the term 'cycle' here as theorised by Amanda Ann Klein, as a set of films with coherent semantics but without a coherent syntax.[23] What makes these films cohere as a cycle, then, despite their disparate genres, subgenres, ideologies and basic narratives, is the semantic resonances between the films – the figure of the hoodie itself, plots that revolve around working-class teens and violence and settings in working-class spaces. This coherent collection of semantic elements grows out of, as Klein argues, the 'easily reproducible elements' of an 'originary film' – in this case, *Kidulthood*.[24]

In addition, the films are also linked by their frequent use of actors who have starred in other hoodie films and working-class dramas. For example, after his success in *Kidulthood*, Adam Deacon took a role in the hoodie horror *Comedown*. There, he acted alongside Jacob Anderson, who had recently been in the hoodie horror *Demons Never Die*, where he worked alongside Jason Maza, who had worked on Andrea Arnold's working-class drama *Fish Tank*. *Fish Tank* also cast Harry Treadaway, who had earlier starred in the hoodie horror *The Disappeared*. Deacon had also starred in the comedy *Anuvahood*, which also cast Ashley Walters, star of the hoodie precursor *Bullet Boy* (Saul Dibb, 2004), who would later appear in *Demons Never Die*. For that film, Walters worked with Jennie Jacques, who went on to act in the hoodie horror *Cherry Tree Lane*, which saw her working alongside Jumayn Hunter.

Hunter would later star as the antagonist in *Attack the Block*. Previously, he had been the only non-white member of the hoodie gang in *Eden Lake*, where he was cast alongside Thomas Turgoose, whose portrayal of a working-class kid who falls into the 1980s skinhead lifestyle in *This Is England* (Shane Meadows, 2006) had won him, and the film, awards and strong praise from critics. Arguably, the casting of Thomas Turgoose is one of the facets of *Eden Lake* that marks it out as knowingly part of the hoodie cycle, given that he had just played an adolescent working-class gang member; his casting signals a self-conscious desire to engage with larger cultural discourses around working-class youths.[25] Both actors worked with Jack O'Connell in *Eden Lake*, and O'Connell went on to act in both *Harry Brown* and *Tower Block*. These actors, and other repeats on the cast lists, provide another key shared semantic element in the cycle that marks out the films as 'hoodie'.

Hoodie films also followed the basic pattern of a cycle. As Klein describes it, the 'originary film . . . launches a cycle [by] tap[ping] into a subject of contemporary relevance, something in which the audience is already emotionally invested'.[26] *Kidulthood* was this film. The figure of the hoodie, and their working-class environs, were both easily recognisable within the logic of 'Broken Britain', a cultural discourse created in the mid-2000s by tabloids like *The Sun*, which is owned by subsidiaries of Rupert Murdoch's News Corp, and the similarly inflammatory *Daily Mail*. This discourse, quickly adopted by the UK's political right, maintained that Britain was more lawless, chaotic and dangerous than ever before. Critics and audiences who helped to perpetuate the hoodie cycle by discussing and viewing these films were already invested in both 'Broken Britain' and the hoodie. When *Kidulthood*'s teens slouched and cursed their way onto the screen in 2006, their easy violence and lack of bourgeois sexual mores 'ruffled feathers', and many critics thought the film would 'put the fear of God into parents everywhere'.[27] For many of these critics, as well as for the film's writer, Noel Clarke, the film's 'essential truth' lies in its depiction of British teens and the way it works to 'document urban teenagers' lives', which makes it '"an essential film for all parents to see"' since '"every child could be at risk"'.[28] The hoodie cycle capitalised upon and tapped into these pre-existing fears.

More than simply an issue of cultural import, though, fears over the hoodie had coalesced into a moral panic. The foundational definition of moral panic comes from Stanley Cohen's work on the Mods and Rockers in 1960s Britain; he defines a moral panic as a cyclically occurring phenomenon when, suddenly, 'a condition, episode, person or group of persons emerges to become defined as a threat to societal values and interests'.[29] The media presents the threat in a stylised and stereotypical way, while 'right-thinking people' publicly denounce it. After a short time, public hostility toward the threat grows until it transforms into a 'folk devil', a 'visible reminder . . . of what we should not be', which in turn prompts experts and politicians to lead a 'moral crusade' to diagnose and treat the problem to save people from the threat. All of these responses contribute to and constitute the moral panic.

Stuart Hall and his co-authors took this theorisation further to posit that moral panics represent a new social construction of an extant thing – for example, a new way of understanding mugging or working-class teenagers. In the moral panic over mugging in the 1970s, as Hall and his co-authors have argued, the act of garrotting, a crime that had been common in large British cities since the 1800s, was redefined using the American word mugging, and the subsequent rise in muggings (because of this semantic change) was attributed in part to the negative influence of American culture, as well as the degradation of British society. This came about because of what Hall and his co-authors call the signification spiral: an issue rises into the public consciousness and is then associated with a 'subversive minority', which leads to 'the prophesy of more troubling times to come' and finally a 'call for "firm steps"'. When 'things threaten to disintegrate', whether that is economic security or 'traditional insignia of class', the mugger, and I would argue the hoodie, 'becomes the bearer of all our social anxieties' and 'we turn against him the full wrath of our indignation'.[30]

In the case of the moral panic over hoodies, an issue, street crime, came to be associated in mainstream public discourse with working-class teenagers. These teens were suddenly defined as a threat to public safety, and their chosen clothing was redefined as well; the hooded sweatshirt was no longer simply sportswear or the clothing supposedly preferred by rappers but the preferred wardrobe of criminal teens and an active impediment to justice. This link between the hoodie, rap and working-class teens is key. Early in the panic, 'Broken Britain' was positioned as having allowed, and also having been shaped by, the import of dangerous American cultural elements like gangsta rap and its associated clothing styles and violence.

The first report on happy-slapping, a piece in the *Times Educational Supplement* (*TES*) in January 2005, asserted that the bullying took 'inspiration from violent reality videos, such as those produced in the United

States', like *Bumfights: A Cause for Concern* (Ryen McPherson, 2002), banned for video release by the BBFC, and the more mainstream *Jackass* television show (2000–7).[31] A number of other early articles laid blame on UK garage music, which was seen as, in the words of political and social commentator Deborah Orr, a 'bad-seed' offshoot of UK youth culture that counted American 'gangsta rap' culture as 'a huge influence'.[32] UK garage is influenced by electronica and house music, as well as rap. While, like rap in the US, UK garage was and is primarily produced by artists of colour from marginalised, often working-class, communities, unlike US gangsta rap, UK garage does not take up gang culture and conflicts with the police as its primary lyrical subject. However, its perceived links to US culture made it a likely scapegoat in the moral panic due to the pervasive anti-Americanisation discourse in British culture.[33] Like the hoodie garment itself, UK garage and the teens who listened to it were redefined, with little attention to reality or nuance, to fit the dominant discourse of the panic; all three discursively became a threat to so-called right-thinking British people. As with moral panics historically, the panic had more to do with white, middle-class fears about foreignness and the racialised Other than with the real people within the demonised group. Americanisation was one of many contributing factors proposed by the media and government to explain the rise of the hoodie, and the 2010 political campaign was essentially the Conservative party's moral crusade against these issues, including the supposed rise of antisocial behaviours and the breakdown of the traditional heteronormative nuclear family.

And yet, by the end of 2012, the hoodie cycle had mostly played itself out, with the exception of Gabe Turner's late-comer *The Guvnors* (2014). As Klein has argued, cycles run for a limited time, in part because they 'capitalize on an audience's interest in a subject before it moves on to something else' – and it is this interest in capturing a fickle audience's fleeting interest in a subject that makes film cycles 'small, detailed snapshots of that culture at a single moment in time'.[34] This decline in interest synchronised with the decline of the moral panic itself.

There appear to be a number of reasons why the moral panic wound down. First, there was a gradual de-escalation of political rhetoric around hoodies after the Conservatives won in 2010. While the media and government still spoke of hoodies in derogatory terms, after the 2011 riots, the government and media moved from bemoaning and diagnosing the problem to proposing and implementing solutions. Hoodies were spoken of less often as the focus changed instead to '"gangs," "problem families," and immigration', a shift that allowed the Conservative government to implement many of the policies they said would fix 'Broken Britain' nationwide.[35] It also seems likely that in the aftermath of the August 2011 riots, films about violent, and sometimes killer, hoodies may have increasingly seemed uncomfortably real to Brits who bought into the Tory's fearmongering and unhelpful to people who recognised the reality of Britain's growing income inequality issue. Of course, having won the 2010 election through campaigns largely centred on fear, it also would have been politically expedient for the Tories to de-escalate their rhetoric around 'Broken Britain' to maintain power, as they would have no longer had a vested interest in agitating the public toward political change.

In addition, 2012 was an eventful year in the UK: the Summer Olympic Games were held in London; Queen Elizabeth II had her Diamond Jubilee; the Scottish Government announced its intention to hold the 2014 referendum on Scottish independence; there was record flooding in several parts of the country; unemployment and government debt both hit an all-time high and the economy was thought to have entered a double-dip recession early in the year, though later analysis showed the country had narrowly avoided a second recession. All of these events changed the cultural discourse, and hoodies were no longer the primary concern. The desire to gloss over social ills during the Olympics and the Jubilee, with international attention focused on the country, and London especially, would have been a powerful motivation.

Because of its concentrated run, the hoodie cycle presents a unique window into the moral panic over hoodies. Indeed, I argue that the generic borrowings of *Eden Lake* and *Attack the Block* are part of what allows the films to participate in and comment upon the panic that manifested in the hoodie film more broadly. That is, it is specifically through its transnational genre hybridity that each film engages with the hoodie panic. By reworking backwoods horror via the lens of the hoodie, *Eden Lake* taps into debates around working-class families and spaces, contributing to the panic. The film works as an expression of white middle-class anxiety, driven by fear of economic precarity and projected onto a working-class Other who represents what individuals in the middle class fear they may become if made downwardly mobile. This is also a fear of foreignness and a perceived foreignness thought to be possessed by people of colour – corrupting influences from outside the cultural sphere of white, middle-class Britain, like rap music and gangsta culture, are thought to have undue impact on these working-class teens, pulling their behaviour further out of line from hegemonic white bourgeois norms. *Attack the Block* responds to this same moral panic but instead critiques it by presenting its protagonists as complex individuals with limited choices and reasonable motivations. That both films rework American genres, reshaping those genres' class and racial politics to address domestic concerns, further signals their engagement with and place within the panic itself because of its early and persistent roots in fears over Americanisation, which shaped the way the hoodie was defined and represented.

'"Gated Community"? Who Are They so Afraid of?': Working-Class Spaces and the Discourse of Real-Life Fears in *Eden Lake*

The height of the American backwoods horror subgenre was in the 1970s, prefaced by *Two Thousand Maniacs* (US, Hershell Gordon Lewis, 1964). The more influential of these backwoods horror films are *Straw Dogs*, *The Texas Chainsaw Massacre* and *The Hills Have Eyes*. *Texas Chainsaw* has an especially interesting history in the UK, as it was not denied exhibition by the BBFC and was briefly distributed on video before being banned on video, with those videos being pulled from the shelves. The film did not pass censors for exhibition and distribution in the UK until 1999.[36] Kendall Phillips has argued that *Texas Chainsaw Massacre* embodies the pervasive feeling in the 1970s that the American dream had died and that the world as people knew it was 'ending and that behind the layers of cultural illusion [lay] a deep, inner truth about our nature'.[37] I would extend this argument to the other backwoods horror films of the 1970s as well; these films present rural America as a place failed by both the capitalist economy and the government, filled with people whose isolation from the civilising influence of the city and the national economy has made them devolve – the speed and intensity of these regressions reveal a profound anxiety about economic precarity, the instability of class boundaries and fears of what base desires and behaviours the civilising influence of urban spaces and capital keep the urban middle classes from experiencing or acknowledging within themselves.

Backwoods horror films generally follow several urban-dwellers as they travel into the countryside to temporarily escape city life only to run into rural peoples, sometimes inbred and often dirty and mentally unstable, who terrorise them in psychologically disturbing and graphic ways. Often, early in the film, as in *Texas Chainsaw* and *The Hills Have Eyes*, the city-dwellers stop at an outpost of civilisation, like a gas station, where the carnage to come is foreshadowed. Later, they return to this outpost for help, only to realise that the outpost is either populated and run by the rural maniacs they are attempting to escape from or is about to be overrun by them. While there were several British films mixing comedy with backwoods horror in the 2000s – including *Severance* (Christopher Smith, 2006), *The Cottage* (Paul Andrew Williams, 2008) and the intended-to-be-comedic *Inbred* (Alex Chandon, 2011) – *Eden Lake* stands out as one of the first non-comedic British horror films to take on the subgenre. The film follows Steve (Michael Fassbender) and Jenny (Kelly Reilly), an urban, middle-class couple, as they travel into the countryside for a romantic weekend vacation, only to be terrorised by local hoodies. Like the casts of most backwoods horror films, the town and hoodie gang are pretty overwhelmingly white; Jumayn Hunter's Mark and James Gandhi's Adam are the only characters of colour and neither has much dialogue, screen time or character individuation. The plot of *Eden Lake* clearly draws on backwoods horror's narrative conventions – a journey from city to country, the stop in a small town whose violence foreshadows the violence to come in the film and the later return to that outpost, which has been revealed as dangerous. The film also uses certain tropes from the subgenre, such as the uncivilised, insular nature of the hoodies and people in their community and Jenny's descent into violence that mirrors the hoodies' violence (problematically referred to in discussions of the backwoods genre as 'going native').

The journey from the city to the country presented in the first few minutes of the film foreshadows much of what is to come in terms of the film's concern with hoodies and devolved rural working-class populations, as well as introducing the outpost of civilisation where a feeling of 'wrongness' begins to build. As Johnny Walker argues, in *Eden Lake*, 'the countryside is a metaphor for Broken Britain', and this brokenness emerges as soon as the couple begin their journey out of the city.[38] While Steve drives, a programme plays on the radio discussing delinquent teens and the parents who fail to discipline them as images of first the city, then the motorway and finally the country visualise the couple's journey. The small town in which the Crown Inn operates is the outpost of civilisation. Steve and Jenny's entry into the town is met with two instances of aggressive driving, where the rules of the road, both written and unwritten, are ignored, foreshadowing both the hoodies' and their parents' lack of regard for institutional and cultural laws regarding behaviour. First, several youths on bicycles speed through a red light at an intersection, so that Steve must stop short to avoid hitting them. Then, when Steve and Jenny arrive at the Crown Inn, another car rushes into the parking space that Steve had been waiting for, with his turn signal on.

This focus on middle-class norms of social behaviour, as well as the law, continues when Jenny and Steve sit down for a lager at the Inn. While drinking in the outdoor patio space behind the pub, they witness a mother hitting her screaming child. Jenny and the mother share a moment of sustained eye contact wherein the mother appears outwardly hostile and aggressive toward Jenny, as though she is daring her to say something in judgment. Jenny looks away rather than respond, and via long shot the mother continues, with her arms crossed defensively, to cast angry glances at Jenny. The mother is, tellingly, wearing a hooded sweatshirt over her low-cut tank top and short denim skirt. Though an adult, her hooded sweatshirt connects her to the hoodies who later torture the couple. Indeed, the mother's costuming, in addition to her violence, shows her disregard for middle-class norms of appearance, as her outfit is both age-inappropriate and over-sexualised compared to Jenny's girlishly feminine pink dress, with a modest neckline and hemline falling below her knees. The unnecessary hostility and violence in this scene foreshadow the violence the local youths will later inflict on Jenny and Steve, as well as their hostile attitudes and disregard for legal and social norms.

This scene also establishes Steve and Jenny as wannabe enforcers of norms. When the children run around their table, Steve asks, 'A bit past their bed time, isn't it?', and when one child screams repeatedly, he says, 'That child. Needs a good . . .' Of course, his recommendation is broken off when the mother slaps the child. Jenny's look of horror at the mother is also a look of rebuke and outrage; the brief interaction at the start of the film between Jenny and the young children she teaches, as well as her reaction to the shouting children ('Poor things must be exhausted'), position her as gentle and sympathetic toward children. Like the frustration Steve displays earlier when the rules of the road are broken, Steve's actions in this scene position him as someone who not only believes in prevailing social norms related to public behaviour but who, like the commentators on the radio programme earlier, would like to police the behaviour of others and feels worthy of that task.

However, neither he nor Jenny confront the mother about her actions or the couple fighting loudly in the parking lot that they later complain to each other about, in part because that would be breaking social norms as well, as they would not be minding their own business and would be creating social discord. Instead, Jenny looks away, and Steve pushes away his discomfort with irony, asking Jenny, 'Another pint of wifebeater?' Instead of solving the problems they see, Steve and Jenny both turn away from them, hoping they will be fixed by someone else; in this working-class space, the weight of their social disapproval does not function as a deterrent for behaviour in the way that panoptic social monitoring and the potential for social shaming function in their urban home, again showing how far removed they are from the social and legal norms of the city – how far the working-class people have devolved.

Following a common trope in backwoods horror, Jenny is so influenced by the combination of the violent locals and lack of policing that she eventually devolves as well. While the film aligns viewers with Jenny and Steve in an assumption of shared middle-classness, Jenny's education and middle-class, urban values cannot save her from 'going native', adopting the violence shown by the working-class youths who terrorise the couple. When she is being pursued by Brett (Jack O'Connell), the main and most violent hoodie, and another boy after escaping from the fire in which they tried to burn her alive with Steve's corpse, Jenny stumbles into a broken-down rest area that contains markers of the quarry's former life as a nature preserve and park. However, like the larger environment of the park, the rest area has been long neglected. The map Jenny finds is faded and covered in dirt. The glass in front of the map is covered in a thin patina of dirt and mould. Without the trappings of authority, with no social map of how to deal with what she is experiencing, Jenny is at a loss. She hides from her pursuers in a dumpster thick with sludgy filth.

Jenny's experience in the dumpster is brief but transformative. After the hoodies have gone, she opens the dumpster lid and gasps, taking in a huge breath, like the first breath of a newborn. Her skin is covered not only in brown sludge but reddish filth that looks like blood. These visual cues indicate Jenny's rebirth as a creature of the working-class space. Covered in the filth of the environment, metaphorically and literally, Jenny cannot help but succumb and 'go native' by adopting the violence displayed by working-class characters. Not even a minute later, after ripping a strip of fabric off her dress to fashion a knife from a shard of glass, Jenny ruthlessly stabs Cooper (Thomas Turgoose), the gentlest and most reluctant of the hoodies. Cooper approaches her, remorseful and guilty as he looks around to make sure none of the others are nearby. He calls to Jenny softly, saying 'Miss?' She quickly turns around, baring her teeth, and stabs him in the neck, making an animalistic grunting noise as she does so. She rips her improvised knife out of his neck and blood gushes down his front. Even as, with one hand, she tries to stop the flow of blood from his wound, she takes quick, darting glances around herself and tries to stifle Cooper's coughing with her other hand. Her violence mirrors the violence the hoodies display earlier in the film when Brett coerces each of them, except Paige (Finn Atkins), to stab Steve.

While Jenny displays some remorse for this first kill, her second kill is in cold blood, showing her further descent into depravity. When she kills Cooper, Jenny weeps afterward. Combining that with the way the baby-faced Thomas Turgoose played the character of Cooper, as the young one afraid to engage in violence but also afraid of the consequences of not participating, the audience is set up to feel sympathy for both Cooper and Jenny – Cooper because he was the least guilty hoodie and Jenny because of what she has gone through and become. But later, when Jenny runs down and hits the girl hoodie Paige with a stolen truck, the moment is framed as a victory. Jenny grunts as she slams on the gas pedal and the car accelerates into the young girl; as Paige flips over the top of the truck and rolls lifelessly into the ditch behind the speeding truck, the film cuts to a close-up of Jenny's face, warped in a grin that is also a grimace. It is a satisfied look, and she grunts again as the music swells. As she drives away, she lets out a loud sigh of relief and lifts her head high.

While Cooper's death is an unthinking moment of violence and tragedy for him and Jenny alike, Paige's death is a victorious moment of revenge. Jenny has 'gone native' and appropriated the hoodies' own tactics. Brett's attempts to kill Jenny are framed as his idea of warped vigilante justice for Steve accidentally killing his dog Bonnie. When Steve says that killing the dog was an accident, Brett responds, 'Well, there's going to be another accident when I find that bitch of yours', aligning dog and woman. Jenny's murder of Paige is a similarly outsized and misplaced act of vengeance. Paige's participation in the hoodies' activities is strictly passive; she only records the violence on her phone. Paige becomes, as Jenny was for Brett, just another 'bitch' who can be killed in order to revenge oneself upon the man, or young men, to whom she is connected. The Jenny who was sympathetic to the unruly children who were up past their bedtimes at the Crown Inn is gone.

However, Jenny is not implicated in her own violence in the same way that the hoodies are; while the hoodies are presented as naturally violent and bad, Jenny's learned, adopted violence is presented as an unfortunate side effect of being in the rural, working-class community. Her violence allows the audience to feel, however momentarily, as though the hoodies have been punished. But, her increasing adoption of the hoodie mindset, from thoughtlessly stabbing Cooper to speeding up to hit Paige, also serves as a warning, common in backwoods horror, that, without the social norms and legal institutions of the middle-class urban environment, even those who seem to be good people can easily descend into horrific behaviour. As in films like *Straw Dogs*, the film envisions a base quality to humanity that reveals itself in dire circumstances, a vileness that cuts across class and upbringing.

After she escapes the hoodies, Jenny returns to the local village, and this return draws upon the narrative conventions of the return to the outpost of civilisation in backwoods horror. As in those films, Jenny hopes to find protection but instead finds only further terror. Similar to the start of the film, as Jenny approaches the town, a driver ignores the rules of the road and pulls out right in front of her. However, while this reckless driving was merely a frustration to Steve, now it causes Jenny to careen off the road and toward the backyard of a local home, where she crashes through a fence and into a parked car. Now, rather than a scene of physical and verbal violence, Jenny stumbles into a hedonistic backyard gathering. Adults in bathing suits frolic in an above-ground swimming pool filled with foamy bubbles, while others bounce in a child's bounce house. A bonfire blazes and the sound of cheery music and wild cries of delight fill the air. Once inside the house, Jenny recognises the family dog (Clyde, brother Bonnie) and begins to panic as Brett's dad, Jon (Shaun Dooley), refuses her pleas to call an ambulance or the police. (The dogs' names are likely a nod toward the negative influence of American culture on the community, referencing the American outlaws who famously antagonised the police, popularised by Arthur Penn's 1967 New Hollywood film *Bonnie and Clyde*.) When Jenny escapes to the bathroom, she walks in on a couple having sex in the shower stall. Again, the outpost of civilisation has proven to be uncivilised and out of sync with middle-class social norms of appropriate adult behaviour.

Just as the community's actions demonstrate how far their behaviour is from Jenny and Steve's urban middle-class standards, their distrust of the police and other institutional authorities like the ambulance service belie the community's physical and ideological isolation from civilisation. The town's insularity is signalled early in the film. The bartender ignores Jenny and Steve in favour of chatting with his local customers. When Steve asks their waitress if she has seen any kids on bikes, after the hoodies ruin Steve and Jenny's food and slash one of their vehicle's tyres, the waitress fondly calls the hoodies 'little terrors' and laughs at Steve. When he tells her that the kids slashed their tyres, the actress immediately scowls and changes her tone from friendly to darkly offended, saying 'not my kids'. This unwillingness to see fault, further evidenced by the fact that she is present at the party at the end of the film, reflects a wilful ignorance and prickly defensiveness that firmly maintains the borders of 'them' and 'us'. In this scene, Steve and Jenny go from being an 'us' who the waitress can joke with to a 'them' who is trying to get her kids in trouble.

This 'us versus them' dynamic is at work, too, in the resistance to institutional authority. The locals' initial unwillingness to contact an ambulance or the police persists after the hoodie teens return and tell their parents that Jenny killed one of them and stole the eldest boy's car (which is, in part, true). As Brett's dad Jon says, 'What good are they, eh? What good are they to him [Brett]?' Instead, after Jenny attacks him, Jon decides they will administer their own brand of justice because, as he says, 'she killed a little one'. Even though they know that the dead children will mean the police will come around, Jon says, 'that doesn't mean they're gonna get any answers, does it? We look after our own 'round here'. The working-class community sees the police as 'them', as an antagonistic force that threatens their community, because they do not see themselves as part of the middle-class community or recognise the authority of its laws or institutionalised law enforcement. Three of the men take Jenny into the bathroom, and the last audiences hear of her is her screams. Like a backwoods horror film of the 1970s, returning to the outpost of civilisation only reveals an utter lack of civilisation and leads to the protagonist's doom.

The ways *Eden Lake* draws on the narrative conceits of backwoods horror are important because of how that reframing allows the film to reference and revise the political project of the subgenre and, in so doing, contribute to the hoodie panic. Backwoods horror films show the deadening effect of a bad economy on rural areas of America in the 1970s. As David Roche notes, economic necessity pervades *Texas Chainsaw*, whether it is Hitchhiker (Edwin Neal) complaining that new slaughterhouse technology put him and his family out of work or Old Man (Jim Siedow) griping that the 'cost of electricity is enough to drive a man out of business' after he conscientiously turns out all the lights at his gas station while locking up.[39] It is not just their physical distance from the urban centre's law, civilisation and structures of authority but their increasing irrelevance to the economy that marks them as Other. As Bernice Murphy has argued, the antagonists in backwoods horror films often express a deep resentment against the middle-class, urban outsiders who invade their rural territory.[40] Pitting the urban middle class against the rural working class means the confrontations in these films are between those who perform hard labour in undesirable jobs with little to no opportunity for economic mobility and those who profit from that labour and use that privilege to climb higher on the economic ladder: as Carol Clover puts it, capitalist 'exploiters and their victims'.[41] In *Texas Chainsaw*, for example, the ancestral home that Sally and her brother travel to was owned by their grandfather, who raised the cattle that Leatherface (Gunnar Hansen) and Hitchhiker's family slaughtered; the now-urban family is tainted by the fact that they profited from the physical labour of the rural working class and then left them behind. However, the films work to align viewers with the middle-class protagonists; the monstrosity of the working-class, rural Other is framed as justifying the hegemony of both capitalism (the Other is lesser and therefore deserves and receives less) and associated middle-class social norms.

Eden Lake's political project is broadly similar to the project of 1970s American backwoods horror but ultimately nationally and historically specific, as well as cycle-specific: revealing what the film considers to be the dirty underbelly of British society by implicating rural working-class families in the violence inflicted by hoodies and positioning that violence as an integral, and infectious, part of working-class spaces. A number of subtle but key changes make this shift possible. The film focuses on hoodie teens rather than adults as the major antagonists, and there is one main instigator pressuring the others to, mostly reluctantly, participate in the violence he takes glee in. While in the backwoods horror film, antagonists are often marked out as such by physical deformity (like the mutants in *The Hills Have Eyes*) or the appearance of below-average intelligence (as with Hitchhiker in *Texas Chainsaw*), the physical indicators of monstrosity for the teens of *Eden Lake* are what marks them out as hoodies: their attire, their chosen music (rap) and the fact that they record their violence (as with happy-slapping incidents).

These differences also manifest in the rural communities more broadly. While the rural families in backwoods horror films often subvert traditional gender norms (as when Leatherface takes on the domestic duties and a more feminine appearance in *Texas Chainsaw Massacre*), the families in *Eden Lake* conform strictly to those norms, with the men clearly in charge of decisions and the women there as either sex objects or caretakers. These roles are clear in the final scene, when the women all hover around Jenny, telling her she is safe because there are 'big, ugly men about' to protect her. These women cannot call an ambulance or the police for Jenny, because it is not their place to protect her, so instead they ask Jon to do it. He refuses, patronisingly telling Jenny 'you're safe here, love', implying that the rural men are all the protection she needs (not what she needs protection from). In addition, the film clearly demonstrates its interest in the service economy by explicitly placing the hoodies' parents in tradesperson service jobs: Brett's dad is a house painter, Brett's older brother is a home electrician and one of the mothers is a waitress. In making these adjustments, the film signals its place within the hoodie cycle, as it takes up and perpetuates strands of the discourses around the moral panic that tap into longer-running political discourses that have worked to shift the coding of the working class from respectable to disreputable and to prop up middle-class culture.

Owen Jones argues that, under Thatcher, working-class identity shifted in cultural value from an identity to take pride in to an identity that must be escaped through upward mobility. The hoodie's acquisition (legal and otherwise) and wearing of clothing and accessories from expensive brands (or knock-offs) is a physical manifestation of this desire for upward mobility that is not and has not been accessible in the UK's economy. In *Eden Lake*, this desire bubbles up when Brett steals Steve's Ray-Ban sunglasses and later admires himself in the mirror. Jones frames this inaccessibility as the fault of the Thatcher government's cultural and economic attacks on the working class through union-busting, rising housing prices, a tax burden that shifted from the wealthy to the poor, and the cultural shift toward framing the working classes as racist, feral and to blame for their economic situation. This shift in cultural values 'made respectable . . . the idea that, more often than not, less fortunate people had only themselves to blame', making it possible for both conservatives and liberals to use the spectre of the working class to reduce the social safety net and frighten middle-class people into voting for them.[42] This cultural attitude persisted from the 1980s through the 2000s, when the economy began shifting for young working-class people as temporary and part-time employment (underemployment) proliferated and the service industry grew.[43]

Critics responding to *Eden Lake* largely recognised how it taps into this discourse and perpetuates negative attitudes toward working-class people. Critics from *The Sun* and *The Telegraph* roundly condemned the film for 'express[ing] fear and loathing of ordinary English people'[44] and being an 'exploitative, patronizing' film that suggests 'that all working-class people are thugs'.[45] But, other critics felt that the film, while exploitative, also tapped into real middle-class fears. *Sight & Sound*'s Rebecca Davies and the *Guardian*'s Libby Brookes both saw *Eden Lake* as preying upon the middle-class fear of working-class children.[46] Some critics, though, read the film along political lines. As Anthony Quinn, for *The Independent*, notes, the film suggests 'a consciousless underclass . . . as a red rag to more conservative souls'.[47] Critics may not have agreed upon who exactly was taken in, or not, by the film's ideological message, but their reactions to the film confirm its place within the hoodie panic, regardless of whether that contribution was seen as extreme and repulsive or just indicative of the extremely repulsive nature of the class hatred in the panic itself.

And yet it is not just the portrayal of the hoodies and their parents that constitute the contribution *Eden Lake* makes to the moral panic, but also the portrayal of the rural space inhabited by the working-class community and their relationship to that space. In backwoods horror films, trouble comes about when middle-class protagonists seeking leisure enter the rural living spaces of working-class antagonists, usually coming to or passing through the space while on vacation. This invasion, treating the working and living space of a rural working-class community as a public leisure or tourist space, brings up lingering resentments, whether caused by economic displacement (as with *Texas Chainsaw*) or innate misanthropy (as with the cannibal family in *The Hills Have Eyes*). The tension between the different uses of space available to the characters in the films frames leisure time as a key element of middle-class-ness. Part of the monstrousness of the working-class antagonists is that they are allowed no leisure, as they must struggle at all times to survive, whether that means trying to scam money from travellers (like Hitchhiker in *Texas Chainsaw*) or butchering them for meat (as with Leatherface in *Texas Chainsaw* and the family in *Hills Have Eyes*).

In *Eden Lake*, however, the class conflict plays out in a space of leisure that is used as such by both protagonist and antagonist. The park and lake where Steve and Jenny run afoul of the hoodies, Slapton Quarry, is a space of leisure in transition. The space started out as a quarry – a potential workspace for the working-class inhabitants of the nearby town. When the quarry was flooded, however, it became a space of leisure. This change resonates, in part, with the larger changes in the British economy since the Thatcher era, as the economy was deindustrialised and the job market shifted away from traditional physical labour like mining. This space of leisure was public and open to all. However, the leisure activities indulged in by Steve and Jenny, the hoodies and the hoodies' parents represent clear class distinctions that mark out the working-class characters as Other.

Jenny and Steve engage in a variety of leisure activities at the quarry, all of which are enabled by having money to spend on moderately expensive non-essential goods that function as markers of class status. While Jenny lays out on the beach wearing a pristine, newly purchased bikini, savouring the silence and sun, Steve uses scuba gear to dive in the lake. To navigate around the area, they use a GPS that provides spoken directions and can pair with Steve's phone via Bluetooth. Jenny and Steve's leisure is defined by both a Romantic, somewhat distanced appreciation of the wonders of nature and access to expensive clothing and equipment through which to increase their enjoyment. When they lie out on the beach and chat, or even when they engage in a make-out session, Jenny and Steve are framed as relaxing appropriately in public.

And yet, when Brett and his companions sit on the beach, joke with each other and listen to music, they are framed as loitering and disturbing the peace – 'the peace' being Jenny and Steve's. Their more destructive actions are framed as delinquent and increasingly monstrous but do not appear to be their normal leisure activities, as they all occur in response to actions taken by Steve and Jenny. After Steve first confronts them, they flash Jenny and put a bottle under the back tyre of the couple's vehicle; after Steve complains to their parents, they steal Steve's vehicle and drive it recklessly around the park; and, finally, after Steve tries to fight them and kills Brett's dog, they fatally torture Steve and hunt Jenny. But their misunderstanding of what constitutes proper leisure-time activities is mirrored, to a lesser extent, by their parents, who, in parody of the popular foam parties at dance clubs in large cities in the UK, fill their temporary above-ground pool with foam and dance in it. These foam parties are usually more the domain of single twenty-somethings rather than parents in their forties, and the hoodie parents' inability to recognise age-appropriate behaviour is part of their classed misunderstanding of leisure.

This attitude is directly connected to discourses that privilege middle-class norms regarding the use of public space, as well discourses that generally stereotype working-class Brits as engaging in leisure and consumer activities in a fundamentally 'wrong' way. Owen Jones has noted that the word 'chav' has been used in the 2000s as a way to express 'distaste towards [white] working-class people who have embraced consumerism, only to spend their money in supposedly tacky and uncivilized ways rather than with the discreet elegance of the bourgeoisie'.[48] As consumerism is so often imbricated in leisure, this so-called tackiness extends, I argue, to leisure activities as well as consumer goods. This seems particularly true because many of the fashion trends related to the 'chav' stereotype are connected to leisure, including the hoodie itself, tracksuits, baseball caps and sneakers. Because these items are not used by working-class people only while engaging in athletic activity but as everyday casualwear, their use is deemed 'tacky' in an effort to police behaviour. In the same way, Brett and his friends' leisure time in Slapton Quarry is deemed uncivilised because they are not quietly appreciating nature with the 'discreet elegance' of Jenny and Steve. While Steve, and later Jenny, fails at policing their behaviour, the hoodies will be punished for their misuse of the space because the land will soon be off-limits, gated off and used as housing for those with greater class status and economic capital.

The hoodies' use of the space of Slapton Quarry can also be considered part of the film's contribution to the moral panic because of how mastery of the space is classed. The space of Slapton Quarry represents a space of freedom for Brett and his hoodie companions, where they can listen to music as loudly as they wish, ride their bikes and take out their frustrations on smaller children. They can also escape their parents and, potentially, the horizontal violence those parents may inflict on them after long days at work. The film takes pains to twice draw attention to the hole punched in a door in Brett's house, presumably by Brett's father based on his nonchalant attitude toward the damage, and when Brett's father gets home and thinks Brett is upstairs, his first response is anger and shouting. Later, in the final scene, Brett's father hits him for speaking out of turn. None of this behaviour is treated as out of the ordinary, making it likely that one reason the hoodies spend so much time at the park is to avoid their parents, or at least Brett's father. In their frequent escapes to Slapton, the hoodies have developed mastery over the space. This is made clear in the way that they continually track down and find Steve and Jenny in the large wooded area. This mastery positions the rural space as one that no longer safely accommodates middle-class leisure-seekers. Once the hoodies begin pursuing Jenny, she has no chance of escape; even after she kills two of them and steals their car, she ends up in Brett's house, surrounded and eventually killed by his family.

The coming of the gated community shows that the only way to remain safe from the hoodies, and their parents, is to fence oneself off. While Jenny and Steve may not be able to defeat the hoodies or their parents, the gated community is still coming, and it will take possession of the space over which the hoodies feel mastery, not only reducing the spaces where they can go but also reducing, or even eliminating, their feelings of mastery over spaces within their community. Indeed, gated communities were seen as a response to fears of rising crime rates and increasingly uncontrollable youths. Gated communities proliferated in the UK in the early 2000s, with nearly 1,000 built between 2002 and 2007.[49] This phenomenon is generally cited as having trickled over from the United States, where the gated community arose in the 1980s. These developments placed a wall or fence between the residents and the outside world and often took further measures to ensure safety, such as guards, CCTV and legally binding codes of conduct for residents.[50] These communities 'reflect and reinforce social divisions'.[51]

More than that, as Rowland Atkinson and John Flint showed in their study of British gated communities, this segregation can lead to 'an increased sensitivity to problems' and 'fear of outsiders' instead reducing 'the fear of crime'.[52] Residents in gated communities were likely to overestimate the amount of crime in their neighbourhood, sometimes grossly, and many expressed direct fears about 'youths'. In news reports in the 2000s, gated communities were often explicitly tied to hoodies, who were portrayed as standing just outside the gates, but not going in.[53] This link was strong enough within the public imagination that the *Guardian*'s Steve Rose published a parodic column urging first-time home buyers to read and then watch the films in his 'Hoodie Information Pack' guide to housing and horror films in Britain.[54] *Eden Lake* was on the list.

Eden Lake draws on specific narrative elements and tropes of the American backwoods horror subgenre but changes them from their original political project. These changes allow the film to fit into the hoodie cycle and respond to the moral panic over hoodies more broadly within Britain. Its contribution to the moral panic is a reactionary one, surely. Hoodies, as well as their parents, are positioned as monstrous because of their class position and the way that class position is racialised and associated with cultural practices outside white, middle-class norms. Even if they appropriately aspire to middle-class-ness, their methods of acquiring the trappings of middle-class-ness are not sanctioned by the film. This reliance on reactionary discourses around supposedly lazy and violent working-class parents and teens, borne out from the initial radio discussion at the start of the film, defines the 'hoodie problem' as one of innate behaviours possessed by working-class people and infecting working-class spaces to such an extent that vulnerable middle-class people will 'go native' once there. The couple's misreading of Slapton Quarry, a man-made space, as a beautiful beach vacation spot and safe space of rural idyll shows a basic disconnect, wherein middle-class people are unable to appropriately 'read' working-class spaces whose infectious values present a moral and mortal danger to them.

In the end, only reinforced borders prevail. According to the ideology of the film, working-class spaces must be limited. But more importantly, elite spaces must be protected because of how the middle classes are vulnerable to descent or backsliding toward working-class behaviours and mores. This is why the film endorses the gated community that Steve and Jenny are initially dismayed to see; what seems like the couple's initially correct dislike and distrust of the company's plan to take over the space of Slapton Quarry is ultimately shown to be naïve ignorance on their part. In response to the hoodie panic, *Eden Lake* breeds mistrust of not only hoodies and the working class but other people within the target middle-class audience.

'It Would've Been Okay to Mug Me If I Didn't Live Here? That's How It Works?': *Attack the Block* and Community Expansion, from Tower Blocks to a United Kingdom

This message promoting paranoia and class segregation runs counter to how the tower block in *Attack the Block* is portrayed negatively as a space of class segregation. While both films participate in the hoodie panic, *Attack the Block* critiques discourses within the panic that stereotyped hoodies as monstrous and Other. In part, the film achieves its critique by drawing upon narrative, character and visual elements of 1970s cult American gang films, specifically *Assault on Precinct 13* and *The Warriors*, and changing the class and racial politics of those films to fit into the hoodie cycle. *Attack the Block* follows a racially diverse group of hoodies from the fictional Wyndham Tower estate/tower block: the leader Moses (John Boyega), his second in command Pest (Alex Esmail), the bookish Jerome (Leeon Jones), scrapper Dennis (Franz Drameh) and charmer Biggz (Simon Howard). The boys mug a young woman, Sam (Jodie Whittaker), who they must then team up with to defend their community from aliens.

Attack the Block is clearly on the side of the hoodies, innocuous poseurs whose roughness pales in comparison to actual local gangster Hi-Hatz (Jumayn Hunter, also of *Eden Lake*). The hoodies are complex characters who have made bad decisions due to negative pressures within their urban working-class communities and, for Moses, a lack of oversight at home, rather than being innately monstrous due to their class status or, as in the 1970s gang films, as a faceless mob. *Attack the Block* counters the stereotypes, presented in films like *Eden Lake*, of working-class people who exist in insular communities beyond the reach of middle-class norms and institutions. Instead, it is a breakdown of various levels of community, perpetuated by the isolating and anonymising geography of the tower block, that allows crime to take hold.

While *Attack the Block* features significant science fiction (SF) elements, and often has been talked about as an SF film, it was marketed and recognised in the UK as a hoodie horror/SF hybrid. The film's main trailer calls the hoodies 'the deadliest species in the galaxy', playing on cultural fears of hoodies while also, through hyperbole, satirising those fears, particularly the connection between the racial component of the hoodie panic and, taking those views to their most extreme conclusion, racist pseudo-science that sees races as separate species. (The line also, of course, signals the film's extra-terrestrial concerns.) Early on, bloggers identified the film as part of the hoodie cycle; at *The List*, a leading entertainment site in the UK at the time, Paul Gallagher argues the film turns 'the hoodie horror genre on its head' and 'has done a good turn for the ASBO generation'.[55] The marketing of the film reinforced the film's genre hybridity. The main poster emphasises the SF elements, showing the hoodie gang and Sam outside the tower block, looking frightened by the alien pods streaking down through the sky above them. A later poster introduced a week before the film's premiere emphasises the film's ties to horror, featuring a black background and huge, threatening glowing alien teeth framing the poster's text.

The film's use of practical effects and models rather than primarily using digital effects ties to it the SF/horror hybrids of the 1950s and 1980s, like Hawks's *The Thing from Another World* (1951) and Carpenter's 1982 reboot. For *Attack the Block*, special effects workers created giant, fuzzy black alien suits, reminiscent of gorillas but for their massive, glowing, razor-sharp teeth; the suits were worn by real actors and mostly filmed at the same time as the rest of filming, not added in post-production. This decision was motivated at least partly by budget, but the decision was also both ideological and stylistic: a rejection of what Joe Cornish has called the 'aesthetic of hyper-detail, . . . an obsession with texture, fidelity to "truthful" texture which seems disingenuous' that is common in Hollywood.[56] The film's low-budget aesthetics act as a rebellion from prevailing Americanised film conventions like the heavy use of CGI, much like the film's treatment of hoodies represents a critique of established narratives of the hoodie panic.

The film's troubling of negative stereotypes persistent within panic comes out through the ways in which the film draws on, and changes, elements of 1970s cult American gang films. Some of the links between the films are straightforward, like the film's villainous gangster, Hi-Hatz, being named after the gang of mimes, the Hi-Hats, in *The Warriors*. (It is tempting to read Hi-Hatz's name as a nod toward his seemingly performative mimicry of the stereotype of the 'hard man', as he, like Moses, seems to have ended up in his position because of a series of bad choices he made to survive.) The gang's south London slang also harkens back to *The Warriors*'s complicated lingo. There are also strong narrative links between the films. For example, like Carpenter's gang film *Assault on Precinct 13*, *Attack* features a Black protagonist who teams up with a motley crew, including a competent young white woman, to resist a mostly anonymous, but deadly, enemy's assault on a building. The enemy is defeated via an explosion that requires teamwork between two leads who are positioned on opposite sides of the law.

Attack plays out the key tropes that *Assault* borrowed from its primary intertext, Howard Hawks's *Rio Bravo* (1959): 'heroes that are trustworthy professionals pitted with impossible odds against an evil wrongdoer, the strong bond between seemingly opposed characters, the continuing battle of the sexes, and the collapse of authority institutions'.[57] The nurse whom the boys mug, Sam, represents the trustworthy professional; her nursing expertise is called upon when she helps patch up Pest's leg wound. The boys, particularly Moses and Pest, form an alliance and eventual bond with Sam, which they use to help them defeat the aliens. Moses confirms this bond when he allows Sam to enter his apartment, which allows her to see how young and neglected he is. The group of girls in the film help to established the 'battle of the sexes' theme, particularly through the contentious relationship between Moses and Tia (Danielle Vitalis). Tia confronts Moses about his bad behaviour several times, as when she calls him a 'bad breed' after learning he killed the female alien. Finally, the police's ineptitude in capturing the boys after they mug Sam, and their focus on petty criminals like the boys rather than harder criminals like Hi-Hatz, show the collapse of their authority. Sam knows the police cannot be counted on and says as much after the attack, much as Biggz shouts at the end of the film that the police 'always arrest the wrong people'.

Visually, *Attack the Block* also borrows from *Assault* in terms of its depiction of its antagonists. The aliens are black in colour, gorilla-like and aggressive; they resonate with the depiction of hoodie kids in more reactionary hoodie films. However, they are also an undifferentiated, faceless, Othered mob, akin to the gang that attacks the police precinct in *Assault*, which is made up of unnamed people of colour who are portrayed as largely exchangeable. For example, in the scene where the gang begins shooting the windows of the police station to break in, none of the gang members are shown for more than a few seconds at a time, and the quick cuts make their faces difficult to distinguish. Often, the gang members are broken down by the shots into mere body parts – anonymous hands holding a gun. This is in distinct contrast to how the film's protagonists are most often shown, in close-ups that emphasise their faces and individuate them. *Attack the Block* takes this to a more extreme level of anonymity with their aliens; all but the single female alien look exactly alike, and the aliens' fur was rotoscoped in post-production to make them appear two-dimensional, so that when they overlap in a shot, it is impossible to differentiate their bodies (see Figure 3).

Additionally, the lighting in *Attack the Block* draws from similar lighting schemes in not only *Assault on Precinct 13* but also *The Warriors* and *The Thing*. *Attack the Block* has several shots similar to ones in *Assault*, wherein the aliens emerge from the shadows in the mid-ground of a shot and run forward toward the hoodies, mirroring how the gang emerges from the shadows in the mid-ground when they start surrounding the police station (see Figure 3). In both cases, cars and the landscape are cast in shadow, and these shadows are used to hide the antagonists. This strategy of using high-contrast lighting and having the antagonists emerge from the inky black shadows was also done in *The Warriors* and *The Thing*. Another element of lighting tying all four films together is the colour. As director Joe Cornish discusses in his director's commentary with executive producer Edgar Wright, he and cinematographer Thomas Townend decided early in the project to primarily use a greenish-blue lighting scheme to mimic the light colours and tones of those earlier films. *Assault* and *The Warriors* had this greenish-blue colour because the cities where their outdoor scenes were shot had lampposts that used mercury-vapour bulbs, which produced that colour of light.

Figure 3. Top, *Attack the Block*, Moses, played by John Boyega, being pursued by the flattened, undifferentiated mob of aliens. Bottom, *Assault on Precinct 13*, the gang members emerge from the shadows in the midground in the police station parking lot.

While *Attack the Block* draws on certain narrative and stylistic elements from these films, it also makes key changes that shape its engagement with the hoodie panic. The political project of films like *Assault on Precinct 13* and *The Warriors* is somewhat unclear. *The Warriors* resists a straightforward ideological reading of class and race because while members of all of the gangs commit reprehensible crimes like rape and murder, the film only frames those actions as 'bad' when done by the main villains, the Rogues gang. Robin Woods discusses how *Assault*'s gang represents the monstrous repressed Other of 'ethnic groups' and the 'proletariat'.[58] Tony Williams reads the film as part of a 'tradition of simplistic right-wing movies where conservative individualism', as displayed by the cop and prisoner, conflicts with and then conquers the 'unindividualized violent totalitarianism' of the faceless gang.[59] Taking a more positive tack, John Kenneth Muir argues that the film shows that 'race, sex, and even the law are not important . . . when things come down to issues of honor, decency, and morality', showing that 'we all *can* get along' (emphasis in original).[60] Yet, Steve Smith has refuted both perspectives through a close reading of the film's ending. When Leigh (Laurie Zimmer) walks off, and Lieutenant Bishop (Austin Stoker) volunteers to lead Wilson (Darwin Joston) outside rather than letting another police officer do it, Smith reads the scene as a 'reassertion of the outside world, in which things are a little more complex', and in which police officers and criminals, and Black men and white women, cannot openly fraternise.[61] He argues that the middle of the film, wherein these three main characters break the stereotypes associated with them, serves to critique this reassertion. Because of the film's ideological equivocality, all of these readings seem equally plausible.

While *The Warriors* and *Assault*'s political projects are ambiguous at best, *Attack the Block* presents its politics clearly, largely through its differences from those films. While the visual depiction of the aliens in *Attack the Block* has many commonalities with the depiction of the gang in *Assault*, their characterisation is incredibly different. The gang in *Assault* is written off as anarchically evil because their desire for revenge consistently exceeds logical boundaries and involves innocent people. After several gang members are killed in a raid by police, the gang begins killing civilians, including a young girl trying to purchase ice cream. When her father kills one of them, the gang again escalates the situation, following him to the precinct and then proceeding to try to kill everyone inside.

The aliens in *Attack the Block*, though, pursue Moses, and anyone who came in physical contact with him or the female alien he killed, because he is covered with a pheromone that they use to track the female, who landed on the planet before them. Their attack on the block is less about revenge than it is about finding their female; their victims simply made the mistake of getting in the way of their driving purpose. Moses even acknowledges that the attack was a consequence of his earlier retributive violence toward the female alien. When the female alien attacked him at the start of the film, it had just crash-landed into a car and was likely disoriented; when Moses climbed into the car to see if there was anything he could steal, he likely startled the creature, which defended itself and then escaped. The violence likely would have ended there if Moses had not decided to pursue and kill the alien in an act of performative machismo – as he tells the other boys, 'I'm chasing that down. I'm killing that. Watch'. Unlike the villainous gang in *Assault*, the villainous aliens in *Attack the Block* are acting out of a biological logic, and their attack is not framed in terms of their innate or anarchic evil but instead as the foreseeable consequence of Moses's bad behaviour. Because Moses does not control his desire for violent revenge and macho approval, more people die, including gentle Jerome and aggressive Dennis.

Moreover, the film uses the aliens to confront and critique racist stereotypes about people of colour in the UK. Critics have read the aliens primarily in terms of the way in which they, not the Black hoodie characters, embody negative stereotypes of British Blackness. Lorrie Palmer reads the aliens as 'literalis[ing] monstrosity, thereby disconnecting its symbolic stigma from the gang' and 'distinguish[ing] truly alien blackness . . . from non-white British citizenship'.[62] Similarly, Sarah Ilott argues that the film 'portrays black characters as inherently British rather than Britain's Other, challenging the way that racist rhetoric attempts to position those of non-white ethnicity'.[63] However, the film's treatment of the aliens also shows how quickly and easily one group can stereotype and turn against another group they assume are invading the space they consider home.

The scene where the hoodies confront and kill the female alien exemplifies this behaviour. Jerome's comments especially play into racist tropes about Black British people: he describes the alien as 'some orangutan-type thing' and 'some exotic creature, like a monkey thing'. The aliens do physically resemble, as one of the boys later puts it, a 'gorilla wolf', particularly in terms of the way that they move and the position of their bodies when they are on all fours, but the decision to have the aliens physically embody those stereotypes, as well as being so black as to stop reflecting any light, helps them to serve also as an exaggeration and critique of those stereotypes. The assumptions the boys make about the aliens also play into negative stereotypes in the UK about non-white immigrants. Pest theorises that the aliens 'have come from space, trying to take over Earth', despite the fact that they have only seen a single alien, who ran away quickly to escape them – hardly the behaviour of an aggressive coloniser.

Once they've established the 'foreignness' of the alien, the boys in the gang are quick to justify killing the creature because it was in their block. Dennis quips, 'Welcome to London, motherfucker', while Biggz adds, 'Welcome to the ends, brother'. Pest continues the train of thought, saying 'This is the block. Nobody fucks with the block, get me?' When the boys heft the alien carcass aloft, they repeatedly chant 'Block'. The alien, of course, represents the ultimate outsider, the ultimate foreign invader, because it comes from an entirely different planet. Its arrival, like the arrival of many immigrants in Britain, is greeted with territoriality and violence. Similar reactions have come from multiple segments of British society during the immigrant crises of the 2000s and 2010s, with conservative media figures like Katie Hopkins calling immigrants 'cockroaches' who, to paraphrase, ought to be shot before their boats reach Britain.[64]

And yet, the major revelation of *Attack the Block* is that the attack on the block was less the fault of the aliens and more a consequence, as noted earlier, of Moses's impulsive violence. Here, the film critiques multiple narratives about race and 'foreigners' in Britain by showing how these narratives are rooted in thoughtless stereotyping of immigrants of colour as violent and an inappropriate impulse to violently defend the space of home, broadly conceived, from these 'outsiders'. Going back to Palmer and Ilott's arguments, the film encourages the audience to take these lessons and apply them to the hoodies as well as to actual immigrants and descendants of immigrants of colour in Britain.

The film itself takes this lesson to heart, particularly in its depiction of Moses. While *Assault on Precinct 13* portrays its criminal lead as friendly and honourable within the context of the siege, he is still a mass-murderer, and no motivation is given for his crime. He never indicates remorse, just a general bemusement that he is imprisoned; his heroism is ambiguous. Changing these qualities allows *Attack the Block* to counter stereotypes about hoodies. While Moses and his crew do mug Sam, and Moses pulls a knife on her, in the end, the film also gives Moses a fleshed-out backstory that provides him with motivation for his criminal acts. While the other boys in the gang appear to live in well-kept homes, surrounded by loving families (e.g. Biggz's phone conversations with his mother), Moses lives alone with his uncle in an untidy, poorly maintained apartment. He is obviously neglected, as his uncle is away more often than he is around. The film brings this neglect to the emotional fore when Sam, and the audience, sees Moses's bare room and the crumpled-up Spiderman comforter on his bed – he's only fifteen. These details make it easier to understand why Moses might be tempted by the cash and status offered through working for Hi-Hatz, who drives his own car, appears to command outward respect in the community and has the money to produce his own music. Again, these changes from *Assault* to *Attack* work to humanise the hoodies.

Moses also learns a valuable lesson and regrets his criminal actions, unlike Wilson. As he says, 'Wished I'd never chased after that thing. Wish we never murked you [mugged Sam]. Wish I never took that white [drugs] off Hi-Hatz'. He also tells Sam that they did not know she lived in the block and would not have mugged her if they had known they were neighbours. His failure, with regard to Sam, was a failure to recognise a member of his community. In the end, Moses and Pest even adopt the middle-class white pothead Brewis into their community, broadening their definitions of what it means to be part of the block. Moses also realises that he should not have included Hi-Hatz, and his drug-dealing, in that community. His recognition of these failures works to not only humanise him but helps make him a clear hero rather than villain or anti-hero.

Like in *Assault*, the villains are defeated using an explosion that requires teamwork between the criminal protagonist and the protagonist representing institutional authority – Moses and Sam. In *Assault*, Lieutenant Bishop stands side-by-side with Wilson and fires the shot that causes the explosion; he is therefore slightly more responsible for saving the day. But in *Attack*, Sam prepares Moses's apartment by turning on the gas, and it is Moses alone who charges into his apartment and lights the firecracker that causes the explosion. This shift is key, because it allows Moses to repay his debt to Sam and fully make the shift to hero. As Ilott notes, the film's most 'emblematic image . . . shows the hero, Moses, hanging out of a window; the only thing preventing him from plummeting to his death is the Union Jack flag that he clasps'.[65] While Ilott reads this as an affirmation of Moses's, and the hoodie gang's, belonging in British society, I would argue that the image of Moses hanging from the flag works directly with the previous scene, wherein he apologises to Sam and accepts her as part of his community. Taken together, these two scenes show not only that Moses is part of the larger national community, but that he must realise that fact and broaden his idea of who should not be murked. This scene serves a dual purpose, then, in countering stereotypes about innately bad hoodies, too lazy to change, but also in pushing working-class youths to see themselves as part of the national community and not fall prey to predators like Hi-Hatz.

The film's exploration of the tower block itself implicates the space in this damaging attitude of insularity. In her article on *Attack the Block*, Lorrie Palmer argues that the 'characters define the spaces, not the other way around', in that per De Certeau, spaces only acquire meaning through the human activities that occur within them.[66] The film does rewrite the hoodies' spaces of intimate habitation – their family apartments, which, with the exception of Moses's apartment, are well-cared-for spaces filled with family who care about the boys – to counter the stereotype of dirty, drug-filled flats. Palmer notes that partway through the film, the boys in the gang introduce themselves to Sam in the hallway outside her apartment, 'rewriting the anonymous corridor as a site of community'.

While there are moments wherein the families and boys recode the spaces of the block, turning anonymity into community, it is important to note that the core problems within the diegesis are caused by that anonymity: contra Palmer, the spaces are not there to be defined by their inhabitants but actively work against them. As Oscar Newman noted in his foundational study of public housing, the anonymity of the public spaces in tower blocks, be they hallways, elevators, stairwells, entryways, etc., make it 'impossible for residents to develop an accord on what [is] acceptable behaviour in these areas, impossible for them to feel or exert proprietary feelings' that would cause them to care for the spaces, and 'impossible to tell resident from intruder'.[67] This isolation makes inhabitants 'incredibly vulnerable to criminals'.[68] In the film, the bare hallways look the same on each floor; with the exception of Tia's gated apartment door, every doorway is identical. The very design of the building works to separate people, confining them to their apartments and encouraging the bounds of their communities to shrink from neighbourhood to immediate family and friends from school or work. These spaces work against community by promoting anonymity and, according to Newman, making it difficult to tell who is even a part of the community.

This brings us back to the key lesson that the film pushes Moses to learn: to broaden his community by making others less anonymous to him and himself less anonymous to others. He must fight the very architecture of his home to achieve this goal, though. As discussed above, part of Moses's turn from hoodlum to hoodie hero involves accepting Sam, and even Brewis, into his community, and during the final scene where he hangs from the Union Jack, perhaps even the broader British community at large. However, part of his turn also necessitates letting others in, literally. In the scene when all of the boys retrieve weapons from their apartments to hunt the aliens, every boy's apartment is shown except Moses's. The camera follows him to the door but cuts before he opens it. The audience is not allowed to see or know Moses through his home, keeping his hard man façade intact. The later scene where he asks Sam to go into his home, then, proves, more than his apology to her, that he has accepted not only her role in his community but his role in hers. The viewer, too, is implicated within this community by the frequent point-of-view shots; we move through and observe the intimate space of Moses's apartment with Sam. As Sherryl Vint notes, *Attack the Block* asks viewers to question their 'image of hoodie-wearing, generally non-white, teenagers' and their stereotypical media representation.[69] The film not only pushes Moses to broaden his community, but it pushes the viewer to include hoodies within their own communities.

This message is made especially clear by the film's ending. After the police have arrested Moses and Pest, Sam tells the police, 'Those boys. No, I know them. They're my neighbours'. The community, standing outside, crowds together around the foundation of the block and begins to chant Moses's name. For one of the first times in the film, Moses smiles. The community has taken back the anonymous spaces of the tower block; they recognise Moses, and the hoodies, who instigate and lead the chant, as part of the community. The long shots showing the crowd of residents stretching out from the base of the block literalises this message, as their bodies broaden the foundation of the block, the community. While the world reasserts itself in *Assault on Precinct 13* and the utopian community must collapse, that community is maintained in *Attack the Block*, pushing the film's agenda of inclusivity and understanding, as well as critiquing the reactionary, Othering discourses within the hoodie panic.

Conclusions

Eden Lake and *Attack the Block* position themselves as part of the larger hoodie cycle by engaging with the moral panic over hoodies. The films work within and against the discourses of the panic through their transnational genre hybridity. By drawing on 1970s cult American gang films and backwoods horror films, these films use familiar narrative language but make key changes that advance their specific political projects. Writing on *Eden Lake* in 2008, *The Guardian*'s Peter Bradshaw described the film as having 'taken the famous news picture of the hoodie making the "gun" gesture behind David Cameron's back – and photoshopped a real weapon into his hand'.[70] At the film's end, societal connection collapses in 'a realist moment of despair and blundering horror'. This is in stark contrast, for Bradshaw, to *Attack the Block*, about which he later writes, '[the film has] a cheerful, unfashionably optimist belief in a happy outcome' if only opposing groups 'discover common ground that should have been cultivated anyway'.[71]

Bradshaw's comments capture the key differences in how the films interact with the moral panic over hoodies. *Eden Lake* perpetuates reactionary discourses within the panic that echo and amplify former Prime Minister Margaret Thatcher's infamous claim that 'there is no such thing as society'. The hoodies and parents in the film visualise the breakdown of society, from disregarding middle-class social norms, to not acknowledging the authority of social institutions like law enforcement, to breaking down the bodies of the middle-class couple who ventures into their working-class space. Both Steve and Jenny also embody this breakdown in the ways that their behaviour becomes increasingly more like the hoodies' and parents' behaviour the longer they remain in the space. There may be, as Steve tries to convince the hoodies, a big beach, but the film shows that there is not room there for everyone. Just as the monstrous hoodies and their parents make certain traditional spaces of middle-class leisure unavailable to Jenny and Steve, the gated community will turn Slapton Quarry into Eden Lake soon after the film's end, effectively condensing the space in which both working-class and middle-class people can live, work and play. The film implies that order will eventually reassert itself, fencing off safe space to protect elites and keep the working and middle classes outside, where they will only have each other to prey upon.

On the other hand, *Attack the Block* troubles these conclusions about the hoodie panic and society, pushing instead for both hoodies and viewers of all classes to broaden their conception of community to include each other. Even the aliens are not made into a completely evil Other, as their violence is a consequence of Moses's own actions. The film shows that even an anonymising, antisocial space like a tower block can be reclaimed and recoded as a community if the residents are willing to see others as part of their community and to see themselves, and make themselves available as, a part of others' communities. Critics picked up on the film's serious treatment of the hoodie panic, describing the film using language that links it to social realist cinema: 'a potential Ridley Scott blockbuster . . . hijacked by the social concerns of a Ken Loach film' and providing 'sharp social commentary'.[72] The name-dropping of Loach not only makes the link between this hoodie horror and social realism clear but cements that link with the high level of cultural capital associated with this giant of British cinema. *Attack the Block*, then, fits into a longer tradition of British cinema that has concerned itself with humanely examining and exposing the plight of the working class.

Both films, despite their disparate political agendas, use transnational genre hybridity to legitimise British horror within middlebrow British film culture by proving able to confront and contribute to ongoing cultural discourses in British society, carrying forward a similar filmic project to *28 Days Later* and *Shaun of the Dead*. However, rather than creating a new, British version of an American genre, *Eden Lake* and *Attack the Block* position themselves within an existing, contemporary British film cycle.

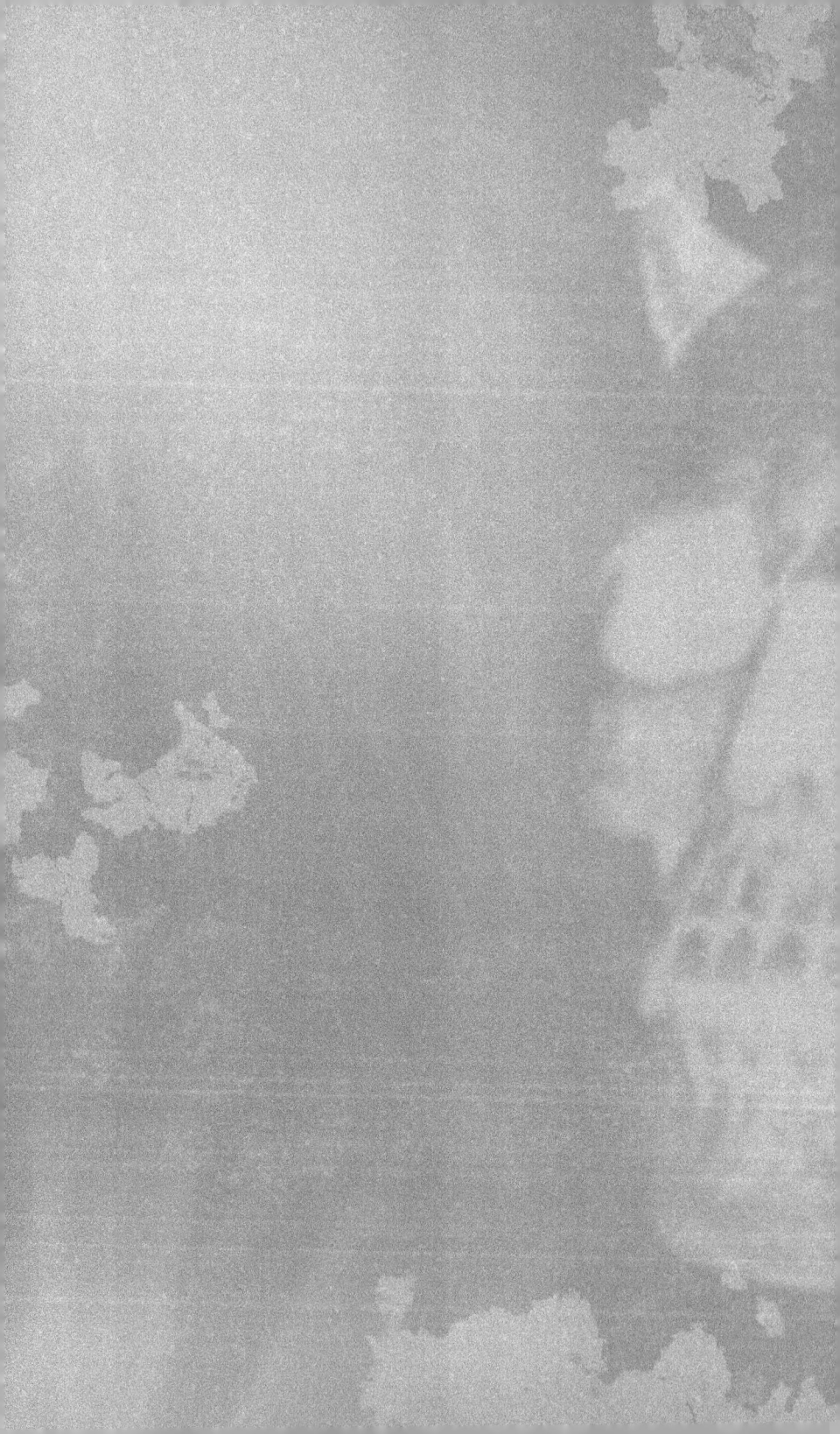

4

'A Famous Corpse'

Resurrecting Hammer's Transnational Appeal

[O]wning a famous corpse is just the beginning; making it walk, talk and earn money again – that's the real challenge. (Adam Dawtrey, writing on the attempted Hammer revival in the early 2000s[1])

IN THIS CHAPTER, I turn to look at the third way that transnational genre hybridity has manifested in films of the British horror resurgence – *trans-* not as between or thoroughly changing but as *beyond* the national. This articulation of transnational genre hybridity is exemplified by the revived Hammer Films' Gothic film *The Woman in Black* (James Watkins, 2012), an adaptation of British author Susan Hill's 1983 novella of the same name. The film is set ostensibly during the Edwardian era, though its temporally muddled *mise-en-scène* is filled with nods to the Victorian and Edwardian periods as well as the First World War. *The Woman in Black* tells the story of a young and recently widowed lawyer, Arthur Kipps (Daniel Radcliffe), who, upon trying to execute a deceased woman's will, discovers an angry ghost who terrorises the local villagers in Crythin Gifford. The generic hybridity in *The Woman in Black* is not between discrete genres, as in previous chapters. Instead, the generic hybridity is tied to the film's use of different national and historical manifestations of the Gothic mode, which encompasses a wide range of traditions and tropes as well as permeating both national and generic boundaries.

The Woman in Black and the discourses around the film draw upon key cultural legacies that have haunted the critical conversation about 2000s British horror cinema – namely, those of the literary Gothic as it manifested in the late Romantic and Victorian eras of British literature and Hammer's celebrated Gothic films from the 1950s and 60s, including those films' links to British costume drama and heritage films. However, the film and its paratexts reframe these legacies by presenting *The Woman in Black* as a product whose appeal and genre reach beyond the national to appeal to foreign markets, whether through the use of visual tropes from internationally popular Japanese horror films from the late 1990s and early 2000s (commonly referred to as J-horror) or the international appeal of the film's star, Daniel Radcliffe (who played Harry Potter in the *Harry Potter* film series).

The film is fraught with tension, and not the kind you would expect from a Gothic chiller. Despite a clear nostalgia for classic Hammer, the film also foregrounds its aesthetic debt to J-horror. While Hammer is invoked in and around the film, the film itself has primarily superficial connections to the classic Hammer brand it was said to be helping revive. The 'Britishness' of the film via Hammer's history is foregrounded in both the film and its paratexts but connections to other domestic British Gothic media (such as the BBC's *A Ghost Story for Christmas*) are effaced. Daniel Radcliffe's casting was part of the film's appeal to teens inclined toward the safe Gothic shared by *Woman* and the *Harry Potter* films, which contrasts with the adult appeal of the film's links to classic Hammer and the heritage genre. While the film and its marketing espouse a desire for connection with multiple elements of the past, those pasts are used superficially and evacuated of meaning.

However, these simulacra of the past create a productive tension with the film's more contemporary elements, and it was this tension that allowed the film to be financially and critically successful by appealing, however superficially, to younger, older, British and foreign audiences on a multiplicity of levels. The film's dual focus on the past and present ultimately serves a single common goal: positioning the film as appealing *beyond* the national. This *beyond* serves a number of functions. For British audiences, the film's connections to J-horror framed the film as *beyond*, or surpassing, more traditional British horror offerings, while the links to classic Hammer positioned the film as capable of success outside Britain. For foreign audiences, the use of J-horror tropes and Daniel Radcliffe's starring role helped to frame the film as explicitly acknowledging and courting a transnational audience in a way that British fare for domestic audiences, like the BBC's *A Ghost Story for Christmas*, does not. In this way, the film's transnational genre hybridity operates as an industrial strategy that both solicits and allows for transnational audience appeal. The use of transnational genre hybridity in *The Woman in Black* allows it to draw upon the cultural capital of Hammer and British Gothic while simultaneously casting off the weight of those legacies and appearing as the new face of a Hammer, and a Gothic, ready to compete at both the worldwide and domestic box office.

'Do You Believe in Ghosts?': New Hammer and Nostalgia

There is still a broad consensus that Hammer is and has been, for all practical purposes, synonymous with British horror since its classic Gothic cycle of films took hold in the late 1950s. Indeed, many sources use just that word, 'synonymous', to link Hammer and British horror. For the BBC and Channel 4, Hammer 'became synonymous with the horror genre in the 1950s' and is 'the British movie brand synonymous with horror'.[2] For Barry Forshaw, in his *British Gothic Cinema*, Hammer is 'synonymous' with horror like Penguin is with the paperback – which is to say that it has exceeded its original boundaries as a term and become a generic description applicable to films made by other companies but in 'the Hammer template'.[3] Johnny Walker and Sarah Street have also picked up and used this 'synonymous' language: 'the sobriquet "Hammer Horror" has, for many, become synonymous with British horror cinema', and Hammer's frequent pairing of 'director Terence Fisher and actors Christopher Lee and Peter Cushing provided a style of film which became synonymous with British horror'.[4] Of course, while Hammer has come to be popularly synonymous with British horror, it does not encompass all British horror nor account for every association of the words British and horror. As Mark Jancovich has argued, 'Englishness was associated with horror long before the success of Hammer', mostly due to the significant presence of British talent and locations in 1930s and 40s American horror films.[5] Alison Peirse has done strong work mapping a counter-history of non-Hammer horror in the UK.[6] Other British film-makers and studios, such as Amicus, have also made key contributions to British horror.

And yet, Hammer haunts British horror – in terms of expected style but also anticipated cultural import and impact. But what exactly does this mean? Hutchings argues that Hammer dominated not just because of its prolific output but also because its films 'draw upon, represent and are always locatable in relation to much broader shifts and tendencies in British social history'.[7] In other words, classic Hammer horror films play out and contribute to cultural conversations around issues like class, gender and family structure within their historical moment. While Hammer films were considered, and aimed, to be disreputable in their day, they have come to be seen as culturally significant and often fairly tame.

Known as Hammer Productions before its bankruptcy in the 1930s, as Hammer Film Productions during its 'golden age', very briefly as Hammer Films Limited as it went bankrupt in the late 1970s and as Hammer Films today (dubbed 'Hammer 2.0' by film journalist Naila Scargill), Hammer has gone by a variety of names throughout its chequered history. Throughout this chapter, I have attempted to simplify by just calling the company Hammer whenever possible, particularly because my interest is less in the company's industrial history and more its legacy and the way its current leaders speak about what it means to be 'Hammer'. Where more clarification is necessary, I refer to 1950s to 70s Hammer as classic Hammer and post-2007 Hammer as new Hammer.

Founded in 1934, Hammer produced a variety of titles, including non-horror films. While Hammer began their horror production with Val Guest's sci-fi/horror film *The Quatermass Xperiment* (1955), the company quickly turned to producing the Gothic horror films that would become their legacy, starting with two staples of Gothic literature: Mary Shelley's *Frankenstein* (*Curse of Frankenstein*, Terence Fisher, 1957) and Bram Stoker's *Dracula* (*Horror of Dracula*, Terence Fisher, 1958). After solidifying an agreement that allowed them to remake films from Universal's 1930s horror cycle, Hammer went on to make *The Mummy* (Terence Fisher, 1959), a number of sequels to that film, *Curse of Frankenstein* and *Horror of Dracula*. The company also produced a cycle of prehistoric exploitation films (including Don Chaffey's 1966 *One Million Years B.C.*, which starred Raquel Welch in what would become an iconic fur bikini) and a number of psychological thrillers.

Hammer's horror films became increasingly sexualised during the 1960s, arguably culminating with the trilogy of lesbian vampire sexploitation films catering to the heterosexual male gaze in the early 1970s – *The Vampire Lovers* (Roy Ward Baker, 1970), *Lust for a Vampire* (Jimmy

Sangster, 1971) and *Twins of Evil* (John Hough, 1971). However, while British films in general were, at that time, pushing the boundaries of what could and could not be shown on film, partly to compete with television, and were generally reflective of a more permissive cultural attitude, Hammer's sexploitation films failed to perform at the box office. Unable to cope when American funding to British studios largely dried up in the 1970s, the company fell into insolvency shortly before its final film of the twentieth century, a remake of Hitchcock's *The Lady Vanishes* (Anthony Page, 1979), premiered.[9]

Hammer films have long been a primary site of investigation for British horror film studies. This is true in part because of their financial success and cultural visibility. However, it is also due to their expression of national anxieties. From the 1970s through the mid-1990s, one of the key lines of scholarly inquiry in British cinema studies was concerned with establishing British cinema as a distinctive national cinema. Studies of the British horror film, then, could more easily claim legitimacy for this maligned genre by framing it as distinctively national. For example, in his foundational study *Hammer and Beyond* (1993), one of two key early texts on the British horror film, Peter Hutchings reads *The Quatermass Xperiment* as a meditation on British post-war masculinity. Like many soldiers post-Second World War, Victor, the film's monster and a Royal Air Force (RAF) pilot, returns from the war unable to reintegrate into society, treated as Other because of physical and emotional changes caused by his time in the war – of course, while many soldiers had war-related trauma, Victor is infected by an alien.[10] On a more general level, Hammer's horror films tended to reflect the dominant bourgeois sensibilities of post-war Britain by valorising professional men, depicting aristocrats as predators or parasites and portraying the working class as either a dangerous mob or mere comic relief.[11] Hutchings links British horror films and British social concerns and attitudes to argue that the mid-1950s to mid-1970s boom is 'part of a specifically national cinema', wherein national fears were expressed through horror films.[12] He argues that this period of British horror was defined by the post-war crisis in masculinity, as well as, in the 1970s, changes to family structure caused by the concurrent rise of the feminist movement and authority-rejecting youth culture. These issues seemed to crystallise in films dealing with the family and with deviations from the bourgeois hegemonic norm of heterosexual desire (for example, the lesbian vampire film *The Vampire Lovers* (Roy Ward Baker, 1970)).

Similarly, several early scholars could position Hammer as deserving of scholarly interest because of the connection between its iconic early films and British Gothic novels, and thus the longer history of the British Gothic. After the success of *Curse of Frankenstein* and *Horror of Dracula*, Hammer quickly followed up with numerous sequels and other Gothic tales like *The Gorgon* (Terence Fisher, 1964), many directed by house director Terence Fisher. The proliferation of Gothic horror films led David Pirie to conclude, in the first full-length study of the British horror film, published in 1973, that Gothic horror like Hammer's was 'the only staple cinematic myth which Britain can properly claim its own'.[13] Framing the British horror film as the continuance of an enduring Gothic tradition allowed Pirie to position the films of the period as 'in no way imitative of American or European models but derived in general from literary sources' and thus a legitimate part of a distinctly British national arts culture.

Hammer briefly resurfaced in the 1980s with their ITV series *Hammer House of Horror* (1980–1) and *Hammer House of Mystery and Suspense* (1984–5), which were somewhat successful, but film production would not resume until after the millennium.[14] Hammer was bought in 2000 by an investment consortium run by 'leading lights in the UK film, music, publishing and advertising sectors'.[15] Part of their original remit was to 'develop a series of films – both remakes of Hammer classics and fresh properties – and starting shooting them back-to-back' in 2002 'using a lot of the same cast and crew'. In other words, new Hammer wanted to largely follow the business model used for classic Hammer films. However, the company also aimed to eschew 'the campness' of some classic Hammer films, endeavouring instead to make more psychological and adult-oriented Gothic fare in line with films like *Sleepy Hollow* (Tim Burton, 1999), *The Sixth Sense* (M. Night Shyamalan, 1999) and *What Lies Beneath* (Robert Zemeckis, 2000).

After 'a couple of fallow years', Hammer was bought again in 2007 by another investment consortium, this time composed of European investors headed by a Netherlands-based company, Cyrte Investments.[16] These new investors potentially wanted to remake some of Hammer's older films, but they also wanted to 'reinvigorate the classic Hammer brand "for a new generation"'. Simon Oakes, one of the heads of the new management team, stated in 2007, 'Hammer is a great British brand – we intend to take Hammer back into production and develop its global potential'.[17] They planned to do so by not only tapping into the audience of cinephiles familiar with Hammer's name but also by targeting young people, in part through the use of new technologies like streaming, mobile devices and other web-based tools.[18] The company wanted *The Woman in Black* to be 'full of dread, but with no body count and no torture porn', so that it could 'scare both a 14-year-old and a 40-year-old'. Much as classic Hammer's turn toward gore from the 1950s to the 1970s signalled an appeal to the growing teen audience, new Hammer's turn away from gore also signalled an appeal to teen audiences, now seduced by the safe Gothic elements in popular family and teen films of the 2000s, like the *Twilight* and *Harry Potter* series. This use of safe Gothic in *The Woman in Black*, combined with the casting of Daniel Radcliffe, works to appeal to a segment of both the teen and adult markets not served by the then-dominant international body horror cycle. In contrast to US torture porn, French New Extremism and New Asian Horror like Japan's *Audition* (Takashi Miike, 1999), Hammer would make 'enlightened horror'.[19] Indeed, Hammer may be responsible for fomenting the beginnings of the 'elevated horror' discourse that has come to dominate discussions of horror at this time of writing, but that is an argument for another time.

As Matt Hills has argued, this new Hammer set itself up with a 'contradictory identity' – one typified by both 'modernization' and 'nostalgia'.[20] New Hammer attempted to solidify its latest brand image while capitalising on the prestige associated with classic Hammer and its back catalogue. Part of that decision can be attributed to basic business sense, but the decision was also influenced by what Hills calls 'the shadow of a previous golden age [that] looms large over its output'.[21] By adapting a known Gothic property that had seen success across multiple media, *The Woman in Black* was carrying on a Hammer tradition. Susan Hill's source novel had, by 2012, achieved saturation in the UK. A stage adaptation had been on the West End stage in one iteration or another since 1987; the story had been adapted as a TV-movie in 1989. The book itself was a best-seller and had been adopted by the national curriculum.[22] In much the same way as the classic Hammer horror films that adapted Gothic literature worked to 'bridge the gap between high and low cultures' to help culturally legitimise the horror film, the association between Hammer's *The Woman in Black* and both the page and the stage brings additional cultural capital to the film to try to culturally legitimise Hammer's new horrors, as well as new Hammer.[23]

For new Hammer, and Oakes, *The Woman in Black* was 'the poster child for what [the revived studio] want[ed] Hammer to be, because it plays on [the company's] Britishness and . . . literary tradition'.[24] Classic

Hammer was inspired by the more corporeal monsters from Universal's 1930s horror cycle, as well as from Gothic novels, and had not made a true ghost story before *The Woman in Black*. Both *Taste of Fear* (Seth Holt, 1961) and *Paranoiac* (Freddie Francis, 1963) are sometimes erroneously referred to as ghost stories, but neither contains an actual ghost, in much the same way as Christine's 'ghost' in *The Phantom of the Opera* (Terence Fisher, 1962) turns out to be just a living person. Of course, the Gothic is more than ghost stories; it is a contested and contingent term whose manifestations must be considered within their cultural and historical contexts, as well as in terms of medium specificity. Gothic literature introduced a new way of speaking about evil and terror when it emerged in the 1790s, amidst the riots and beheadings of the French Revolution.[25] The Gothic has been used, in places as diverse as carnivals and museums, to indicate an interest in history and heritage, as well as to indicate a certain 'desirable "popular culture" cachet'.[26] As Xavier Aldana Reyes argues, the Gothic horror film's 'distinctiveness lies in its reliance on specific Gothic atmospheres, settings, music, tropes or figures' meant to inspire or evoke feelings of dread, fright, disgust and tension.[27] The world envisioned is one wherein good struggles against evil, but it is also a world wherein the uncanny proliferates, so that boundaries are constantly being questioned and shifted. Often, it is a world wherein evil triumphs over good and where good has no hope of success because of fate or the continuing influence of the past. In those cases, when evil cannot be ameliorated or escaped, it can only be accepted.

Within this worldview, the Gothic horror film has accumulated a shifting set of semantic elements through which to signify Gothicness. We can trace Gothic horror films forward from Méliès's *The Haunted Castle* (1896), with its occult conjurings, transformations and disappearances; bats, demons, witches, skeleton, ghosts and Christian iconography; and reliance on creating fear from the tension between what is seen versus what is not seen.[28] German Expressionism introduced high-contrast lighting. Large, isolated mansions set on foggy heaths often served as an optimal setting in which to play out these tropes. Since the 1960s, though, Aldana Reyes argues that Gothic horror films have become increasingly interested in the body, through the 'increasing corporealization of the ghost', 'a strong fascination with monsters and their sexuality' and the 'opening up' and transformation of the body into a 'site of Gothic inscription'.[29] This focus has led Gothic horror films toward more explicit depictions of the body, as in the bloody *giallo* films from Italian directors like Dario Argento, Mario

Bava and Lucio Fulci in the 1960s and 70s; American cannibal films from the 1970s like *Texas Chainsaw Massacre* (Tobe Hooper, 1974) and *The Hills Have Eyes* (Wes Craven, 1977); and the 2000s multinational cycle of extreme body horror, from the American Saw series to Marina de Van's French New Extremism film *In My Skin* (*Dans ma peau*, 2002).

The Woman in Black takes up a number of these Gothic tropes and aesthetic strategies and, in doing so, links itself to older Gothics. Narratively, the film establishes itself as Gothic through its reliance on classic Gothic tropes. First, there is the woman herself, Jennet (Liz White), a ghost with malevolent intent toward the living; as the film's title implies, she is dressed all in black, including a long black veil, to signal that she still mourns for her son, Nathaniel (Ashley Foster). She haunts a huge, crumbling old mansion near an isolated town that is frequently foggy. The film's temporal setting in the Edwardian era also signals its connection to the Gothic, as Gothic tales tend to be set in the past.

Toward the start of the film, Kipps's dead wife Stella (Sophie Stuckey) appears behind him in his shaving mirror, and the camera lingers on a newspaper story about séances that Kipps had been reading. These early images establish the film's interest in hauntings of many kinds: not simply malicious hauntings like the woman in black, but also benign hauntings and the way that grief can haunt a person who has lost a loved one. These narrative tropes are paired with several classic Gothic aesthetic choices, such as high-contrast lighting, shallow depth of field, tight framing and the frequent use of medium and close-up shots, all of which help the film to use its off-screen space to inspire terror, mostly through the use of unexpected or creepy noises.

The more recent Gothic focus on bodily visibility is also clear in *The Woman in Black*, whether in the often decidedly corporeal ghosts of Jennet and her son or the claustrophobic camerawork that emphasises the vulnerability of Kipps's body. The film's downbeat ending also ties the film to the triumph of evil in Gothic horror. Even after Kipps pulls Jennet's dead son's body from the bog and reunites their corpses, Jennet's desire for revenge remains unsated, and she tempts Kipps's son into the middle of the train tracks, where he and Kipps are hit and killed by the train that would have taken them home. And yet, the ending is more complicated than 'evil wins'. Kipps remains haunted by memories of his wife, and perhaps by her ghost, throughout the film. At the end of the film, Kipps and his son are reunited with her, and the family unit is restored. While the onlookers appear horrified, the entire Kipps family is smiling – this is only Kipps's second smile in the film, the first coming near the beginning of the film, when he is presented with his son, before he learns that his wife has died. Jennet's victory, then, can oddly be read simultaneously as the best possible ending for the entire Kipps family: Kipps can stop grieving and experience happiness again, the son gets a mother and a father who will never leave him again and Mrs Kipps regains her son and husband. Jennet gets the final frame of the film, but the more powerful image, arguably, is the Kipps family walking into the fog, hand in hand, that comes just before. Matt Hills has argued that with this ending, 'Hollywood ideology aimed at the restoration of connotative normality is thus recuperated'.[30] Killing Kipps is less a victory for chaotic evil than a draw. In this way, the film ends on conservative note, promoting the reunification of the fractured nuclear family.

While the Gothic manifests in *The Woman in Black* in part through its period setting and costumes, those tropes also signal the film's participation in the tradition of Hammer 'quality'. Within Britain, period settings and costumes gave the films a veneer of quality that linked them to broader taste hierarchies in British cinema, even as they were simultaneously devalued as low, genre cinema. And, as Sue Harper has noted, Hammer's turn towards historical horror was also 'a key factor' in their international box office strategy – they differentiated British horror from the modern settings of American horror while also 'packag[ing] European history so as to give American audiences a strong flavour of the exotic, and to give everyone else a version of the past that retained some familiar elements', because two-thirds of the studio's profits came from abroad.[31]

The heritage and period elements of *The Woman in Black* function in a similar way. Hammer's self-proclaimed 'enlightened horror' is implicitly positioned against mainstream body horror with largely contemporary settings coming out of the US and other countries. Both the first international trailer and the second trailer focus, when they are not showing close-ups of Daniel Radcliffe, on the manor house and village where the film is set. In the second trailer, the first shot after the logos of the associated studios (Momentum and Hammer) is of a dark and dusty-looking child's bedroom, stage-dressed in the Edwardian style, with period furniture and heavy draperies. This image is followed by shots of creepy, period-specific toys, long shots of the manse itself, interior shots of the great foyer and images of Daniel Radcliffe and the village children costumed in Victorian and Edwardian-era mainstays such as the three-piece suit, dress with pinafore and jacket with short pants. While the costuming and toys provide an explicit link to costume and heritage cinema, the focus on the spaces inside and outside the mansion also reflect a common aesthetic of heritage cinema, as discussed in Chapter 2. The international trailer also links itself with costume and heritage, though more so via Radcliffe's costuming, as images of his body and face dominate the trailer, though brief external and internal shots of the film's manse also contribute.

Of course, as Helen Wheatley has argued about televised Gothic, while heritage costume drama intends for audiences to feel good about their country's culture and literature because of the way the subgenre valorises the past, Gothic costume dramas are '"feel bad"' texts because they 'offer the viewer narratives of fear and anxiety set in a past which is not only marked by a sense of decay or dilapidation, but which is also disturbed by uncanny happenings and supernatural events'.[32] These Gothic costume dramas are 'less stable and pleasant than the past offered to the viewer in the more traditional heritage text' because they disallow 'the sanitization of nostalgia' by 'remov[ing] the surety of the past as a haven'.[33] However, while the links to heritage and costume in *The Woman in Black* may not appeal to audiences in terms of presenting a nostalgic, safe past, *Woman* packages British history as a consumable aesthetic that signals a certain level of production quality and that can simultaneously read as exotic to Americans and vaguely familiar to European audiences. By visual linking itself with the tropes of the heritage genre, *The Woman in Black* and its trailers put forth a clear appeal to that genre's primarily adult audience, as well as older audiences who would remember seeing classic Hammer's historical horror in cinemas and on television.

While Hammer executives wanted to reinvigorate and capitalise on previous iterations of the brand after the 2007 buyout, their language also defines new Hammer differently from classic Hammer. As demonstrated in the 2013 feature on the Gothic in *Sight & Sound*, within middlebrow British film culture, Hammer is still thought of as provocative, vigorous and masculine – as 'Terence Fisher push[ing] the boundaries by engorging Hammer Films' creations with as much Technicolor blood, gore and sex appeal as the censors could abide, every scene a sumptuous coronation for those Kings of Horror, Peter Cushing and Christopher Lee'.[34] As Brian Wilson notes, classic Hammer films set themselves apart from the earlier cycle of Universal horror films and contemporary horror films through 'excessive forms of graphic violence and gore'.[35] The florid Technicolor of the creature's unhealed facial stitches and the heaving bosoms of Dracula's women victims, both of which at turns worried and shocked censors, are what classic Hammer films are known for.

This heritage was hardly the 'enlightened horror' discussed by new executives. *The Woman in Black* contains not a single heaving bosom nor a testosterone-fuelled grapple, and aside from one brief scene with a small amount of bright red blood, the film is a study in blues and greys. Rather than revelling in the campy excess of Hammer classics like *The Vampire Lovers*, in which partially nude women giggle as they gleefully chase each other around a bedroom, blatantly pandering to the heterosexual male gaze, *The Woman in Black* takes a serious approach that is both understated and fairly humourless. New Hammer executives seemed, as Johnny Walker has noted, determined to 'distance [the company] from its anachronistic former self'.[36] By bringing forward key elements of classic Hammer, including the brand name and association with heritage settings and costumes, new Hammer could appeal to past fans of the studio's films while also shedding elements that could be considered outdated (camp) or too similar to competing horror films (gore).

By the time Hammer made *The Woman in Black*, they had already made four other films: *Beyond the Rave* (Matthias Hoene, 2008), a vampire film set in England that was partially distributed on the online social platform Myspace as a twenty-part serial; the US-set film *Let Me In* (Matt Reeves, 2010), an inferior remake of the Swedish film *Let the Right One In* (Tomas Alfredson, 2008); a second US-set film, *The Resident* (Antti Jokinen, 2011), which features a cameo by renowned classic Hammer star Christopher Lee; and the Irish-set, Irish co-production *Wake Wood* (David Keating, 2009). However, none of the films achieved the combination of critical praise, box-office success and wide exhibition of *The Woman in Black*, which was the culmination of the new Hammer's brand strategy.

When it opened in the UK the weekend of 12 February 2012, *The Woman in Black* had the 'highest ever opening for a Hammer film in the UK' ($4.9 million) following its strong opening weekend in the US the previous weekend ($21 million).[37] By the end of its theatrical run, it had become the highest-grossing British horror film on record at the UK box office. Hammer claimed that the film's financial success was proof that 'British audiences enjoy intelligent genre, which are the types of films Hammer is known for'. The film's success, combined with its reworking of Gothic tropes, allowed Hammer to position itself as continuing a larger history of successful Gothic Hammer films while also eschewing the historical reception of those films as gore-filled and excessive.

Critics seemed to make a similar rhetorical move. Writing for *Sight & Sound*, Lisa Mullen argues that the film 'gives notice of [Hammer's] return to its classic strengths as a purveyor of deadpan but terrifically entertaining period frightfests' – it delivers what one 'hope[s] to get from the best Hammer films: a thoroughly enjoyable hour and a half of jumps, screams and prickling neck hair'.[38] *Screen International* calls the film a 'good old-fashioned gothic horror' driven by Radcliffe's 'restrained adult performance', cinematographer Tim Maurice-Jones's 'atmospheric cinematography' and Watkins's 'respect for the rules of gothic horror'.[39] By positioning the film as 'thoroughly enjoyable' for its 'good old-fashioned gothic' and 'restrained' acting, these critics, like the Hammer film executives, revise classic Hammer's reputation to take the bite out of the original films and position them, and current Hammer productions, against the excessive and the unsettling.

Of course, not all critics praised the film or aligned with Hammer's rhetoric. David Noh's scathing review mocked the film's serious tone, lamented the lack of the 'sense of fun so necessary to all good horror' (which Noh defined as James Whale films) and delivered a rather personal jab at Ciaran Hinds's 'morose joke of a face'.[40] Ad hominem attack aside, Noh's review provides an important counterbalance and reminder that horror, like all genres, is defined in multiple, shifting ways – much as Hammer, and some critics, wanted to assert that the financial success of the film showed that audiences desired something other than torture porn and link the film to a longer lineage of restrained British Gothic horror films, there were audiences who preferred the campier tone of classic Hammer films and rejected *The Woman in Black* precisely because it feels like 'enlightened horror'.

'What Did[n't] They See?': *The Woman in Black* and Made-For-Television British Gothic Films

New Hammer foregrounded the connection between *The Woman in Black* and one conception of classic Hammer and the British Gothic tradition. Similar to how classic Hammer's gore and camp are denied or downplayed, the connections between *The Woman in Black* and made-for-television British Gothic films are effaced within the discourse around the film. This is done, I argue, to distance the film and brand from the domestic to emphasise the more exportable elements of both, positioning the film as *beyond* the national.

As noted earlier, Hammer had not previously made a ghost film; however, there was a major cultural touchstone within British visual culture that had produced a variety of ghost stories and from which *The Woman in Black* clearly draws aesthetic inspiration: the BBC's *A Ghost Story for Christmas* series. As Derek Johnston has shown, the idea of broadcasting ghost stories at Christmas dates at least as early as the 1920s, with seasonal radio broadcasts, though the idea of telling ghost stories at Christmas is an older tradition that became popular during the early Victorian era, though the Victorians themselves may have been reviving an oral cultural tradition of earlier provenance.[41] The first televised Christmas ghost story dates back to 1936, with 'Bransby Williams's two live appearances in the character of [Dickens's] Scrooge on Christmas Eve'.[42] The Christmas ghost story was of such importance, Johnston notes, that both ITV and Channel 4 attempted to 'start their own Christmas ghost story tradition' when they began broadcasting in 1955 and 1985, respectively.[43] Starting in 1972, Christmas broadcasting line-ups across the channels were filled with Universal's classic 1930s horror films, Jacques Tourneur's 1940s horror films and 'more recent films from the likes of Hammer and Amicus'.[44] In fact, the original ITV production of *The Woman in Black* premiered on Christmas Eve and was thus a part of this tradition of ghost stories at Christmas.

The most sustained entry in this broadcast television ghost story tradition came from the BBC itself in its *A Ghost Story for Christmas* series. The series was inspired by the 1968 BBC *Omnibus* production *Whistle and I'll Come to You* (Jonathan Miller), which is often considered to be part of the series despite being a forerunner and despite the fact that it was initially broadcast in May, making its Christmas showing a rebroadcast. The series proper started in 1971 with *The Stalls of Barchester* (Lawrence Gordon Clark) and ended in 1978 with *The Ice House* (Derek Lister). Throughout the 1980s and 1990s, these films were rebroadcast during the Christmas season.[45] The series was briefly revived in the 1980s via the BBC's *Classic Ghost Stories* (1986) and *Spine Chillers* (1980) and then brought back more fully in the 2000s with BBC's *Ghost Stories for Christmas with Christopher Lee* (2000), as well as several new and remade full-length films, such as Mark Gatiss's *The Tractate Middoth* (2013). These 2000s reboots explicitly and 'intentionally drew upon nostalgia for the television Christmases of the 1970s'.

The Woman in Black has key cinematographic and aural, as well as narrative, similarities to a number of the BBC *A Ghost Story for Christmas* productions, from the frequent long shots of the woman herself to the claustrophobicness of the camerawork that focuses on Kipps. In terms of narrative, the *A Ghost Story for Christmas* films follow a certain structure; as Derek Johnston has described it, 'A Researcher travels to a New Location, where they uncover a Past Narrative. The discovery awakens a supernatural Guardian, leading to a Death, usually the Researcher's'.[47] For example, *A Warning to the Curious* (Lawrence Gordon Clark, 1972) tells the story of Mr Paxton (Peter Vaughan), an amateur archaeologist who lived as a lowly clerk before deciding to try to find a hidden and protected ancient Anglo-Saxon artefact said to keep England safe from invasion. He takes a train from London to the coast, where he is met by suspicious and surly locals. Once he finds the artefact, he is pursued by its ghost protector. The film ends somewhat ambiguously, as Paxton has either gone mad or been frightened so badly that he will likely die shortly from the shock. Kipps in *The Woman in Black* follows a similar path, as a young solicitor who must travel to Eel Marsh House, where he uncovers the story and ghost of Jennet, who then proceeds to kill a number of children before killing Kipps and his son.

Some of the narrative similarities between *The Woman in Black* and the films of *A Ghost Story for Christmas* are also consistent with Hill's novel, but these similarities become more significant when considered alongside the aesthetic similarities between *Woman* and the series, especially *A Warning to the Curious*. In both films, the aesthetics of shooting the ghost using a shallow depth of field keep it fuzzy and somewhat obscure; these ghosts menace from a distance. In *The Woman in Black*, Jennet often hovers in the background, her presence only discernible when she moves, as in the film's first jump scare, when Kipps is fiddling with the taps at the kitchen sink and an out-of-focus Jennet suddenly moves several feet toward him in the background. The ghosts in these films are brought into close view only at a few key moments, in darkened rooms, to punctuate the tension the films have been building – in *A Warning*, this happens as Paxton tries to sleep the night after stealing the artefact, and, in *The Woman in Black*, when Kipps has discovered that Nathaniel was Jennet's son and Jennet's ghost re-enacts her death scene. As Helen Wheatley notes, the BBC's *A Ghost Story for Christmas* films 'centr[e] on the *suggestion* of a ghostly presence rather than the horror of visceral excess and abjection' (emphasis in original).[48] *The Woman in Black* continues this aesthetic tradition; the *A Ghost Story for Christmas* series embodies the 'enlightened horror' that new Hammer tries to link to classic Hammer.

Moreover, the films' sound designs allow the lack of 'visceral excess and abjection' to be made more terrifying via a corresponding *lack* of sound. The best example of this technique from the *A Ghost Story for Christmas* series is its *Omnibus* forerunner, *Whistle and I'll Come to You*. Professor Parkin (Michael Hordern), a considerably eccentric academic, takes a trip to the eastern coast, finds and takes a whistle that was buried in a graveyard and is subsequently haunted by a ghost. As with *A Warning to the Curious*, the ghost figure is shot in the background, out of sharp focus, until the Professor's shocking confrontation with the spectre in his darkened bedchamber.

But unlike *Warning*, *Whistle* proceeds mostly without dialogue or either diegetic or extradiegetic music, and the protagonist is aurally accompanied on his 'good trudge[s]' across the countryside and during his researches in the hotel by only his own mumbles, hums, harrumphs and single-word interjections. After Parkin's first nightmare about his ghost, the camera hems him in throughout the remainder of film, ranging between medium shots and extreme close-ups. Similarly, in *The Woman in Black*, a significant chunk of the film plays without dialogue (at least thirty-five of the ninety-five minutes) and with only a sparse soundtrack, populated mostly with Foley work to match Kipps's footfalls and breathing. Likewise, while there are long shots of Kipps, he is primarily shot between medium and close-up shots. In both of these films, viewers are tightly bound to the body of the protagonist – we hear his breathing and footfalls, and we are most often looking at his face. As Johnston argues about Christmas ghost films more broadly, 'the viewers experience the investigation, the warnings and the resolution much as the protagonist does, and so feel the message of the narrative as much as they experience and understand it intellectually'.[49]

These aesthetic links, when combined with the narrative similarities, show clear resonances between the BBC *A Ghost Story for Christmas* films and *The Woman in Black*, suggesting the series' unacknowledged influence at the very least and at most, I argue, a conscious effacement of these intertextual links in the discourse around the film put forward by Hammer. That Hammer's films, and the original ITV *The Woman in Black*, were included in Christmas broadcast line-ups since the 1970s makes new Hammer's total failure to recognise or mention the links between *Woman* and the seasonal ghost story tradition even more striking. This conclusion is only strengthened by the enduring popularity of the *Ghost Stories* series, such that it was briefly brought back in the 2000s with Hammer legend Christopher Lee. The connections here could easily have been picked up on by domestic audiences familiar with the *Ghost Stories* tradition. Indeed, the BBFC, when rating the film, appeared to have recognised the similarities, stating in their report that the 'period setting [of *The Woman in Black*] provides a degree of separation between the film and contemporary reality, and is in the tradition of classic ghost stories such as those of M. R. James'.[50] The UK community cinema non-profit Moving Image also noticed that the *Ghost Stories* served as inspiration for *Woman*.[51]

Explicitly acknowledging the links between *The Woman in Black* and these domestic, televised films would work against Hammer's positioning of the film as appealing to audiences outside the UK. Unlike the film's links to heritage films and classic Hammer, this link is glossed over because its potential appeal is essentially only domestic – while heritage films and classic Hammer appealed to domestic audiences, they were also both exportable and bankable, meaning their intertextual links with *The Woman in Black* imply that this film, too, will have multiple appeals to older domestic and foreign audiences. Hammer's effacement of the *Ghost Story* connection is one more way of emphasising the appeal of the film *beyond* the national, by denying appeals that are almost entirely domestic.

Instead, potential connections to the *Ghost Stories* were repurposed within the discourse around the film to serve other purposes. For example, the director's commentary for the film acknowledges the film's 'stripped down' soundtrack but attributes it to a conscious effort to avoid Americanisation; as director James Watkins states, they 'kept the sound design very, very muted' because 'In a lot of American horror films, they're really wallpapered with music, and the cue really leads the scare. And we didn't want that at all, we wanted it to be much more – not telling people when to be scared but let them feel it more, I suppose. But it's very stripped down, very spare'. Here, the film's sound is used to signal that the film is not Americanised. This is also another way of positioning the film as enlightened horror, since American horror films use loud sounds before scares to tell their audience when to be afraid, either because the audience is not canny enough to know when to be frightened or the films' scares are low quality and not frightening enough to provoke a response.

The Woman in Black and the Global Gothic, or 'The Ring for the Downton Abbey Crowd'[52]

The Woman in Black foregrounds its connections to an exportable British cinematic past, including British Gothic horror and British heritage films, but also has a dual emphasis on elements of film linked firmly to the present: the aesthetics of J-horror films and the safe Gothic associated with Radcliffe and the *Harry Potter* series. Both of these connections also share significant exportability and are part of what positions *The Woman in Black* as having appeal *beyond* the national, both in terms of what is appealing about the film itself and which audiences it is thought to appeal to.

Thus far, this chapter has framed *The Woman in Black* and the Gothic in terms of how scholars have traditionally talked about the British Gothic, in part because the Gothic is often assumed to be the domain of the Brits. However, as work by scholars like Glennis Byron has shown, the Gothic has 'progress[ed] far beyond being fixed in terms of any one geographically circumscribed mode'.[53] The Gothic has increased in popularity and visibility on a global scale since the 1990s because of economic globalisation and the fact that the Gothic offers a 'ready-made language to describe whatever anxieties might arise in an increasingly globalised world'.[54] As Byron puts it, 'the gothic is globalised – reproduced, consumed, recycled – and globalisation is gothicked – made monstrous, spectral, vampiric'.[55] This new Gothic, what Byron terms 'globalgothic', is not 'the "Gothic" in its traditional Western sense as the shadow side of Enlightenment modernity' and the infliction of that Gothic on non-European cultures; the globalgothic represents global cultural flows and the manifestation of a global Gothic in which 'we recognise the use of specific tropes and conventions'.[56] So, while recognisably Gothic texts and rhetorics have emerged in new locations, those Gothics are not simply reflective of a straightforward colonisation but a 'Trend to Blend' old tropes that existed within these cultures with tropes from the Gothics of other cultures.[57]

As Byron notes, one of the strongest examples of this globalgothic comes from Japan. In part because of their economic growth post-Second World War and focus on technology, Japan 'led the way' in the globalgothic.[58] Of course, this blending of the Gothic with Japanese traditions was easier because they were similar to the British Gothic. The Japanese theatrical traditions of *Noh* and *Kabuki* theatres have long aimed to inspire feelings of horror and the uncanny in audiences.[59] Elements of these cultural traditions began to blend with elements of the traditional Gothic and Western horror in post-Second World War Japanese horror cinema, particularly in *kaidan* (avenging spirit) films. The first *kaidan* film may have been, as Ruth Goldberg argues, *A Page of Madness* (Kinugasa Teinosuke, 1926), an *avant-garde* film about an uncanny mother.[60] However, the *kaidan* film only became popular in Japan during the 1950s, with Arai Ryohei's *Ghost Cat* films (1953–68). Kaneto Shindô's *Onibaba* (1964) and Tanaka Tokuzo's *Kwaidan* (1964) have also come to be regarded as classics of the subgenre.[61] Modern examples include, but are not limited to, *Ringu*

(Hideo Nakata, 1998), *Ju-on: The Grudge* (Takashi Shimizu, 2002) and *Dark Water* (Hideo Nakata, 2002). These films received international critical acclaim, and *Ringu* grossed over $13 million at the box office worldwide.[62] All three films were remade by American studios seeking (and largely failing) to capitalise on their appeal.

The avenging spirits in these films are most often women returning to seek revenge for wrongs inflicted on them during life.[63] These women, with their wide, staring eyes and long black hair are, as D. P. Martinez has argued, 'both a source of danger to the norm and the very means of perpetuating that norm', as they are both 'symbolically dangerous' and, as women, considered culturally to also be 'the source of all that is Japanese'.[64] While the avenging of crimes in these films serves to help to solidify social norms around social responsibility, the way in which the women ghosts go about seeking and achieving revenge may instead undermine those norms.[65] Writing on the *kaidan* figure, both Jay McRoy and Susan Napier attribute this dual nature of the woman ghost to changes in the workforce in Japan in the 1950s and 60s, as well as the 1990s and 2000s, that caused crises of masculinity in Japan.[66]

These changes also produced a new plot within modern Japanese horror. As Steffen Hantke notes, in films like Takashi Miike's *Audition*, 'the object of the revenge does not, properly speaking, deserve to be punished', and there is no 'sense of social justice that is being reinstated' through the living woman protagonist's actions.[67] As Napier argues, following trends in Japanese literature, women in these films become something that men must escape; they are 'agents of entrapment', 'increasingly other, unreachable, even demonic'.[68] Indeed, many of the J-horror *kaidan* films dealt with maternal failure as integral to family dysfunction.[69] For example, *Ringu*'s spirit Samara seeks revenge in part because her mother's failure as a psychic, failure in choosing a romantic partner and failure to protect Samara led to the girl's death. The film also characterises its divorced, single mother protagonist Reiko as endangering her child by working. The lead in Hideo Nakata's *Dark Water* (2002), Yoshimi, is characterised similarly as endangering her daughter in part because of her status as a divorced working mother, and the film's girl-child spirit is only appeased when Yoshimi submits to acting as its mother and dying. On the other hand, *Ju-on: The Grudge*'s primary spirits are a mother and son murdered by the family patriarch.[70]

While it is easy to draw facile similarities between narrative trends within *kaidan* films and *The Woman in Black*, from the trope of the avenging woman spirit who was wronged via family dysfunction to the focus on motherhood, the links between J-horror and *The Woman in Black* go beyond narrative and help the film reach beyond the British Gothic to the globalgothic. Partly, this link comes out through Liz White's character performance as Jennet, as well as her costuming, the costuming and performance of Ashley Foster, who plays Nathaniel, and the film's cinematography.

Take, for example, the way Jennet moves. As Kipps sits, obliviously reading paperwork about Nathaniel's death and then gently dozing, Jennet can be seen in the background of several shots, first opening a door and quickly slipping into view. The camera cuts to a shot behind Kipps; Jennet's reflection floats forward in a mirror in the upper left of the frame before the camera cuts to her point-of-view shot as she takes over the camera's perspective, which then slides forward with her, toward Kipps. Her movement here and in other, similar scenes, is disturbing because of its uncanniness; she appears human but her movements are too smooth and quick. Nathaniel, too, also moves with preternatural speed and smoothness, as when he slips across the margins of the frame just before Kipps sees Jennet's ghost re-enact her suicide. These uncanny movements are reminiscent of the movements of the ghosts in J-horror. For example, Nathaniel's movements are similar to the quick, smooth movements of the small ghost boy Toshio in *Ju-on: The Grudge* as he darts around the margins of the frame while terrorising social work volunteer Rika. Uncanny or inhuman movement is part of the list of 'techniques for representation of the ghost' developed by screenwriter Hiroshi Takahashi, who wrote *Don't Look Up* (Hideo Nakata, 1996) and both *Ringu* and *Ringu 2* (Hideo Nakata), as well as working as a creative consultant on *Ju-on: The Grudge*.[71]

Jennet and Nathaniel's bodies visually echo ghosts from *kaidan* films in other ways as well. Jennet's long black veil, while correct costuming for the period, also visually echoes the long black hair typical of women ghosts like Samara in *Ringu* or Kayako in *Ju-on: The Grudge*. In addition, at some points during the film, Jennet takes the form of a black, smoke-like substance when attempting to touch Kipps, like Kayako when she tries to touch the older woman, Sachie (see Figure 4).

Jennet and Nathaniel, like Toshio in *Ju-on: The Grudge*, are often placed in the *mise-en-scène* in easy-to-miss ways that can inspire paranoia and additional fear in viewers, who then search the corners and background of the frame. As Jay McRoy argues about *Ju-on: The Grudge*: 'by frequently relegating frightening images to the extreme edges of the frame, as fleeting,

Figure 4. Top, Jennet's smoky black ghost hand on Kipps's left shoulder. Bottom, the smoke-like ghost of Kayako hovering over Sachie.

yet troubling figures glimpsed peripherally but never completely', the film 'creat[es] the impression that we may have just witnessed a flash of something disquieting'.[72] In *The Woman in Black*, Jennet and Nathaniel serve a similar purpose, as when Kipps first visits the graveyard near the house, passing first Nathaniel, camouflaged among the trees, and then Jennet, who slips past in the foreground and could (almost) be confused for a tree.

There is also the strong visual similarity between Nathaniel and Toshio, small boys with roundish faces and bowl haircuts. There are shots of Nathanial that echo shots of Toshio. For example, when Kipps finally finds his matches to relight his candle after dropping it in shock when he sees Jennet hang herself, the light from the match illuminates the screeching face of Nathaniel. This bears strong similarity to the scene in *Ju-on: The Grudge* when the businessman Katsuya searches the room where he finds his wife Kazumi lying catatonic on the bed. Toshio rises from behind the bed, mouth also open in a screech. In terms of both shots and both boys, the focus is on the mouth – in *Ju-on: The Grudge*, this is achieved through a close-up shot that centres the mouth in the frame, while *The Woman in Black* keeps the adult in the frame and achieves a focus on the mouth via lighting (see Figure 5). The wide-open roundness of the screeching mouths ties them together visually, further highlighting how *The Woman in Black* links itself to J-horror and the globalgothic.

These links between *The Woman in Black* and J-horror are both explicit allusion (as with the mirrored shots of Toshio and Nathaniel's mouths) and stylistic influence (for example, Jennet's hovering at the edges, background and foreground of the shots). The general stylistic influence serves a key function in that it presents recognisable tropes from J-horror that can be easily recognised by reviewers, as well anyone generally familiar with J-horror – even those who have not seen these films may be familiar with the general aesthetics from trailers or popular parodic treatments like those found in the *Scary Movie* franchise and *Saturday Night Live* sketches. On the other hand, the more direct allusions appeal to cinephilic audiences and horror fans. These audiences can feel they are 'in' on the shared cultural (and/or subcultural) reference that these allusions represent. The connections between *The Woman in Black* and J-horror addresses the film to multiple audiences, positioning the film as relevant across audiences traditionally separated by age and geography.

Also, though, the film's connection to J-horror connects the film to new Hammer's 'enlightened horror' – at least within British film culture. As Daniel Martin has shown in his research on the reception of *Ringu*

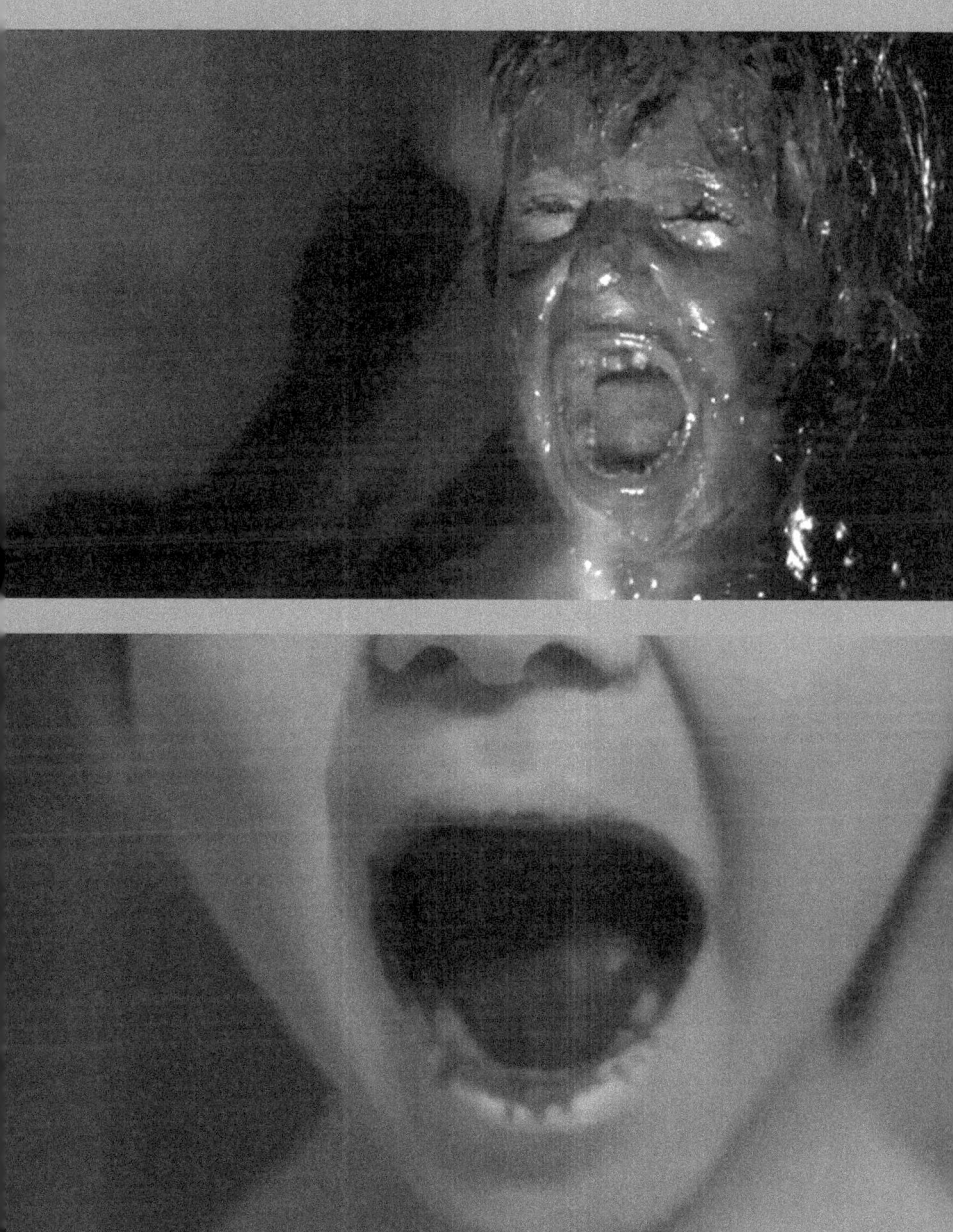

Figure 5. Top, Nathaniel in *The Woman in Black*. Bottom, Toshio in *Ju-on: The Grudge*.

within British film criticism, while subsequent J-horror films were valued for their 'foreign credentials', *Ringu* was valued because it represented 'an alternative to the dominant Hollywood cycle of horror films' represented by *Scream* (Wes Craven, 1996) by privileging 'subtlety and restraint' over 'violence and shock tactics'.[74] *Ringu* and subsequent J-horror films were esteemed in part because of their connection to the longstanding discourse in British film culture linking quality and restraint.[75] Interestingly, according to Martin, a number of critics at the time compared *Ringu* to the ghost stories of M. R. James, whose stories comprise the majority of the BBC's *A Ghost Story for Christmas* series, even going so far as to cite his stories as inspiration for *Ringu*, though that seems more like the product of British critics' cultural imperialist imaginations than fact.[76]

Critical responses to *The Woman in Black* participate in this discourse elevating J-horror. As *The Guardian*'s Phil Hoad put it, *The Woman in Black* and J-horror share an 'emphasis on atmosphere over cheap shocks'.[77] Jane Goldman, the scriptwriter, also expressed a similar sentiment during the promotional tour for the film and within the director's commentary on the US DVD release, linking the film with J-horror because of how both 'take the business of being frightening seriously. There is no attempt at postmodernism or humour. They are incredibly melancholy, with a strong emotional core, while remaining absolutely terrifying'.[78] This shared investment in serious scares was also discursively linked to the influence of classic Hammer on both *The Woman in Black* and key J-horror directors.[79]

The popularity of J-horror in Britain, and internationally, meant that *The Woman in Black*'s connections to J-horror positioned the film as doing something respectable, enlightened and also new and popular that, at the same time, represented the influence of celebrated classic Hammer films. Critics picked up on these appeals when the film was released, and the film's connection to J-horror was seen as a positive and savvy contribution to the film's repertoire of scare techniques, while also rhetorically positioning the film as both akin to and different from classic Hammer horror. Leslie Felperin writes that Watkins and Goldman 'judiciously combine moves from the classic scare-'em-ups with new tricks from recent J-horror pics', so that 'only shot-by-shot analysis will reveal whether there really are figures and face lurking, barely seen, at the edge of the frame, which contribute very subtly to the atmosphere of unease, or whether they are just figments of the imagination'.[80]

The Woman in Black, then, was rhetorically positioned as the product of the proliferation and influence of British Gothic seeping outward through the flows of the global economy, influencing Japanese horror, only to have that influence flow back to and manifest in the new Hammer. Scholars writing on Japanese horror, and the globalgothic more broadly, reject this imperialist discourse, which positions British Gothic as the 'one true' Gothic from which other nations derive their own traditions. Rather than 'conflat[ing] globalization with Americanization or Westernization', writers like Glennis Byron have encouraged 'a new emphasis on multi-directional exchanges'.[81] In other words, while British Gothic has likely influenced Japanese horror, British Gothic was already influenced by transnational flows from other cultures and forms of the Gothic, whether that means, for example, the original influence of the German *Sturm und Drang* movement in the late 1700s or the postcolonial Caribbean Gothic. Nonetheless, the use of aesthetic and narrative tropes from J-horror in *The Woman in Black* allows for multiple readings of the film's Gothicness to suit domestic and international audiences.

'*Harry Potter and the Scary Ghost Lady*': Daniel Radcliffe's Transnational Stardom and *The Woman in Black*[82]

The connection between *The Woman in Black* and J-horror is not the film's only connection to contemporary films. The film's main character, Arthur Kipps, is played by international film star Daniel Radcliffe of *Harry Potter* fame. While the minimal sound design and the camera's tight focus on Kipps in *The Woman in Black* can be seen as aesthetic connections to older cultural touchstones within British Gothic visual media, as discussed above, these techniques also provide an international audience of fans with the opportunity to get closer to Radcliffe (and thus, Potter), even if that closeness is mediated by the camera. The marketing for *The Woman in Black* plays up Radcliffe's presence in the film, in part by visually mimicking aspects of the marketing for Radcliffe's final *Potter* film, *Harry Potter and the Deathly Hallows – Part 2* (David Yates, 2011). These connections position the film as rooted in the present and appealing to a broad audience via Radcliffe's star power and connections to the *Potter* phenomenon.

As Stephen Hinerman has argued, 'stardom permeates the globalized economy' as 'one imaginary glue of globalization'.[83] Stars become common images that have the potential for recognition across national and linguistic borders. In a globalised economy saturated by, and arguably driven by, multinational news and entertainment corporations, stars 'provide individuals with shared communication experiences'.[84] *The Woman in Black*, then, in its focus on Radcliffe's body, uses that image as a means of appealing to an international audience bound together as a pre-constituted viewership by the common coin of Radcliffe's image.

In 2012, Radcliffe was an in-demand, highly recognisable and recognisably British actor. Theatrically exhibited in sixty-five different countries by the end of 2011, the final film of the *Potter* series brought in a worldwide box office gross of over $1.341 billion, making it one of the top ten films in terms of all-time worldwide gross. The UK market made up a little under 9 per cent of the film's worldwide box office and the US around 28 per cent, meaning that around 63 per cent of the total box office gross came from outside the US and UK. The ten most profitable of these countries were Japan ($124 million), Germany ($78 million), France ($67 million), China ($60 million), Australia ($51 million), Russia ($36 million), Brazil ($35 million), Mexico ($34 million), South Korea ($32 million) and Italy ($29 million). It was also the fourth highest-grossing English-language film at the Turkish box office that year and the third highest-grossing film overall in the Philippines. *Deathly Hallows 2* was not only a success in the United States and Europe but across much of the globe.[85]

This box-office draw makes Radcliffe one of biggest selling points of *The Woman in Black*. With this in mind, the film can be seen as more than just a ghost story starring Daniel Radcliffe but instead as a film experience that brings fans closer to Radcliffe, via Kipps – that promises and delivers a certain amount of access to the actor's body and presence in his return to cinemas post-*Potter*. The film, both in terms of its aesthetics and promotional paratexts, capitalises on Radcliffe's transnational stardom to position itself, and by extension British horror, as an exportable product that *Potter* fans in audiences across the globe will desire.

Given Daniel Radcliffe's well-known desire for privacy, his star image was still primarily informed by the *Potter* films and related promotional work. He had done work on other films, first playing the young David in the BBC TV movie *David Copperfield* (Simon Curtis, 1999), then taking a small role in *The Tailor of Panama* (John Boorman, 2001), but these films were significantly less well-known. Radcliffe had tried, unsuccessfully, to break out of his Potter image by starring in the West End staging of *Equus* in early 2007, which required him to be nude onstage; playing a young teen entering a period of sexual awakening in *December Boys* (Rod Hardy, 2007); and taking the role of the eponymous Jack in *My Boy Jack* (Brian Kirk, 2007), a made-for-television period drama centring on Rudyard

Kipling's search for his son during the Second World War. Instead, these artistic ventures became known as roles Radcliffe had taken out of desperation because the character 'wasn't Harry Potter', and even complimentary reviews proclaiming Radcliffe had '[shaken] off the mantle of Harry Potter' still framed him in *Potter*'s terms, with one article describing his *Equus* performance as 'no flash in the magic pan'.

Critical reactions to *The Woman in Black* also bear this out. Hannah Dowle's piece for *Variety*, 'Things Getting Scarier for Harry and "Woman"', not only conflates Potter and Radcliffe in the title but begins by asserting that Radcliffe had moved on from the 'jovial ghouls of Hogwarts'.[87] Sally Williams's odd, fawning interview with Radcliffe for the UK's *Telegraph Magazine* performs a strikingly similar rhetorical move, advertising Radcliffe's story of 'life after the broomstick' and framing Radcliffe throughout the article, including its title ('And For My Next Trick'), via the lens of Potter, with references in nearly every paragraph – whether it is describing Radcliffe's now adult body by saying 'gone are the Potter glasses and soft curves of childhood' or discussing the physicality of his turn in the musical *How to Succeed in Business Without Really Trying* (in its 2011–12 Broadway revival) as 'unbelievably exotic after years of seeing him wave a wand'.[88] Williams conflates the costuming and bodily performance of the character with the appearance and bodily comportment of the actor. With titles like 'The Ghost of Harry Potter' and 'Harry Potter Grows Up', many other reviews and interviews performed a similar conflation, unable to see Radcliffe without also seeing Potter, unable to discuss new work without mentioning *Potter*.[89]

In essence, to borrow M. J. Simpson's sublime phrasing, *The Woman in Black* was, for many audience members, '*Harry Potter and the Scary Ghost Lady*'.[90] This slippage between actor and character is one that can be common for stars who have either played an iconic role or been consistently typecast. Richard DeCordova argues that, for stars,

> the body that appears in fiction films actually has an ambiguous and complex status: at any moment one can theoretically locate two bodies in the one: a body produced (that of the character) and a body producing (that of the actor). Attention to the former draws the spectator into the representation of character within the fiction. Attention to the latter, on the other hand, draws the spectator into a specific path of intertextuality that extends outside the text as a formal system.[91]

At this stage in his career, however, there were three bodies locatable within Radcliffe's image. Most dimly visible, there was the body produced in the film in question – here, Kipps. Second most visible, in DeCordova's terms, is Radcliffe's producing body. However, the body most visible is that of Harry Potter, the body produced by Radcliffe in the *Harry Potter* films and which had come, by this point in his career, to possess his image and screen presence. Critics and audiences could not see Daniel Radcliffe, or any of his characters, without also seeing Harry Potter, and *The Woman in Black* capitalises upon this reality.

Matt Hills has argued that Hammer 'aimed to exploit' previous *Potter* marketing 'by ostensibly completing the arc of the *Harry Potter* brand, implying that Radcliffe had matured into full adulthood by moving genres from juvenile fantasy to a harder-edged ghost story'.[92] However, Radcliffe's star image was not, in 2012, one of 'full adulthood'. For example, in the interviews discussed above, there is a constant emphasis on Radcliffe's youth and maturity. He, and his star image, are caught in a liminal state between childhood and adulthood. For Williams, Radcliffe appears 'boyish and enthusiastic', with 'glimpses of a grown man'; Patterson's interview starts with Radcliffe complimenting the author – 'my mum sent me a column you wrote' – and frames his favourite book, Bulgakov's classic *The Master and Margarita*, as 'magic for a child wizard who has grown up'.[93]

The film-makers took pains to make Radcliffe appear older in *The Woman in Black*, giving him stubble and sideburns, as well as swapping liquor for the hot chocolate Kipps and Mr Daily (Ciaran Hinds) were originally scripted to drink together.[94] However, reviews on Radcliffe's adult-ish appearance were mixed. *Screen International* claimed that the *Potter* films were 'firmly behind' Radcliffe, who appears 'adult and tortured by memories of his late wife', but others, like reviewer Leslie Felperin, felt Radcliffe was 'too puppyish to convince as a parent'.[95] These differing interpretations of Radcliffe's status belie the fact that his star image remained liminal at this time.

So, while Hammer intended, as Hills argues, to exploit Radcliffe's *Potter* fame and branding, I would argue that *The Woman in Black* actually capitalises less on Radcliffe as adult and more on his status as in between. To see Radcliffe on screen at this point in his career was to see, specifically, a Radcliffe whose body was both child and adult, that had produced Potter and whose career was now defined as an attempt to move past the character that still possessed his image and presence – the very act of defining Radcliffe as post-Potter meant that he was still, in fact, being defined by that role.

This layered star image becomes clear in the promotional posters for the film, which bear distinct similarities to the posters for *Deathly Hallows 2* and encourage potential audiences for *The Woman in Black* to see all three potential bodies in the image – Kipps, Radcliffe and Potter. In the promotional poster for *The Woman in Black* that features the tagline 'Fear her curse', Radcliffe's body is positioned with his right arm hanging straight down at his side and his left arm slightly away from his body; his left shoulder is angled to be a little higher and a little further forward than his right. His body is facing the camera directly, and he is staring intensely into the camera. His lips are set in a straight line, his jaw set. Centred in foreground of the image, Radcliffe's body is positioned as the most important element. These descriptions could apply in equal measure to the main international poster for *Deathly Hallows 2*, the English-language and translated/localised versions. Radcliffe's body appears in almost the exact same position as it does in the 'Fear' poster, and his facial expression is nearly identical. The posters also share a similar hue and tone, cast in a desaturated, blueish grey. The lighting pattern on Radcliffe's face is also similar, though in reverse; in 'Fear', the right side of Radcliffe's face is illuminated with a bright light, while in 'Trio', the left side of his face is illuminated with a bright light. Even these differences, though, are another continuity, in that one side of his face is brightly lit in both posters. These similarities highlight how the poster campaign for *The Woman in Black* attempted to code the body in the photos as not only Radcliffe and Kipps, but also Potter.

These appeals are also present in the film's first, and primary, trailer, which was released both in the UK and internationally. At least in terms of the French and German-language version of this first international trailer, there are no major differences from the English-language version. The trailer delivers multiple images of Radcliffe – of the 1:41 length of the trailer, 1:05 shows images of Kipps, most often in close-up and medium shots, placing the focus on Radcliffe's image to capitalise on viewer recognition. The first diegetic sound in the trailer is that of a train whistle, which plays over the opening production company logos, followed by a brief interlude of whimsical but mysterious staccato music reminiscent of that from a music box. The next image is a train chugging across the frame, trailing steam and smoke, followed by a close-up of Kipps on the train, leaning against the window next to his seat. Train noises and imagery evoke, arguably for audiences with even passing familiarity with the *Potter* series, Platform 9 and 3/4 and Harry's journeys to Hogwarts, which recurs in several of the films. The music-box style music is reminiscent of the opening measures of John Williams's 'Hedwig's Theme', which introduced the *Harry Potter and the Chamber of Secrets* and *Deathly Hallows Part 2* trailers and functioned as a main theme throughout all of the films, though with some tonal variation as the series delved into darker themes and situations.

Both the posters for the film and the first trailer sell *The Woman in Black* via a promise of sustained access to Radcliffe's on-screen presence, as well as, by extension, a continuance of Harry Potter's on-screen presence. Returning to *The Woman in Black*, one can see the promise of the film's marketing fulfilled. One of the primary pleasures available to audiences of the film is the ability to not only see Radcliffe but to feel as though one is with him, insofar as that is possible through the mediation of the screen. In other words, the claustrophobic cinematography and minimal sound design take on additional meanings when Radcliffe's star image is taken into consideration. While the dialogue-free middle section of the film that follows Kipps as he pursues and is pursued by Jennet and Nathaniel best represents the fulfilment of the film's promise of closeness to Radcliffe (and thus Potter), it is his initial foray into Eel Marsh House that sets up that expectation within the film itself.

As Kipps gets his first up-close glimpse of the house, the camera shifts to his perspective and there is a clear sound of the walkway's gravel crunching under his feet as he walks up the path. There is a cut, and then the camera is facing Kipps, framing him in a medium close-up as he walks, his footsteps forming a sound bridge between the shots. As Kipps enters the house, there is a similar pair of shots: the door creaks open and the camera shoots from Kipps's perspective as he surveys the front room and grand staircase, then cuts so the camera is in front of Kipps, framing him in a close-up. The sound of his footsteps and the faint sound of his breathing runs during both shots, linking them via sound bridge. In cutting between Kipps's perspective and a close perspective on Kipps, these shots invite viewers to align their perspective with Kipps's; the sound design aurally places the viewer with Kipps, so close as to hear him breathing. These shots, and those like them throughout the rest of the first sequence where Kipps is alone in the house, introduce and establish the level of intimacy viewers are invited to physically feel with not only Kipps but also Radcliffe, and by extension Potter. This level of aural and physical closeness is maintained throughout both stretches of the film where Kipps wanders around Eel Marsh House alone.

As Goldman notes in the DVD director's commentary, *The Woman in Black* allows the viewer to 'sort of experienc[e things] in the same way that [Kipps] is in a sense, when it's quiet', and she agrees with Watkins that the mostly silent middle section of the film is the most gripping part because the viewer gets to be 'alone with Arthur [Kipps]'. Watkins also acknowledges a purposeful focus on the main character – they did not want a 'slasher gory horror' film 'where the character just has to be killed' but instead wanted to 'slow down and advance the character' so that audiences would be 'rooting for him'.[96] Here, Goldman and Watkins position the heavy focus on Radcliffe as serving the narrative and the audience's mental and emotional connection to that narrative. However, as Paul McDonald has argued about Hollywood stars, character is the 'figure of the narrative' while the actor is 'a figure of spectacle'.[97] Focusing on Kipps may help to move the narrative forward, but it also presents Radcliffe's body as spectacle. So, while the idea Goldman and Watkins put forward supports a certain narrative about their creative intentions and abilities, the narrative and cinematographic focus on Kipps also serves to fulfil audiences' desires 'be with' Radcliffe/Potter.

The appeal of Radcliffe's layered star text, his possession by his previous role as Potter, is clear not only in the film's cinematography, sound design and marketing but also in the discourse around and backlash against the film's rating, 12A in the UK and PG-13 in the US. As Adam Dawtrey notes in *Variety*, Radcliffe's casting, combined with the rating, 'guaranteed a huge awareness for the movie among kids who grew up alongside the boy wizard, but for whom Hammer was a previously unknown name', as his presence 'mobilized a wider audience of all ages than would normally have turned out for a horror pic or a literary period piece'.[98] This is true, Dawtrey contends, because the 'increasingly Gothic elements of the Potter franchise', including 'ghosts, werewolves, and spooky Victoriana', 'groomed its young audience for a further step into the dark side with *The Woman in Black*'. Even in rating the film, the BBFC considered that 'as Daniel Radcliffe was starring in *The Woman in Black* (his first major film role since finishing the Harry Potter series), the film might attract a younger audience, that may not usually choose to watch a scary film'.[99]

However, the film also represents a turn away from the bodily degradation and mutilation that accompanied many other Gothic horror films of the time (as mentioned above). Instead, the Gothic in *The Woman in Black* is a safe Gothic that would have appealed not only to young *Potter* fans but also teens and adults who were underserved by or uninterested in contemporaneous body horror. As Emma McEvoy has argued, the performance of the Gothic can be used for different ends than fear. As with the figure of Count von Count on the popular children's programme *Sesame Street*, it can be used 'to signify scary without actually being scary'.[100] While *The Woman in Black* contains intense situations, as when Jennet compels a young girl to set herself on fire, audiences can feel safely distanced from the potential fear the film evokes because its temporal setting removes much of the immediacy of any threats. Surely, children are in danger in *The Woman in Black*, but they are young girls wearing pinafores and young boys wearing blazers and short pants – they are not today's children. In addition, children are the only population truly endangered within the film, as Jennet seems able to compel only children to take their own lives, not teens or adults. The *Potter* series accomplishes similar distancing through its fantastical setting within a wizarding world that is hidden from non-magical humans. However, this is not to say that the film does not have frightening moments – rather, there are Gothic and horror elements, including the ubiquitous jump scare, that, in addition to potentially actually being frightening, signal to audiences that something frightening is occurring. Going back to Hammer's desire to produce 'enlightened horror', part of the potential pleasure of this safe Gothic is being allowed intellectual recognition of frightening situations while also being distanced enough not to viscerally feel the effects.

Despite this, the expectations linked to Radcliffe's post-*Potter* star image led to controversy after parents took young fans to *The Woman in Black*, despite the cuts the BBFC required for the film to obtain a 12A rating.[101] This controversy led to *The Woman in Black* being the BBFC's most-complained about film for 2012 and one of the two most-complained about films from 2010 to 2014, with most complaints due to '"confounded expectations"'.[102] These complaints were mostly parents who thought the film '"too scary" for their children', who were 'more used to seeing Radcliffe at Hogwarts'.[103] The film was clearly marketed as horror, from the ghostly atmosphere and images of the posters to the high-speed, tension-inducing editing and jump scares of the trailers. A 12A rating marked out the film as inappropriate for children under twelve, particularly because in 12A films, 'moderate physical and psychological threat may be permitted', 'providing disturbing sequences are not frequent or sustained'.[104] Moreover, the film was a pre-sold property, in that Susan Hill's novel and the stage adaptation are widely known in the UK. And yet, by creating a heavy visual link between *Woman* and *Potter* in the marketing materials, Hammer set up the film to be seen as a similarly safe, 'enlightened' Gothic.

These 'confounded expectations' are attributable to the presence of Daniel Radcliffe and viewers' inability to see past his possession by Potter, as well as the ties between the films established through marketing, which encouraged this conflation. As one BBFC spokeswoman put it, "'People have certain expectations about films with Daniel Radcliffe in them'".[105] Audiences expect that while they are getting Gothic fare from *Woman*, as with the *Potter* franchise, it will be a safe Gothic that is appropriate viewing for children (which is what precipitated their complaints that a horror film was frightening). The first three *Potter* films garnered a PG rating in the UK, while the subsequent five films were rated 12A. Despite containing more gore and violence than *The Woman in Black* – characters are often spattered with blood; the dead bodies of numerous secondary characters and bystanders, some children, are shown; and a main character has his neck slit open – *Deathly Hallows 2* passed the BBFC without cuts. The BBFC described the film as containing 'moderate threat, injury detail and language', while *Woman* contained 'intense supernatural threat and horror'.[106]

I would argue that these ratings are less reflective of the actual content of the films and more reflective of certain expectations about *Potter* as a children's series and *Woman*'s encouraging of audiences to see Kipps as Potter in a less fantastical, more adult setting, which made even a lesser amount of violence, gore and intense situations seem more frightening. Viewer complaints against *Woman*, and the relative lack of complaints against *Deathly Hallows*, would have been influenced by the same logic. By taking advantage of the marketing strategy for *Deathly Hallows 2*, *The Woman in Black* could capitalise on Radcliffe's star image and sell their film as safe, 'enlightened' Gothic horror. But these associations also led some audience segments to see the film as more frightening and objectionable than they may have otherwise, allowing the film to be positioned as both safe and scary and, in so doing, to appeal to a multiplicity of audiences.

Conclusions

In 2013, the BFI launched a Gothic cinema season, including 'more than 150 films and around 1,000 screenings throughout the UK' from August 2013 to January 2014, a score of public events and lectures, a major Education programme outlining thirteen Gothic films children should watch by the time they are thirteen years old, Gothic television programming, the DVD release of a number of older Gothic films and the publication of an essay collection from film-makers and scholars.[107] Films were chosen from around the world; *The Woman in Black* capped off the exhibition season, which included celebrated Gothic films like *The Cabinet of Dr Caligari* (Robert Wiene, 1920), *Night of the Demon* (Jacques Tourneur, 1957), *Throne of Blood* (Akira Kurosawa, 1957), Fisher's *Horror of Dracula* and *The Mummy* (1959), *The Masque of the Red Death* (Roger Corman, 1964), *Nosferatu the Vampyre* (Werner Herzog, 1979) and *The Shining* (Stanley Kubrick, 1980). While this renewed focus on the Gothic had likely been in the works at the BFI before *The Woman in Black* came out, both the film and the cinema season were products of (and helped to maintain) the larger turn toward and appeal to the globalgothic. Rather than a focus on British Gothic, or the Gothic as specifically British, both *Woman* and the BFI's Gothic season turned their gaze beyond the national, toward the transnational, reframing classic Hammer's Gothic horror by situating it within a broader Gothic tradition.

Whether it is the discourse around *The Woman in Black*, the promotional paratexts, or the film itself, genre and stardom link the film to concerns, audiences and traditions *beyond* the national. These links work not only to construct an international audience for the film, as well as Hammer studio products and British horror more broadly, but also to appeal to those audiences. Nigel Sinclair, co-chairman of Exclusive Media Group, which owns Hammer, has said that the critical and financial success of *The Woman in Black* caused the media group to 'realiz[e] that Britishness is an asset' and decide to set films in the UK going forward.[108] Oakes added, 'Hammer is a heritage brand, and we want to reinvent it in the same way as Burberry reinvented its legacy for a modern audience'. And after *The Woman in Black*, Hammer did turn to focus on films set in Britain, starring British actors. *The Quiet Ones* (John Pogue, 2014), set in Oxford and starring Jared Harris, was filmed in the famous Bodleian Library and Oxford's Merton College.[109] The sequel to *The Woman in Black*, *The Woman in Black 2: Angel of Death* (Tom Harper, 2014), revisits the sites of Crythin Gifford and Eel Marsh House.

However, neither film recaptured the explosive critical and financial success of *The Woman in Black*. *The Quiet Ones* took in a little over $17.8 million worldwide, which is a good return on an estimated $200,000 budget. *The Woman in Black 2: Angel of Death* managed over $36.7 million on a $15 million budget. Both are a far cry from the $127.7 million grossed by *The Woman in Black* on its $15 million budget. Additionally, both films received mixed reviews. Responses to *The Quiet Ones* praised

Jared Harris's performance, but there was a pervasive emphasis on the calculated, commercial nature of the film – it was 'a shrewd bit of retrofitting' but 'too business-minded to be distinctively scary', an unconvincing 'pair of cut-price x-ray specs'.[110] *The Woman in Black 2*, on the other hand, was called a 'commercially driven sequel' lacking 'the charge of the first story'.[111] These critical comments underline the fact that Hammer's subsequent films played too heavily on what the studio had decided was the strength of *The Woman in Black*: not only Britishness in setting and cast, but also in terms of being set in the past and depicting and embodying a certain version of British heritage. *The Woman in Black* could avoid wallowing in the past because its transnational genre hybridity placed its pastness and presentness in tension. Its use of J-horror tropes and Radcliffe's presence gestured towards the present, via his star image. At the same time, the film also borrowed certain elements from the British heritage genre and was presented as reviving classic Hammer, even though it mostly superficially capitalised on nostalgia for that studio's works rather than substantively carrying on its traditions of gore and camp.

These tensions between the nostalgic and the contemporaneous allow the film to capitalise on the most marketable elements of classic Hammer, as well as its reputation as an internationally bankable product, and position itself as tapping into popular (and, again, profitable) contemporary trends like J-horror and the *Harry Potter* franchise. But Hammer's subsequent films have lacked these elements. They also lacked transnational genre hybridity, a key part of what helped *Woman* address a potentially wider and more international audience. Hammer would not make another film again until *The Lodge* (Veronika Franz and Severin Fiala), an American co-production which was well received at the Sundance Film Festival in 2019 but would not see cinema screens until after this time of writing. To draw again on Adam Dawtrey's words: new Hammer might own a famous corpse, but they still need to make it 'walk, talk and earn money again'.[112] While the studio has yet to achieve this in a sustained way, the sheer breadth of the globalgothic offers a wealth of possibilities from which Hammer could draw.

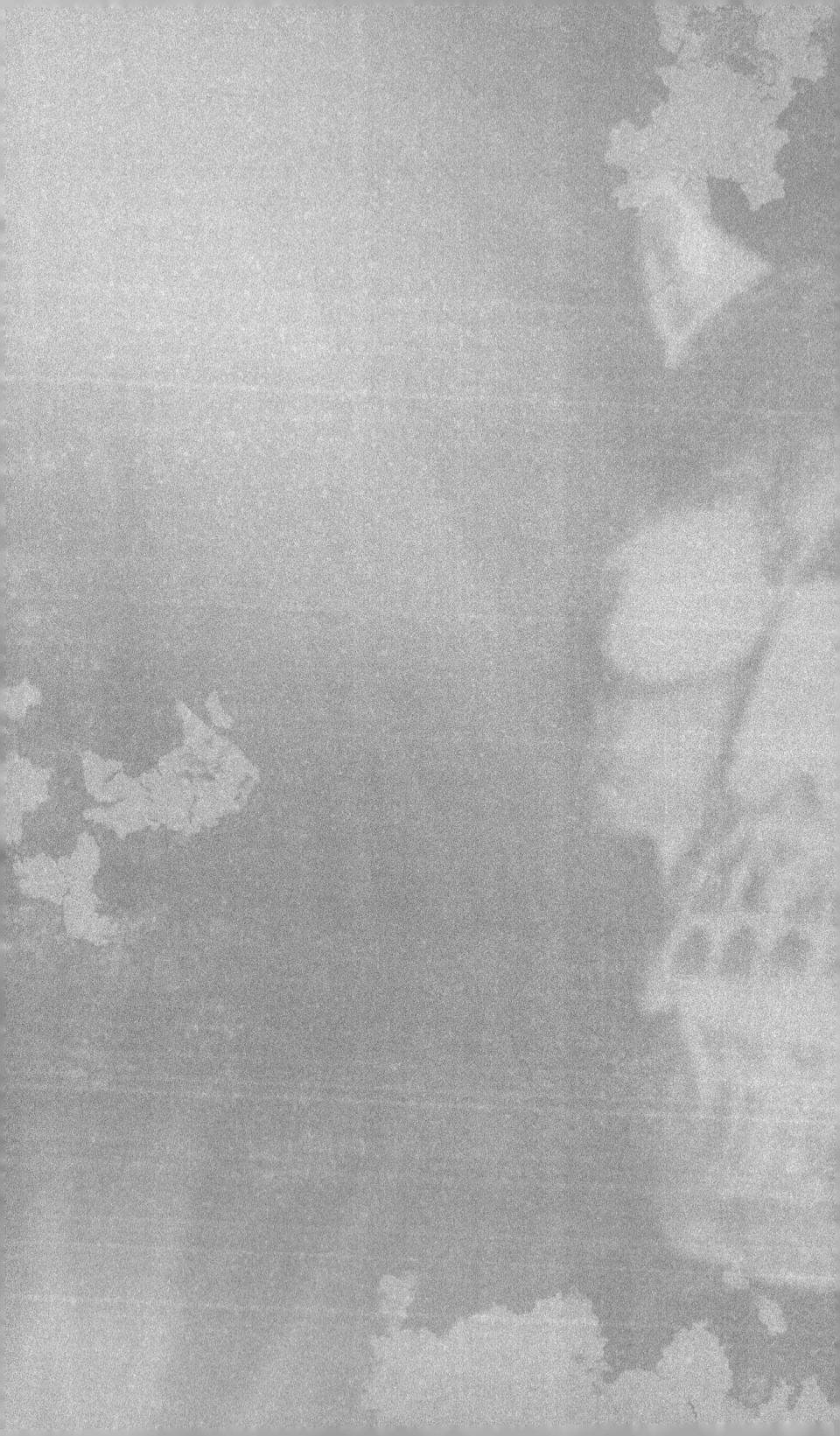

Conclusion: British Horror's Perpetually 'Dying Light'[1]

THERE WERE MULTIPLE indicators in the early 2010s that British horror had achieved a measure of cultural legitimacy. *The Woman in Black* was cited as 'an immovable obstacle at the top of the box-office charts' and further publicised as 'the biggest British horror title since accurate reporting began'.[2] Additionally, in November 2012, *Sight & Sound* featured a British horror film, Ben Wheatley's *Sightseers* (2012) on their cover (see Figure 6), as well as devoting a feature story to the film. The trend continued in 2013 and early 2014; in 2013, the magazine devoted three of its covers to British horror. June's cover featured Neil Jordan's *Byzantium* (a British/Irish/US co-production, 2012), while October displayed an iconic burning wicker man from the classic *The Wicker Man* (Robin Hardy, 1973). November was a special issue on the Gothic, and while a number of classic Gothic characters feature on the cover, Christopher Lee's Dracula has pride of place at the centre, his face double the size of the next largest face on the cover. A haunting image of Scarlett Johansson's character in *Under the Skin* graces the April 2014 cover. In comparison, between May 2014 and December 2019, there was only one more cover of *Sight & Sound* focused on British horror, 2016's April cover showcasing Ben Wheatley's *High Rise* (2015).

Figure 6. The cover of the November 2012 issue of *Sight & Sound*.

The Woman in Black was not the final horror film using transnational genre hybridity to come out of Britain – there was one last gasp in 2013, with *A Field in England* (Ben Wheatley) and *Under the Skin* (Jonathan Glazer). Like *Woman*, the transnational genre hybridity in both films positions them as *beyond* the national through their hybridisation of horror and art cinema. Art cinema tends to designate films that conspicuously differ from the formal and narrative norms of Hollywood film but maintain an element of commercial viability that experimental and avant-garde films eschew. Directors are often framed as auteurs with singular artistic vision that they work to express across the films in their *oeuvre*. Art cinema tends toward ambiguity, not only in terms of character motivation and plot resolution, but also extradiegetically in terms of nation. As Rosalind Galt and Karl Schoonover note in their collection, *Global Art Cinema*, this 'elastically hybrid category' 'demands that we watch across cultures and see ourselves through foreign eyes, binding spectatorship and pleasure into an experience of geographical difference, or potentially of geopolitical critique', even as it also works to 'draw our attention to the perils of thinking the global'.[3] Art cinema, then, is positioned as a key mode through which to think about the global, as well as the transnational.

Dubbed an 'art-horror hybrid' by critic Kim Newman, Wheatley's *A Field in England* fits the category, and not just because Wheatley patterned its black and white cinematography after 'arthouse films from the 60s and 70s' and Peter Watkins's *Culloden* (1964), which was meant for mass consumption but became an arthouse favourite.[4] Reminiscent of Michael Reeves's *Witchfinder General* (1968), particularly in terms of costuming, and set around the time of the English Civil War, the film is difficult to summarise. It tells the story of Whitehead (Reece Shearsmith), an alchemist's apprentice who meets several army deserters while searching for the alchemist (Michael Smiley) who stole some of his master's belongings. Fairy circles, psychedelic mushrooms and mind control feature heavily. In the end, after Whitehead defeats the alchemist in a mind-bending battle, he stumbles away from the scene only to see himself and two of his once-deceased colleagues standing beside each other, all in a row. Cause and effect have been suspended. Indeed, the film is aggressively ambiguous and contradictory, requiring audiences to participate actively in the construction of the film's meaning.

The film also calls attention to its formal play, particularly in terms of sound and editing. In several scenes, the characters remain still, in a variety of positions that convey the power dynamics most recently established within the group. These shots are *tableaux vivant*, not stills, as the wind causes their clothing and hair to flutter and the actors can be seen to breathe and move ever so slightly, insofar as it is not possible to hold completely still. Here, the divide between photo and film comes into sharp relief, as what we assume is a photograph is soon shown to be a live scene that can only partially freeze before our eyes. These scenes do not advance the narrative, breaking traditional mandates about narrative economy. The same could be said of the shots, scattered throughout the film, of the field itself, focusing on the stillness of the grass itself, or the way it, at times, ripples in the wind like waves in the ocean – these images, often shot low to the ground, are reminiscent of similar shots in Kaneto Shindô's famous art-horror film *Onibaba* (1964), a Japanese film that is also set in the past (during one of Japan's civil wars) and concerned with the occult. These shots serve to call attention to not only the film's self-conscious concern with the formal elements of film, but also its place within a longer lineage of films that hybridise the tropes of art cinema, historical drama and horror.

In the scene during and after Whitehead's ingestion of hallucinogenic mushrooms, the editing cuts from shot to shot at a lightning-fast pace to produce a viscerally nauseating, stroboscopic effect. At the end of the scene, as Whitehead's body is brought into itself, swallowed by the kaleidoscopic divide in the centre of the screen (see Figure 7), the high-pitched whistling wind-sound and metallic lowing drop out of the mix as a grinding sound and an organic, fleshy sound of tearing and squishing come to dominate. The scene culminates with Whitehead's body disappearing into the centre of the screen, followed by a cut to black timed with an audio cut to silence followed quickly by a clear popping sound. Reality itself has been altered, much as this kaleidoscopic sequence calls attention to how the filmic image can be manipulated in post-production.

As with *A Field in England*, Jonathan Glazer's *Under the Skin* is light on exposition. The film follows an unnamed alien (Scarlett Johansson) as she hunts men in Glasgow and the surrounding countryside before seemingly having an identity crisis and trying to escape her handler. It is not clear why the alien hunts down human men, nor what happens to their innards once they end up on the red-lit conveyor belt (or how they get there in the first place, or what the inky black room is). From its opening scene, the film positions itself as art cinema, in part by visually citing Stanley Kubrick's *2001: A Space Odyssey* (1968). A small, dim pinprick of light in the centre of the screen suddenly explodes into a bright blue light; a

Figure 7. Whitehead's body is turned into itself.

black ball drifts towards a white, doughnut-shaped object; suddenly, white light floods the screen and the white sphere and black sphere come into extreme close-up on the screen. The spheres shift on screen and darken, until white light again floods the screen, and we see that the spheres have come together to construct a human-like eye (see Figure 8). Throughout, a disembodied voice first recites letters, as though learning or testing, then words, all over a steady, droning, ominously mechanical soundtrack. As the eye's pupil dilates and contracts, the eye appears oddly more alien, rather than more human or organic, than when it is being constructed. Kubrick is evoked not only through the tight close-up on the constructed, robotic eye (as with *2001*'s HAL) and human-like eye (as with Bowman's eye during his final journey), but also the early shots where the component parts of the as-yet-unassembled eye look like planets in space, invoking the early planetary alignment scene in *2001*.

The alien's kills are visually striking; the men follow her into an inky black, seemingly dimension-less room, where they sink into the floor, underneath which they will slowly die, the innards sucked from their bodies, leaving behind only a floating skin sac in the twilight of the goo. Her hunting, though, is lensed using an observational documentary style, to great effect. Glazer filmed Johansson as she cruised around Glasgow in rumpled black wig, talking to unsuspecting strangers, capturing their unscripted conversations and Johansson's improvisations. This documentary style contrasts with the more visually experimental, stylised segments of the film. This contrast creates a productive tension by encouraging viewer immersion during the kill scenes, particularly through the suspenseful stringed accompaniment and slow, rhythmic drums, and then revoking that immersion and encouraging the viewer to be more aware of their position as a spectator during the hunting scenes.

The film's horror also asks the viewer to consider their position as spectator; the camera consistently disavows the male gaze and instead adopts a predatory gaze that is then aimed at men. From the van, viewers watch with the alien as she appraises hundreds of human men. We watch her coldly scan them, looking for weakness. The camera often takes on the alien's perspective during these scenes, and viewers begin to, or are encouraged to begin to, see these men through her eyes. This kind of point of view shot flips the traditional power dynamic of the camera's gaze, and without safely couching itself in a similar visual language of physical desire (like, for example, what has been described as a female gaze in Gregory Jacobs's 2015 film *Magic Mike XXL*). The men here are not sexualised,

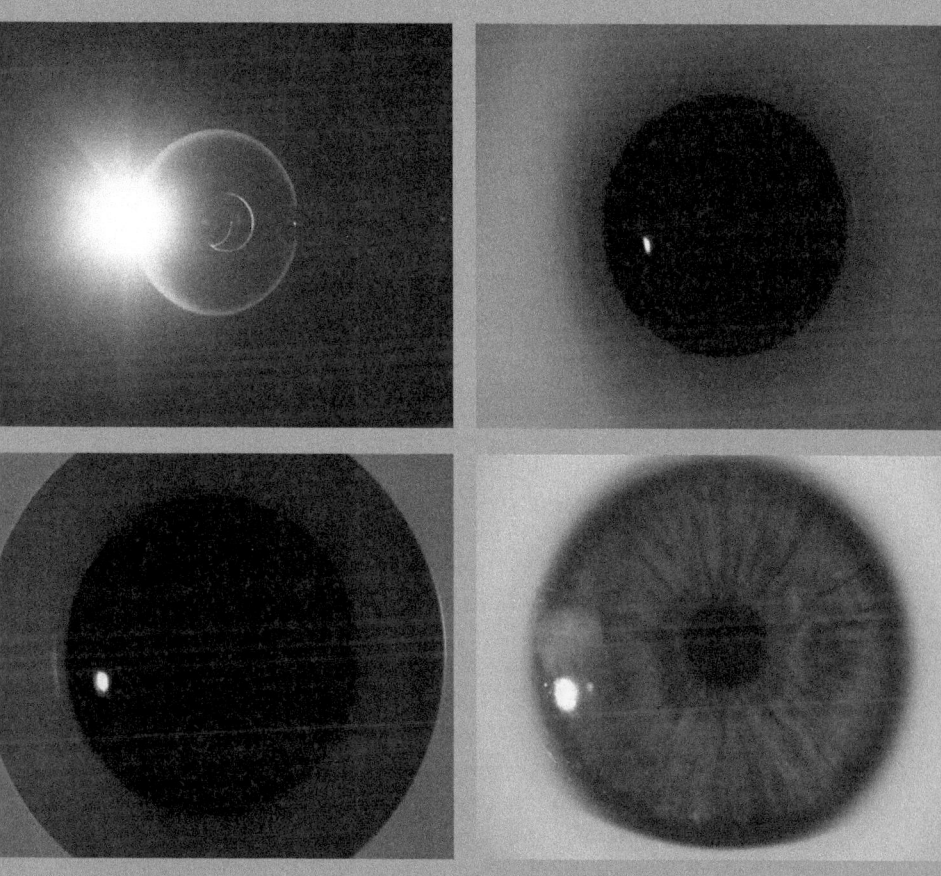

Figure 8. From left to right, top to bottom, making an eye in *Under the Skin*.

nor is the alien. The camerawork reveals the power dynamics that underlie the male gaze of traditional camerawork, which, without the excuse of sexualization, are more rooted in power, an attitude of superiority and the assumption of control. This formal experimentation, combined with the film's finale of attempted rape and murder, serve as a critique of the male gaze in horror, where it is far more common for the point-of-view shot to be used for men hunters to stalk their women prey.

Importantly, within middlebrow British film culture, *Under the Skin* was positioned by several critics as one of a set of films that demonstrated how the industry had been saved, playing into the saved/doomed binary. In a piece in *Variety* considering whether British critics had finally 'come around' on British film, writer and interviewer Leo Barraclough cites several British film critics who mention *Under the Skin* by name as part of a banner year for British film, one which produced films 'considerably better ... than the French' did (as the *Evening Standard*'s Derek Malcolm put it).[5] *Under the Skin* was used in a rhetorically similar way in Geoffrey Macnab's piece 'The British Are Coming! Again!' for *The Independent* – as one of a number of films contributing to a '"richness" of current British cinema' during a 'vintage period for independent and art house cinema' full of 'very strong director-driven films bound to stand the test of time'.[6] Finally, Ben Roberts used *Under the Skin*, including its long production history, to mount a defence of the UK's system of tax relief for films, as well as public film funding, positioning *Under the Skin* as 'tough sell' that may not have been made or released without tax relief and public funding, but which is nonetheless a film the industry can be proud of.[7] Indeed, the film was part of what led Film4 to subsequently sign a development deal with Glazer.[8]

Like *The Woman in Black*, both films use transnational genre hybridity to signal their Britishness as well as their global appeal – and significantly, while both films were discussed as fitting into the British horror resurgence, they were also seen as part of British cinema's new wave of art cinema. The mid-2000s saw a number of important art films released to critical acclaim, including Andrea Arnold's *Red Road* (2006), Shane Meadows's *This is England* (2006), Joanna Hogg's *Unrelated* (2007), Duane Hopkins's *Better Things* (2008), Meadows's *Somers Town* (2008), Steve McQueen's *Hunger* (2008), Gideon Koppel's *Sleep Furiously* (2008), Arnold's *Fish Tank* (2009) and Peter Strickland's *Katalin Varga* (2009).[9] Critics like *The Guardian*'s Andrew Pulver began to speculate in the late 2000s that British cinema was 'on the verge of a new wave', a 'rebirth of the British art film'. The wave would continue with films like Duncan Jones's UK/US co-production *Moon* (2009), Hogg's later film *Archipelago* (2010), Lynne Ramsay's *We Need to Talk about Kevin* (2011) and Strickland's *Berberian Sound Studio* (2012), as well as *A Field in England* and *Under the Skin*. As Pulver notes, the film-makers of this new wave of art cinema can be seen as heirs to the legacies of 1980s British art cinema auteurs like Derek Jarman, Peter Greenaway, Sally Potter and Terence Davies. We can also see them as heirs to the experimental legacies of late 1960s and early 1970s films like *Witchfinder General* (Michael Reeves, 1968) and *The Wicker Man* (Robin Hardy, 1973).

Hybridising the horror genre and art cinema mode represents a natural extension of the global turn in British horror's transnational genre hybridity – like *The Woman in Black*'s reliance on the globalgothic – even as it also works to firmly link horror to modern trends in British cinema. The move towards a transnational genre hybridity that marks itself out as simultaneously global and domestic, rooted in current trends and a longer national filmic history, shows that transnational genre hybridity built up British horror. It addressed concerns in British film culture that horror was not British enough, or culturally worthy, by self-consciously demonstrating that it was. And the hybridity between horror and art cinema demonstrated by these films represents a key development in the cultural legitimation of horror: the return of the horror auteur. While Hammer Studios's Terence Fisher has long been regarded as an auteur, and discussed as such by scholars like David Pirie and Peter Hutchings, his last horror film came out in 1974.[10] Certainly, arguments for his status as an auteur were an important part of why classic Hammer films, and other films of the era, achieved their current culturally elevated status.

Despite the scholarly debunking of classical auteur theory, auteurism persists as a key element of cultural capital within a variety of film cultures and some academic circles. Both Wheatley and Glazer have been singled out by middlebrow British film culture as potential auteurs. Glazer was held up as a hopeful to revive the British film industry by elevating the horror genre in the early 2000s, when he began the project that would eventually become *Under the Skin*.[11] Wheatley, on the other hand, only became a darling of British film culture after his second feature, the *Wicker Man*-inspired *Kill List* (2011), was a hit at the SXSW Film Festival; critics hoped, predictably, he could 'breathe life into Britain's film industry' through his innovative use of genre.[12] Soon after, he was named in *The Guardian*'s list of the '23 best film directors in the world today'.[13] It is important to note, though, that both directors have worked outside the horror genre, with feature-length debut crime films – Wheatley with *Down Terrace* (2009) and Glazer with *Sexy Beast* (2000). While they are talked about as burgeoning auteurs (Glazer has even been hailed as the 'new Kubrick'), before 2013, they had not been talked about as horror auteurs; the emphasis fell on how their personal vision allowed them to act as 'genre-redefining figure[s]'.[14] Their status as auteur allows for a discursive redemption of their status as directors of horror films, as British horror's turn toward art cinema helps the genre to solicit prestige.

Transnational genre hybridity played a vital part in allowing horror to gain a measure of cultural legitimacy, and it was used by the most successful films of the period, but it was not a dominant practice. And after 2013, British horror film-makers' use of the strategy appears to have come to an end, or at least an extended pause. In part, it had served its purpose by engaging with and countering and changing, though not fully dismantling, the anti-Americanisation, saved/doomed binary and anti-horror discourses in middlebrow British film culture. Increasing streaming opportunities, and the increasing difficulty of cracking cinema screens dominated by Hollywood studio mega-franchises, likely also played a part.

Since 2013, film-makers have produced numerous British horror films that have been successful critically, financially or both. These films include, but are not limited to: international co-productions, including the British/Irish/French co-production *The Little Stranger* (Lenny Abrahamson, 2018), some directed by international directors like André Øvredal (*The Autopsy of Jane Doe*, 2016) and Yorgos Lanthimos (*The Killing of a Sacred Deer*, 2017); US/UK co-productions from directors like Johannes Roberts, who directed *The Other Side of the Door* (2016), *47 Meters Down* (2017), *47 Meters Down: Uncaged* (2019); the wave of women horror directors, including Alice Lowe (*Prevenge*, 2016), Kate Shenton (*Egomaniac*, 2016) and Aislinn Clarke (*The Devil's Doorway*, 2018); genre hybrids like *The Girl With All the Gifts* (Colm McCarthy, 2016), *Anna and the Apocalypse* (John McPhail, 2017) and the sublime *Annihilation* (Alex Garland, 2018); and innovative horror like the incredible *Under the Shadow* (Babak Anvari, 2016), *Ghost Stories* (Jeremy Dyson and Andy Nyman, 2017) and *In Fabric* (Peter Strickland, 2018).

Surveying the key books on the British horror film, it seems unsafe to issue any predictions about the future of the genre. David Pirie's original *A Heritage of Horror*, published in 1973, ended by expressing the hope that Gothic horror would continue to be successful at the box office. The genre was subsequently decimated by the film industry crisis of the mid-1970s.

On the other hand, Steve Chibnall and Julian Petley's excellent edited collection *British Horror Cinema*, published in 2002, ends with the prophetic-feeling 'Dying Light: An Obituary for the Great British Horror Movie', from Richard Stanley – a prophecy which turned out to be exactly wrong, since the genre was on the verge of an unpredicted resurgence. I have no plans, then, to issue any predictions of my own as to the future success or failure of British horror cinema.

But I will issue a small plea to middlebrow British film culture. British horror may be a perpetually dying light, a candle flickering, shining bright one second and guttering the next. Perhaps that is the struggle of film-making outside a mega-industry like Hollywood, Bollywood or China. But I would argue this condition has less to do with the films and film-makers themselves and everything to do with the way that middlebrow British film culture sees fit to frame British horror. Writers continue to frame the genre by asking, during boom periods of production and critical acclaim, whether these films 'can ever really compete with their US rivals'.[15] And yet, despite the pervasiveness of the anti-Americanisation discourse, these same critics became positively besotted with the 'elevated' horror coming out of the US starting in 2014, with films like David Robert Mitchell's *It Follows* (2014) and Robert Eggers's *The Witch* (2015). In 2015, in *Sight & Sound*, Ben Roberts praises *It Follows* in one breath and in the following laments that 'we're not making films like it here, and we could'.[16] But British film-makers were already making, to use Roberts's words, 'intelligent and unnerving' films; they had been since 2000. Some writers in middlebrow British film culture are more interested in painting a picture of a doomed industry than championing the good work being done in British horror. That is good for neither British horror nor a healthy British film culture.

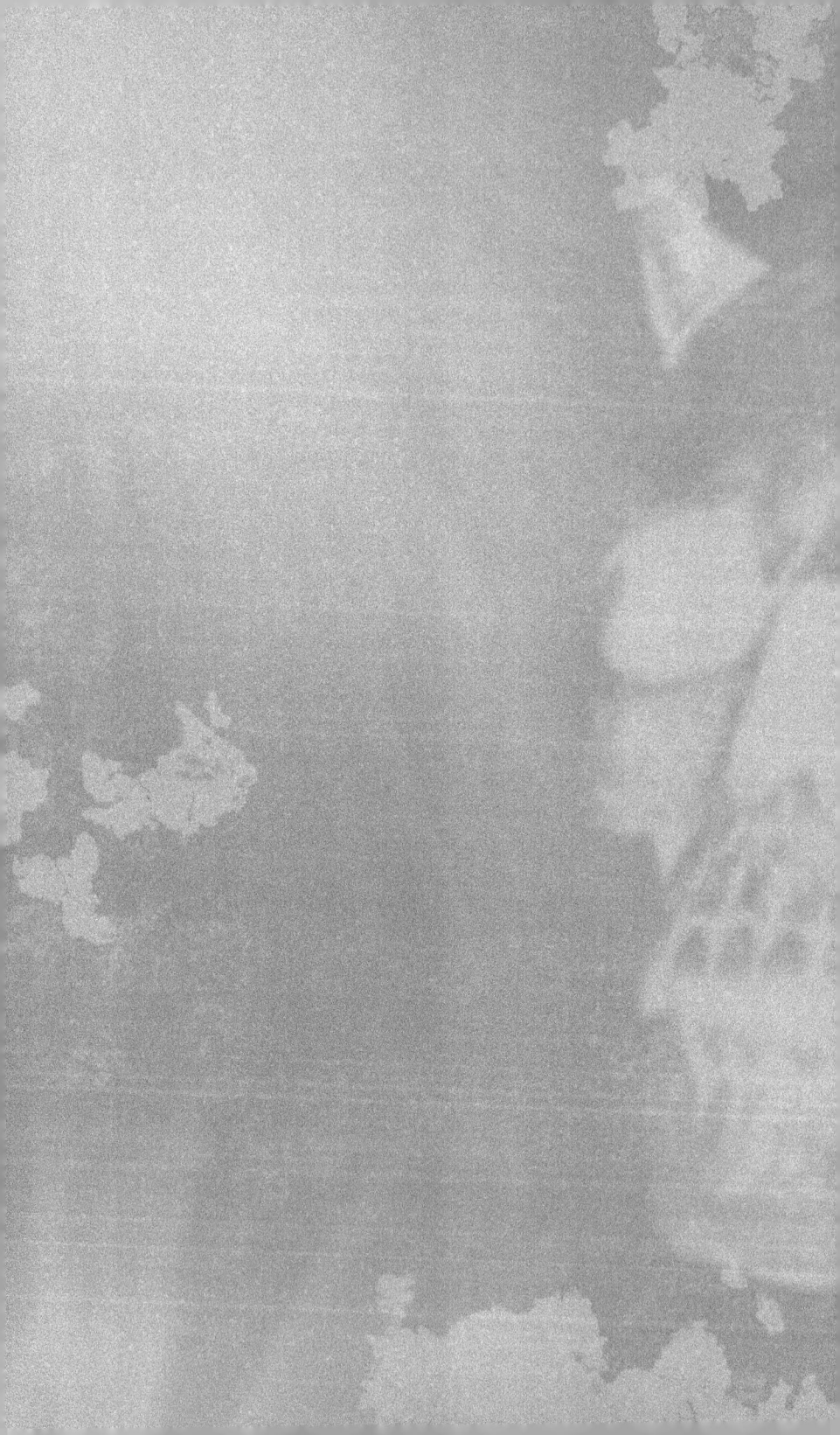

Notes

Introduction

1. James Leggott, *Contemporary British Cinema: From Heritage to Horror* (London: Wallflower, 2008), p. 61.
2. Geoffrey Macnab, 'A Bloodthirsty Bunch of Fans', *The Independent*, 4 November 2005. Anne Billson, 'A Feast of Horror', *The Telegraph*, 4 May 2008.
3. Andrew Higson, 'The Limiting Imagination of National Cinema', in Mette Hjort and Scott MacKenzie (eds), *Cinema and Nation* (New York: Routledge, 2000), p. 63.
4. See Elizabeth Ezra and Terry Rowden (eds), *Transnational Cinema: The Film Reader* (London: Routledge, 2006); Nataša Durovicová and Kathleen E. Newman (eds), *World Cinemas, Transnational Perspectives* (Abingdon, UK: Routledge, 2009); Rosalind Galt and Karl Schoonover (eds), *Global Art Cinema: New Theories and Histories* (New York: Oxford University Press, 2010); and Iain Robert Smith, *Hollywood Meme* (Edinburgh: Edinburgh University Press, 2017).
5. Deborah Shaw, 'Deconstructing and Reconstructing "Transnational Cinema"', in Stephanie Dennison (ed.), *Contemporary Hispanic Cinema: Interrogating the Transnational in Spanish and Latin American Film* (Rochester: Tamesis, 2013), pp. 47–65; Deborah Shaw, 'Transnational Cinema: Mapping a Field of Study', in Rob Stone, Paul Cooke, Stephanie Dennison and Alix Marlow-Mann (eds), *Routledge Companion to World Cinema* (New York: Routledge, 2017), pp. 290–8; Will Higbee and Song Hwee Lim, 'Concepts

of Transnational Cinema: Towards a Critical Transnationalism in Film Studies', *Transnational Cinemas*, 1/1 (2010), 7–21; Mette Hjort, 'On the Plurality of Cinematic Transnationalisms', in Nataša Ďurovičová and Kathleen E. Newman (eds), *World Cinemas, Transnational Perspectives* (Abingdon, UK: Routledge, 2009), pp. 12–33; Austin Fisher and Iain Robert Smith, 'Transnational Cinemas: A Critical Roundtable', *Frames Cinema Journal*, 9 (2016), n. p., framescinemajournal.com/article/transnational-cinemas-a-critical-roundtable/; Austin Fisher and Iain Robert Smith, 'Second Phase Transnationalism: Reflections on Launching the SCMS Transnational Cinemas Scholarly Interest Group', *Transnational Screens*, 10/2 (2019), 114–25.
6. Deborah Shaw, 'Deconstructing and Reconstructing "Transnational Cinema"', pp. 54 and 58–9.
7. Mette Hjort, 'On the Plurality of Cinematic Transnationalisms', p. 13.
8. Lindsey Decker, 'Ana Lily Amirpour's Transnational Gaze', in Alison Peirse, *Women Make Horror* (Newark, NJ: Rutgers University Press, forthcoming).
9. Andrew Higson, *Waving the Flag* (Oxford: Clarendon Press, 1995), pp. 278–9.
10. British Film Institute, 'Summary of Cultural Test Points', *British Film Institute*, www.bfi.org.uk/film-industry/british-certification-tax-relief/cultural-test-film (accessed 5 January 2020).
11. Sarah Street, *British National Cinema* (New York: Routledge, 2009), p. 1.
12. John Hill, 'British Cinema as National Cinema: Production, Audience and Representation', in Robert Murphy (ed.), *The British Cinema Book* (New York: Palgrave Macmillan, 2009), p. 19.
13. Susan Hayward, 'Framing National Cinemas', in Mette Hjort and Scott MacKenzie (eds), *Cinema and Nation* (New York: Routledge, 2000), p. 88.
14. Ian Conrich, 'Traditions of the British Horror Films', in Robert Murphy (ed.), *The British Cinema Book* (New York: Palgrave Macmillan, 2009), p. 104. John Fitzgerald, *Studying British Cinema: 1999–2009* (London: Auteur, 2010); Pirie, *A New Heritage of Horror* (New York: I.B. Tauris, 2007), p. 224. Leggott, *Contemporary British Cinema*, p. 59.
15. Lucy Mazdon, '"Kings of the Middle Way": Continental Cinema on British Screens', in Sally Faulkner (ed.), *Middlebrow Cinema* (New York: Routledge, 2016), p. 184.
16. Mazdon, '"Kings of the Middle Way"', p. 182.
17. Janet Harbord, *Film Cultures* (London: Sage, 2002).
18. See Chapter 1 for a more detailed discussion.
19. Ryan Gilbey, '"Yes, We Did Betray Ewan"', *The Independent*, 25 October 2002.

20. Laurence Phelan, 'Five Best Revivals', *The Independent*, 13 September 2008. Peter Bradshaw, 'Film Reviews: In Too Deep', *The Guardian*, 12 September 2008.
21. Jane Graham, 'Too Cool for School', *The Guardian*, 6 May 2011. Peter Bradshaw, 'Film Reviews: Enemies of the State', *The Guardian*, 13 May 2011.
22. Phil Hoad, 'The *Cabin in the Woods* Shows Horror Speaks an International Language', *The Guardian*, 10 April 2012.
23. See Johnny Walker, 'Low Budgets, No Budgets and Digital-video Nasties: Recent British Horror and Informal Distribution', in Richard Nowell (ed.), *Merchants of Menace* (New York: Bloomsbury, 2014), pp. 215–28.
24. M. J. Simpson, *Urban Terrors: New British Horror Cinema, 1998–2002* (Baltimore, MD: Midnight Marquee Press, 2013).
25. John Fitzgerald, *Studying British Cinema: 1999–2009*; James Rose, *Beyond Hammer* (Leighton Buzzard, UK: Auteur, 2009); Ian Cooper, *Frightmares: A History of British Horror Cinema* (Leighton Buzzard, UK: Auteur, 2016); James Leggott, *Contemporary British Cinema*; Barry Forshaw, *British Gothic Cinema* (New York: Palgrave Macmillan, 2013).
26. Steven Gerrard, *The Modern British Horror Film* (Newark, NJ: Rutgers University Press, 2017).
27. Peter Hutchings, *Hammer and Beyond: The British Horror Film* (New York: St Martin's Press, 1993), p. 24.
28. Hutchings, *Hammer and Beyond*, pp. 38–9.
29. Alison Peirse, 'The Feminine Appeal of British Horror Cinema', *New Review of Film and Television Studies*, 13/4 (2015), 387.
30. Hutchings, *Hammer and Beyond*, p. 1.
31. I. Q. Hunter, *British Trash Cinema* (London: Palgrave Macmillan, 2013), p. 9.
32. Pirie, *A New Heritage of Horror*, p. 202.
33. Pirie, *A New Heritage of Horror*, p. 202.
34. Steve Chibnall and Julian Petley, 'Return of the Repressed? British Horror's Heritage and Future', in Steve Chibnall and Julian Petley (eds), *British Horror Cinema* (New York: Routledge, 2002), p. 8.
35. Richard Stanley, 'Dying Light: An Obituary for the Great British Horror Movie', in Steve Chibnall and Julian Petley (eds), *British Horror Cinema* (New York: Routledge, 2002), p. 194.
36. Rose, *Beyond Hammer*, pp. 7–9.
37. Linnie Blake, *The Wounds of Nations* (New York: Manchester University Press, 2008), p. 158.
38. Johnny Walker, *Contemporary British Horror Cinema: Industry, Genre and Society* (Edinburgh: Edinburgh University Press, 2016).

39. Here I reference Hutchings's chapter title, 'For Sadists Only? The Problem of British Horror', from *Hammer and Beyond*.
40. Adam Minns, 'UK Production Trend Develops into Horror', *Screen International*, 29 November 2001.
41. James Russell, 'Hollywood Blockbusters and UK Production Today', in I. Q. Hunter, Laraine Porter and Justin Smith, *The Routledge Companion to British Cinema History* (New York: Routledge, 2017), p. 377.
42. See Mark Kermode, *The Good, The Bad and The Multiplex* (London: Random House, 2011).
43. Kermode, *The Good, The Bad and The Multiplex*, p. 227.
44. Kermode, *The Good, The Bad and The Multiplex*, p. 234.
45. Mark Glancy, *Hollywood and the Americanization of Britain: From the 1920s to the Present* (New York: I.B. Tauris, 2014), pp. 3–4 and 17–18.
46. Genevieve Abravanel, *Americanizing Britain: The Rise of Modernism in the Age of the Entertainment Empire* (Oxford: Oxford University Press, 2012), pp. 3–4.
47. Abravanel, *Americanizing Britain*, p. 8. 'Home Rule for Britain', *World Film News* 2/8 (November 1937), p. 5, unavailable to this author despite valiant searching, quoted in Abravanel, p. 181, footnote five to chapter three. Same quotation cited from the same source, quoted in James Stone, '"I Used to Like Gangsters and Newspaper Films, But I'm Not So Sure Now": The Hollywood Dreams of Jessie Matthews and the British Film Industry', in Rocío G. Davis (ed.), *The Transnationalism of American Culture: Literature, Film, and Music* (New York: Routledge, 2013), p. 78.
48. Tom Ryall, *Britain and the American Cinema* (Thousand Oaks, CA: SAGE, 2001), p. 154.
49. Abravanel, *Americanizing Britain*, p. 1.
50. Ryall, *Britain and the American Cinema*, p. 19.
51. Glancy, *Hollywood and the Americanization of Britain*, p. 5.
52. Richard Nowell (ed.), *Merchants of Menace* (New York: Bloomsbury, 2014); Dana Och and Kirsten Strayer (eds), *Transnational Horror across Visual Media: Fragmented Bodies* (New York: Routledge, 2014); Sophia Siddique and Raphael Raphael (eds), *Transnational Horror Cinema: Bodies of Excess and the Global Grotesque* (London: Palgrave Macmillan, 2016).
53. Nick James, 'British Cinema's US Surrender – A View from 2001', in Robert Murphy (ed.), *The British Cinema Book* (New York: Palgrave Macmillan, 2009), p. 27. Ryan Gilbey, 'The New Wave of British Horror Films', *The Guardian*, 10 June 2010.

Chapter 1 The 'Bastard Child of Mainstream Cinema'

1. John Hamilton, *X-Cert: The British Independent Horror Film 1951–1970* (Baltimore, MD: Midnight Marquee Press, 2012), p. 208.
2. Geoffrey Nowell-Smith and Christophe Dupin, 'Introduction', in Geoffrey Nowell-Smith and Christophe Dupin (eds), *The British Film Institute, Government and Film Culture, 1933–2010* (New York: Manchester University Press, 2012), p. 1.
3. Geoffrey Nowell-Smith, 'The *Sight & Sound* Story, 1932–1992', in Geoffrey Nowell-Smith and Christophe Dupin (eds), *The British Film Institute, Government and Film Culture, 1933–2010* (New York: Manchester University Press, 2012), p. 250.
4. Based on data for print readership from the National Readership Survey (NRS), historical data accessible via *www.nrs.co.uk*. ABC1 refers to NRS reader designations for upper middle class (A), middle class (B) and lower middle class (C1).
5. See '*The Guardian* and *Observer* Reader Profile', *image.guardian.co.uk/sys-files/Guardian/documents/2012/08/22/Printreaderprofile.pdf* (accessed 5 January 2020).
6. Data on *The Guardian* is from 2013 and is available from their website, both in the story '*The Guardian*, Our Readers and Circulation', *www.theguardian.com/advertising/guardian-circulation-readership-statistics* (accessed 5 January 2020), and in '*The Guardian* and *Observer* Reader Profile'. Data on *Sight & Sound* is from their 2011 readership survey, the data for which is available from *Sight & Sound* in their Media Pack, available from the magazine by request.
7. '*Screen International* Media Information 2012', originally accessed via the *Screen Daily* website, now available via the Internet Archive, *https://web.archive.org/web/20130420073849/www.screendaily.com/Journals/2012/03/08/t/a/y/SCRN122-Screen-media-pack-2012.pdf* (accessed 5 January 2020).
8. David Pirie, *A Heritage of Horror: The English Gothic Cinema 1946–1972* (London: Gordon Fraser, 1973).
9. Charles Barr, *All Our Yesterdays* (London: BFI, 1986). Peter Hutchings, *Hammer and Beyond: The British Horror Film* (New York: St Martin's Press, 1993).
10. Jonathan Rigby, *English Gothic: A Century of Horror Cinema* (Surrey: Reynolds & Hearn, 2000); Steve Chibnall and Julian Petley (eds), *British Horror Cinema* (New York: Routledge, 2002); David Pirie, *A New Heritage of Horror* (New York: I.B. Tauris, 2007).

11. John Hill, *British Cinema in the 1980s* (Oxford: Clarendon Press, 1999), p. 43.
12. Budget data from John Pym, *Film on Four 1982/1991* (London: BFI, 1992), pp. 116–18.
13. Box office information taken from the Internet Movie Database (IMDB).
14. Sarah Street and Margaret Dickinson, *Cinema and State: The Film Industry and the Government 1927–1984* (London: BFI, 1985), p. 247.
15. *Film Policy*, Cmnd 9319 (London: HMSO, 1984).
16. See HC Deb. 19 July 1984, vol. 64, col. 523, hansard.millbanksystems.com/commons/1984/jul/19/film-industry-policy (accessed 5 January 2020), and HL Deb. 19 July 1984, vol. 454, cols 1643–5, hansard.millbanksystems.com/lords/1984/jul/19/film-industry (accessed 5 January 2020).
17. Sarah Street, *British National Cinema* (New York: Routledge, 2009), p. 19.
18. Street, *British National Cinema*, p. 19.
19. Hill, *British Cinema in the 1980s*, pp. 35–6.
20. See HC Deb. 19 July 1984, vol. 64, col. 525, hansard.millbanksystems.com/commons/1984/jul/19/film-industry-policy (accessed 5 January 2020).
21. Hill, *British Cinema in the 1980s*, p. 39.
22. Mark Sweney, 'Big-Screen Boom: UK Cinemas on Track for Best Year Since 1971', *The Guardian*, 14 December 2018.
23. Phil Hoad, 'How Multiplex Cinemas Saved the British Film Industry 25 Years Ago', *The Guardian*, 11 November 2010.
24. Alan Stanbrook, 'When the Lease Runs Out', *Sight & Sound*, summer 1984, 172–3.
25. This quotation is unattributed but several publications quoted it as being said in the meeting. It may have been spoken by Lew Wasserman, CEO of MCA, then the parent company of Universal. See 'An Active Agenda', *Screen International*, 23 June 1990.
26. Derek Malcolm, 'Mrs. Thatcher's Saving Grace?', *The Guardian*, 14 June 1990.
27. 'UK Film Back on Political Agenda' and Ralf Ludemann, 'US Product Gains Ground in European Territories', *Screen International*, 2 June 1990.
28. 'Editorial: Made in Europe', *Sight & Sound*, February 1992, 3.
29. Nowell-Smith, 'The *Sight & Sound* Story', p. 247.
30. Nowell-Smith, 'The *Sight & Sound* Story', p. 250.
31. Ajax Scott, 'Blue Moves', *Screen International*, 17 April 1992, 9–11.
32. Scott, 'Blue Moves', 9.
33. Michael Relph, 'A Major Step For British Film', *Screen International*, 24 April 1992, 6.

34. 'Editorial: In Bed Together', *Sight & Sound*, June 1992, 3.
35. Alan Burton and Steve Chibnall, 'Palace Pictures', in *The Historical Dictionary of British Cinema* (Lanham, MD: Scarecrow Press, 2013), p. 323.
36. British Film Institute, 'Palace Pictures', BFI *Screen Online*, www.screenonline. org.uk/film/id/477684 (accessed 5 January 2020).
37. This quotation from Justice Morland was reported in numerous newspaper accounts of the trial, but I have taken it from Edward Pilkington, 'Boys Guilty of Bulger Murder – Detention Without Limit for "Unparalleled Evil"', *The Guardian*, 25 November 1993, reprinted at *The Guardian Online* in the section on original trial reports from the James Bulger Murder, www.theguardian. com/uk/1993/nov/25/bulger1 (accessed 5 January 2020).
38. Steve Simkin, 'Wake of the Flood: Key Issues in UK Censorship, 1970-5', in Edward Lamberti (ed.), *Behind the Scenes at the BBFC: Film Classification from the Silver Screen to the Digital Age* (London: BFI, 2012), p. 86.
39. Letter from Stephen Murphy, BBFC Director, to the distributor, 1 June 1973, BBFC file: *Bloody Friday*. Quoted in Simkin, 'Wake of the Flood', p. 86. Letter from Stephen Murphy, BBFC Director, to the distributor, 8 July 1974, BBFC file: *The Last House on the Left*. Quoted in Simkin, 'Wake of the Flood', p. 86.
40. Guy Osborn and Alex Sinclair, 'The "Poacher Turned Gamekeeper": James Ferman and the Increasing Intervention of the Law', in Edward Lamberti (ed.), *Behind the Scenes at the BBFC: Film Classification from the Silver Screen to the Digital Age* (London: BFI, 2012), pp. 94–5.
41. Julian Petley, *Film and Video Censorship in Modern Britain* (Edinburgh: Edinburgh University Press, 2011), p. 17.
42. Mark Kermode, 'The British Censors and Horror Cinema', in Steve Chibnall and Julian Petley (eds), *British Horror Cinema* (New York: Routledge, 2002), p. 17.
43. Petley, *Film and Video Censorship in Modern Britain*, p. 23. Peter Chippendale, 'How High Street Horror Is Invading the Home', *The Sunday Times*, 30 May 1982.
44. Petley, *Film and Video Censorship in Modern Britain*, pp. 18–19.
45. Michael Brooke, 'The Video Nasties', *BFI Screen Online*, www.screenonline. org.uk/film/id/591919/ (accessed 5 January 2020).
46. Petley, *Film and Video Censorship in Modern Britain*, pp. 24 and 29.
47. Petley, *Film and Video Censorship in Modern Britain*, p. 45. Originally published as 'Two or Three Things I Know About "Video Nasties"', *Monthly Film Bulletin*, April 1984, pp. 350–2.
48. Petley, *Film and Video Censorship in Modern Britain*, p. 19.

49. Petley, *Film and Video Censorship in Modern Britain*, p. 108.
50. See the discussion of this incident in 'Editorial: The Sensible Party', *Sight & Sound*, May 1994, 3.
51. David Sharrock, Maggie O'Kane and Edward Pilkington, 'Two Youngsters Who Found a New Rule to Break', *The Guardian*, 25 November 1993.
52. 'Judge's Remarks Prompt MPs' Horror Video Curb Call', *The Guardian*, 25 November 1993.
53. Barrie Gunter and Jill McAleer, *Children and Television* (London: Routledge, 1997), p. 94.
54. Sally Weale, '*Child's Play 3* – The Movie', *The Guardian*, 26 November 1993.
55. See Paula Skidmore, 'Report: The "Effects" Tradition – Its Problems, Politics and Supersession, London, 26–27 November 1994', *Screen*, 36/2 (summer 1995), 156–8.
56. David Elstein, 'Demonising a Decoy', *The Guardian*, 22 December 1993.
57. Julian Petley, 'Who's Behind the "Nasty" Panic?', *The Guardian*, 27 December 1993.
58. 'Opinion: Danger Signals', *Screen International*, 4 February 1994. 'Opinion: Political Hot Line', *Screen International*, 22 April 1994.
59. 'Editorial: Rewinding the Panic', *Sight & Sound*, January 1994, 3.
60. Criminal Justice and Public Order Act 1994 (c. 33), Part VII, s. 90(1), inserting s. 4A(1)–(2) into the Video Recordings Act 1984 (c. 39): available from Legislation.Gov.UK, *www.legislation.gov.uk/ukpga/1994/33/part/VII/crossheading/video-recordings/enacted* (accessed 5 January 2020).
61. Kermode, 'The British Censors and Horror Cinema', p. 20.
62. Kay Dickinson, *Off Key: When Film and Music Won't Work Together* (Oxford: Oxford University Press, 2008), p. 87.
63. 'Editorial: Cinema Wars', *Sight & Sound*, November 1993, 3.
64. 'Needing to Make a Free Trade Mark', *The Guardian*, 15 November 1993.
65. Quoted in 'GATT Away!' *Screen International*, 1 October 1993.
66. Michael Billington, 'Last Chance Saloon', *The Guardian*, 11 December 1993.
67. Michael Relph, 'Home Truths', *Screen International*, 1 October 1993.
68. Harbord, *Film Cultures* (London: Sage, 2002), pp. 104–5.
69. The discourse of American cultural products as invaders is pervasive, but the particular phrasing here is taken from Zoe Hall's 'Jurassic Perplexity: Cinema Is Not A Tin of Peas', *The Guardian*, 29 December 1993. Frederick Studemann, 'Resist Hollywood or Bust, Film-Makers Warn; Cinema in Europe Fading Out As America's Cultural Invaders Snatch the Big Box Office. Guardian Reporters Ask If the Cameras Must Stop Rolling Across the Continent', *The Guardian*, 19 February 1994.

70. Nick Roddick, 'Welcome to the Multiplex', *Sight & Sound*, June 1994, 26.
71. David Puttnam, 'Puttnam: A Lesson in Positive Thinking', *Screen International*, 17 December 1993.
72. Andy Medhurst, 'Spaced Out', *Sight & Sound*, June 1993, 45.
73. While I've tried to correctly identify the national backgrounds of various contributors, I am drawing from existing public data and regret any potential errors here.
74. Paul Giles, 'History With Holes', in Lester Friedman (ed.), *Fires Were Started: British Cinema and Thatcherism* (Minneapolis, MN: U of Minnesota P, 1993), p. 84.
75. Mary Desjardins, 'Free From the Apron Strings', in Lester Friedman (ed.), *Fires Were Started: British Cinema and Thatcherism* (Minneapolis, MN: University of Minnesota Press, 1993), p. 139.
76. '1995: Killer Ronnie Kray Dies', *BBC News, BBC On This Day Online*, 17 March 1995, news.bbc.co.uk/onthisday/hi/dates/stories/march/17/newsid_2524000/2524249.stm (accessed 5 January 2020).
77. Dick Hobbs, 'Obituary: Ron Kray', *The Independent*, 18 March 1995.
78. Susan Torrey Barber, 'The Films of Stephen Frears', in Lester Friedman (ed.), *Fires Were Started: British Cinema and Thatcherism* (Minneapolis, MN: University of Minnesota Press, 1993), p. 226.
79. Local Government Act 1988 (c. 9), Part IV, section 28, www.legislation.gov.uk/ukpga/1988/9/section/28 (accessed 5 January 2020).
80. Manthia Diawara, 'Power and Territory', in Lester Friedman (ed.), *Fires Were Started: British Cinema and Thatcherism* (Minneapolis, MN: University of Minnesota Press, 1993), p. 149.
81. Medhurst, 'Spaced Out', 45.
82. Christopher Bray, 'Always Miserable', *The Times Literary Supplement*, 15 October 1993.
83. Jane Sillars, 'Review', *Screen*, 35/1 (1994), 109.
84. Jane Sillars, 'Review', 110.
85. Jane Sillars, 'Review', 110.
86. Google Scholar, 'Andrew Higson – Google Scholar Citations', scholar.google.com/scholar?cites=5715149606530011462&as_sdt=5,33&sciodt=0,33&hl=en (accessed 5 January 2020).
87. Maggie Magor and Philip Schlesinger, '"For This Relief Much Thanks": Taxation, Film Policy and the UK Government', *Screen*, 50/3 (fall 2009), 304.
88. Magor and Schlesinger, '"For This Relief Much Thanks"', 305.
89. Dan Glaister, 'Boom or Bust Time for British Movie Makers', *The Guardian*, 24 December 1997.

90. Louise Tutt, 'High Hopes in UK After Labour Election Victory', *Screen International*, 9 May 1997.
91. 'Editorial: An Even Break', *Sight & Sound*, August 1997, 3.
92. Stuart Kemp, 'Strainspotting?', *Screen International*, 22 August 1997.
93. 'Table of Contents', *Sight & Sound*, October 1998, 1.
94. Geoffrey Nowell-Smith, 'Towards the Millennium', in Geoffrey Nowell-Smith and Christophe Dupin (eds), *The British Film Institute, Government and Film Culture, 1933–2010* (New York: Manchester University Press, 2012), pp. 294–5.
95. Nowell-Smith, 'Towards the Millennium', pp. 296–7.
96. Quoting a Home Office spokeswoman, in Lucy War, 'Chief Censor Accuses Home Secretary of Blocking Liberalisation Moves', *The Guardian*, 13 January 1998.
97. Quoted in Dan Glaister, 'Controversial Ferman Quits as Chief Film Censor', *The Guardian*, 28 March 1998.
98. Mark Kermode and Julian Petley, 'The Censor and the State', *Sight & Sound*, May 1998, 14.
99. Kermode and Petley, 'The Censor and the State', 14.
100. Kamal Ahmed, 'Film Violence Link to Teenage Crime', *The Guardian*, 8 January 1998.
101. 'New Labour, New Austerity?', *Screen International*, 23 January 1998.
102. Glaister, 'Controversial Ferman Quits as Chief Film Censor', p. 2.
103. See Colin Hughes, 'Jack Straw: Jack of All Tirades', *The Guardian*, 24 July 1999.
104. Brian Pendreigh, 'Everything Was in Place for a Clampdown on Sex and Violence. So Where Is It?', *The Guardian*, 30 April 1999.
105. See the cover of *Sight & Sound*, July 1998.
106. Pendreigh, 'Everything Was in Place', p. 106.
107. Petley, *Film and Video Censorship in Modern Britain*, p. 167. Originally published as '"The Way Things Are Now": An Interview with Robin Duval', *Sight & Sound*, December 2001.
108. Mark Kermode, 'My Life of Porn and Violence', *The Observer*, 18 September 2004.
109. Andy Richards, 'Lighthouse', *Sight & Sound*, August 2002, 43.
110. Nowell-Smith, 'Towards the Millennium', pp. 299–300.
111. Nowell-Smith, 'Towards the Millennium', p. 300.
112. 'Editorial: Gangbusters', *Sight & Sound*, May 2000.
113. Fiachra Gibbons, 'Help For Film Makers Taking on Hollywood', *The Guardian*, 2 May 2000.

114. This incident is discussed in numerous publications across the decades. For this iteration, see Jonathan Romney, 'Box Office Isn't Everything', *The Guardian*, 5 May 2000.
115. Street, *British National Cinema*, p. 27. For the statistical information here, see IMDB.
116. 'British Film Industry Will Suffer If the Government Closes the UK Film Council', *The Telegraph*, 5 August 2010.
117. Quoted in Mark Brown and Maev Kennedy, 'UK Film Council Axed', *The Guardian*, 26 July 2010.
118. Johnny Walker, 'A Wilderness of Horrors? British Horror Cinema in the New Millennium', *Journal of British Cinema and Television*, 9/3 (2012), 441.
119. Quoting Katie Hayes, Film4's Marketing Manager for Drama and Acquisitions. Quoted in Wendy Mitchell, 'Film4 Signs on as Headline Sponsor for UK's FrightFest', *Screen International*, 8 May 2007.
120. Ryan Gilbey, 'British Cinema Special: Reasons to Be Cheerful', *Sight & Sound*, October 2002, 14.
121. Walker, 'A Wilderness of Horrors?', 442.
122. Walker, 'A Wilderness of Horrors?', 442.
123. Robert Murphy, summarising Geoff Brown's chapter in his introduction to *British Cinema of the 90س*. Robert Murphy, 'Introduction', in Robert Murphy (ed.), *British Cinema of the 90s* (London: BFI, 2000), p. ix.

Chapter 2 The Golden Age of British Cinema is Undead

1. Nick Roddick, 'Mr. Busy: Another Scary Movie', *Sight & Sound*, January 2009, 14.
2. Danny Boyle, 'Director Danny Boyle Here. Hello Reddit! AMA', *Reddit*, 15 March 2013, www.reddit.com/r/IAmA/comments/1acxl7/director_danny_boyle_here_hello_reddit_ama/ (accessed 5 January 2020).
3. Andrew Higson, *Waving the Flag* (Oxford: Clarendon Press, 1995).
4. Linnie Blake, *The Wounds of Nations* (New York: Manchester University Press, 2008), pp. 166 and 173.
5. Nicole LaRose, 'Gangsters, Zombies, and Other Rebels: Alternative Communities in Late Twentieth-Century British Novels and Films' (PhD dissertation, University of Florida, 2006), p. 75; Barbara Korte, 'Envisioning a Black Tomorrow? Black Mother Figures and the Issues of Representation in *28 Days Later* (2003) and *Children of Men* (2006)', in Lars Eckstein, Barbara

Korte, Eva Uldrike Pirker and Christoph Reinfandt (eds), *Multi-Ethnic Britain 2000+: New Perspectives in Literature, Film and the Arts* (New York: Rodopi, 2008), pp. 332–4.
6. Blake, *The Wounds of Nations*, p. 169.
7. Kim Edwards, 'Moribundity, Mundanity and Modernity: *Shaun of the Dead*', *Screen Education*, 50 (January 2008), 103.
8. Johnny Walker, *Contemporary British Horror Cinema: Industry, Genre and Society* (Edinburgh: Edinburgh University Press, 2016), pp. 20–1.
9. Peter Dendle, 'The Zombie as Barometer of Cultural Anxiety', in Niall Scott (ed.), *Monsters and the Monstrous: Myths and Metaphors of Enduring Evil* (New York: Rodopi, 2007), p. 54.
10. Gretchen Bakke, 'Dead White Men: An Essay on the Changing Dynamics of Race in US Action Cinema', *Anthropological Quarterly*, 83/2 (2010), 400–28.
11. Nick Muntean and Matthew Thomas Payne, 'Attack of the Livid Dead: Recalibrating Terror in the Post-September 11 Zombi Film', in Andrew Schopp and Matthew B. Hill (eds), *The War on Terror and American Popular Culture: September 11 and Beyond* (Cranbury, NJ: Fairleigh Dickinson University Press, 2009), pp. 246–7.
12. Michael Newbury, 'Fast Zombie/Slow Zombie: Food Writing, Horror Movies, and Agribusiness Apocalypse', *American Literary History*, 24/1 (spring 2012), 87–114.
13. Paul McDonald, 'Britain: Hollywood, UK', in Paul McDonald and Janet Wasko (eds), *The Contemporary Hollywood Film Industry* (Malden, MA: Blackwell, 2008), pp. 223 and 220.
14. Steven Applebaum, 'Off the beach', *The Scotsman* (Edinburgh), 17 October 2002.
15. Tom Charity, '*28 Days Later*', *Time Out*, 30 October 2002.
16. Jo Wiltshire, 'A World Gone Mad', *Mail on Sunday*, 20 October 2002.
17. Brigid Cherry, 'A Cosy Catastrophe: Genre, National Cinema and Fan Responses to *28 Days Later*', in Tobias Hochscherf and James Leggott (eds), *British Science Fiction Film and Television* (Jefferson, NC: McFarland, 2011), p. 158.
18. See Jim Leach, *British Film* (Cambridge: Cambridge University Press, 2004).
19. Allan Hunter, '*28 Days Later*', *Screen International*, 24 October 2002.
20. See Amy Raphael, *Danny Boyle: In His Own Words* (London: Faber and Faber, 2011).
21. Bishop, *American Zombie Gothic* (Jefferson, NC: McFarland, 2010), p. 34.
22. Quoted in Raphael, *Danny Boyle*, p. 171.

23. Information taken from the Internet Movie Database (IMDB). Also, see *www.screenonline.org.uk/people/id/470997/credits.html*.
24. Leach, *British Film*, pp. 48–65.
25. Graham Murdock, 'Reservoirs of Dogma: An Archaeology of Popular Anxieties', in Martin Barker and Julian Petley (eds), *Ill Effects: The Media/Violence Debate* (New York: Routledge, 1997), p. 150. Martin Barker, 'The Newson Report: A Case Study in "Common Sense"', in Martin Barker and Julian Petley (eds), *Ill Effects: The Media/Violence Debate* (New York: Routledge, 1997), p. 12.
26. Jason Bennetto and John Davison, 'Police Blame Hollywood for Rise of Hit-Men', *The Independent*, 28 December 1998.
27. Andrew Culf, 'Put Blame on Hollywood for Screen Violence, Says Censor', *The Guardian*, 12 December 1996.
28. Andreas Whittam Smith, 'To Believe Nothing Flows from TV Violence is Implausible: As President of the British Board of Film Classification I Do Sentry Duty in this Area', The Independent, 14 June 1999.
29. Mark Kermode, 'I Was a Teenage Horror Fan: Or, How I Learned to Stop Worrying and Love Linda Blair', in Martin Barker and Julian Petley (eds), *Ill Effects: The Media/Violence Debate* (New York: Routledge, 1997), p. 134.
30. See the *BBFC Annual Reports*, in particular 2004, page 51, *www.bbfc.co.uk/about-bbfc/annual-reports* (accessed 5 January 2020).
31. Julian Petley, 'Us and Them', in Martin Barker and Julian Petley (eds), *Ill Effects: The Media/Violence Debate* (New York: Routledge, 1997), p. 176.
32. R. C. Zachner, 'The Rot that Infests the *Clockwork Orange*', *The Times*, 22 July 1972.
33. David Buckingham, 'Electronic Child Abuse? Rethinking the Media's Effects on Children', in Martin Barker and Julian Petley (eds), *Ill Effects: The Media/Violence Debate* (New York: Routledge, 1997), p. 63.
34. Bishop, *American Zombie Gothic*, p. 35.
35. Victoria Burnett, 'Socialism's Sacred Cows Suffer Zombie Attack in Popular Cuban Film', *The New York Times*, 10 December 2011.
36. Dendle, 'The Zombie as Barometer of Cultural Anxiety', p. 54; Sarah Lauro and Karen Embry, 'A Zombie Manifesto: The Nonhuman Condition in the Era of Advanced Capitalism', *Boundary 2*, 35/1 (2008), 107; Muntean and Payne, 'Attack of the Livid Dead', pp. 246–7.
37. Paul Peachey, 'Animal Rights', *The Independent*, 17 February 2001; Sylvia Pfeifer, 'Huntingdon Demands Law to Ban Animal-Rights Thugs', *Sunday Business* (London), 29 April 2001.
38. Raphael, *Danny Boyle*, p. 172.

39. Stephen Barber, 'An Indescribable Blur: Film and London', in Gail Cunningham and Stephen Barber (eds), *London Eyes: Reflections in Text and Image* (New York: Berghahn Books, 2007), p. 125.
40. Charlotte Brunsdon, *London in Cinema: The Cinematic City Since 1945* (London: BFI, 2007), p. 49.
41. Brunsdon, *London in Cinema*, p. 50.
42. Nick James, 'British Cinema's US Surrender – A View from 2001', in Robert Murphy (ed.), *The British Cinema Book* (New York: Palgrave Macmillan, 2009), p. 26.
43. Higson, *Waving the Flag*, p. 213.
44. Higson, *Waving the Flag*, pp. 179 and 213.
45. Higson, *Waving the Flag*, pp. 230–1.
46. Aidan Power, 'Invasion of the Brit-Snatchers', in Tobias Hochscherf and James Leggott (eds), *British Science Fiction Film and Television* (Jefferson, NC: McFarland and Co., 2011), p. 152.
47. Fred Botting, 'Zombie London: Unexceptionalities of the New World Order', in Lawrence Phillips and Anne Witchard (eds), *London Gothic: Place, Space and the Gothic Imagination* (New York: Continuum, 2010), p. 156.
48. Botting, 'Zombie London', p. 128.
49. Owen Gleiberman, '*28 Days Later* (2003)', *Entertainment Weekly*, 27 June 2003.
50. Geoffrey Macnab, 'British Cinema Special: That Shrinking Feeling', *Sight & Sound*, October 2002, 18.
51. Unpublished research essay by Ian Conrich, quoted in Robert Murphy, 'A Path through the Moral Maze', in Robert Murphy (ed.), *British Cinema of the 90s* (London: BFI, 2000), p. 2.
52. John Fitzgerald, *Studying British Cinema: 1999–2009* (London: Auteur, 2010), p. 186.
53. Andrew Pulver, 'Where There's Brass...', *The Guardian*, 13 January 2004.
54. Stephen Armstrong, 'Back From the Dead', *The Sunday Times*, 14 March 2004.
55. Bonnie Greer, 'Dying for a Laugh', *Mail on Sunday*, 14 March 2004.
56. Pulver, 'Where There's Brass...'.
57. David Pirie, *A New Heritage of Horror* (New York: I.B. Tauris, 2007), p. 212.
58. Paul English, 'The Razz: Why I Made the World's First Zom-Rom-Com', *Daily Record* (Glasgow), 9 April 2004, pp. 52–3.
59. Greer, 'Dying for a Laugh', p. 29.
60. Wendy Ide, '*Shaun of the Dead*', *Screen International*, 20 March 2004.
61. Kim Newman, '*Shaun of the Dead*', *Sight & Sound*, May 2004, 73.
62. Budgets and worldwide box office gross are taken from IMDB.

63. Tim Dams, 'BBC Viewers Vote for Best Films of 2004', *Screen International*, 23 December 2004.
64. Brent Simon, 'Land of the Dead', *Screen International*, 22 June 2005.
65. John Fitzgerald, *Studying British Cinema: 1999–2009*, p. 205.
66. Linda McDowell, 'Changing Cultures of Work: Employment, Gender and Lifestyle', in David Morely and Kevin Robins (eds), *British Cultural Studies: Geography, Nationality and Identity* (Oxford: Oxford University Press, 2001), p. 350.
67. Jane Millar, *Keeping Track of Welfare Reform: The New Deal Programmes*, Joseph Rowntree Foundation (York, UK: York Publishing Services, 2000), p. 41.
68. Simon Rogers, John Burn-Murdoch and Ami Sedghi, 'Unemployment: The Key UK Data and Benefit Claimants for Every Constituency', *The Guardian*, 15 May 2013.
69. McDowell, 'Changing Cultures of Work', p. 345.
70. Kenneth Tynan, 'Ealing: The Studio in Suburbia', *Films and Filming*, November 1955, p. 4.
71. Tim O'Sullivan, 'Ealing Comedies 1947–57', in I. Q. Hunter and Laraine Porter (eds), *British Comedy Cinema* (New York: Routledge, 2012), pp. 68–9.
72. Tynan, 'Ealing', p. 4.
73. O'Sullivan, 'Ealing Comedies', p. 71.
74. Nigel Mather, *Tears of Laughter* (Manchester University Press: New York, 2006), 25. Philip Simpson, 'Directions to Ealing', *Screen Education*, 24 (1977), 14.
75. Charles Barr, *Ealing Studios* (Berkeley, University of California Press, 1998), pp. 96–7.
76. Blake, *Wounds of Nations*, p. 170.
77. Sean Nixon, 'Resignifying Masculinity', in David Morely and Kevin Robins (eds), *British Cultural Studies: Geography, Nationality and Identity* (Oxford: Oxford University Press, 2001), pp. 379–83.
78. McDowell, 'Changing Cultures of Work', p. 346.
79. Blake, *Wounds of Nations*, p. 167.
80. Andy Medhurst, *A National Joke* (Routledge: New York, 2007).
81. Leon Hunt, *Cult British TV Comedy* (Manchester University Press: New York, 2013), p. 51.
82. Medhurst, *A National Joke*, p. 112.
83. Hunt, *Cult British TV Comedy*, p. 177.
84. Jeffrey S. Miller, *Something Completely Different: British Television and American Culture* (Minneapolis: University of Minnesota Press, 2000), p. 111.

85. Miller, *Something Completely Different*, p. 132.
86. Murphy, 'A Path through the Moral Maze', p. 4.
87. Robert Murphy 'Bright Hopes, Dark Dreams: A Guide to New British Cinema', in Robert Murphy (ed.), *The British Cinema Book*, 3rd edition (New York: Palgrave Macmillan, 2009), p. 407.
88. Ryan Gilbey, 'The New Wave of British Horror Films', *The Guardian*, 10 June 2010.

Chapter 3 Hybrid Hoodie Horrors

1. Jane Graham, 'Hoodies Strike Fear in British Cinema', *The Guardian*, 5 November 2009.
2. Imogen Tyler, 'Chav Scum: The Filthy Politics of Social Class in Contemporary Britain', *MC Journal: A Journal of Media and Culture*, 9/5 (November 2006), *www.journal.media-culture.org.au/0610/09-tyler.php* (accessed 5 January 2020). See also Keith Hayward and Majid Yar's 'The "Chav" Phenomenon: Consumption, Media and the Construction of a New Underclass', *Crime Media Culture*, 2/1 (April 2006), 9–28.
3. Peter Bradshaw, '*Attack the Block*', *The Guardian*, 12 May 2011.
4. Chris Hewitt, '*Attack the Block* Review', *Empire Online*, *www.empireonline.com/movies/attack-block/review/* (accessed 5 January 2020).
5. Peter Bradshaw, '*Eden Lake*', *The Guardian*, 11 September 2008.
6. The quotation appears to have been poorly transcribed for the written interview. Watkins is quoted as saying 'On this one particularly I though [sic] you take the old backwards [sic] horror, horror in the worlds [sic]'. However, it seems clear from context that Watkins actually said 'I thought, you take the old backwoods horror, horror in the woods'. Den of Geek, 'James Watkins Interview: *Eden Lake*, Modern Horror and *The Descent 2*', *Den of Geek*, 23 January 2009, *www.denofgeek.us/movies/13937/james-watkins-interview-eden-lake-modern-horror-the-descent-2* (accessed 5 January 2020).
7. John Fitzgerald, *Studying British Cinema: 1999–2009* (London: Auteur, 2010), p. 216.
8. Sherryl Vint, 'Visualizing the British Boom: British Science Fiction Film and Television', *CR: The New Centennial Review*, 13/2 (fall 2013), 174.
9. Linn Lönroth, 'Hoodie Horror: The New Monster in Contemporary British Horror Movies', *Journal of Media, Cognition and Communication*, 2/1 (2014), p. 4–20.

10. Mark Featherstone, '"Hoodie Horror": The Capitalism Other in Postmodern Society', *Review of Education, Pedagogy and Cultural Studies*, 35/3 (2013), 193.
11. Johnny Walker, 'A Wilderness of Horrors? British Horror Cinema in the New Millennium', *Journal of British Cinema and Television*, 9/3 (2012), 450–1.
12. Walker, 'A Wilderness of Horrors?', 448.
13. Joe Cornish, '*Attack the Block* Final Shooting Script (Including Reshoots)', 10 November 2010, *162mc.files.wordpress.com/2012/11/attack-the-block.pdf* (accessed 5 January 2020).
14. Tyler, 'Chav Scum: The Filthy Politics of Social Class in Contemporary Britain'. See also Hayward and Yar, 'The 'Chav' Phenomenon: Consumption, Media and the Construction of a New Underclass'.
15. Owen Jones, *Chavs* (New York: Verso, 2011). See also Ferdinand Mount, *Mind the Gap: The New Class Divide in Britain* (London: Short Books, 2004); Michael Collins, *The Likes of Us: A Biography of the White Working Class* (London: Granta Books, 2004); Imogen Tyler, *Revolting Subjects: Social Abjection and Resistance in Neoliberal Britain* (London: Zed Books, 2013); Will Atkinson, Steven Roberts and Mike Savage (eds), *Class Inequality in Austerity Britain: Power, Difference and Suffering* (New York: Palgrave Macmillan, 2013).
16. Stephen Shafer, 'An Overview of the Working Classes in British Feature Film from the 1960s to the 1980s: From Class Consciousness to Marginalization', *International Labor and Working Class History*, 59 (April 2001), 12–13.
17. See Chapters 1 and 2 of this book for more substantive discussions of the Bulger murder and its effect on cinema. Máire Messenger Davies, '"Crazyspace": The Politics of Children's Screen Drama', *Screen*, 46/3 (Autumn 2005), 394.
18. Samantha Booth, 'That Bling Bling Thing', *Daily Record* (Glasgow), 27 March 2003.
19. Katy Weitz, Gaby Hinsliff and Martin Bright, 'The Youth Debate', *The Observer*, 15 May 2005.
20. BBC News, 'Mall Bans Shoppers' Hooded Tops', *BBC News Online*, 11 May 2005, *news.bbc.co.uk/2/hi/uk_news/england/kent/4534903.stm* (accessed 5 January 2020). For a nuanced discussion of the Bluewater ban and moral panic, see Dan Lett, Sean Hier, Keven Walby and Andre Smith's 'Panic, Regulation and the Moralization of British Law and Order Politics', in Sean Hier (ed.), *Moral Panics and the Politics of Anxiety* (New York: Routledge, 2011), pp. 155–70.
21. Harry Honigsbaum, 'Concern over Rise of "Happy-Slapping" Craze', *The Guardian*, 25 April 2005.

22. Introduced in 1998 by Tony Blair to punish minor crimes that would not usually warrant arrest or trial, ASBOs are Antisocial Behaviour Orders that can be given to citizens over ten years of age who have perpetrated antisocial behaviour like drunken or intimidating behaviour, vandalism, or playing music too loudly after dark. These orders can restrict where the recipients can go and who they can spend time with. *Doctor Who*, Series 2, Episode 3, 'School Reunion', dir. James Hawes (29 April 2006, BBC One).
23. Amanda Ann Klein, *American Film Cycles: Reframing Genres, Screening Social Problems, and Defining Subcultures* (Austin, TX: University of Texas Press, 2011), p. 18.
24. Klein, *American Film Cycles*, p. 11.
25. Johnny Walker also notes how Turgoose's casting signals the film's concern with class. *Contemporary British Horror Cinema: Industry, Genre and Society* (Edinburgh: Edinburgh University Press, 2016), p. 97.
26. Klein, *American Film Cycles*, p. 11.
27. Miranda Sawyer, 'The Film That Speaks to Britain's Youth in Words They Understand', *The Guardian*, 25 February 2006. Liz Hoggard, 'Hoodie UK', *The Independent*, 19 February 2006.
28. Sawyer, 'The Film That Speaks'. Hoggard, 'Hoodie UK'.
29. Stanley Cohen, *Folk Devils and Moral Panics: The Creation of the Mods and Rockers* (New York: Routledge, 2002), pp. 1–2.
30. Stuart Hall, Chas Crotchet, Tony Jefferson, John Clarke and Brian Roberts, *Policing the Crisis: Mugging, the State, and Law and Order* (New York: Holmes and Meier, 1978), pp. 29, 6, 3, 21, 26 and 161–2.
31. The *Times Educational Supplement* is a UK publication published weekly and aimed at primary school teachers. Michael Shaw, 'Bullies Film Fights by Phone', *Times Educational Supplement*, 21 January 2005.
32. Deborah Orr, 'A Statement of the Bleeding Obvious', *The Independent*, 17 May 2005. See also Honigsbaum, 'Concern over Rise of "Happy-Slapping" Craze'; Nicola Stow, 'Women Assaulted in Capital's First "Happy Slapping" Attacks', *Evening News* (Edinburgh), 13 June 2005; Pete Samson, 'Myleene in Happy Slapping Terror', *Daily Record* (Glasgow), 8 December 2005; Andrew Picken, '"Happy Slapping Attack" On Man By 15-Year-Old Yobs', *Evening News* (Edinburgh), 3 February 2006.
33. For more information on the hoodie panic's misinterpretation of UK garage, see Darren Waters, 'Garage Scene Denies Glorifying Guns', *BBC News Online*, 6 January 2003, news.bbc.co.uk/2/hi/entertainment/2631401.stm (accessed 5 January 2020). See also *UK Garage: Brandy*

and Coke, dir. Ewen Spencer, produced by Somesuch & Co. Broadcast on Channel 4 and available for streaming on the Dazed Online website, www.dazeddigital.com/artsandculture/article/19531/1/watch-music-nation-brandy-coke-full-length-channel-4-uk-garage-documentary.
34. Klein, *American Film Cycles*, pp. 13 and 19.
35. Daniel Briggs, 'Concluding Thoughts', in Daniel Briggs (ed.), *The English Riots of 2011: A Summer of Discontent* (Hook, UK: Waterside Press, 2012), p. 392.
36. '*The Texas Chainsaw Massacre*', BBFC Case Studies, www.bbfc.co.uk/case-studies/texas-chain-saw-massacre (accessed 5 January 2020).
37. Kendall Phillips, *Projected Fears* (Westport, CT: Praeger, 2005), pp. 106–7.
38. Walker, *Contemporary British Horror Cinema*, p. 102.
39. David Roche, *Making and Remaking Horror in the 1970s and 2000s* (Jackson, MS: University of Mississippi Press, 2014), pp. 22–3.
40. Bernice Murphy, *The Rural Gothic in American Popular Culture* (New York: Palgrave Macmillan, 2013), p. 149.
41. Carol Clover, *Men, Women, and Chain Saws* (Princeton, NJ: Princeton University Press, 1992), pp. 124–6.
42. Jones, *Chavs*, p. 74.
43. Anoop Nayak, 'Displaced Masculinities: Chavs, Youth and Class in the Post-Industrial City', *Sociology*, 40/5 (2006), 814.
44. Philip Horne, 'DVD Reviews: *Eden Lake*', *The Daily Telegraph*, 24 January 2009.
45. 'Something for the Weekend', *The Sun*, 12 September 2008.
46. Rebecca Davies, '*Eden Lake*', *Sight & Sound*, September 2008, 58. Libby Brooks, 'Comment and Debate: Forget Zombie Dawn. Now It's Day of the Feral Youth', *The Guardian*, 18 September 2008.
47. Anthony Quinn, '*Cherry Tree Lane* (18)', *The Independent*, 3 September 2010.
48. Jones, *Chavs*, p. 8.
49. Paul Vallely, 'Welcome to Gated Britain', *The Independent*, 3 February 2007.
50. Sarah Blandy and David Parsons, 'Gated Communities in England: Rules and Rhetoric of Urban Planning', *Geographica Helvetica* (2003), 314.
51. Blandy and Parsons, 'Gated Communities in England', 322.
52. Rowland Atkinson and John Flint, 'Fortress UK? Gated Communities, the Spatial Revolt of the Elites and Time-Space Trajectories of Segregation', *Housing Studies*, 19/6 (2004), 880.
53. See, for example, Paul Vallely, 'Welcome to Gated Britain' or Mira Katbamna, 'Office Hours', *The Guardian*, 12 June 2006.

54. Steve Rose, 'The Guide: Let's Not Move To...', *The Guardian*, 4 September 2010.
55. Paul Gallagher, 'Attack the Block – Joe Cornish Interview', *The List Online*, 28 April 2011, *film.list.co.uk/article/34094-attack-the-block-joe-cornish-interview/* (accessed 5 January 2020).
56. Eva Wiseman, 'Joe Cornish Interview: The Hoodie Horror', *The Observer*, 16 April 2011.
57. Marco Lanzagorta, 'John Carpenter', *Senses of Cinema* (2003), *sensesofcinema.com/2003/great-directors/carpenter/* (accessed 5 January 2020).
58. Robin Wood, 'The American Nightmare: Horror in the 70s', in Mark Jancovich (ed.), *Horror the Film Reader* (Routledge: New York, 2002), p. 29.
59. Tony Williams, '*Assault on Precinct 13*: The Mechanics of Repression', in Robin Wood and Robert Lippe (eds), *The American Nightmare: Essays on the Horror Film* (Toronto: Festival of Festivals, 1979), p. 70.
60. John Kenneth Muir, *The Films of John Carpenter* (Jefferson, NC: McFarland, 2000), p. 71.
61. Steve Smith, 'A Siege Mentality? Form and Ideology in Carpenter's Early Siege Films', in Ian Conrich and David Woods (eds), *The Cinema of John Carpenter* (Wallflower Press: London, 2004), p. 46.
62. Lorrie Palmer, '*Attack the Block*: Monsters, Race, and Rewriting South London's Outer Spaces', *Jump Cut*, 56 (2014), *www.ejumpcut.org/archive/jc56.2014-2015/PalmerAttackBlock/index.html* (accessed 5 January 2020).
63. Sarah Ilott, '"We Are the Martyrs, You're Just Squashed Tomatoes!": Laughing through the Fears in Postcolonial British Comedy: Chris Morris's *Four Lions* and Joe Cornish's *Attack the Block*', *Postcolonial Text*, 8/2 (2013), 3.
64. Zoe Williams, 'Katie Hopkins Calling Migrants Vermin Recalls the Darkest Events of History', *The Guardian*, 19 April 2015.
65. Ilott, '"We Are the Martyrs"', 3.
66. Palmer, '*Attack the Block*'.
67. Oscar Newman, 'Defensible Space – A New Physical Planning Tool for Urban Revitalization', *Journal of the American Planning Association*, 61/2 (1995), 150.
68. Oscar Newman, 'Defensible Space', 155.
69. Vint, 'Visualizing the British Boom', p. 174.
70. Bradshaw, '*Eden Lake*'.
71. Bradshaw, '*Attack the Block*'.
72. Allan Hunter, 'Rich Pickings', *Screen International*, 16 December 2011. Bradshaw, '*Attack the Block*'.

Chapter 4 'A Famous Corpse'

1. Adam Dawtrey, 'U.K. Pix Strike Up the Brand', *Variety*, 21–27 July 2003, p. 73.
2. 'Hammer Horror Classics to be Restored', *BBC News, Arts and Entertainment*, 19 January 2012, *www.bbc.com/news/entertainment-arts-16629619* (accessed 5 January 2020); Stephanie West, 'Hammer Films Releases Vampire Horror Let Me In', *Channel4 News Online*, 4 November 2010, *www.channel4.com/news/hammer-films-releases-vampire-horror-let-me-in* (accessed 5 January 2020).
3. Barry Forshaw, *British Gothic Cinema* (New York: Palgrave Macmillan, 2013), p. 80.
4. See the abstract for Walker's presentation at the Centre for the Interdisciplinary Study of Film and the Moving Image at the University of Kent in February 2015, '"From the Makers of *The Woman in Black*": Hammer Films and Contemporary Horror Cinema', *blogs.kent.ac.uk/artsnews/2015/01/16/film-research-events-for-spring-term-2015-announced/* (accessed 5 January 2020). Sarah Street, *British National Cinema* (New York: Routledge, 2009), p. 88.
5. Mark Jancovich, '"It's About Time British Actors Kicked Against These Roles in 'Horror' Films": Horror Stars, Psychological Films, and the Tyranny of the Old World in Classical Horror Cinema', *Historical Journal of Film, Radio, and Television*, 33/2 (2013), 214.
6. Alison Peirse, 'The Feminine Appeal of British Horror Cinema', *New Review of Film and Television Studies*, 13/4 (2015), 385–402.
7. Peter Hutchings, *Hammer and Beyond: The British Horror Film* (New York: St Martin's Press, 1993), p. 1.
8. Naila Scargill, 'Hammer 2.0 – CEO Simon Oaks Reveals Studio's Future Plans', originally accessed via the *MovieScope* website, now available via the Internet Archive, *https://web.archive.org/web/20150918224205/http://www.moviescopemag.com/market-news/featured-editorial/hammer-2-0-ceo-simon-oakes-reveals-studios-future-plans/* (accessed 5 January 2020).
9. Hutchings, *Hammer and Beyond*, p. 1. Denis Meikle, *A History of Horrors: The Rise and Fall of the House of Hammer* (Lanham, MD: Scarecrow Press, 2009), p. 223.
10. Hutchings, *Hammer and Beyond*, pp. 41–50.
11. Hutchings, *Hammer and Beyond*, p. 67.
12. Hutchings, *Hammer and Beyond*, pp. 18–19.

13. David Pirie, *A Heritage of Horror: The English Gothic Cinema 1946–1972* (London: Gordon Fraser, 1973), p. 9. See also Barry Forshaw, *British Gothic Cinema*; Jonathan Rigby, *English Gothic: Classic Horror Cinema 1897–2015* (Cambridge: Signum Books, 2015).
14. Paul Moody, 'Hammer Horror', *BFI ScreenOnline*, www.screenonline.org.uk/film/id/445975/ (accessed 5 January 2020).
15. Adam Minns, 'Hammer Teams with Sturridge to Scare Up Six Films', *Screen International*, 13 May 2001.
16. Dawtrey, 'U.K. Pix Strike Up the Brand', p. 1. Wendy Mitchell, 'Hammer Film Relaunched with European Investors Including Cyrte', *Screen International*, 10 May 2007.
17. Mitchell, 'Hammer Film Relaunched'.
18. Adam Dawtrey, 'Hammer Scares Up Coin From a New Generation', *Variety*, 26 March – 1 April 2012, p. 7.
19. Dave McNary, 'Indie Team Wields Classic Hammer', *Variety*, 3–9 May 2010, p. 8.
20. Matt Hills, 'Hammer 2.0: Legacy, Modernization and Hammer Horror as a Heritage Brand', in Richard Nowell (ed.), *Merchants of Menace* (New York: Bloomsbury, 2014), p. 230.
21. Hills, 'Hammer 2.0', p. 246.
22. '*The Woman in Black*', *BBFC Case Studies*, www.bbfc.co.uk/case-studies/woman-black (accessed 5 January 2020).
23. Brian Wilson, 'Notes on a Radical Tradition: Subversive Ideological Applications in the Hammer Horror Films', *Cineaction*, 72 (2007), 55.
24. Wilson, 'Notes on a Radical Tradition', 55.
25. See Joseph Crawford, *Gothic Fiction and the Invention of Terrorism: The Politics and Aesthetics of Fear in the Age of the Reign of Terror* (New York: Bloomsbury, 2013), pp. viii, x–xii and 192.
26. Emma McEvoy, '"Boo! To Taboo" Gothic Performance at British Festivals', in Justin Edwards and Agnieszka Soltysik Monnet (eds), *The Gothic in Contemporary Literature and Popular Culture* (New York: Routledge, 2012), pp. 178–9.
27. Xavier Aldana Reyes, 'Gothic Horror Film, 1960–Present', in Glennis Byron and Dale Townshend (eds), *The Gothic World* (New York: Routledge, 2014), p. 388.
28. James Morgart, 'Gothic Horror Film from *The Haunted Castle* (1896) to *Psycho* (1960)', in Glennis Byron and Dale Townshend (eds), *The Gothic World* (New York: Routledge, 2014), pp. 376–7.
29. Aldana Reyes, 'Gothic Horror Film', p. 389. While Fred Botting writes in this same collection on the post-millennial monster, I do not substantively

include his discussion here. Botting argues that by the millennium, there were no more monsters, as they had been thoroughly domesticated and were no longer Other, only 'simulated [monsters] sought out by isophrenic individuals desperately seeking Otherness'. I disagree with this claim, as well as Baudrillard's original theorisation of the isophrenic and its strikingly insensitive and ableist co-optation of psychological terminology for conditions like schizophrenia and autism for use as signifiers of postmodern problems. Botting, 'Post-Millennial Monsters: Monstrosity-no-more', in Glennis Byron and Dale Townshend (eds), *The Gothic World* (New York: Routledge, 2014), p. 500. Jean Baudrillard, *Cool Memories*, trans. Chris Turner (Cambridge: Polity Press, 1996).
30. Hills, 'Hammer 2.0', p. 237.
31. Sue Harper, 'The Scent of Distant Blood: Hammer Films and History', in Tony Barta (ed.), *Screening the Past: Film and the Representation of History* (Westport, CT: Praeger, 1998), p. 111.
32. Helen Wheatley, *Gothic Television* (Manchester: Manchester University Press, 2006), p. 49.
33. Wheatley, *Gothic Television*, p. 50.
34. Rhidian Davis, 'Shadowlands', *Sight & Sound*, November 2013, 26.
35. Brian Wilson, 'Notes on a Radical Tradition', 55.
36. Johnny Walker, 'A Wilderness of Horrors? British Horror Cinema in the New Millennium', *Journal of British Cinema and Television*, 9/3 (2012), 444.
37. '*The Woman in Black* Scares Away *The Muppets* to Take UK Box Office Crown', *Screen International*, 13 February 2012. Throughout, all box office figures taken from or verified with the Internet Movie Database (IMDB).
38. Lisa Mullen, '*The Woman in Black*', *Sight & Sound*, March 2012, 78.
39. '*The Woman in Black*', *Screen International*, 25 January 2012.
40. David Noh, '*The Woman in Black*', *Film Journal International*, March 2012, p. 59.
41. Derek Johnston, *Haunted Seasons: Television Ghost Stories for Christmas and Horror for Halloween* (New York: Palgrave Macmillan, 2015), pp. 66 and 127.
42. Johnston, *Haunted Seasons*, p. 155.
43. Johnston, *Haunted Seasons*, pp. 67 and 70.
44. Johnston, *Haunted Seasons*, p. 71.
45. Johnston, *Haunted Seasons*, p. 155.
46. Johnston, *Haunted Seasons*, p. 172.
47. Johnston, *Haunted Seasons*, p. 162.
48. Wheatley, *Gothic Television*, p. 55.

49. Johnston, *Haunted Seasons*, p. 170.
50. '*The Woman in Black*', *BBFC Case Studies*.
51. '*Woman in Black* (12A)', *Moving Image*, www.movingimage.org.uk/woman-in-black-12a/ (accessed 5 January 2020).
52. Mike Snoonian, 'Is *The Woman in Black* J-Horror in Victorian Clothing?', *FilmThrills*, 16 February 2012, *filmthrills.com/is-the-new-woman-in-black-j-horror-in-victorian-clothing/* (accessed 5 January 2020).
53. Glennis Byron, 'Introduction', in Glennis Byron (ed.), *Globalgothic* (New York: Manchester University Press, 2013), p. 1.
54. Byron, 'Introduction', p. 2.
55. Byron, 'Introduction', p. 5.
56. Byron, 'Introduction', p. 3.
57. Byron, 'Introduction', p. 4.
58. Byron, 'Introduction', p. 4.
59. Richard Hand, 'Aesthetics of Cruelty: Traditional Japanese Theatre and the Horror Film', in Jay McRoy (ed.), *Japanese Horror Cinema* (Honolulu: University of Hawai'i Press, 2005), p. 22.
60. Ruth Goldberg, 'Demons in the Family: Tracking the Japanese "Uncanny Mother Film" from *A Page of Madness* to *Ringu*', in Barry Keith Grant and Christopher Sharrett (eds), *Planks of Reason: Essays on the Horror Film* (Lanham, MD: Scarecrow, 2004), pp. 370–85.
61. Hand's work tracing the influence of *Noh* and *Kabuki* theatre provides the category of '*kaidan* films' with a great deal of nuance. Richard Hand, 'Aesthetics of Cruelty'. Also useful in this regard is Colette Balmain, *Introduction to Japanese Horror Film* (Edinburgh: Edinburgh University Press, 2008).
62. Box office figures taken from IMDB.
63. Jay McRoy, 'Introduction', in Jay McRoy (ed.), *Japanese Horror Cinema* (Honolulu: University of Hawai'i Press, 2005), p. 3.
64. D. P. Martinez, 'Gender, Shifting Boundaries and Global Cultures', in D. P. Martinez (ed.), *The Worlds of Japanese Popular Culture: Gender, Shifting Boundaries and Global Cultures* (New York: Cambridge University Press, 1998), p. 7.
65. See also Valerie Wee, *Japanese Horror Films and Their American Remakes: Translating Fear, Adapting Culture* (New York: Routledge, 2014).
66. McRoy, 'Introduction', p. 4; Susan Napier, *Anime from Akira to Princess Mononoke: Experiencing Contemporary Japanese Animation* (New York: Palgrave, 2001), p. 80.
67. Steffen Hantke, 'Japanese Horror Under Western Eyes: Social Class and Global Culture in Miike Takashi's *Audition*', in Jay McRoy (ed.), *Japanese Horror Cinema* (Honolulu: University of Hawai'i Press, 2005), p. 60.

68. Susan Napier, *The Fantastic in Modern Japanese Literature: A Subversion of Modernity* (New York: Routledge, 1996), pp. 54 and 56–7.
69. Wee, *Japanese Horror Films and Their American Remakes*, pp. 55 and 106.
70. Many contemporary *kaidan* films also focus on technology. See Jinhee Choi and Mitsuyo Wada-Marciano, 'Introduction', in Jinhee Choi and Mitsuyo Wada-Marciano (eds), *Horror to the Extreme: Changing Boundaries in Asian Cinema* (Hong Kong: Hong Kong University Press, 2009), pp. 1–11. See also Matt Hills, 'Ringing the Changes: Cult Distinctions and Cultural Differences in US Fans' Readings of Japanese Horror Cinema', in Jay McRoy (ed.), *Japanese Horror Cinema* (Edinburgh: Edinburgh University Press, 2005), pp. 161–74.
71. Chika Kinoshita, 'The Mummy Complex: Kurosawa Kiyoshi's *Loft* and J-horror', in Jinhee Choi and Mitsuyo Wada-Marciano (eds), *Horror to the Extreme: Changing Boundaries in Asian Cinema* (Hong Kong: Hong Kong University Press, 2009), p. 115. Choi and Wada-Marciano, 'Introduction', pp. 1–12.
72. Jay McRoy, *Nightmare Japan: Contemporary Japanese Horror Cinema* (New York: Rodopi, 2008), pp. 97–8.
73. In particular, the basic plots of *Scary Movie 3* (David Zucker, 2003) and *Scary Movie 4* (David Zucker, 2006) borrow from and parody the plots and tropes of *Ringu* and *Ju-On* respectively.
74. Daniel Martin, 'Japan's *Blair Witch*: Restraint, Maturity, and Generic Canons in the British Critical Reception of *Ring*', *Cinema Journal*, 48/3 (2009), 35 and 36.
75. For a concise discussion of the discourse of quality within British cinema, see Jim Leach, *British Film* (Cambridge: Cambridge University Press, 2004).
76. Martin, 'Japan's *Blair Witch*', p. 47.
77. Phil Hoad, 'The *Cabin in the Woods* Shows Horror Speaks an International Language', *The Guardian*, 10 April 2012.
78. Jane Goldman, quoted in an interview by Kate Kellaway, 'Touched By Evil: Susan Hill and Jane Goldman on What Inspired *The Woman in Black*', *The Guardian*, 4 February 2012.
79. Phil Hoad, 'The *Cabin in the Woods* Shows Horror Speaks an International Language'.
80. Leslie Felperin, 'Review: *The Woman in Black*', *Variety*, 25 January 2012.
81. Byron, 'Introduction', p. 3.
82. M. J. Simpson, *Urban Terrors: New British Horror Cinema, 1998–2002* (Baltimore, MD: Midnight Marquee Press, 2013), p. 284.
83. Stephen Hinerman, 'Star Culture', in James Lull (ed.), *Culture in the Communication Age* (New York: Routledge, 2001), p. 196.

84. Hinerman, 'Star Culture', p. 202.
85. All statistics taken from IMDB. There is not much information available on how *Deathly Hallows 2* did in African countries. Information was unavailable for India and Indonesia.
86. Helen Pidd, '"If The Script Says Have Sex, I Have Sex"', *The Guardian*, 7 September 2007. Paul Majendie, 'Potter Star Radcliffe Wins Rave Reviews in "Equus"', *Reuters*, 28 February 2007, *www.reuters.com/article/2007/02/28/us-arts-potter-idUSL2723314820070228* (accessed 5 January 2020).
87. Hannah Dowle, 'Things Getting Scarier for Harry and "Woman"', *Variety*, 30 January – 5 February 2012.
88. Sally Williams, 'And For My Next Trick . . .', *Telegraph Magazine*, 28 January 2012.
89. David Wildman, 'The Ghost of *Harry Potter*', *Worchester Magazine*, 2–9 February 2012. Christina Patterson, 'Harry Potter Grows Up', *The Independent*, 1 December 2012.
90. Simpson, *Urban Terrors*, p. 284.
91. Richard DeCordova, *Picture Personalities: The Emergence of the Star System in America* (Urbana, IL: University of Illinois Press, 1990), pp. 19–20. See also Paul McDonald's Hollywood Stardom (Malden, MA: Wiley-Blackwell, 2013) and Richard Maltby, *Hollywood Cinema* (Malden, MA: Blackwell, 2003).
92. Hills, 'Hammer 2.0', p. 237.
93. Williams, 'And For My Next Trick . . .'. Christina Patterson, 'Harry Potter Grows Up', *The Independent*, 1 December 2012.
94. Watkins reveals this in the DVD director's commentary.
95. '*The Woman in Black*', *Screen International*. Felperin, 'Review: *The Woman in Black*'.
96. 'Radcliffe Mania', *Screen International*, 14 February 2012.
97. McDonald, *Hollywood Stardom*, p. 195.
98. Dawtrey, 'Hammer Scares Up Coin from a New Generation', p. 7.
99. '*The Woman in Black*', *BBFC Case Studies*.
100. McEvoy, '"Boo! To Taboo"', p. 178.
101. '*The Woman in Black*', *BBFC Case Studies*.
102. Ben Child, 'Film Classifiers Rewrite Horror Rules After *Woman in Black* Complaints', *The Guardian*, 13 January 2014; Andreas Wiseman, 'BBFC To Adopt Tougher Line on Unclassified Video Content, Black Swan Most Complained About Film in Cinemas Last Year', *Screen International*, 11 July 2012.
103. Hannah Furness, 'Daniel Radcliffe's First Film After *Harry Potter* "Too Scary"', *The Telegraph Online*, 11 July 2012.
104. '*The Woman in Black*', *BBFC Case Studies*.

105. Furness, 'Daniel Radcliffe's First Film After *Harry Potter* "Too Scary"'.
106. '*Harry Potter and the Deathly Hallows – Part 2*', BBFC Insight, *www.bbfc.co.uk/releases/harry-potter-and-deathly-hallows-part-2-2011-0* (accessed 5 January 2020).
107. Michael Rosser, 'BFI Unveils Gothic Cinema Season', *Screen International*, 27 June 2013.
108. Dawtrey, 'Hammer Scares Up Coin from a New Generation', p. 7.
109. 'Hammer Horror *The Quiet Ones* Wraps in Oxford', *BBC News*, 17 July 2012, *www.bbc.com/news/uk-england-oxfordshire-18871710* (accessed 5 January 2020).
110. Mike McCahill, '*The Quiet Ones* Review', *The Guardian*, 15 April 2014. Xan Brooks, '*The Quiet Ones* Review', *The Guardian*, 12 April 2014.
111. Peter Bradshaw, '*The Woman in Black 2: Angel of Death* Review', *The Guardian*, 25 December 2014.
112. Dawtrey, 'U.K. Pix Strike Up the Brand', p. 73.

Conclusion

1. Richard Stanley, 'Dying Light: An Obituary for the Great British Horror Movie', in Steve Chibnall and Julian Petley (eds), *British Horror Cinema* (New York: Routledge, 2002).
2. Charles Gant, '*The Woman in Black* Slaughters Top British Horror Titles at the UK Box Office', *The Guardian*, 1 March 2012.
3. Rosalind Galt and Karl Schoonover, 'Introduction: The Impurity of Art Cinema', in Rosalind Galt *and Karl Schoonover (eds),* Global Art Cinema: New Theories and Histories (New York: Oxford University Press, 2010), pp. 1 and 11.
4. Kim Newman, 'This Spectred Isle', *Sight & Sound*, July 2013, 48. Ben Wheatley, as quoted in Henry Northmore, 'Ben Wheatley, Director of *A Field in England* – Interview', *The List*, 24 June 2013, *film.list.co.uk/article/52082-ben-wheatley-director-of-a-field-in-england-interview/* (accessed 5 January 2020).
5. Leo Barraclough, 'You Like Us? You Really Like Us?', *Variety*, 3 December 2013.
6. In the first two quotations, Macnab quotes from and paraphrases remarks by Sony Pictures Classics co-founder and co-president Michael Barker. Geoffrey Macnab, 'The British are Coming! Again!' *The Independent*, 14 December 2013.

7. Ben Roberts, 'What a Relief', *Sight & Sound*, May 2015, 16.
8. Andreas Wiseman, 'Film4 Inks Deal with Jonathan Glazer', *Screen International*, 4 February 2015.
9. Andrew Pulver, 'Rebirth of the British Art Film', *The Guardian*, 23 July 2009. See also Jonathan Romney, 'Hats Off! It's the Year of the Auteur', *The Independent* (London), 6 January 2013. David Locke, 'A Haven for Art Films', *Sight & Sound*, November 2012, 18.
10. David Pirie, *A Heritage of Horror: The English Gothic Cinema 1946–1972* (London: Gordon Fraser, 1973) and *A New Heritage of Horror* (New York: I.B. Tauris, 2007); Peter Hutchings's *Terence Fisher* (Manchester: Manchester University Press, 2002).
11. Adam Minns, 'UK Production Trend Develops Into Horror', *Screen International*, 29 November 2001.
12. Danny Leigh, 'Can *Kill List* Breathe Life into Britain's Film Industry?', *The Guardian*, 2 September 2011.
13. Ali Catterall, Charlie Lyne, Gwilym Mumford and Damon Wise, 'The 23 Best Film Directors in the World Today', The Guardian, 31 August 2012.
14. Danny Leigh, 'Under the Skin: Why Did This Chilling Masterpiece Take a Decade?', *The Guardian*, 6 March 2014. Catterall, Lyne, Mumford and Wise, 'The 23 Best Film Directors in the World Today'.
15. Ryan Gilbey, 'The New Wave of British Horror Films', *The Guardian*, 10 June 2010.
16. Ben Roberts, 'Scream Test', *Sight & Sound*, June 2015, 17.

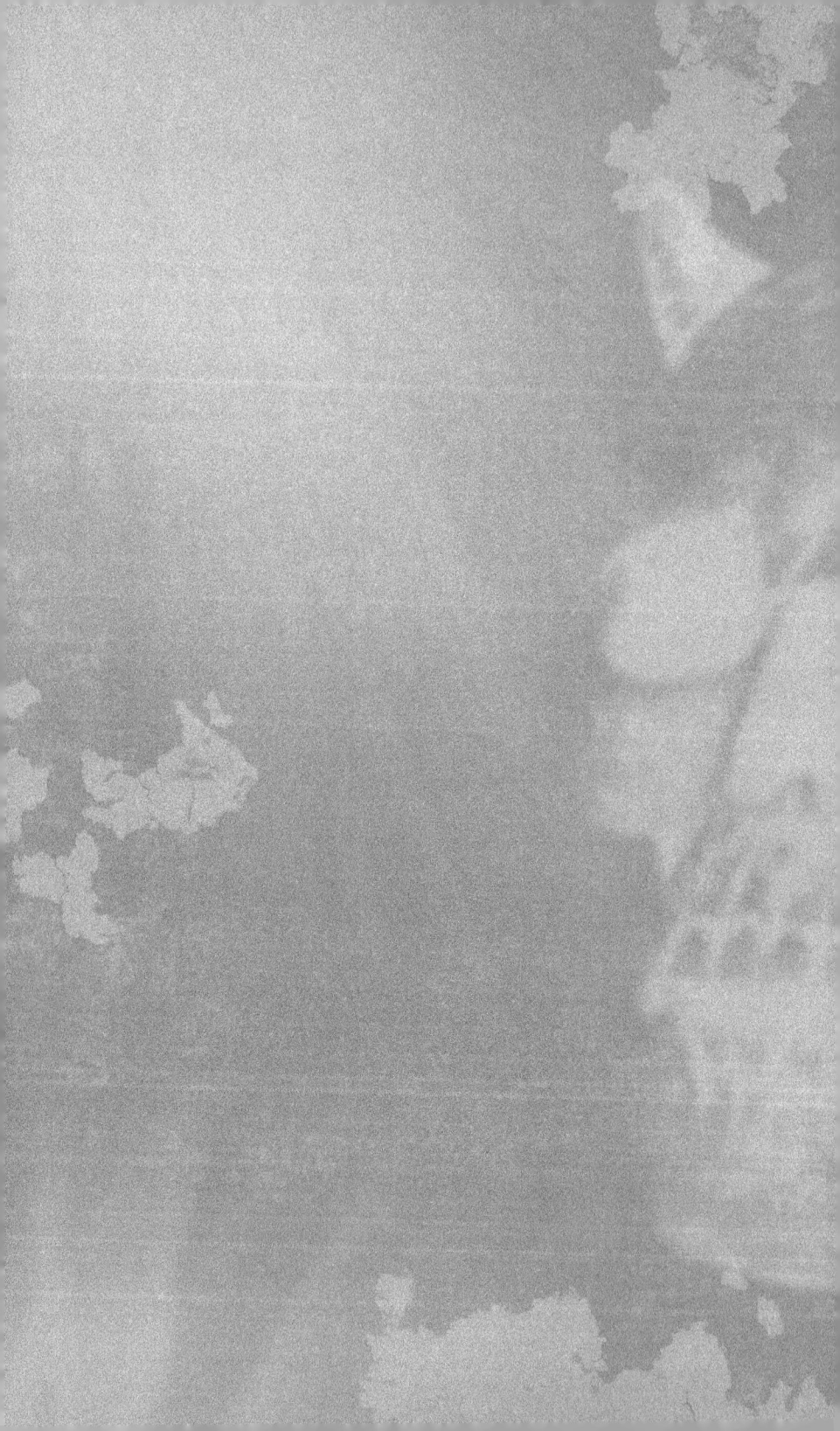

References

'1995: Killer Ronnie Kray Dies', *BBC News*, *BBC On This Day Online*, 17 March 1995, news.bbc.co.uk/onthisday/hi/dates/stories/march/17/newsid_2524000/2524249.stm (accessed 5 January 2020).

Abravanel, Genevieve, *Americanizing Britain: The Rise of Modernism in the Age of the Entertainment Empire* (Oxford: Oxford University Press, 2012).

Ahmed, Kamal, 'Film Violence Link to Teenage Crime', *The Guardian*, 8 January 1998.

Aldana Reyes, Xavier, 'Gothic Horror Film, 1960–Present', in Glennis Byron and Dale Townshend (eds), *The Gothic World* (New York: Routledge, 2014), pp. 388–98.

'An Active Agenda', *Screen International*, 23 June 1990.

Applebaum, Steven, 'Off the beach', *The Scotsman* (Edinburgh, UK), 17 October 2002.

Armstrong, Stephen, 'Back From the Dead', *The Sunday Times*, 14 March 2004.

Atkinson, Rowland and John Flint, 'Fortress UK? Gated Communities, the Spatial Revolt of the Elites and Time-Space Trajectories of Segregation', *Housing Studies*, 19/6 (2004), 875–92.

Atkinson, Will, Steven Roberts and Mike Savage (eds), *Class Inequality in Austerity Britain: Power, Difference and Suffering* (New York: Palgrave Macmillan, 2013).

Bakke, Gretchen, 'Dead White Men: An Essay on the Changing Dynamics of Race in US Action Cinema', *Anthropological Quarterly*, 83/2 (2010), 400–28.

Balmain, Colette, *Introduction to Japanese Horror Film* (Edinburgh: Edinburgh University Press, 2008).

Barber, Stephen, 'An Indescribable Blur: Film and London', in Gail Cunningham and Stephen Barber (eds) *London Eyes: Reflections in Text and Image* (New York: Berghahn Books, 2007), pp. 123–34.

Barker, Martin, 'The Newson Report: A Case Study in "Common Sense"', in Martin Barker and Julian Petley (eds), *Ill Effects: The Media/Violence Debate* (New York: Routledge, 1997), pp. 11–27.

Barr, Charles, *All Our Yesterdays* (London: BFI, 1986).

——, *Ealing Studios* (Berkeley, University of California Press, 1998).

Barraclough, Leo, 'You Like Us? You Really Like Us?' *Variety*, 3 December 2013.

Baudrillard, Jean, *Cool Memories*, trans. by Chris Turner (Cambridge: Polity Press, 1996).

BBC News, 'Mall Bans Shoppers' Hooded Tops', *BBC News Online*, 11 May 2005, news.bbc.co.uk/2/hi/uk_news/england/kent/4534903.stm (accessed 5 January 2020).

BBFC Annual Reports, *www.bbfc.co.uk/about-bbfc/annual-reports* (accessed 5 January 2020).

Bennetto, Jason and John Davison, 'Police Blame Hollywood for Rise of Hit-Men', *The Independent*, 28 December 1998.

Billington, Michael, 'Last Chance Saloon', *The Guardian*, 11 December 1993.

Billson, Anne, 'A Feast of Horror', *The Telegraph*, 4 May 2008.

Bishop, Kyle, *American Zombie Gothic* (Jefferson, NC: McFarland, 2010).

Blake, Linnie, *The Wounds of Nations* (New York: Manchester University Press, 2008).

Blandy, Sarah and David Parsons, 'Gated Communities in England: Rules and Rhetoric of Urban Planning', *Geographica Helvetica* (2003), 314–24.

Booth, Samantha, 'That Bling Thing', *Daily Record* (Glasgow), 27 March 2003.

Botting, Fred, 'Post-Millennial Monsters: Monstrosity-no-more', in Glennis Byron and Dale Townshend (eds), *The Gothic World* (New York: Routledge, 2014), pp. 498–509.

——, 'Zombie London: Unexceptionalities of the New World Order', in Lawrence Phillips and Anne Witchard (eds), *London Gothic: Place, Space and the Gothic Imagination* (New York: Continuum, 2010), pp. 153–71.

Boyle, Danny, 'Director Danny Boyle Here. Hello Reddit! AMA', *Reddit*, 15 March 2013, *www.reddit.com/r/IAmA/comments/1acxl7/director_danny_boyle_here_hello_reddit_ama/* (accessed 5 January 2020).

Bradshaw, Peter, '*Attack the Block*', *The Guardian*, 12 May 2011.

——, '*Eden Lake*', *The Guardian*, 11 September 2008.

——, 'Film Reviews: Enemies of the State', *The Guardian*, 13 May 2011.

——, 'Film Reviews: In Too Deep', *The Guardian*, 12 September 2008.

——, '*The Woman in Black 2: Angel of Death* Review', *The Guardian*, 25 December 2014.
Bray, Christopher, 'Always Miserable', *The Times Literary Supplement*, 15 October 1993.
Briggs, Daniel, 'Concluding Thoughts', in Daniel Briggs (ed.), *The English Riots of 2011: A Summer of Discontent* (Hook, UK: Waterside Press, 2012), pp. 381–401.
'British Film Industry Will Suffer If the Government Closes the UK Film Council', *The Telegraph*, 5 August 2010.
British Film Institute, 'Palace Pictures', *BFI Screen Online*, www.screenonline.org.uk/film/id/477684 (accessed 5 January 2020).
——, 'Summary of Cultural Test Points', *British Film Institute*, www.bfi.org.uk/film-industry/british-certification-tax-relief/cultural-test-film (accessed 5 January 2020).
Brooke, Michael, 'The Video Nasties', *BFI Screen Online*, www.screenonline.org.uk/film/id/591919/ (accessed 5 January 2020).
Brooks, Libby, 'Comment and Debate: Forget Zombie Dawn. Now It's Day of the Feral Youth', *The Guardian*, 18 September 2008.
Brooks, Xan, '*The Quiet Ones* Review', *The Guardian*, 12 April 2014.
Brown, Mark and Maev Kennedy, 'UK Film Council Axed', *The Guardian*, 26 July 2010.
Brunsdon, Charlotte, *London in Cinema: The Cinematic City Since 1945* (London: BFI, 2007).
Buckingham, David, 'Electronic Child Abuse? Rethinking the Media's Effects on Children', in Martin Barker and Julian Petley (eds), *Ill Effects: The Media/Violence Debate* (New York: Routledge, 1997), pp. 28–40.
Burnett, Victoria, 'Socialism's Sacred Cows Suffer Zombie Attack in Popular Cuban Film', *The New York Times*, 10 December 2011.
Burton, Alan and Steve Chibnall, *The Historical Dictionary of British Cinema* (Lanham, MD: Scarecrow Press, 2013).
Byron, Glennis, 'Introduction', in Glennis Byron (ed.), *Globalgothic* (New York: Manchester University Press, 2013).
Catterall, Ali, Charlie Lyne, Gwilym Mumford and Damon Wise, 'The 23 Best Film Directors in the World Today', *The Guardian*, 31 August 2012.
Charity, Tom, '*28 Days Later*', *Time Out*, 30 October 2002.
Cherry, Brigid, 'A Cosy Catastrophe: Genre, National Cinema and Fan Responses to *28 Days Later*', in Tobias Hochscherf and James Leggott (eds), *British Science Fiction Film and Television* (Jefferson, NC: McFarland, 2011), pp. 156–66.

Chibnall, Steve and Julian Petley, 'Return of the Repressed? British Horror's Heritage and Future', in Steve Chibnall and Julian Petley (eds), *British Horror Cinema* (New York: Routledge, 2002), pp. 1–9.

Chibnall, Steve and Julian Petley (eds), *British Horror Cinema* (New York: Routledge, 2002).

Child, Ben, 'Film Classifiers Rewrite Horror Rules After *Woman in Black* Complaints', *The Guardian*, 13 January 2014.

Chippendale, Peter, 'How High Street Horror Is Invading the Home', *The Sunday Times*, 30 May 1982.

Choi, Jinhee and Mitsuyo Wada-Marciano, 'Introduction', in Jinhee Choi and Mitsuyo Wada-Marciano (eds), *Horror to the Extreme: Changing Boundaries in Asian Cinema* (Hong Kong: Hong Kong University Press, 2009), pp. 1–11.

Clover, Carol, *Men, Women, and Chain Saws* (Princeton, NJ: Princeton University Press, 1992).

Cohen, Stanley, *Folk Devils and Moral Panics: The Creation of the Mods and Rockers* (New York: Routledge, 2002).

Collins, Michael, *The Likes of Us: A Biography of the White Working Class* (London: Granta Books, 2004).

Conrich, Ian, 'Traditions of the British Horror Films', in Robert Murphy (ed.), *The British Cinema Book* (New York: Palgrave Macmillan, 2009), pp. 96–105.

Cooper, Ian, *Frightmares: A History of British Horror Cinema* (Leighton Buzzard, UK: Auteur, 2016).

Cornish, Joe, '*Attack the Block* Final Shooting Script (Including Reshoots)', 10 November 2010, *162mc.files.wordpress.com/2012/11/attack-the-block.pdf* (accessed 5 January 2020).

Crawford, Joseph, *Gothic Fiction and the Invention of Terrorism: The Politics and Aesthetics of Fear in the Age of the Reign of Terror* (New York: Bloomsbury, 2013).

Criminal Justice and Public Order Act 1994 (c. 33), Part VII, s. 90(1), inserting s. 4A(1)–(2) into the Video Recordings Act 1984 (c. 39), available from Legislation.Gov.UK, *www.legislation.gov.uk/ukpga/1994/33/part/VII/crossheading/video-recordings/enacted* (accessed 5 January 2020).

Culf, Andrew, 'Put Blame on Hollywood for Screen Violence, Says Censor', *The Guardian*, 12 December 1996.

Dams, Tim, 'BBC Viewers Vote for Best Films of 2004', *Screen International*, 23 December 2004.

Davies, Rebecca, '*Eden Lake*', *Sight & Sound*, September 2008, 58.

Davis, Rhidian, 'Shadowlands', *Sight & Sound*, November 2013, 24–8 and 30.

Dawtrey, Adam, 'Hammer Scares Up Coin from a New Generation', *Variety*, 26 March – 1 April 2012.

——, 'U.K. Pix Strike Up the Brand', *Variety*, 21–27 July 2003, 1 and 73.

Decker, Lindsey, 'Ana Lily Amirpour's Transnational Gaze', in Alison Peirse, *Women Make Horror* (Newark, NJ: Rutgers University Press, forthcoming 2020).

DeCordova, Richard, *Picture Personalities: The Emergence of the Star System in America* (Urbana, IL: University of Illinois Press, 1990).

Den of Geek, 'James Watkins Interview: *Eden Lake*, Modern Horror, and *The Descent 2*', *Den of Geek*, 23 January 2009, *www.denofgeek.us/movies/13937/james-watkins-interview-eden-lake-modern-horror-the-descent-2* (accessed 5 January 2020).

Dendle, Peter, 'The Zombie as Barometer of Cultural Anxiety', in Niall Scott (ed.), *Monsters and the Monstrous: Myths and Metaphors of Enduring Evil* (New York: Rodopi, 2007), pp. 45–57.

Desjardins, Mary, 'Free From the Apron Strings', in Lester Friedman (ed.), *Fires Were Started: British Cinema and Thatcherism* (Minneapolis, MN: University of Minnesota Press, 1993), pp. 130–44.

Diawara, Manthia, 'Power and Territory', in Lester Friedman (ed.), *Fires Were Started: British Cinema and Thatcherism* (Minneapolis, MN: University of Minnesota Press, 1993), pp. 147–60.

Dickinson, Kay, *Off Key: When Film and Music Won't Work Together* (Oxford UK: Oxford University Press, 2008).

Dowle, Hannah, 'Things Getting Scarier for Harry and "Woman"', *Variety*, 30 January–5 February 2012.

Durovicová, Nataša and Kathleen E. Newman (eds), *World Cinemas, Transnational Perspectives* (Abingdon, UK: Routledge, 2009).

'Editorial: An Even Break', *Sight & Sound*, August 1997, 3.

'Editorial: Cinema Wars', *Sight & Sound*, November 1993, 3.

'Editorial: Gangbusters', *Sight & Sound*, May 2000.

'Editorial: In Bed Together', *Sight & Sound*, June 1992, 3.

'Editorial: Made in Europe', *Sight & Sound*, February 1992, 3.

'Editorial: Rewinding the Panic', *Sight & Sound*, January 1994, 3.

'Editorial: The Sensible Party', *Sight & Sound*, May 1994, 3.

Edwards, Kim, 'Moribundity, Mundanity and Modernity: *Shaun of the Dead*', *Screen Education*, 50 (January 2008), 99–103.

Elstein, David, 'Demonising a Decoy', *The Guardian*, 22 December 1993.

English, Paul, 'The Razz: Why I Made the World's First Zom-Rom-Com', *Daily Record* (Glasgow), 9 April 2004.

Ezra, Elizabeth and Terry Rowden (eds), *Transnational Cinema: The Film Reader* (London: Routledge, 2006).

Featherstone, Mark, '"Hoodie Horror": The Capitalism Other in Postmodern Society', *Review of Education, Pedagogy and Cultural Studies*, 35/3 (2013), 178–96.

Felperin, Leslie, 'Review: *The Woman in Black*', *Variety*, 25 January 2012.
Film Policy, Cmnd 9319, London: HMSO, 1984.
Fisher, Austin and Iain Robert Smith, 'Transnational Cinemas: A Critical Roundtable', *Frames Cinema Journal*, 9 (2016), n. p., framescinemajournal.com/article/transnational-cinemas-a-critical-roundtable/.
——, 'Second Phase Transnationalism: Reflections on Launching the SCMS Transnational Cinemas Scholarly Interest Group', *Transnational Screens*, 10/2 (2019), 114–25.
Fitzgerald, John, *Studying British Cinema: 1999–2009* (London: Auteur, 2010).
Forshaw, Barry, *British Gothic Cinema* (New York: Palgrave Macmillan, 2013).
Furness, Hannah, 'Daniel Radcliffe's First Film After *Harry Potter* "Too Scary"', *The Telegraph Online*, 11 July 2012.
Gallagher, Paul, 'Attack the Block – Joe Cornish Interview', *The List Online*, 28 April 2011, *film.list.co.uk/article/34094-attack-the-block-joe-cornish-interview/* (accessed 5 January 2020).
Galt, Rosalind and Karl Schoonover, 'Introduction: The Impurity of Art Cinema', in Rosalind Galt and Karl Schoonover (eds), *Global Art Cinema: New Theories and Histories* (New York: Oxford University Press, 2010), pp. 1–27.
Gant, Charles, '*The Woman in Black* Slaughters Top British Horror Titles at the UK Box Office', *The Guardian*, 1 March 2012.
'GATT Away!', *Screen International*, 1 October 1993.
Gerrard, Steven, *The Modern British Horror Film* (Newark, NJ: Rutgers University Press, 2017).
Gibbons, Fiachra, 'Help for Film Makers Taking on Hollywood', *The Guardian*, 2 May 2000.
Gilbey, Ryan, 'British Cinema Special: Reasons to Be Cheerful', *Sight & Sound*, October 2002, 14–17.
——, 'The New Wave of British Horror Films', *The Guardian*, 10 June 2010.
——, '"Yes, We Did Betray Ewan"', *The Independent*, 25 October 2002.
Giles, Paul, 'History with Holes', in Lester Friedman (ed.), *Fires Were Started: British Cinema and Thatcherism* (Minneapolis, MN: University of Minnesota Press, 1993), pp. 70–91.
Glaister, Dan, 'Boom or Bust Time for British Movie Makers', *The Guardian*, 24 December 1997.
——, 'Controversial Ferman Quits as Chief Film Censor', *The Guardian*, 28 March 1998.
Glancy, Mark, *Hollywood and the Americanization of Britain: From the 1920s to the Present* (New York: I.B. Tauris, 2014).
Gleiberman, Owen, '*28 Days Later* (2003)', *Entertainment Weekly*, 27 June 2003.

Goldberg, Ruth, 'Demons in the Family: Tracking the Japanese "Uncanny Mother Film" from *A Page of Madness* to *Ringu*', in Barry Keith Grant and Christopher Sharrett (eds), *Planks of Reason: Essays on the Horror Film* (Lanham, MD: Scarecrow, 2004), pp. 370–85.

Google Scholar, 'Andrew Higson – Google Scholar Citations', *scholar.google.com/scholar?cites=5715149606530011462&as_sdt=5,33&sciodt=0,33&hl=en* (accessed 5 January 2020).

Graham, Jane, 'Hoodies Strike Fear in British Cinema', *The Guardian*, 5 November 2009.

——, 'Too Cool for School', *The Guardian*, 6 May 2011.

Greer, Bonnie, 'Dying for a Laugh', *Mail on Sunday*, 14 March 2004.

'*The Guardian* and *Observer* Reader Profile', *image.guardian.co.uk/sys-files/Guardian/documents/2012/08/22/Printreaderprofile.pdf* (accessed 5 January 2020).

'*The Guardian*, Our Readers and Circulation', *www.theguardian.com/advertising/guardian-circulation-readership-statistics* (accessed 5 January 2020).

Gunter, Barrie and Jill McAleer, *Children and Television* (London: Routledge, 1997).

Hall, Stuart, Chas Crotchet, Tony Jefferson, John Clarke and Brian Roberts, *Policing the Crisis: Mugging, the State, and Law and Order* (New York: Holmes and Meier, 1978).

Hall, Zoe, 'Jurassic Perplexity: Cinema Is Not A Tin of Peas', *The Guardian*, 29 December 1993.

Hamilton, John, *X-Cert: The British Independent Horror Film 1951–1970* (Baltimore, MD: Midnight Marquee Press, 2012).

'Hammer Horror Classics to be Restored', *BBC News, Arts and Entertainment*, 19 January 2012, *www.bbc.com/news/entertainment-arts-16629619* (accessed 5 January 2020).

'Hammer Horror *The Quiet Ones* Wraps in Oxford', *BBC News*, 17 July 2012, *www.bbc.com/news/uk-england-oxfordshire-18871710* (accessed 5 January 2020).

Hand, Richard, 'Aesthetics of Cruelty: Traditional Japanese Theatre and the Horror Film', in Jay McRoy (ed.), *Japanese Horror Cinema* (Honolulu: University of Hawai'i Press, 2005), pp. 18–28.

Hantke, Steffen, 'Japanese Horror Under Western Eyes: Social Class and Global Culture in Miike Takashi's *Audition*', in Jay McRoy (ed.), *Japanese Horror Cinema* (Honolulu: University of Hawai'i Press, 2005), pp. 54–65.

Harbord, Janet, *Film Cultures* (London: Sage, 2002).

Harper, Sue, 'The Scent of Distant Blood: Hammer Films and History', in Tony Barta (ed.), *Screening the Past: Film and the Representation of History* (Westport, CT: Praeger, 1998), pp. 109–25.

'*Harry Potter and the Deathly Hallows – Part 2*', BBFC Insight, *www.bbfc.co.uk/releases/ harry-potter-and-deathly-hallows-part-2-2011-0* (accessed 5 January 2020).

Hayward, Keith and Majid Yar, 'The "Chav" Phenomenon: Consumption, Media and the Construction of a New Underclass', *Crime Media Culture*, 2/1 (April 2006), 9–28.

Hayward, Susan, 'Framing National Cinemas', in Mette Hjort and Scott MacKenzie (eds), *Cinema and Nation* (New York: Routledge, 2000), pp. 88–102.

HC Deb. 19 July 1984, vol. 64, col. 523, *hansard.millbanksystems.com/commons/ 1984/jul/19/film-industry-policy* (accessed 5 January 2020).

HC Deb. 19 July 1984, vol. 64, col. 525, *hansard.millbanksystems.com/commons/ 1984/jul/19/film-industry-policy* (accessed 5 January 2020).

Hewitt, Chris, '*Attack the Block* Review', Empire Online, *www.empireonline.com/ movies/attack-block/review/* (accessed 5 January 2020).

Higbee, Will and Song Hwee Lim, 'Concepts of Transnational Cinema: Towards a Critical Transnationalism in Film Studies', *Transnational Cinemas*, 1/1 (2010), 7–21.

Higson, Andrew, 'The Limiting Imagination of National Cinema', in Mette Hjort and Scott MacKenzie (eds), *Cinema and Nation* (New York: Routledge: 2000), pp. 63–74.

——, Waving the Flag (Oxford: Clarendon Press, 1995).

Hill, John, 'British Cinema as National Cinema: Production, Audience and Representation', in Robert Murphy (ed.), *The British Cinema Book* (New York: Palgrave Macmillan, 2009), pp. 13–20.

——, *British Cinema in the 1980s* (Oxford: Clarendon Press, 1999).

Hills, Matt, 'Hammer 2.0: Legacy, Modernization and Hammer Horror as a Heritage Brand', in Richard Nowell (ed.), *Merchants of Menace* (New York: Bloomsbury, 2014), pp. 229–49.

——, 'Ringing the Changes: Cult Distinctions and Cultural Differences in US Fans' Readings of Japanese Horror Cinema', in Jay McRoy (ed.), *Japanese Horror Cinema* (Edinburgh: Edinburgh University Press, 2005), pp. 161–74.

Hinerman, Stephen, 'Star Culture', in James Lull (ed.), *Culture in the Communication Age* (New York: Routledge, 2001), pp. 193–211.

Hjort, Mette, 'On the Plurality of Cinematic Transnationalisms', in Nataša Ďurovičová and Kathleen E. Newman (eds), *World Cinemas, Transnational Perspectives* (Abingdon, UK: Routledge, 2009), pp. 12–33.

HL Deb. 19 July 1984, vol. 454, cols 1643–5, *hansard.millbanksystems.com/ lords/1984/jul/19/film-industry* (accessed 5 January 2020).

Hoad, Phil, 'How Multiplex Cinemas Saved the British Film Industry 25 Years Ago', *The Guardian*, 11 November 2010.

——, 'The *Cabin in the Woods* Shows Horror Speaks an International Language', *The Guardian*, 10 April 2012.
Hobbs, Dick, 'Obituary: Ron Kray', *The Independent*, 18 March 1995.
Hoggard, Liz, 'Hoodie UK', *The Independent*, 19 February 2006.
Honigsbaum, Harry, 'Concern over Rise of 'Happy-Slapping' Craze', *The Guardian*, 25 April 2005.
Horne, Philip, 'DVD Reviews: *Eden Lake*', *The Daily Telegraph*, 24 January 2009.
Hughes, Colin, 'Jack Straw: Jack of All Tirades', *The Guardian*, 24 July 1999.
Hunt, Leon, *Cult British TV Comedy* (Manchester University Press: New York, 2013).
Hunter, Allan, '*28 Days Later*', *Screen International*, 24 October 2002.
——, 'Rich Pickings', *Screen International*, 16 December 2011.
Hunter, I. Q., *British Trash Cinema* (London: Palgrave Macmillan, 2013).
Hutchings, Peter, *Hammer and Beyond: The British Horror Film* (New York: St Martin's Press, 1993).
——, *Terence Fisher* (Manchester: Manchester University Press, 2002).
Ide, Wendy, '*Shaun of the Dead*', *Screen International*, 20 March 2004.
Ilott, Sarah, '"We Are the Martyrs, You're Just Squashed Tomatoes!": Laughing through the Fears in Postcolonial British Comedy: Chris Morris's *Four Lions* and Joe Cornish's *Attack the Block*', *Postcolonial Text*, 8/2 (2013), 1–17.
James, Nick, 'British Cinema's US Surrender – A View from 2001', in Robert Murphy (ed.), *The British Cinema Book* (New York: Palgrave Macmillan, 2009), pp. 21–7.
Jancovich, Mark, '"It's About Time British Actors Kicked Against These Roles in 'Horror' Films": Horror Stars, Psychological Films, and the Tyranny of the Old World in Classical Horror Cinema', *Historical Journal of Film, Radio, and Television*, 33/2 (2013), 214–33.
Johnston, Derek, *Haunted Seasons: Television Ghost Stories for Christmas and Horror for Halloween* (New York: Palgrave Macmillan, 2015).
Jones, Owen, *Chavs* (New York: Verso, 2011).
'Judge's Remarks Prompt MPs' Horror Video Curb Call', *The Guardian*, 25 November 1993.
Katbamna, Mira, 'Office Hours', *The Guardian*, 12 June 2006.
Kellaway, Kate, 'Touched by Evil: Susan Hill and Jane Goldman on What Inspired *The Woman in Black*', *The Guardian*, 4 February 2012.
Kemp, Stuart, 'Strainspotting?', *Screen International*, 22 August 1997.
Kermode, Mark, 'The British Censors and Horror Cinema', in Steve Chibnall and Julian Petley (eds), *British Horror Cinema* (New York: Routledge, 2002), pp. 10–22.

—, *The Good, The Bad and The Multiplex* (London: Random House, 2011).

—, 'I Was a Teenage Horror Fan: Or, How I Learned to Stop Worrying and Love Linda Blair', in Martin Barker and Julian Petley (eds), *Ill Effects: The Media/Violence Debate* (New York: Routledge, 1997), pp. 48–55.

—, 'My Life of Porn and Violence', *The Observer*, 18 September 2004.

Kermode, Mark and Julian Petley, 'The Censor and the State', *Sight & Sound*, May 1998, 14.

Kinoshita, Chika, 'The Mummy Complex: Kurosawa Kiyoshi's *Loft* and J-horror', in Jinhee Choi and Mitsuyo Wada-Marciano (eds), *Horror to the Extreme: Changing Boundaries in Asian Cinema* (Hong Kong: Hong Kong University Press, 2009), pp. 103–22.

Klein, Amanda Ann, *American Film Cycles: Reframing Genres, Screening Social Problems, and Defining Subcultures* (Austin, TX: University of Texas Press, 2011).

Korte, Barbara, 'Envisioning a Black Tomorrow? Black Mother Figures and the Issues of Representation in *28 Days Later* (2003) and *Children of Men* (2006)', in Lars Eckstein, Barbara Korte, Eva Uldrike Pirker and Christoph Reinfandt (eds), *Multi-Ethnic Britain 2000+: New Perspectives in Literature, Film and the Arts* (Amsterdam and New York: Rodopi, 2008), pp. 315–25.

Lanzagorta, Marco, 'John Carpenter', *Senses of Cinema* (2003), sensesofcinema.com/2003/great-directors/carpenter/ (accessed 5 January 2020).

LaRose, Nicole, 'Gangsters, Zombies, and Other Rebels: Alternative Communities in Late Twentieth-Century British Novels and Films' (PhD dissertation, University of Florida, 2006).

Lauro, Sarah and Karen Embry, 'A Zombie Manifesto: The Nonhuman Condition in the Era of Advanced Capitalism', *Boundary 2*, 35/1 (2008), 85–108.

Leach, Jim, *British Film* (Cambridge: Cambridge University Press, 2004).

Leggott, James, *Contemporary British Cinema: From Heritage to Horror* (London: Wallflower, 2008).

Leigh, Danny, 'Can *Kill List* Breathe Life into Britain's Film Industry?', *The Guardian*, 2 September 2011.

—, 'Under the Skin: Why Did This Chilling Masterpiece Take a Decade?', *The Guardian*, 6 March 2014.

Lett, Dan, Sean Hier, Keven Walby and Andre Smith, 'Panic, Regulation and the Moralization of British Law and Order Politics', in Sean Hier (ed.), *Moral Panics and the Politics of Anxiety* (New York: Routledge, 2011), pp. 155–70.

Local Government Act 1988 (c. 9), Part IV, s. 28, www.legislation.gov.uk/ukpga/1988/9/section/28 (accessed 5 January 2020).

Locke, David, 'A Haven for Art Films', *Sight & Sound*, November 2012, 18.

Lönroth, Linn, 'Hoodie Horror: The New Monster in Contemporary British Horror Movies', *Journal of Media, Cognition and Communication*, 2/1 (2014), p. 4–20.

Ludemann, Ralf, 'US Product Gains Ground in European Territories', *Screen International*, 2 June 1990.

Macnab, Geoffrey, 'A Bloodthirsty Bunch of Fans', *The Independent*, 4 November 2005.

——, 'British Cinema Special: That Shrinking Feeling', *Sight & Sound*, October 2002, 18–20.

——, 'The British are Coming! Again!', *The Independent*, 14 December 2013.

Magor, Maggie and Philip Schlesinger, '"For This Relief Much Thanks": Taxation, Film Policy and the UK Government', *Screen*, 50/3 (fall 2009), 299–317.

Majendie, Paul, 'Potter Star Radcliffe Wins Rave Reviews in "Equus"', *Reuters*, 28 February 2007, www.reuters.com/article/2007/02/28/us-arts-potter-idUSL2723314820070228 (accessed 5 January 2020).

Malcolm, Derek, 'Mrs. Thatcher's Saving Grace?', *The Guardian*, 14 June 1990.

Maltby, Richard, *Hollywood Cinema* (Malden, MA: Blackwell, 2003).

Martin, Daniel, 'Japan's *Blair Witch*: Restraint, Maturity, and Generic Canons in the British Critical Reception of *Ring*', *Cinema Journal*, 48/3 (2009), 35–51.

Martinez, D. P., 'Gender, Shifting Boundaries and Global Cultures', in D. P. Martinez (ed.), *The Worlds of Japanese Popular Culture: Gender, Shifting Boundaries and Global Cultures* (New York: Cambridge University Press, 1998), pp. 1–18.

Mather, Nigel, *Tears of Laughter* (Manchester University Press: New York, 2006).

Mazdon, Lucy, '"Kings of the Middle Way": Continental Cinema on British Screens', in Sally Faulkner (ed.), *Middlebrow Cinema* (New York: Routledge, 2016), pp. 181–95.

McCahill, Mike, '*The Quiet Ones* Review', *The Guardian*, 15 April 2014.

McDonald, Paul, 'Britain: Hollywood, UK', in Paul McDonald and Janet Wasko (eds), *The Contemporary Hollywood Film Industry* (Malden, MA: Blackwell, 2008), pp. 220–31.

——, *Hollywood Stardom* (Malden, MA: Wiley-Blackwell, 2013).

McDowell, Linda, 'Changing Cultures of Work: Employment, Gender and Lifestyle', in David Morely and Kevin Robins (eds), *British Cultural Studies: Geography, Nationality and Identity* (Oxford: Oxford University Press, 2001), pp. 343–60.

McEvoy, Emma, '"Boo! To Taboo" Gothic Performance at British Festivals', in Justin Edwards and Agnieszka Soltysik Monnet (eds), *The Gothic in Contemporary Literature and Popular Culture* (New York: Routledge, 2012), pp. 165–81.

McNary, Dave, 'Indie Team Wields Classic Hammer', *Variety*, 3–9 May 2010.

McRoy, Jay, 'Introduction', in Jay McRoy (ed.), *Japanese Horror Cinema* (Honolulu: University of Hawai'i Press, 2005), pp. 1–11.

——, *Nightmare Japan: Contemporary Japanese Horror Cinema* (New York: Rodopi, 2008).

Medhurst, Andy, *A National Joke* (Routledge: New York, 2007).

——, 'Spaced Out', *Sight & Sound*, June 1993, 45.

Meikle, Denis, *A History of Horrors: The Rise and Fall of the House of Hammer* (Lanham, MD: Scarecrow Press, 2009).

Messenger Davies, Máire, '"Crazyspace": The Politics of Children's Screen Drama', *Screen*, 46/3 (Autumn 2005), 389–99.

Millar, Jane, *Keeping Track of Welfare Reform: The New Deal Programmes* (Joseph Rowntree Foundation (York, UK: York Publishing Services, 2000).

Miller, Jeffrey S., *Something Completely Different: British Television and American Culture* (Minneapolis: University of Minnesota Press, 2000).

Minns, Adam, 'Hammer Teams with Sturridge to Scare Up Six Films', *Screen International*, 13 May 2001.

——, 'UK Production Trend Develops into Horror', *Screen International*, 29 November 2001.

Mitchell, Wendy, 'Film4 Signs on as Headline Sponsor for UK's FrightFest', *Screen International*, 8 May 2007.

——, 'Hammer Film Relaunched with European Investors Including Cyrte', *Screen International*, 10 May 2007.

Moody, Paul, 'Hammer Horror', *BFI ScreenOnline*, www.screenonline.org.uk/film/id/445975/ (accessed 5 January 2020).

Morgart, James, 'Gothic Horror Film from *The Haunted Castle* (1896) to *Psycho* (1960)', in Glennis Byron and Dale Townshend (eds), *The Gothic World* (New York: Routledge, 2014), pp. 376–87.

Mount, Ferdinand, *Mind the Gap: The New Class Divide in Britain* (London: Short Books, 2004).

Muir, John Kenneth, *The Films of John Carpenter* (Jefferson, NC: McFarland, 2000).

Mullen, Lisa, '*The Woman in Black*', *Sight & Sound*, March 2012, 78–9.

Muntean, Nick and Matthew Thomas Payne, 'Attack of the Livid Dead: Recalibrating Terror in the Post-September 11 Zombi Film', in Andrew Schopp and Matthew B. Hill (eds), *The War on Terror and American Popular Culture: September 11 and Beyond* (Cranbury, NJ: Fairleigh Dickinson University Press, 2009), pp. 239–58.

Murdock, Graham, 'Reservoirs of Dogma: An Archaeology of Popular Anxieties', in Martin Barker and Julian Petley (eds), *Ill Effects: The Media/Violence Debate* (New York: Routledge, 1997), pp. 56–73.

Murphy, Bernice, *The Rural Gothic in American Popular Culture* (New York: Palgrave Macmillan, 2013).

Murphy, Robert, 'A Path through the Moral Maze', in Robert Murphy (ed.), *British Cinema of the 90s* (London: BFI, 2000), pp. 1–16.

——, 'Bright Hopes, Dark Dreams: A Guide to New British Cinema', in Robert Murphy (ed.), *The British Cinema Book*, 3rd edition (New York: Palgrave Macmillan, 2009), pp. 395–407.

——, 'Introduction', in Robert Murphy (ed.), *British Cinema of the 90s* (London: BFI, 2000), pp. ix–xi.

Napier, Susan, *Anime from Akira to Princess Mononoke: Experiencing Contemporary Japanese Animation* (New York: Palgrave, 2001).

——, *The Fantastic in Modern Japanese Literature: A Subversion of Modernity* (New York: Routledge, 1996).

Nayak, Anoop, 'Displaced Masculinities: Chavs, Youth and Class in the Post-Industrial City', *Sociology*, 40/5 (2006), 813–31.

'Needing to Make a Free Trade Mark', *The Guardian*, 15 November 1993.

'New Labour, New Austerity?', *Screen International*, 23 January 1998.

Newbury, Michael, 'Fast Zombie/Slow Zombie: Food Writing, Horror Movies, and Agribusiness Apocalypse', *American Literary History*, 24/1 (spring 2012), 87–114.

Newman, Kim, '*Shaun of the Dead*', *Sight & Sound*, May 2004, 72–3.

——, 'This Spectred Isle', *Sight & Sound*, July 2013, 48–51.

Newman, Oscar, 'Defensible Space – A New Physical Planning Tool for Urban Revitalization', *Journal of the American Planning Association*, 61/2 (1995), 149–55.

Nixon, Sean, 'Resignifying Masculinity', in David Morely and Kevin Robins (eds), *British Cultural Studies: Geography, Nationality and Identity* (Oxford: Oxford University Press, 2001), pp. 373–86.

Noh, David, '*The Woman in Black*', *Film Journal International*, March 2012.

Northmore, Henry, 'Ben Wheatley, Director of A Field in England – Interview', *The List*, 24 June 2013, *film.list.co.uk/article/52082-ben-wheatley-director-of-a-field-in-england-interview/* (accessed 5 January 2020).

Nowell, Richard (ed.), *Merchants of Menace* (New York: Bloomsbury, 2014).

Nowell-Smith, Geoffrey, 'The *Sight & Sound* Story, 1932–1992', in Geoffrey Nowell-Smith and Christophe Dupin (eds), *The British Film Institute, Government and Film Culture, 1933–2010* (New York: Manchester University Press, 2012), pp. 237–51.

——, 'Towards the Millennium', in Geoffrey Nowell-Smith and Christophe Dupin (eds), *The British Film Institute, Government and Film Culture, 1933–2010* (New York: Manchester University Press, 2012), pp. 272–303.

Nowell-Smith, Geoffrey and Christophe Dupin, 'Introduction', in Geoffrey Nowell-Smith and Christophe Dupin (eds), *The British Film Institute, Government and Film Culture, 1933–2010* (New York: Manchester University Press, 2012), pp. 1–13.

Och, Dana and Kirsten Strayer (eds), *Transnational Horror across Visual Media: Fragmented Bodies* (New York: Routledge, 2014).

'Opinion: Danger Signals', *Screen International*, 4 February 1994.

'Opinion: Political Hot Line', *Screen International*, 22 April 1994.

Orr, Deborah, 'A Statement of the Bleeding Obvious', *The Independent*, 17 May 2005.

Osborn, Guy and Alex Sinclair, 'The "Poacher Turned Gamekeeper": James Ferman and the Increasing Intervention of the Law', in Edward Lamberti (ed.), *Behind the Scenes at the BBFC: Film Classification from the Silver Screen to the Digital Age* (London: BFI, 2012), pp. 93–104.

O'Sullivan, Tim, 'Ealing Comedies 1947–57', in I. Q. Hunter and Laraine Porter (eds), *British Comedy Cinema* (New York: Routledge, 2012), pp. 66–76.

Palmer, Lorrie, '*Attack the Block*: Monsters, Race, and Rewriting South London's Outer Spaces', *Jump Cut*, 56 (2014), www.ejumpcut.org/archive/jc56.2014-2015/PalmerAttackBlock/index.html (accessed 5 January 2020).

Patterson, Christina, 'Harry Potter Grows Up', *The Independent*, 1 December 2012.

Peachey, Paul, 'Animal Rights', *The Independent*, 17 February 2001.

Peirse, Alison, 'The Feminine Appeal of British Horror Cinema', *New Review of Film and Television Studies*, 13/4 (2015), 385–402.

Pendreigh, Brian, 'Everything Was in Place for a Clampdown on Sex and Violence. So Where Is It?', *The Guardian*, 30 April 1999.

Petley, Julian, *Film and Video Censorship in Modern Britain* (Edinburgh: Edinburgh University Press, 2011).

——, 'Us and Them', in Martin Barker and Julian Petley (eds), *Ill Effects: The Media/Violence Debate* (New York: Routledge, 1997), pp. 74–86.

——, 'Who's Behind the "Nasty" Panic?', *The Guardian*, 27 December 1993.

Pfeifer, Sylvia, 'Huntingdon Demands Law to Ban Animal-Rights Thugs', *Sunday Business* (London), 29 April 2001.

Phelan, Laurence, 'Five Best Revivals', *The Independent*, 13 September 2008.

Phillips, Kendall, *Projected Fears* (Westport, CT: Praeger, 2005).

Picken, Andrew, '"Happy Slapping Attack" On Man By 15-Year-Old Yobs', *Evening News* (Edinburgh), 3 February 2006.

Pidd, Helen, '"If the Script Says Have Sex, I Have Sex"', *The Guardian*, 7 September 2007.

Pilkington, Edward, 'Boys Guilty of Bulger Murder – Detention Without Limit for "Unparalleled Evil"', *The Guardian*, 25 November 1993, reprinted at *The Guardian Online*, *www.theguardian.com/uk/1993/nov/25/bulger1* (accessed 5 January 2020).

Pirie, David, *A Heritage of Horror: The English Gothic Cinema 1946–1972* (London: Gordon Fraser, 1973).

——, *A New Heritage of Horror* (New York: I.B. Tauris, 2007).

Power, Aidan, 'Invasion of the Brit-Snatchers', in Tobias Hochscherf and James Leggott (eds) *British Science Fiction Film and Television* (Jefferson, NC: McFarland and Co., 2011), pp. 143–55.

Pulver, Andrew, 'Rebirth of the British Art Film', *The Guardian*, 23 July 2009.

——, 'Where There's Brass ...', *The Guardian*, 13 January 2004.

Puttnam, David, 'Puttnam: A Lesson in Positive Thinking', *Screen International*, 17 December 1993.

Pym, John, *Film on Four 1982/1991* (London: BFI, 1992).

Quinn, Anthony, '*Cherry Tree Lane* (18)', *The Independent*, 3 September 2010.

'Radcliffe Mania', *Screen International*, 14 February 2012.

Raphael, Amy, *Danny Boyle: In His Own Words* (London: Faber and Faber, 2011).

Relph, Michael, 'A Major Step for British Film', *Screen International*, 24 April 1992.

——, 'Home Truths', *Screen International*, 1 October 1993.

Richards, Andy, 'Lighthouse', *Sight & Sound*, August 2002, 43.

Rigby, Jonathan, *English Gothic: A Century of Horror Cinema* (Surrey: Reynolds & Hearn, 2000).

——, *English Gothic: Classic Horror Cinema 1897–2015* (Cambridge: Signum Books, 2015).

Roberts, Ben, 'Scream Test', *Sight & Sound*, June 2015, 17.

——, 'What a Relief', *Sight & Sound*, May 2015, 16.

Roche, David, *Making and Remaking Horror in the 1970s and 2000s* (Jackson, MS: University of Mississippi Press, 2014).

Roddick, Nick, 'Mr. Busy: Another Scary Movie', *Sight & Sound*, January 2009, 14.

——, 'Welcome to the Multiplex', *Sight & Sound*, June 1994, 26–8.

Rogers, Simon, John Burn-Murdoch and Ami Sedghi, 'Unemployment: The Key UK Data and Benefit Claimants for Every Constituency', *The Guardian*, 15 May 2013.

Romney, Jonathan, 'Box Office Isn't Everything', *The Guardian*, 5 May 2000.

——, 'Hats Off! It's the Year of the Auteur', *The Independent* (London), 6 January 2013.

Rose, James, *Beyond Hammer* (Leighton Buzzard, UK: Auteur, 2009).

Rose, Steve, 'The Guide: Let's Not Move To...', *The Guardian*, 4 September 2010.

Rosser, Michael, 'BFI Unveils Gothic Cinema Season', *Screen International*, 27 June 2013.

Russell, James, 'Hollywood Blockbusters and UK Production Today', in I. Q. Hunter, Laraine Porter and Justin Smith, *The Routledge Companion to British Cinema History* (New York: Routledge, 2017), pp. 377–86.

Ryall, Tom, *Britain and the American Cinema* (Thousand Oaks, CA: SAGE, 2001).

Samson, Pete, 'Myleene in Happy Slapping Terror', *Daily Record* (Glasgow), 8 December 2005.

Sawyer, Miranda, 'The Film That Speaks to Britain's Youth in Words They Understand', *The Guardian*, 25 February 2006.

Scargill, Naila, 'Hammer 2.0 – CEO Simon Oaks Reveals Studio's Future Plans', *MovieScope*, 26 August 2011, originally accessed via the *MovieScope* website, now available via the Internet Archive, *https://web.archive.org/web/20150918224205/http://www.moviescopemag.com/market-news/featured-editorial/hammer-2-0-ceo-simon-oakes-reveals-studios-future-plans/* (accessed 5 January 2020).

Scott, Ajax, 'Blue Moves', *Screen International*, 17 April 1992.

'Screen International Media Information 2012', originally accessed via the *Screen Daily* website, now available via the Internet Archive, *https://web.archive.org/web/20130420073849/www.screendaily.com/Journals/2012/03/08/t/a/y/SCRN122-Screen-media-pack-2012.pdf* (accessed 5 January 2020).

Shafer, Stephen, 'An Overview of the Working Classes in British Feature Film from the 1960s to the 1980s: From Class Consciousness to Marginalization', *International Labor and Working Class History*, 59 (April 2001), 3–14.

Sharrock, David, Maggie O'Kane and Edward Pilkington, 'Two Youngsters Who Found a New Rule to Break', *The Guardian*, 25 November 1993.

Shaw, Deborah, 'Deconstructing and Reconstructing "Transnational Cinema"', in Stephanie Dennison (ed.), *Contemporary Hispanic Cinema: Interrogating the Transnational in Spanish and Latin American Film* (Rochester: Tamesis: 2013), pp. 47–66.

—, 'Transnational Cinema: Mapping a Field of Study', in Rob Stone, Paul Cooke, Stephanie Dennison and Alix Marlow-Mann (eds), *Routledge Companion to World Cinema* (New York: Routledge, 2017), pp. 290–8.

Shaw, Michael, 'Bullies Film Fights by Phone', *Times Educational Supplement*, 21 January 2005.

Siddique, Sophia and Raphael Raphael (eds), *Transnational Horror Cinema: Bodies of Excess and the Global Grotesque* (London: Palgrave Macmillan, 2016).

Sillars, Jane, 'Review', *Screen*, 35/1 (1994), 109.

Simkin, Steve, 'Wake of the Flood: Key Issues in UK Censorship, 1970–5', in Edward Lamberti (ed.), *Behind the Scenes at the BBFC: Film Classification from the Silver Screen to the Digital Age* (London: BFI, 2012), pp. 72–86.
Simon, Brent, 'Land of the Dead', *Screen International*, 22 June 2005.
Simpson, M. J., *Urban Terrors: New British Horror Cinema, 1998–2002* (Baltimore, MD: Midnight Marquee Press, 2013).
Simpson, Philip, 'Directions to Ealing', *Screen Education*, 24 (1977), 5–19.
Skidmore, Paula, 'Report: The "Effects" Tradition – Its Problems, Politics and Supersession, London, 26–27 November 1994', *Screen*, 36/2 (summer 1995), 156–8.
Smith, Iain Robert, *Hollywood Meme* (Edinburgh: Edinburgh University Press, 2017).
Smith, Steve, 'A Siege Mentality? Form and Ideology in Carpenter's Early Siege Films', in Ian Conrich and David Woods (eds), *The Cinema of John Carpenter* (Wallflower Press: London, 2004), pp. 35–48.
Snoonian, Mike, 'Is The Woman in Black J-Horror in Victorian Clothing?', *FilmThrills*, 16 February 2012, *filmthrills.com/is-the-new-woman-in-black-j-horror-in-victorian-clothing/* (accessed 5 January 2020).
'Something for the Weekend', *The Sun*, 12 September 2008.
Spencer, Ewan, *UK Garage: Brandy and Coke*, Somesuch & Co., *Dazed Digital*, 1 February 2015, Film, https://www.dazeddigital.com/artsandculture/article/19531/1/watch-music-nation-brandy-coke-full-length-channel-4-uk-garage-documentary.
Stanbrook, Alan, 'When the Lease Runs Out', *Sight & Sound*, summer 1984, 172–3.
Stanley, Richard, 'Dying Light: An Obituary for the Great British Horror Movie', in Steve Chibnall and Julian Petley (eds), *British Horror Cinema* (New York: Routledge, 2002), pp. 183–95.
Stone, James, '"I Used to Like Gangsters and Newspaper Films, But I'm Not So Sure Now": The Hollywood Dreams of Jessie Matthews and the British Film Industry', in Rocío G. Davis (ed.), *The Transnationalism of American Culture: Literature, Film, and Music* (New York: Routledge, 2013), pp. 78–87.
Stow, Nicola, 'Women Assaulted in Capital's First "Happy Slapping" Attacks', *Evening News* (Edinburgh), 13 June 2005.
Street, Sarah, *British National Cinema* (New York: Routledge, 2009).
Street, Sarah and Margaret Dickinson, *Cinema and State: The Film Industry and the Government 1927–1984* (London: BFI, 1985).
Studemann, Frederick, 'Resist Hollywood or Bust, Film-Makers Warn; Cinema in Europe Fading Out As America's Cultural Invaders Snatch the Big Box Office. Guardian Reporters Ask If the Cameras Must Stop Rolling Across the Continent', *The Guardian*, 19 February 1994.

Sweney, Mark, 'Big-Screen Boom: UK Cinemas on Track for Best Year Since 1971', *The Guardian*, 14 December 2018.

'Table of Contents', *Sight & Sound*, October 1998, 1.

'*The Texas Chainsaw Massacre*', BBFC Case Studies, www.bbfc.co.uk/case-studies/texas-chain-saw-massacre (accessed 5 January 2020).

Torrey Barber, Susan, 'The Films of Stephen Frears', in Lester Friedman (ed.), *Fires Were Started: British Cinema and Thatcherism* (Minneapolis, MN: University of Minnesota Press, 1993), pp. 221–36.

Tutt, Louise, 'High Hopes in UK After Labour Election Victory', *Screen International*, 9 May 1997.

Tyler, Imogen, 'Chav Scum: The Filthy Politics of Social Class in Contemporary Britain', *MC Journal: A Journal of Media and Culture*, 9/5 (November 2006), www.journal.media-culture.org.au/0610/09-tyler.php (accessed 5 January 2020).

——, *Revolting Subjects: Social Abjection and Resistance in Neoliberal Britain* (London: Zed Books, 2013).

Tynan, Kenneth, 'Ealing: The Studio in Suburbia', *Films and Filming*, November 1955.

'UK Film Back on Political Agenda', *Screen International*, 2 June 1990.

Vallely, Paul, 'Welcome to Gated Britain', *The Independent*, 3 February 2007.

Vint, Sherryl, 'Visualizing the British Boom: British Science Fiction Film and Television', *CR: The New Centennial Review*, 13/2 (fall 2013), 155–78.

Walker, Johnny, 'A Wilderness of Horrors? British Horror Cinema in the New Millennium', *Journal of British Cinema and Television*, 9/3 (2012), 436–56.

——, *Contemporary British Horror Cinema: Industry, Genre and Society* (Edinburgh: Edinburgh University Press, 2016).

——, '"From the Makers of *The Woman in Black*": Hammer Films and Contemporary Horror Cinema', blogs.kent.ac.uk/arts-news/2015/01/16/film-research-events-for-spring-term-2015-announced/ (accessed 5 January 2020).

——, 'Low Budgets, No Budgets and Digital-video Nasties: Recent British Horror and Informal Distribution', in Richard Nowell (ed.), *Merchants of Menace* (New York: Bloomsbury, 2014), pp. 215–28.

War, Lucy, 'Chief Censor Accuses Home Secretary of Blocking Liberalisation Moves', *The Guardian*, 13 January 1998.

Waters, Darren, 'Garage Scene Denies Glorifying Guns', *BBC News Online*, 6 January 2003, news.bbc.co.uk/2/hi/entertainment/2631401.stm (accessed 5 January 2020).

Weale, Sally, '*Child's Play 3* – The Movie', *The Guardian*, 26 November 1993.

Wee, Valerie, *Japanese Horror Films and Their American Remakes: Translating Fear, Adapting Culture* (New York: Routledge, 2014).

Weitz, Katy, Gaby Hinsliff and Martin Bright, 'The Youth Debate', *The Observer*, 15 May 2005.

West, Stephanie, 'Hammer Films Releases Vampire Horror Let Me In', *Channel4 News Online*, 4 November 2010, *www.channel4.com/news/hammer-films-releases-vampire-horror-let-me-in* (accessed 5 January 2020).

Wheatley, Helen, *Gothic Television* (Manchester: Manchester University Press, 2006).

Whittam Smith, Andreas, 'To Believe Nothing Flows from TV Violence is Implausible: As President of the British Board of Film Classification I Do Sentry Duty in this Area', *The Independent*, 14 June 1999.

Wildman, David, 'The Ghost of *Harry Potter*', *Worchester Magazine*, 2–9 February 2012.

Williams, Sally, 'And for My Next Trick . . .', *Telegraph Magazine*, 28 January 2012.

Williams, Tony, '*Assault on Precinct 13*: The Mechanics of Repression', in Robin Wood and Robert Lippe (eds), *The American Nightmare: Essays on the Horror Film* (Toronto: Festival of Festivals, 1979), pp. 67–73.

Williams, Zoe, 'Katie Hopkins Calling Migrants Vermin Recalls the Darkest Events of History', *The Guardian*, 19 April 2015.

Wilson, Brian, 'Notes on a Radical Tradition: Subversive Ideological Applications in the Hammer Horror Films', *Cineaction* 72 (2007), 53–7.

Wiltshire, Jo, 'A World Gone Mad', *Mail on Sunday*, 20 October 2002.

Wiseman, Andreas, 'BBFC To Adopt Tougher Line on Unclassified Video Content, Black Swan Most Complained About Film in Cinemas Last Year', *Screen International*, 11 July 2012.

——, 'Film4 Inks Deal with Jonathan Glazer', *Screen International*, 4 February 2015.

Wiseman, Eva, 'Joe Cornish Interview: The Hoodie Horror', *The Observer*, 16 April 2011.

'*The Woman in Black*', BBFC Case Studies, *www.bbfc.co.uk/case-studies/woman-black* (accessed 5 January 2020).

'*The Woman in Black*', *Screen International*, 25 January 2012.

'*Woman in Black* (12A)', *Moving Image*, *www.movingimage.org.uk/woman-in-black-12a/* (accessed 5 January 2020).

'*The Woman in Black* Scares Away *The Muppets* to Take UK Box Office Crown', *Screen International*, 13 February 2012.

Wood, Robin, 'The American Nightmare: Horror in the 70s', in Mark Jancovich (ed.), *Horror the Film Reader* (Routledge: New York, 2002), pp. 25–32.

Zachner, R. C., 'The Rot that Infests the *Clockwork Orange*', *The Times*, 22 July 1972.

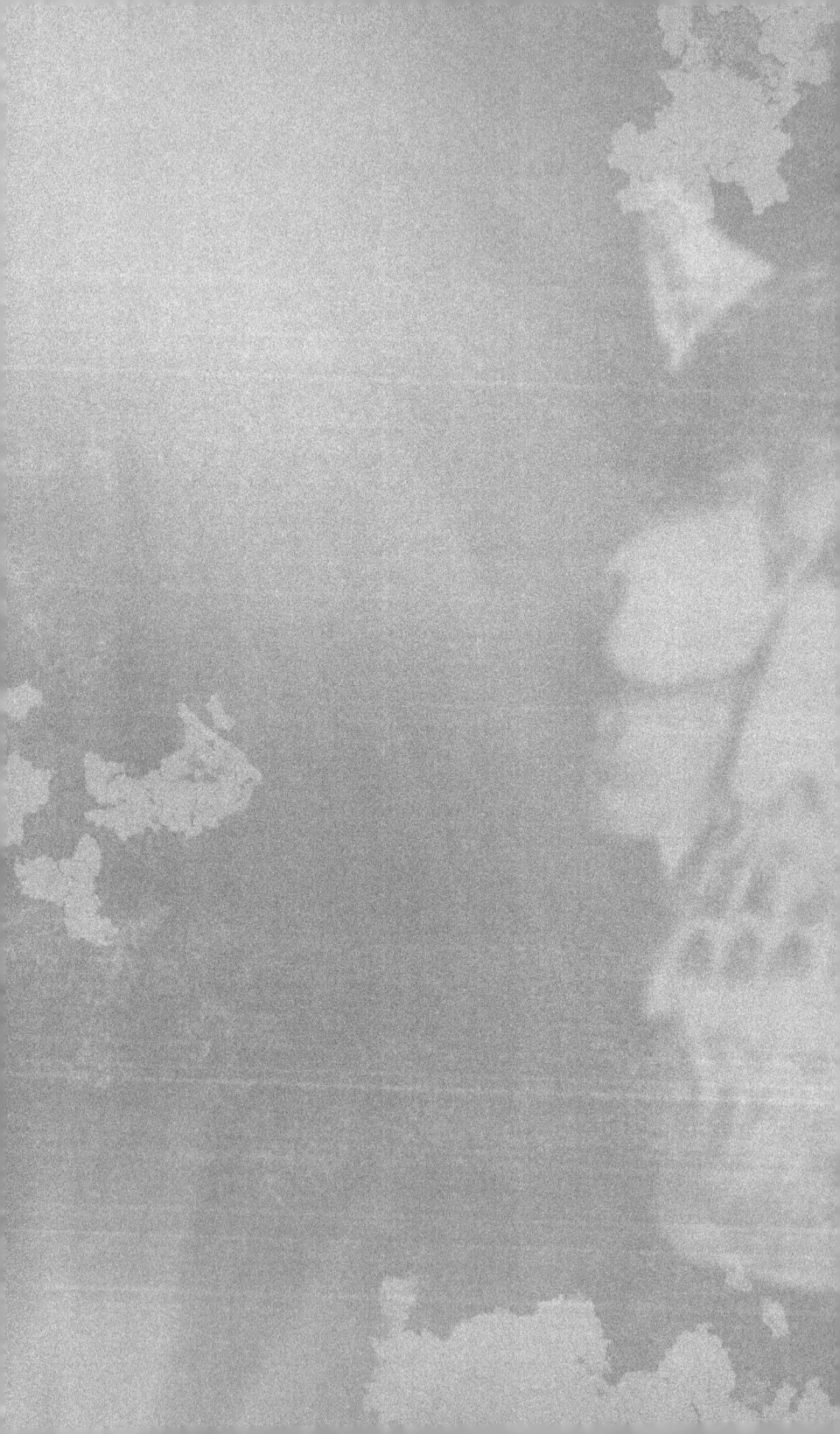

Filmography

2001: A Space Odyssey, dir. Stanley Kubrick (UK/US, 1968).
28 Days Later, dir. Danny Boyle (UK, 2002).
28 Weeks Later, dir. Juan Carlos Fresnadillo (UK/Spain, 2007).
4.3.2.1, dirs Noel Clarke and Mark Davis (UK, 2010).
47 Meters Down, dir. Johannes Roberts (UK/US, 2017).
47 Meters Down: Uncaged, dir. Johannes Roberts (UK/US, 2019).
A Clockwork Orange, dir. Stanley Kubrick (UK/US, 1971).
A Field in England, dir. Ben Wheatley (UK, 2013).
A Girl Walks Home Alone at Night, dir. Ana Lily Amirpour (US, 2014).
A Page of Madness (Kurutta ippêji), dir. Kinugasa Teinosuke (Japan, 1926).
A Room with A View, dir. James Ivory (UK, 1985).
A Warning to the Curious, dir. Lawrence Gordon Clark (UK, 1972).
Absolute Beginners, dir. Julien Temple (UK, 1985).
Anna and the Apocalypse, dir. John McPhail (UK, 2017).
Annihilation, dir. Alex Garland (UK/US, 2018).
Anuvahood, dir. Adam Deacon and Daniel Toland (UK, 2011).
Archipelago, dir. Joanna Hogg (UK, 2010).
Assault on Precinct 13, dir. John Carpenter (US, 1976).
Attack the Block, dir. Joe Cornish (UK/France/US, 2011).

Audition, dir. Takashi Miike (Japan, 1999).

The Autopsy of Jane Doe, dir. André Øvredal (UK, 2016).

Berberian Sound Studio, dir. Peter Strickland (UK, 2012).

The Best Exotic Marigold Hotel, dir. John Madden (UK/US/UEA, 2011).

Better Things, dir. Duane Hopkins (UK, 2008).

Beyond the Rave, dir. Matthias Hoene (UK, 2008).

Billy Elliot, dir. Stephen Daldry (UK/France, 2000).

Black Books, exec. prod. William Burdett-Coutts (UK, Channel 4, 2000–4).

Blackmail, dir. Alfred Hitchcock (UK, 1929).

The Blair Witch Project, dirs Daniel Myrick and Eduardo Sánchez (US, 1999).

Bonnie and Clyde, dir. Arthur Penn (US, 1967).

Boy Eats Girl, dir. Stephen Bradley (Ireland/UK, 2005).

The Broken, dir. Sean Ellis (UK/France, 2008).

Bullet Boy, dir. Saul Dibb (UK, 2004).

Bumfights: A Cause for Concern, dir. Ryen McPherson (US, 2002).

Byzantium, dir. Neil Jordan (UK/Ireland/US, 2012).

The Cabinet of Dr Caligari, dir. Robert Wiene (Germany, 1920).

Chariots of Fire, dir. Hugh Hudson (UK, 1981).

Cherry Tree Lane, dir. Paul Andrew Williams (UK, 2010).

Child's Play 3, dir. Jack Bender (US, 1991).

Citadel, dir. Ciarán Foy (Ireland/UK, 2012).

Classic Ghost Stories, prod. Angela Beeching (UK, BBC, five episodes, 1986).

Colin, dir. Marc Price (UK, 2008).

Comedown, dir. Menhaj Huda (UK, 2012).

Community, dir. Jason Ford (UK, 2012).

The Cottage, dir. Paul Andrew Williams (UK, 2008).

The Crying Game, dir. Neil Jordan (UK/US/Japan, 1992).

Culloden, dir. Peter Watkins (UK, 1964).

The Curse of Frankenstein, dir. Terence Fisher (UK, 1957).

Dark Water, dir. Hideo Nakata (Japan, 2002).

David Copperfield, dir. Simon Curtis (UK/US, BBC and PBS, 1999).

Dawn of the Dead, dir. George Romero (US, 1978).

Day of the Dead, dir. George Romero (US, 1985).
Dead Cert, dir. Steven Lawson (UK, 2010).
Dead of Night, dirs Alberto Cavalanti, Charles Crichton, Basil Dearden and Robert Hamer (UK, 1945).
The Dead Outside, dir. Kerry Anne Mullaney (UK, 2008).
Dead Set, exec. prod. Charlie Brooker (UK, E4, five episodes, 2008).
Deathwatch, dir. Michael J. Bassett (UK/Germany, 2002).
December Boys, dir. Rod Hardy (Australia/Germany/US, 2007).
Demons Never Die, dir. Arjun Rose (UK, 2011).
The Descent, dir. Neil Marshall (UK, 2005).
The Devil's Doorway, dir. Aislinn Clarke (Ireland/UK, 2018).
Dirty Pretty Things, dir. Stephen Frears (UK, 2002).
The Disappeared, dir. Johnny Kevorkian (UK, 2008).
Doctor Who, exec. prods Russell Davies, Julie Gardner and Helen Vallis (UK, BBC One, series 2, episode 3, 'School Reunion', dir. James Hawes, original air date 29 April 2006).
Dog Soldiers, dir. Neil Marshall (UK, 2002).
Don't Look Up, dir. Hideo Nakata (Japan, 1996).
Down Terrace, dir. Ben Wheatley (UK, 2009).
The Draughtsman's Contract, dir. Peter Greenaway (UK, 1982).
Dreams, dir. Akira Kurosawa (Japan/US, 1990).
The Driller Killer, dir. Abel Ferrara (US, 1979).
E.T. the Extra-Terrestrial, dir. Steven Spielberg (US, 1982).
Eden Lake, dir. James Watkins (UK, 2008).
Egomaniac, dir. Kate Shenton (UK, 2016).
Escape from New York, dir. John Carpenter (US, 1981).
The Evil Dead, dir. Sam Raimi (US, 1981).
The Exorcist, dir. William Friedkin (US, 1973).
Eyes Without a Face, dir. Georges Franju (France, 1960).
F, dir. Johannes Roberts (UK, 2010).
Fish Tank, dir. Andrea Arnold (Netherlands/UK, 2009).
Four Weddings and a Funeral, dir. Mike Newell (UK, 1994).

Gandhi, dir. Richard Attenborough (UK, 1982).

Ghost Stories for Christmas with Christopher Lee, prods Richard Downes and May Miller (UK, BBC, four episodes, 2000).

Ghost Stories, dir. Jeremy Dyson and Andy Nyman (UK, 2017).

The Girl with All the Gifts, dir. Colm McCarthy (UK, 2016).

The Gorgon, dir. Terence Fisher (UK, 1964).

Grabbers, dir. Jon Wright (Ireland/UK, 2012).

The Guvnors, dir. Gabe Turner (UK, 2014).

Halloween, dir. John Carpenter (US, 1978).

Hammer House of Horror, exec. prods Brian Lawrence and David Reid (UK, ITV, thirteen episodes, 1980–1).

Hammer House of Mystery and Suspense, exec. prod. Brian Lawrence (UK, ITV, thirteen episodes, 1984–5).

Harlem Nights, dir. Eddie Murphy (US, 1989).

Harry Brown, dir. Daniel Barber (UK, 2009).

Harry Potter and the Deathly Hallows – Part 2, dir. David Yates (US/UK, 2011).

The Haunting, dir. Robert Wise (UK, 1963).

Heartless, dir. Philip Ridley (UK, 2009).

High Rise, dir. Ben Wheatley (UK, 2015).

The Hills Have Eyes, dir. Wes Craven (US, 1977).

Horror of Dracula, dir. Terence Fisher (UK, 1958).

House of America, dir. Marc Evans (UK, 1997).

Housing Problems, dir. Edgar Anstey and Arthur Elton (UK, 1935).

Howards End, dir. James Ivory (UK, 1992).

Hue and Cry, dir. Charles Crichton (UK, 1947).

Hunger, dir. Steve McQueen (UK/Ireland, 2008).

The Hunt for Red October, dir. John McTiernan (US, 1990).

I Spit on Your Grave, dir. Meir Zarchi (US, 1979).

The Ice House, dir. Derek Lister (UK, 1978).

Ill Manors, dir. Ben Drew (UK, 2012).

In Fabric, dir. Peter Strickland (UK, 2018).

In My Skin, dir. Marina de Van (France, 2002).

Inbred, dir. Alex Chandon (UK, 2011).

Independence Day, dir. Roland Emmerich (US, 1996).

The Innocents, dir. Jack Clayton (UK, 1961).

Internal Affairs, dir. Mike Figgis (US/Canada, 1990).

It Follows, dir. David Robert Mitchell (US, 2014).

Jackass, exec. prods Johnny Knoxville, Jeff Tremaine, Spike Jonze (US, MTV, thirty-three episodes, 2000–7).

Jean de Florette, dir. Claude Berri (France/Switzerland, Italy, 1986).

Juan of the Dead, dir. Alejandro Brugués (Spain/Cuba, 2011).

Ju-on: The Grudge, dir. Takashi Shimizu (Japan, 2002).

Katalin Varga, dir. Peter Strickland (UK/Romania, 2009).

Kidulthood, dir. Menhaj Huda (UK, 2006).

Kill List, dir. Ben Wheatley (UK, 2011).

The Killing of a Sacred Deer, dir. Yorgos Lanthimos (UK/Ireland, 2017).

Kind Hearts and Coronets, dir. Robert Hamer (UK, 1949).

The Krays, dir. Peter Medak (UK, 1990).

Kwaidan, dir. Tanaka Tokuzo (Japan, 1964).

The Lady Vanishes, dir. Anthony Page (UK, 1979).

The Ladykillers, dir. Alexander Mackendrick (UK, 1955).

Land of the Dead, dir. George Romero (US, 2005).

Last House on the Left, dir. Wes Craven (US, 1972).

The Lavender Hill Mob, dir. Charles Crichton (UK, 1951).

The League of Gentlemen, exec. prods Jon Plowman, Jeremy Dyson, Mark Gattis, Steve Pemberton and Reece Shearsmith (UK, BBC, nineteen episodes, 1999–2002).

Les Diaboliques, dir. Henri-Georges Clouzot (France, 1955).

Let Me In, dir. Matt Reeves (UK/US, 2010).

Let the Right One In, dir. Tomas Alfredson (Sweden, 2008).

The Lighthouse, dir. Simon Hunter (UK, 1999).

The Likely Lads, dir. Dick Clement (UK, BBC, twenty episodes, 1964–6).

Little Britain, exec. prods Jon Plowman and Myfanwy Moore (UK, BBC, twenty-three episodes, 2003–6).

The Little Stranger, dir. Lenny Abrahamson (UK/Ireland/France, 2018).

Little Voice, dir. Mark Herman (UK, 1998).

Lock, Stock and Two Smoking Barrels, dir. Guy Ritchie (UK, 1998).

Lolita, dir. Adrian Lyne (US/France, 1997).

London to Brighton, dir. Paul Andrew Williams (UK, 2006).

London, dir. Patrick Keiller (UK, 1994).

Look Who's Talking, dir. Amy Heckerling (US, 1990).

Lust for a Vampire, dir. Jimmy Sangster (UK, 1971).

Magic Mike XXL, dir. Gregory Jacobs (US, 2015).

The Man in the White Suit, dir. Alexander Mackendrick (UK, 1951).

Manon des Sources, dir. Charles Berri (France/Switzerland/Italy, 1986).

The Masque of the Red Death, dir. Roger Corman (US/UK, 1964).

Millions Like Us, dir. Sidney Gilliat and Frank Launder (UK, 1943).

Monsters, dir. Gareth Edwards (UK, 2010).

Monty Python and the Holy Grail, dir. Terry Gilliam and Terry Jones (UK, 1975).

Monty Python's Flying Circus, creators Graham Chapman, Eric Idle, Terry Jones, Michael Palin, Terry Gilliam and John Cleese (UK, BBC, forty-six episodes, 1969–74).

Moon, dir. Duncan Jones (UK/US, 2009).

The Morecambe & Wise Show, prods John Ammonds and Ernest Maxin (UK, BBC, seventy episodes, 1968–77).

Mrs Brown, dir. John Madden (UK/Ireland, 1997).

The Mummy, dir. Terence Fisher (UK, 1959).

My Beautiful Laundrette, dir. Stephen Frears (UK, 1985).

My Boy Jack, dir. Brian Kirk (UK, 2007).

My Little Eye, dir. Marc Evans (UK, 2002).

Naked, dir. Mike Leigh (UK, 1993).

Night of the Demon, dir. Jacques Tourneur (UK, 1957).

Night of the Living Dead, dir. George Romero (UK, 1968).

Nightmare City, dir. Umberto Lenzi (Italy/Spain, 1980).

Nosferatu the Vampyre, dir. Werner Herzog (West Germany/France, 1979).

Notting Hill, dir. Roger Michell (UK, 1999).

Nuns on the Run, dir. Jonathan Lynn (UK, 1990).

Nuts in May, dir. Mike Leigh (UK, 1976).

O Lucky Man!, dir. Lindsay Anderson (UK/US, 1973).

The Office, exec. prods Anil Gupta and Jon Plowman (UK, BBC, fourteen episodes, 2001–3).

One Million Years B.C., dir. Don Chaffey (UK/US, 1966).

Onibaba, dir. Kaneto Shindô (Japan, 1964).

The Other Side of the Door, dir. Johannes Roberts (UK/US, 2016).

Paranoiac, dir. Freddie Francis (UK, 1963).

Passport to Pimlico, dir. Henry Cornelius (UK, 1949).

Peeping Tom, dir. Michael Powell (UK, 1960).

The Phantom of the Opera, dir. Terence Fisher (UK, 1962).

Pitch Black, dir. David Twohy (US/Australia, 2000).

Pretty Woman, dir. Garry Marshall (US, 1990).

Prevenge, dir. Alice Lowe (UK, 2016).

Pure Rage: The Making of '28 Days Later', dir. Toby James (UK, 2002).

The Quatermass Xperiment, dir. Val Guest (UK, 1955).

The Quiet Ones, dir. John Pogue (UK, 2014).

Red Road, dir. Andrea Arnold (UK/Denmark, 2006).

The Reeds, dir. Nick Cohen (UK, 2010).

Reservoir Dogs, dir. Quentin Tarantino (US, 1992).

The Resident, dir. Antti Jokinen (UK/US, 2011).

Return of the Living Dead, dir. Dan O'Bannon (US, 1985).

Ringu, dir. Hideo Nakata (Japan, 1998).

Ringu 2, dir. Hideo Nakata (Japan, 1999).

Rio Bravo, dir. Howard Hawks (US, 1959).

Scary Movie 3, dir. David Zucker (US, 2003)

Scary Movie 4, dir. David Zucker (US, 2006)

Scream, dir. Wes Craven (US, 1996).

Séance on a Wet Afternoon, dir. Bryan Forbes (UK, 1964).

Severance, dir. Christopher Smith (UK, 2006).

Sex Lives of the Potato Men, dir. Andy Humphries (UK, 2004).

Sexy Beast, dir. Jonathan Glazer (UK, 2000).
Shallow Grave, dir. Danny Boyle (UK, 1994).
Shank, dir. Mo Ali (UK, 2010).
Shaun of the Dead, dir. Edgar Wright (UK, 2004).
She-Devil, dir. Susan Seidelman (US, 1990).
The Shining, dir. Stanley Kubrick (US/UK, 1980).
Sightseers, dir. Ben Wheatley (UK, 2012).
The Silence of the Lambs, dir. Jonathan Demme (US, 1992).
The Sixth Sense, dir. M. Night Shyamalan (US, 1999).
Sleep Furiously, dir. Gideon Koppel (UK, 2008).
Sleepy Hollow, dir. Tim Burton (US, 1999).
Slumdog Millionaire, dirs Danny Boyle and Loveleen Tandan (UK/India, 2008).
Somers Town, dir. Shane Meadows (UK, 2008).
Spaced, exec. prods Tony Orsten, Nira Park and Lisa Clark (UK, Channel 4, fourteen episodes, 1999–2001).
Spine Chillers, prods Angela Beeching and Anna Home (UK, BBC, twenty episodes, 1980).
The Stalls of Barchester, dir. Lawrence Gordon Clark (UK, 1971).
Straw Dogs, dir. Sam Peckinpah (UK/US, 1971).
Streets of Fire, dir. Walter Hill (US, 1984).
Summer Scars, dir. Julian Richards (UK, 2007).
The Tailor of Panama, dir. John Boorman (US/Ireland, 2001).
Taste of Fear, dir. Seth Holt (UK, 1961),
Texas Chainsaw Massacre, dir. Tobe Hooper (US, 1974).
The Thing, dir. John Carpenter (US, 1982).
The Thing from Another World, dir. Howard Hawks (US, 1951).
This Happy Breed, dir. David Lean (UK, 1944).
This is England, dir. Shane Meadows (UK, 2006).
Throne of Blood, dir. Akira Kurosawa (Japan, 1957).
The Titfield Thunderbolt, dir. Charles Crichton (UK, 1953).
Tower Block, dirs James Nunn and Ronnie Thompson (UK, 2012).
The Tractate Middoth, dir. Mark Gatiss (UK, 2013).

Twins of Evil, dir. John Hough (UK, 1971).

Two Thousand Maniacs, dir. Hershell Gordon Lewis (US, 1964).

Under the Shadow, dir. Babak Anvari (UK, 2016).

Under the Skin, dir. Jonathan Glazer (UK, 2013).

Unrelated, dir. Joanna Hogg (UK, 2007).

The Vampire Lovers, dir. Roy Ward Baker (UK, 1970)

Velvet Goldmine, dir. Todd Haynes (UK/US, 1998).

Wake Wood, dir. David Keating (Ireland/UK, 2011).

Warm Bodies, dir. Jonathan Levine (US, 2013).

The Warriors, dir. Walter Hill (US, 1979).

We Need to Talk about Kevin, dir. Lynne Ramsay (UK/US, 2011).

Went the Day Well?, dir. Alberto Cavalcanti (UK, 1942).

What Ever Happened to the Likely Lads, creators Dick Clement and Ian La Frenais (UK, BBC, twenty-seven episodes, 1973–4).

What Lies Beneath, dir. Robert Zemeckis (US, 2000).

Where Angels Fear to Tread, dir. Charles Sturridge (UK, 1991).

Whisky Galore, dir. Alexander Mackendrick (UK, 1949).

Whistle and I'll Come to You, dir. Jonathan Miller (UK, BBC, original air date 7 May 1968).

The Wicker Man, dir. Robin Hardy (UK, 1973).

Wish You Were Here, dir. David Leland (UK, 1987).

The Witch, dir. Robert Eggers (US, 2015).

The Witches, dir. Nicolas Roeg (UK/US, 1990).

Witchfinder General, dir. Michael Reeves (UK, 1968).

The Woman in Black, dir. James Watkins (UK, 2012).

The Woman in Black 2: Angel of Death, dir. Tom Harper (UK, 2014).

Zombi 3, dir. Lucio Fulci (Italy, 1988).

The Zombie Diaries, dirs Michael Bartlett and Kevin Gates (UK, 2006).

Zombieland, dir. Ruben Fleischer (US, 2009).

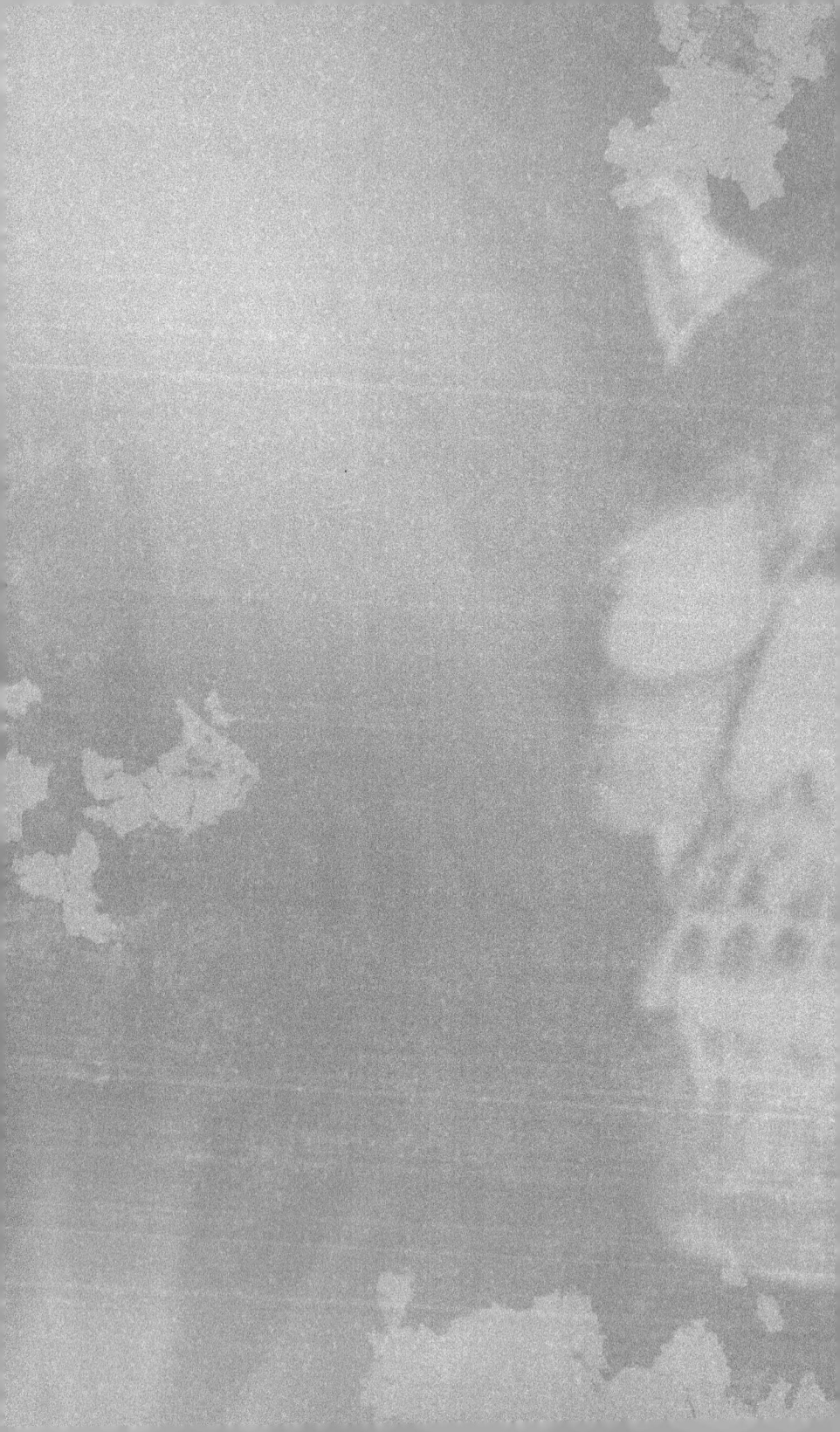

Index

1984 White Paper on film policy 30–1
1985 Film Act 31
2001: A Space Odyssey 180, 182
28 Days Later 10, 56, 63–7, 74–8;
 and Americanisation 18, 68–73;
 Romerian citations in 1–2, 9, 19,
 85–6, 98; and social realism 14,
 61, 79–85, 99
28 Weeks Later 99
47 Meters Down 186

ABC1 28, 193n4
Abravanel, Genevieve 15–16
Academy Awards 29–30
Aldana Reyes, Xavier 148
aliens 126–33, 180–4
Amicus Productions 11–12, 143, 154
animal rights activism 19, 66–7, 72, 78
Anna and the Apocalypse 186
Annihilation 186
anti-Americanisation discourse 15–19,
 32–4, 44–9, 186–7; addressed in
 cinema 64, 67–8, 76–7, 84–6,
 98–9; and hoodie panics 111–13,
 186–7
anti-horror discourse 14–19, 25,
 36–42, 52–60, 64, 69–70, 86
Antisocial Behaviour Orders (ASBOs)
 107, 127, 206n22
Anuvahood 108
Argento, Dario 54, 148–9
Arnold, Andrea 106, 108, 184
arthouse cinema 4, 8–10, 26–7,
 36, 60, 179–80, 184–6; 2000s
 British 'new wave' 184–6
Arts Council of England (ACE) 49
Assault on Precinct 13 9, 20–1, 102–4,
 126–33, 136
Atkinson, Rowland 125
Audition 54, 147, 159
auteurism 8, 14, 179, 185–6
The Autopsy of Jane Doe 186
Attack the Block 9, 20–1, 101–5,
 112–13, 126–38

backwoods horror 20, 101–4, 108,
 112–22, 125, 136–7, 204n6

Bakke, Gretchen 65
banned films 18, 37–8, 42, 110–11, 113
Barber, Susan Torrey 46–7
Barr, Charles 27, 29, 92
Bava, Mario 54, 148–9
Berberian Sound Studio 184–5
The Best Exotic Marigold Hotel 5
Better Things 108, 184
Beyond the Rave 152
BFI 8, 22, 26–7, 34–5, 51, 54–5, 173–4
Blackness 47, 82, 88, 128–32
Blair, Tony 49–50, 65, 72–3, 93, 206n22
The Blair Witch Project 60
Blake, Linnie 13, 65, 92–4
body horror 147–50, 171–2
Boyega, John 126, *130*
Boyle, Danny 56, 63–70, 84–5, 98–9
Bradshaw, Peter 103–4, 137
British Academy of Film and Television Arts (BAFTA) 29–30, 57
British Board of Film Classification (BBFC): censorship by 36–42, 74–5, 110–11, 113, 156–7, 171–3; relaxation of censorship by 14, 18, 25–6, 52–4
British Film Fund Agency (BFFA) 30
British Film Year campaign 31
Britishness 5–9, 48–51, 67–8, 79, 86, 142, 174–5, 184
British Screen Finance Consortium (BSFC) 31–2, 43, 49–50, 55
British Sky Broadcasting (BSkyB) 41
The Broken 56–7
'Broken Britain' 109–12, 114–15
Brunsdon, Charlotte 79

Buckingham, David 77
Bulger murder (James) 26, 28, 195n37, 205n17; and moral panics 19, 36–42, 53–4, 74, 77, 107
Bullet Boy 5, 108
Bumfights 110–11
Byron, Glennis 158, 165
Byzantium 177

Cameron, David 137
Cannes Film Festival 29–30, 58–9
casting 85–7, 142–3, 147, 171, 175; and class concerns 108–9, 206n25; 'star-shy' 67–9; *see also* star image
CCTV 75, 79, 107, 125; *see also* surveillance
Chadha, Gurinder 5
Channel 4 29, 31–3, 47, 56, 70, 84–6, 154
Chariots of Fire 29–30, 45, 50
'chav' (slur) 106, 123–4
Cherry, Brigid 68
Cherry Tree Lane 56–7, 103–5, 108
Chibnall, Steve 12, 29, 187
Child's Play 3 39–41, 53, 74
Cinematograph Films Council (CFC) 30
cinematography 75–83, 129, 136, 182; and *The Woman in Black* 149, 153, 156, 160, 165, 169–71
Citadel 10
class 15–16, 39–40, 47, 65–6, 69, 131, 193n4; representations of 19–21, 86, 95, 99, 103–7, 110–27, 135–8, 144–5; *see also* casting
Classic Ghost Stories 154

Clause 28 47
A Clockwork Orange 75–6
Clover, Carol 120
Colin 56–7, 99
colonialism *see* cultural imperialism
Comedown 108
comedy traditions 9, 19, 85–9, 114; and masculinity 67, 90–9
community 6, 10, 39–40, 80–2; and hoodie panics 20–1, 102–3, 113–14, 117–19, 122, 125–7, 134–8
Community 108
Conrich, Ian 7
consumerism 77–8, 88–90, 123–4
co-productions 3, 10–11, 32–3, 42, 152, 175, 177, 184–6
Cornish, Joe 104, 127–9
The Cottage 114
The Crying Game 36
Culloden 179
cultural imperialism 13, 32–5, 44–5, 48–9, 164–5, 196n69
Curse of Frankenstein 144
Cushing, Peter 143, 151
Cyrte Investments 146

Daily Mail 38, 42, 52–3, 109
Dark Water 158–9
Davis, Lucy 85–6
Dawtrey, Adam 141, 171, 175
Dead Cert 56–7
Dead of Night 54, 90
The Dead Outside 56–7
Dead Set 57
Dead trilogy 64, 69, 77, 87–90; *see also* Romero, George
Deathwatch 13
DeCordova, Richard 167–8

Demons Never Die 103, 108
Dendle, Peter 65
Department for Culture, Media and Sport (DCMS) 26, 49–51, 54–5
Department of National Heritage (DNH) 26, 29–36, 50
Department of Trade and Industry (DTI) 34–5, 50
The Descent 10
Desjardins, Mary 46–7
The Devil's Doorway 10, 186
Diawara, Manthia 46–8
The Disappeared 56–7, 108
Distribution and Exhibition Fund 56
Doctor Who 107, 206n22
documentary 60, 70–3, 79, 99, 106, 182
Dodd, Philip 27, 34
Dog Soldiers 10, 13
Down Terrace 185–6
Downing Street 26, 29–34
The Driller Killer 38, 53
Dupin, Christophe 26
Durgnat, Raymond 27
Duval, Robin 53–4

Eady Levy 30–1
Ealing Studios 9, 19, 54, 67, 79, 86, 90–5
Eccleston, Christopher 57, 72
Eden Lake 56–7, 109, 127; and backwoods horror 9, 20–1, 101–5, 108, 112–14, 119–22, 125–6, 136–8
Egomaniac 10, 186
'elevated' or 'enlightened' horror discourse 22, 147, 150, 152–3, 155–7, 162–4, 172–3, 185–7
Elsaesser, Thomas 46–9

EMI Films 31
Empire 8, 104
Englishness of filmmakers 10–11, 143
Escape from New York 102, 104
Eurimages 42
European Co-Production Fund 32
The Evil Dead 60
Exclusive Media Group 174
The Exorcist 18, 53
exploitation horror 11–12, 15, 38, 103–4

F 104–5
fans 8, 10, 13–14, 28, 47, 74, 97; and *The Woman in Black* 152, 162, 165–6, 171–2
Fassbender, Michael 114
Featherstone, Mark 104–5
Ferman, James 26, 37, 42, 52–5, 74–5
A Field in England 10, 179–80, 185
Film4 14, 54, 56, 59, 84–5, 184, 199n119
The Film Consortium 49
film cycles 12, 20–1, 25, 90–1, 108–9, 111; see also hoodie horror cycle
Film Policy Review 51; see also Department for Culture, Media and Sport (DCMS)
film posters 3, 7, 127, 169–72
film ratings 52, 171–3
film trailers 3, 7, 127, 150–1, 162, 169–72
Fish Tank 108
Fisher, Terence 143, 151, 185
Fitzgerald, John 7, 11, 104
Flint, John 125
foot-and-mouth disease *see* virus
Forshaw, Barry 11, 143

Four Weddings and a Funeral 50–1, 55, 85
Freeman, Martin 85–6
Friedman, Lester: *Fires Were Started* 27, 46–9
FrightFest Film Festival 14, 18, 22, 54, 56–7
Frost, Nick 85–7, 95–6, 104
Fulci, Lucio 148–9
funding 5–7, 13, 30–3, 42–5, 49–50, 55–6, 184; American 29, 145

Galt, Rosalind 179
'gangsta rap' culture 110–12, 120
gated communities 102–3, 113–26, 137
General Agreement on Tariffs and Trade (GATT) 26, 42–9
Gerrard, Steven 7, 11
ghost films 141–2, 148–9, 154–60, 164–8
Ghost Stories 186
A Ghost Story for Christmas 9, 21, 142–3, 154–6, 164
A Girl Walks Home Alone at Night 5
The Girl with All the Gifts 186
Glancy, Mark 15
Glazer, Jonathan 14, 180–6
Gleeson, Brendan 67–8
Gleiberman, Owen 84
Goldberg, Ruth 158
Goldman, Jane 164, 171
The Gorgon 146
Gothic horror 9–10, 21–2, 83, 108, 141–53, 157–65, 171–7, 185–6; globalgothic 158–64, 185; see also *The Woman in Black*
Grabbers 10
Greenaway, Peter 29, 36, 55, 185

The Guardian 8, 17–18, 57, 164, 184–5; and GATT talks 44–5, and hoodie horror 101, 103–4, 122, 125, 137; and media effects discourse 39–40, 52–3, 195n37; readership of 27–8, 193n6; and saved/doomed binary 32, 49, 85–6
The Guvnors 111

Hall, Stuart 110
'Hammer horror' in cultural discourse 37, 141–9, 164–5
Hammer Studios 9–14, 21–2, 56, 144, 150–9, 168–75, 185
Hand, Richard 212n61
Hantke, Steffen 159
happy-slapping 107, 110, 120
Harbord, Janet 8, 44–5
Harper, Sue 150
Harris, Naomie 67, 81–2
Harry Brown 105–6, 108
Harry Potter films 142, 147, 157, 165–75, 214n85
Hayward, Keith 102
Hayward, Susan 6
Heartless 108
heritage cinema 19, 21, 29–30, 67, 83, 142, 150–2, 157, 174–5
High Rise 177
Higson, Andrew 3–6, 46–9, 64, 80–3
Hill, John 6
Hill, Susan 9–10, 141, 147, 172
Hills, Matt 147, 150, 168
The Hills Have Eyes 20, 102, 113, 120, 122, 149
Hinds, Ciaran 153, 168
Hinerman, Stephen 165
Hjort, Mette 3–4

hoodie horror cycle 20–2, 99, 102, 105, 108–12, 120–1, 125–7, 136–8; *see also Attack the Block*; *Eden Lake*
hoodie panic 14, 20–1, 103, 107–22, 126–31, 136–8, 205n20, 206n33
hoof-and-mouth disease *see* virus
Horror of Dracula 21, 144–6, 174
Houston, Penelope 27
Howards End 50–1
Hue and Cry 9, 90
Hunger 184
Hunter, I. Q. 12
Hunter, Jumayn 20, 108–9, 114, 127
Hutchings, Peter 11, 29, 144–5, 185, 192n39

The Ice House 154
Ill Manors 108
Ilott, Sarah 132–4
Inbred 114
In Fabric 186
intertextuality 3–4, 9, 65, 68–9, 77, 156–7, 167–8
Irish Republican Army (IRA) 65
ITV 146, 154, 156

Jackson, Michael (Channel 4 executive) 84
James, M.R. 156–7, 164
James, Nick 18, 80
Jancovich, Mark 143
Jarman, Derek 185
Jennings, Humphrey 79
J-horror (Japanese horror) 5, 10–11, 21, 54, 142–3, 157–65, 175, 180
Johansson, Scarlett 177, 180, 182
Johnston, Derek 154–6
Jones, Owen 106, 121, 123–4

Ju-On: The Grudge 158–63, 213n73
Juan of the Dead 77–8

Kabuki theatre 158, 212n61
kaidan films 158–60, 212n61, 213n70
Katalin Varga 184
Kermode, Mark 15, 26, 38, 52, 54, 76
Kidulthood 105, 108–9
Kill List 10, 185
The Killing of a Sacred Deer 186
Kind Hearts and Coronets 90–2
Klein, Amanda Ann 108–9, 111
Korte, Barbara 65
Kray brothers 33, 47

laddism 86, 93–8
The Lady Vanishes 144–5
The Ladykillers 91–2
Lant, Antonia 46, 48
LaRose, Nicole 65
Last House on the Left 37, 54, 103
The Lavender Hill Mob 79, 91
Lee, Christopher 143, 151–3, 156, 177
Leggott, James 1–2, 7, 9–11
legislation 6, 31, 36, 39–42, 52, 114–15, 119, 206n22
Leigh, Mike 36, 47, 60, 66, 106
Let Me In 152
Let the Right One In 5, 152
The Lighthouse 54, 60
The Likely Lads 67, 86, 95
Loach, Ken 59–60, 66, 106, 138
The Lodge 175
Lolita 52–3
London 67, 79–85, 91, 107, 112, 133
London 9

London to Brighton 106
Lönroth, Linn 104
Lucas, Matt 85–6
Lust for a Vampire 144–5

MacCabe, Colin 51, 54
'mad cow' disease *see* virus
Magor, Maggie 49
Major, John 34, 49–50
male gaze 144–5, 152, 182–4
Martin, Daniel 162–4
Martinez, D. P. 159
masculinity 7, 14, 21, 151, 159; 'new man', shifting forms of 13, 19, 65–7, 90–8; *see also* laddism
Mazdon, Lucy 7–8
McDonald, Paul 66, 171
McDowell, Linda 88–9, 93
McEvoy, Emma 172
McRoy, Jay 159–62
Meadows, Shane 106, 109, 184
Medhurst, Andy 46–9, 95
media effects discourse 19, 40–1, 52, 66–70, 73–8, 82–4
Mellor, David 34, 36, 42–3
Merchant Ivory Productions 29, 50–1
Miller, Jeffrey S. 97
Millions Like Us 80–1
Monsters 10, 56–7
Monthly Film Bulletin (MFB) 27, 34, 39
Monty Python 19, 67, 86, 90, 96–7
Moon 184–5
moral panics *see* hoodie panic; video nasties panic
Morecambe and Wise 19, 67, 86, 95
Morland, Justice 36–9, 53, 195n37
Morvern Callar 57–9
Mrs. Brown 50–1

Muir, John Kenneth 131
multiplexes 15, 26, 31, 45
The Mummy 144, 174
Muntean, Nick 65
Murphy, Bernice 120
Murphy, Cillian 65, 67
Murphy, Robert 98
My Little Eye 57–60

Naked 57–59
Napier, Susan 159
National Film Finance Corporation (NFFC) 30–1
National Lottery Film Franchises 26, 49–51, 55
Newbury, Michael 65–6
New British cinema 2, 4–5, 10–11, 14–18, 55–61
New Cinema Fund 56
New Deal 88–9
New Labour government 49–51, 54–5
Newman, Oscar 135
Nightmare City 69
Nighy, Bill 56, 86–7
Noh theatre 158, 212n61
nostalgia 13–14, 45, 50, 143–53, 175
Notting Hill 9, 51, 55
Nowell, Richard 17
Nowell-Smith, Geoffrey 34, 54–5
Nuts in May 57–9

Oakes, Simon 146–7, 174
Obscene Publications Act (OPA) 37–9
Och, Dana 17
O'Connell, Jack 109, 116
Onibaba 158, 180
The Other Side of the Door 186
'Othering' 20, 48–9, 106, 123, 129, 136–8, 210n29

A Page of Madness 158
Palace Pictures 32, 35–6
Palmer, Lorrie 132–3, 135
pandemic *see* virus
Paranoiac 148
Parker, Alan 55
parody 123–5, 162, 213n73
Passport to Pimlico 90–1
Payne, Matthew Thomas 65
Peeping Tom 12
Pegg, Simon 85–7, 95
Peirse, Alison 12, 143
Penrose, Roy 74
Perry, Simon 50
Petley, Julian 12, 29, 38–41, 52–3, 76, 187
The Phantom of the Opera 148
Phillips, Kendall 113
Pirie, David 2, 7, 12, 29, 86, 146, 185–6
pornography 38, 52, 147, 153; *see also* video nasties panic
Power, Aidan 82
Prevenge 10, 186
public gaze 80–3
Pulver, Andrew 85–6, 184–5
Pure Rage: The Making of '28 Days Later' 70

'quality' film discourse 68, 150–1, 164, 213n75
The Quatermass Xperiment 11, 144
The Quiet Ones 174–5

race 7, 65, 88, 99, 102–6; stereotypes 121, 127, 131–3; *see also* Blackness; whiteness
Radcliffe, Daniel 21, 141–3, 147, 150–3, 157, 165–75

Ramsay, Lynne 14, 57–60, 185
Rank Films 31, 51
Raphael, Raphael 17
Red Road 184
Reilly, Kelly 56, 114
Relph, Michael 35, 44–5
Reservoir Dogs 74
The Resident 152
Rigby, Jonathan 29
Ringu 158–60, 162–4, 213n73
Rio Bravo 128
Roche, David 119
Roddick, Nick 26, 63–4
Romantic era discourses 83, 123, 142
Romero, George 1–2, 9, 19, 66–8, 70, 73, 84–6, 97–9; see also Dead trilogy
A Room with A View 29
Rose, James 11–13
Russell, James 15
Ryall, Tom 16

saved/doomed binary 14–18, 25, 32–6, 45, 50, 59–60, 85–6, 184–6
Scary Movie 162, 213n73
Schlesinger, Philip 49
Schoonover, Karl 179
science fiction (SF) 1–2, 127–8
Scream 103, 163–4
Screen 27–8, 39–41, 48–9
Screen International 8, 17–18, 27–8, 44, 68, 153, 168; on creation of DNH 33–5; critical of moral panics 41, 49–50, 52–3
screen quotas 30–1, 43
Second World War 9–11, 16, 19, 44, 67, 145, 158, 166–7; post-war period 64, 80–3, 90–1

Severance 114
Sex Lives of the Potato Men 87
sexploitation films 144–5, 152
Shafer, Stephen 106
Shaun of the Dead 1–2, 9, 13, 18–19, 64–7, 85–92, 95–101, 138
Shaw, Deborah 3–4
Shearsmith, Reece 85–6, 179
The Shining 174
Siddique, Sophia 17
Sight & Sound 8, 17–18, 41, 122, 151–3, 177–8; and anti-Americanisation discourse 34–5, 44–6, 54, 187; and media effects discourse 50–3; and anti-horror discourse 57–60, 87; readership of 26–8, 193n6
Sightseers 10, 177–9
Sillars, Jane 48–9
Simpson, M. J. 11, 167
Sinclair, Nigel 174
slashers 54, 103, 108, 171
Smith, Andreas Whittam 53, 74
Smith, Steve 131
social realism 7, 13, 19, 60–1, 66–70, 73, 78–80, 86, 105–8, 137–8
Somers Town 184
sound 117–18, 154–7, 169–70, 182
Spaced 85–6, 95
spectatorship 64, 81, 136, 167–71, 179–82
Spine Chillers 154
The Stalls of Barchester 154
Stanley, Richard 12, 187
star image 21–2, 142, 165–75; see also casting
Stevenson, Wilf 35
Straw, Jack 52–3
Straw Dogs 9, 37, 53, 103–4, 113, 118

Strayer, Kirsten 17
Street, Sarah 6, 143
Summer Scars 108
Sundance Film Festival 175
The Sun 109, 121–2
surveillance culture 19, 66–7, 75, 79
SXSW Film Festival 185

Taste of Fear 148
tax relief 30–2, 49–50, 184
Technicolor 151–2
teenagers 13–14, 38, 52–3, 76; and Daniel Radcliffe 142, 147, 166–7, 171–4; and hoodie panic 19–20, 101–14, 119–20, 125–6, 134–6
The Telegraph 56, 121–2
television 8–9, 11, 29–35, 40–3, 56–60; and comedy 67, 85–90, 95–7, 110–11; films made for 50, 151, 153–7, 166–7, 173–4
Tennant, David 107
terrorism 20, 65–6, 78, 113–14, 141, 160
Texas Chainsaw Massacre 20, 53, 102, 149
Thatcher, Margaret 29–33, 37–8, 46–9, 82, 88, 106, 121–3, 137
The Thing 5, 127, 129
This Happy Breed 80
This is England 109, 184
Thorn-EMI Elstree 29, 32
Tigon British Film Productions 11–12
Times Educational Supplement (TES) 110–11, 206n31
'torture porn' 147, 153
Tower Block 108–9
tower blocks 126–38
The Tractate Middoth 154

Turgoose, Thomas 56, 109, 116–17, 206n25
Twins of Evil 144–5
Tyler, Imogen 102, 106
Tynan, Kenneth 91

UK Film Council (UKFC) 55–6
UK garage music 111–13, 206n33
Under the Skin 10, 177–85
Universal Pictures 55, 144, 147–8, 151, 194n25

The Vampire Lovers 144–5
Variety 167, 171, 184
VCRs 35, 38
Video Appeals Committee 54
video nasties panic 13, 19, 27–8, 36–42, 52, 54, 60, 69–70
Video Recordings Act (VRA) 38–9, 42
Vint, Sherryl 104, 136
virus 69–73, 76, 87
VOD (Video On Demand) 10–15

Wake Wood 152
Walker, Johnny 13–14, 56, 60, 65, 105, 114, 144, 152, 206n25, 209n4
A Warning to the Curious 155
The Warriors 20, 102, 104, 126–31
Watkins, James 153, 157, 204n6, 214n94
We Need to Talk about Kevin 184–5
Wheatley, Helen 151, 155
Whisky Galore 90, 92
Whistle and I'll Come to You 154–6
White, Liz 149, 160
whiteness 10–11, 88, 102, 105–6, 111–14, 123–5
Whittaker, Jodie 104, 126

The Wicker Man 177, 185
Williams, Linda 26
Williams, Tony 47, 131
Wilson, Brian 151
Wilton, Penelope 85–7
The Witch 22, 187
Witchfinder General 179, 185
Wollen, Peter 46, 47–8
The Woman in Black 141–3, 154–7, 174–5, 177, 179; and Daniel Radcliffe 165–73; as globalgothic 158–64, 185; and Hammer Studios 9–10, 21, 56, 147–53

Woods, Robin 131
Woodward, John 51
Working Title 2 Productions (WT2), 85
Working Title Films 50–1, 55
World War II *see* Second World War
Wright, Edgar 104, 129

Yar, Majid 102

Zombi 3 69
The Zombie Diaries 99
zombies 9, 19, 65–78, 81–91, 94–9

also in series

Lindsey Decker, *Transnationalism and Genre Hybridity in New British Horror Cinema* (2021)

Stacey Abbott and Lorna Jowett (eds), *Global TV Horror* (2021)

Michael J. Blouin, *Stephen King and American Politics* (2021)

Eddie Falvey, Joe Hickinbottom and Jonathan Wroot (eds), *New Blood: Critical Approaches to Contemporary Horror* (2020)

Darren Elliott-Smith and John Edgar Browning (eds), *New Queer Horror Film and Television* (2020)

Jonathan Newell, *A Century of Weird Fiction, 1832–1937* (2020)

Alexandra Heller-Nicholas, *Masks in Horror Cinema: Eyes Without Faces* (2019)

Eleanor Beal and Jonathan Greenaway (eds), *Horror and Religion: New literary approaches to Theology, Race and Sexuality* (2019)

Dawn Stobbart, *Videogames and Horror: From Amnesia to Zombies, Run!* (2019)

David Annwn Jones, *Re-envisaging the First Age of Cinematic Horror, 1896–1934: Quanta of Fear* (2018)